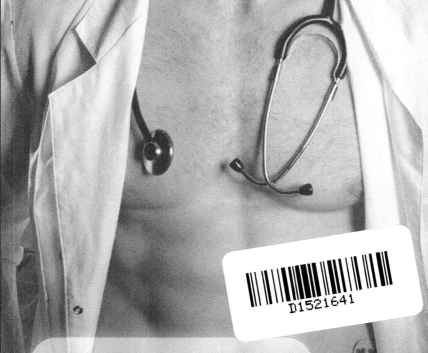

D1521641

Texting

Dr. Stalker

PEPPER WINTERS

Texting Dr Stalker

by
New York Times Bestseller

Pepper Winters

Published: Pepper Winters 2025: pepperwinters@gmail.com
Ebook Design: Cleo Studios
Paperback Design: Cleo Studios
Editing by: Editing-4-Indies (Jenny Sims)
Proofreading by: Christina Routhier

Dedication

*To those green flag heroes who do red flag things...
because love makes us all a little crazy.*

One

Sailor

Hospitals and Ghosts

I SHOULD SEE WHITE LIGHTS AND PEARLY gates, right?

So why can I only see him?

Milton's face burned a permanent nightmare on my eyesight, thanks to him strangling me to death on the rug I'd bought in honour of my nana's birthday. She would've been ninety-nine. We'd often joked that she'd make it to two hundred—

Until time decided it could stop, just like that.

Just like it almost ended for me.

Or rather, *had* ended for me.

Yet here I was, being wheeled at dizzying speed beneath row after row of fluorescent lights, strangers looking down at me with worried frowns, hands touching me with professional inspections.

Everything was a blur as doors banged wide, and the rush made my head swim. I closed my eyes again, but Milton was there, looming and sneering. His hands like iron shackles around my throat, his thumbs digging so painfully.

"Think he's better than me, huh? I'll show you—"

Blocking the memory of his voice, I tried to swallow, but fire-gushing agony looped around my neck.

Time skipped again.

I was grateful for the blips as I suddenly came to on a different bed with different people staring down at me.

Everything hurt.

Every finger and toe.

Every bone and limb.

Tears stung my bruised eyes.

Fear throttled me just like Milton had.

How was I here?

Had he stopped and called for help?

Was he here too? Playing the role of caring boyfriend all while waiting for yet another excuse to kill me?

A wash of full-body terror drenched me at the thought of him still in my house. The house my nana had left me. Prowling through the rooms where I'd always found happiness, contaminating every nook and cranny with his violence.

God, how could I have been so *stupid*?

How could I let him taint my most favourite place in the world?

A nurse poked me with a needle. Another nurse pressed a few buttons on a machine by my head. They looked at each other before glancing at me with a pitying smile. "You'll be okay. You're safe now, alright? He can't get you here."

I wanted to cry.

I might be safe in this chaotic place with doctors and patients and beeping, annoying monitors, but what about my home? How could I ever go back there? How could I ever be in the same room as him again?

The kind nurse with bright coral lips gave me a gentle pat on the shoulder. "Relax now. We've got you."

A fuzzy cloud crept over my mind.

I tried to fight it.

But sleep pulled me under, and the last thing I saw was the ghost of my nana standing at the foot of my bed. Her thick white hair curled perfectly around her chin, the usual pink peony in the top button of her housedress, and a wonderful smile on her gorgeous, wizened face. "Rest, Little Lor. Everything will work out in the end…you'll see."

I slipped into darkness.

"Did the scans show any internal bleeding?" A masculine voice that sounded familiar wriggled through my gluey thoughts.

"No, Dr North. She was lucky."

"Lucky? You call attempted murder lucky?"

"Oh no! Of course not. I just meant…she'll recover. It'll take time, but she'll heal."

"Give me a rundown."

"Of course, Dr North. She's suffered contusions to large areas of her arms and legs, has a hematoma on her hip, multiple abrasions, and a few bruised ribs. Dr Yang did a thorough investigation of her neck and spine, and there doesn't appear to be any skeletal damage. However, he did recommend she doesn't try to speak for up to a week while her larynx heals."

"Thank you, Hayley."

That ruff-gruff, kind voice. It wasn't just familiar—it was one I'd heard almost every day for the past two years—ever since I'd moved in with my nana after she lost Pops. I'd also heard that voice change from teenage crackle to deep baritone as we grew up on either side of the fence.

I forced my heavy eyelids to open.

Fuzzy sight revealed a pretty nurse and a handsome doctor.

His shoes scuffed as he shifted to move away from my bedside. "Let me know when she wakes."

"Will do, Dr—"

"*Wait…*" I tried to speak. It came out like a smoker's cough. And wow, it *hurt.*

Dr North froze. His vibrant green gaze snapped to mine. "Ah, Ms. Rose. Welcome back."

Ms. Rose?

Since when had he ever called me Ms. Rose?

Then again, the man standing over me wasn't the boy who'd teased me when I'd stayed for a week or so every few years to visit my grandparents. There was no sign of the neighbourhood kid who stole my nana's freshly baked cookies and pulled my pigtails.

He was a stranger in a white coat.

He's the reason Milton tried to kill me…

A full-body adrenaline dump had me scrambling out of bed.

I couldn't be around him.

I had to leave.

Now.

Milton can't see me talking to him. He'll—

"Hey! Hey, it's okay." Dr North grabbed my shoulder and elbow and eased me back down. His touch was gentle, but every place he connected, my body ached with a million bruises.

Panting, wincing, gasping with agony and fear and memories, I struggled.

"You're safe. He's not here." Dr North kept me kindly but firmly pressed against my pillow. "Stop moving, please. Otherwise, you'll hurt yourself even more."

The nurse went to my other side and gently laid her hand on my arm. "You're okay. It's a shock waking up in a new place, I know. But Dr North is right. You're safe here. Just take a deep breath for us. That's it."

I swallowed and immediately wished I hadn't.

I'd never felt such fire. Such swollen, molten agony.

My fingers flew to my throat, sure I'd find my neck doubled in size.

The nurse, Hayley, went to stop me, but Dr North gave her a soft smile. "I have it from here. You're free to attend to your other patients."

Hayley nodded, her eyes lingering on him. "Are you sure? She seems a little disoriented."

"I'm sure."

Hayley pursed her lips and stepped back. "I won't be far if you need me." She strode away in her crisp uniform and squeaky sneakers. Dr Alexander North didn't move until she'd gone out of earshot.

His rich red hair straddled the colour spectrums of richest fire and darkest brown, all while his suntanned skin hinted he'd enjoyed the hot summer we'd been having on his days off. His black-framed glasses couldn't hide the tiredness on his face or the dangerous amount of intelligence in his vibrant green eyes.

I'd never seen him in mint-green scrubs before. Whenever we saw each other—on the days we ran into each other, thanks to being neighbours—it was either a courteous wave as we grabbed our mail in mismatched sleepwear or a passing smile as we got into our respective cars to go about our day.

He'd always been friendly but reserved. Kind but standoffish. I supposed that was what happened when our two grandmothers (who'd been best friends since they were fourteen) had bought houses side by side in the fifties to raise their families, expecting their children and grandchildren to act like family.

It hadn't gone quite to plan.

Once he was sure we were alone, he let his professionalism slip a little. His eyes narrowed as they scanned me from head to toe.

I resisted the urge to squirm in the overly starched white sheets of my hospital bed. Memories of Milton accusing me of having an affair with him repeated over and over again.

"You've been banging him. I know you have. Well, you won't be able to anymore, will you?"

Flinching, I shut those thoughts down and forced myself to focus.

I wanted to ask where Milton was. How I ended up here. What on earth happened. But with no voice and barely any energy, all I could do was tremble in bed and blink at the man who was the reason— unknowingly—that I'd almost died.

His face went dark. "Melody would've stabbed that man with her favourite filleting knife if she knew what he did to you."

My mouth fell open.

He'd never shown that sort of passion before—never hinted violence stalked beneath his usual standoffish façade.

I cringed deeper against my pillows.

I'd never been a wallflower, but after what Milton had done and why he did it…it shook the very foundations of my world.

Not noticing my wariness of him, he eyed up the bandage on my left arm. The virginal white wrapping did its best to hide the fingernail gouges Milton had left on me as he threw me into the living room.

He raised an eyebrow. "Are you right-handed?"

I frowned but nodded.

I didn't want to talk to him. I didn't want to talk, period. I wanted to pass out and forget that any of this had ever happened.

Slipping a small white notepad from his scrub's breast pocket, he unclipped one of the pens poking upright and placed both beside my right hand. "Do you know how you ended up here? Do you know who you are? Who I am? Do you have any memory of what happened?"

My heart skipped at the hardness in his voice.

"Go on." He arched his chin at the notepad. "Don't try to speak. You need to let the soft tissue in your throat heal. But if you have questions or concerns, write them down, and I'll do my best to answer." He sniffed. "But answer mine first, please."

Sucking in a breath, I flipped awkwardly to a clean page and clicked the pen.

The sooner I answered him, the sooner he'd leave me alone, and I could breathe again.

My hand shook a little as I scribbled a reply.

I don't know how I ended up here. I'm Sailor Rose. You're Alexander North. And yes, I remember him hurting—

Scowling as tears flushed my eyes, I crossed out ~~hurting~~ and wrote:

*I remember him **killing** me.*

Doing my best to ignore the gush of icy fear to run and never come back, I added: *Where is he? Is he still in my house? How am I not dead?*

Alexander crossed his arms as I held up the notepad for him to read. Glancing left and right, studying the other patients in various states of healing in the large ward, he did his best to shed whatever tension crackled through his shoulders.

"He's been arrested, so no, he's not in Melody's—sorry, *your* house, any longer. You'll have to file a restraining order if he gets out on bail, but for now, he's in custody."

My heart fluttered with fresh terror.

Would he try again?

How long would he be locked up for?

If he knew I was here, speaking to my neighbour…God, he'd do worse than just kill me.

Another tsunami of fear drenched me.

I hated it.

Hated the icy, prickly terror that banded my ribs and suffocated my lungs.

I-I need to leave. Right now.

Straightening his spine, he added, "And you're not dead because Jim's dog slipped his leash while out for his usual walk and bolted to your back door. Jim chased him, saw all the furniture tipped over, you on the floor, and your boyfriend with his hands wrapped around your throat." His voice grew harder. "He didn't think. Didn't hesitate. He strode into the kitchen, grabbed Melody's favourite cast-iron pan and walloped him around the head. He was the one to call for an ambulance and the police. You're alive because of him."

His voice faded as silence fell between us.

I had an overwhelming urge to run home to my neighbourhood and throw my arms around James McNab. The eighty-three-year-old pensioner who'd flirted with my nana, Melody, across the fence most Sundays when they pruned their rose bushes.

Nana had always said he was a sweet young lad, but she didn't do younger men.

At fourteen years his senior, she was perfectly serious, despite them being as wrinkly as the other. I think Jim, me, and the entire street knew Nana's excuse was only because she'd been married to her soulmate for seventy-four years and lost him two years ago.

Placing the notepad back on the bed, I scribbled:

Is Jim okay? Milton didn't hurt him?

Dr North huffed with faint amusement. "He's fine. His dog is too. I believe Jim arranged for a few of his friends to help straighten up the knocked-over furniture, then locked up your house and tucked the spare key under the lavender pot."

I shook my head, once again overwhelmed at the close-knit community of our street. When I'd first moved in, it'd taken some getting used to—having complete strangers know absolutely everything about me had felt like an invasion of privacy. But now, with Nana gone, it felt as if she was still around. Still watching over me.

Nervousness prickled down my spine as I struggled with what to write next.

Dr North must've sensed my flagging energy as he unwound his crossed arms and raked a hand through his glossy red hair. "Just rest. I'll be by later to check on you again. You should be free to go home tomorrow." His professionalism returned, hiding the neighbour I'd spied through lamp-lit windows and fence palings. "If you need anything, just ring that button." He pointed at a remote on the bedside table. "A domestic abuse councillor will want to speak to you before you're discharged. Do you have anyone you'd like me to call to let them know you're alright?"

I managed to hide my flinch.

Funny how the pain could fade but never truly went away whenever I remembered I was the last remaining member of my entire family tree. I wrote: *Could you let my friend, Lily, know? Her number is 555-0987.*

"Of course." He pulled out his phone. "I'll do it right now."

"Eh, Dr North? We need you rather urgently, if you're free?" A different nurse appeared, a frantic look in her eyes.

His fingers flew over the screen, inputting the number into his contacts before slipping the phone into his scrub's pocket. "Sure." Glancing at me, he added, "My apologies. I'll call Lily when I have a spare moment."

He didn't give me a chance to write a reply.

With a lingering look, he vanished with the nurse and left me in a sea of hospital beds.

Two

Zander

Neighbourly Duties

I BECAME A DOCTOR BECAUSE I FELT hopeless as a kid when my dad passed away from cancer. My mom followed him not long after from a hit-and-run when she was leaving work.

I'd been eleven when my two sisters and I moved in with my grandparents. Thanks to them and their unconditional love and acceptance of our losses, I managed to retain my hope in helping people rather than turning to the dark side and getting revenge.

I watched all the superhero movies. I commiserated with the villains as well as the good guys. I read every book I could about men with magic over life and death, yet I could never bring my parents back or stop death.

The closest thing I could get to that sort of power was to wear scrubs and wield a scalpel. And I achieved that goal with a sheer-minded dedication that came at the cost of everything else.

I didn't care that my profession of choice was gruelling on my sleep, love life, and existence in general. I didn't care that medicine and my patients consumed my every waking thought. I'd gone into this career not for money, but to serve, and I'd vowed the Hippocratic Oath with every drop of sincerity I possessed.

Yet now?

Now, I'd give anything to *take* a life instead of save one.

Milton Rild.

The bastard who'd almost killed her.

Not that she was mine to avenge—we'd only ever shared helloes and how are yous—but she was my responsibility in a roundabout way. Her well-being and happiness had been tasked to the six-year-old version of me by Sailor's grandmother on the day of Sailor's birth.

I didn't get to meet her for a few years as her parents never visited, but I had photos shoved in my face and suffered through many a tea-date where my grandmother Mary gossiped with Sailor's grandmother, Melody, about how we'd grow up and fall madly in love and finally join our two houses together.

Needless to say, I wasn't a fan of my unofficially betrothed baby bride who was six years my junior. The first time I met Sailor, she'd been four, and it'd been the first visit Melody's son made. The grumpy bastard brought his equally grumpy wife and painfully shy daughter, and the visit had gone as well as expected.

I knew that'd hurt Melody's and Rory's feelings—that their son didn't want to spend any time with them, let alone share their only child. And I'd taken one look at Sailor Rose and dismissed the annoying request of looking out for her, then flatly refused to marry her—at any age. By the time I was thirteen and she was seven, she came for another visit and scampered behind the shed when I'd shouted hello through the fence.

After that, I didn't see her often. Every couple of years, at the most.

I'd seen her growing up in skips of time. Snippets of skinned knees and braces. Ugly dresses and different hairstyles. With six years between us, she was just the skinny little girl next door.

But that was before she moved back to look after Melody.

Before she started dating that asshole a year ago.

Before I'd taken my responsibility for her a little more seriously now that our grandmothers were gone and their wishes were all that were left.

It was also before my annoyance toward her turned into something *else*. Something I didn't want to name and would flatly deny if anyone asked me. Something that had always been there, slowly building as the years passed by, getting harder and harder to ignore, especially on those lonely nights when I spied her through the window.

But then he'd tried to kill her.

He'd tried to hurt the girl who was supposed to be mine, even if I was too busy, too stubborn, and too exhausted to claim her as my own.

My hands curled into fists again.

I'd first met Milton as he sneaked out of Melody's house at five a.m. I was heading for a shift at the hospital. Not that it was Melody's house anymore—she'd died of a broken heart, leaving yet another hole in my life after I'd lost my own beloved grandparents from various sicknesses over the years.

Dammit, enough!

Shaking my head, I focused on why I'd snuck into the staffroom on my way to see yet another patient. Pulling long shifts always made my mind a mess; my thoughts scrambled with patient data, to-do lists, along with the past and all the promises I'd made and hadn't kept.

At least I could keep this one.

Pulling my phone free, I scrolled to the number Sailor had given me. Pressing call, I paced the small break room.

The scents of coffee teased me with promises of fresh energy as the ringing suddenly switched to a chirpy feminine voice. "Hello? Who's this?"

I stopped pacing and sat in one of the worn vinyl-covered chairs clustered around a crumb-covered table. Considering every doctor and nurse in this place lived in a world of sanitiser and cleanliness, the staffroom was a disaster.

"Is this Lily?"

"Yes…?"

"My name's Zander North. I'm a surgeon at Cedars Hospital."

"Oh my God. Is it my dad? I *told* him he shouldn't have had that white bread. He knows he's celiac but just doesn't listen! He's going to kill himself through wheat!"

Resting my elbow on the table, I nudged up my glasses and pinched the bridge of my nose. Damn, it'd been a long day. "I'm not calling about your father. I'm ringing on behalf of your friend, Sailor. Sailor Rose. She gave me your number to—"

"Sails? Oh no! What happened? Is she okay? What on earth? *Ahhh*, I'm coming right now. I'll get in my car and—"

"She's fine. She suffered a few injuries and…" I paused. The programming that'd been drilled into me to stick to the facts and never give more information than necessary couldn't override the sudden burning violence in my veins. "Do you know her boyfriend? Milton Rild?"

The line went quiet. "Yes, I know him." She sucked in a wary breath. "What did he do to her?"

This was the part where I gave the hospital address and shut down how I truly thought about the patient under my care. But tonight, I just couldn't do it.

Sailor was my neighbour. My shirked responsibility. My childhood destiny if my grandmother had anything to say about it. And I'd had to watch her date that bastard for a full year. I'd had to hold my tongue when she let him move in with her. I'd had to keep my distance even when I had my suspicions of the type of man he was. I'd also come face to face with the awful knowledge that I'd wanted her for years and was too late.

What if Jim's dog, Biscuit, hadn't heard her screaming?

What if Jim hadn't been agile enough to swing that cast iron pan and knock out the bastard?

Sighing heavily, I struggled to contain the growl in my voice. "Milton Rild tried to kill her. She's okay, and he's been arrested, but she could do with a friendly face."

I waited for another river of words, but she was eerily quiet. Finally, she said, "I always knew he didn't deserve her. I'll be there in an hour. I'll swing by her house and grab some things."

Didn't deserve her?

Fuck, that was the understatement of the century.

I hung up before I could tell her exactly what I thought of Sailor Rose, her choice in men, and just how fucking lucky Milton Rild was that Jim had found him instead of me.

Staying in the shadows by the nurses' station on the sixth floor, I peered into the room across the hall. Conveniently, Sailor had been moved into the bed visible from where I stood unseen, the other four beds empty.

However, she wasn't alone.

Lily—her friend who I'd seen popping by quite often over the past two years—sat on a pulled-up chair and laughed as she passed her iPad to Sailor before reading whatever she'd written with the stylus. Patting Sailor's hand, Lily said, "I'll break you out the moment you get the all clear."

Technically, Lily shouldn't be here. It was way past visiting hours, but I'd instructed the nurses to let Sailor have the company. After all, Lily might not be family, but I happened to know that a friend was as close to family as Sailor would get these days. Her parents had died on some excursion in the Middle East after abandoning their teenage daughter at college. For her entire life, they'd acted as if they would have rather never had a kid, and now she didn't have parents.

At least I still had my two sisters—pain in my ass that they were. Sailor truly was an orphan, and that pulled on the part of me that was the ultimate sucker for the hurt and helpless.

Sailor pulled a face, stole the iPad back, then wrote furiously.

Lily read the screen and shook her head. "No, definitely not. We discussed this. You're coming home with me. You can bunk in my room. My roommate won't mind. I don't think you should be alone right now. Especially in that house where he—"

Sailor threw up her bandaged wrist and winced in pain as she tried to speak. She gave up as her swollen throat prevented her vocal cords from making sound. With a huff, she wrote something and shoved the iPad at her friend.

Lily's shoulders slouched as she read it. "I know it's your safe place and it's your home, but…he attacked you in it, Sails. You can't seriously think you can go back and live there after this." Lily shuddered. "You should sell it. Use the inheritance your nan left you and move somewhere else."

Move somewhere else?

The thought pinched like a trapped nerve.

Ever since Melody passed away and left everything to Sailor, I'd expected this day to come. I'd hated the thought of Sailor moving away because whoever bought the quaint two-story home would upset the dynamics on our street. I'd have new neighbours. Strangers who might not be quiet on the days I needed to sleep for graveyard shifts. People with screaming kids or noisy teenagers or annoying pets.

But that wasn't the real reason. The real reason was hidden beneath a lifetime of gaslighting myself that I felt nothing for her.

However, when Sailor showed no signs of selling, she condemned me to live a life of constant torture seeing her everyday instead of just sporadic visits. Each time I saw her, I had fought the very real knowledge that my grandmother had cursed me, and I had an unbearable crush on my neighbour.

I'd even contemplated leaving. I had my own house a few suburbs away that I'd bought when I first moved out. I'd deliberately bought close by to change light bulbs, fix internet issues, and generally keep an eye on my grand folks as they grew older.

When they'd died, I'd found myself spending more and more time at their place until I decided to rent my house out and renovate theirs. I was supposed to do it up in my spare time—*what spare time?*—and then sell it.

But…time had a habit of going too fast, and years ticked by far too quickly.

And now I was hopelessly fucking addicted to spying on the girl who was supposed to be mine and each time I convinced myself I should move on…I couldn't.

"We'll discuss this when you're feeling better." Lily sniffed, passing back the iPad.

Sailor scrunched up her nose and scribbled. Tapping the screen with the stylus, she arched her eyebrows. The black eye that the bastard had left her with glowed even from here. Her sandy-blonde hair was knotted and tangled from fighting for her life.

My hands balled. I had a good mind to call the local police and ask for Milton's location. He deserved to have his throat so bruised he could barely swallow. He deserved to have a lacerated wrist and contusions all over his body.

Sailor's skin recorded every second of the abuse he'd delivered. Every time he'd hit her, thrown her, and kicked her now existed, right there, for anyone to read.

My temper steadily climbed.

How fucking dare he hurt her? How *dare* he steal her sense of safety by—

"Zander?"

My eyes snapped from Sailor and Lily. I struggled to focus on a fellow doctor slouching on the nurses' station desk.

My heart rate picked up at the thought of Sailor catching me watching her. Clicking my fingers, I beckoned my colleague and friend to follow me farther down the hall.

Colin Marx—prosthetic genius and all-around amazing doctor—scowled but obeyed.

I didn't stop until we were well out of earshot. Ignoring the nurses giving me a strange look, I crossed my arms and looked him up and down. "What are you doing here so late?"

He matched me, his biceps popping beneath his black scrubs. "Could ask the same about you." Glancing over his shoulder, he frowned. "Spying on a patient, Zan?"

My initial reaction was to lie and deny, like I usually did when it came to Sailor, but he knew me too well, and it would only arouse his highly suspicious, annoyingly perceptive nature. "Just checking up on someone. She's my neighbour. There's a slight conflict of interest in me treating her, but I wanted to make sure she was recuperating alright."

I had front-row seats to his brain whirring.

He hadn't become the leader of the prosthetic department before his thirty-third birthday by being stupid. I swear he had an eidetic memory most days. It came in useful with patient cases yet downright irritating in everything else.

"Sailor's here?" he asked.

The fact that he knew her name irked me in ways I didn't want to unravel.

Resisting the urge to fidget, I shrugged. "You remember seeing her around whenever you visit?"

"Of course, I remember." He smirked. "She reminds me of a fragile little beanstalk. All legs and no substance."

"No substance?" I bared my teeth, falling right into his trap. "What—"

"Gotcha." He snickered. "I knew you watched her more than you let on." Unwinding his arms, he patted me on the shoulder. "Whenever I'm around at your place, you stiffen if you see her through the windows. In fact, I clearly remember that time when she'd forgotten to close the bathroom blinds, and—"

"Whatever you're about to say, don't." I flicked a look at the nurses still watching us under the guise of sorting paperwork.

"Aw, come on. I know you didn't perve. After all, the window fogged up real quick."

"And how would you know that?"

"Because I'm a man, and *I* sneaked a peek. Just like I'm sure you've sneaked many a peek because you live next door to a beautiful woman who makes you act like a teenage boy who doesn't know how to speak to girls."

I couldn't win with him.

I'd never been able to. Didn't matter I'd graduated with top honours and was the most promising surgeon in this hospital, every brain cell decided to go on the fritz. After such a long shift and a few sleepless nights, I knew better than to even attempt to take him on.

"I'm leaving." Striding down the corridor, I rolled my eyes as he fell into pace with me.

"Going home, huh?" He grinned. "But your sexy neighbour won't be there. What will you watch when her house stays dark with no snippets of her walking from room to room?"

Irrational anger chose that moment to slip free. Snatching his collar, I yanked him into the stairwell and growled. "She's in the hospital, asshole. By the guy who tried to murder her. I will never be able to 'sneak a peek' again. I feel guilty enough as it is."

"Hey, Zan, it's okay, mate." He threw his hands up in surrender, all signs of needling me switching into compassion. "I didn't realise she meant that much to you. I'm sorry. Truly—"

"She doesn't mean anything to me." Smoothing out the collar of his scrubs where I'd yanked him, I backed up. "Sorry. I didn't mean to grab you like that. I'm just…it's been a long day." Pushing my glasses up my nose, I shrugged. "She's the granddaughter of my gran's best-friend, that's all. I've told you this. I feel…responsible for her. Just like I felt responsible for Melody in her later years."

He pursed his lips and wisely said nothing.

Raking a hand through my hair, I huffed. "Whatever. I need to go to bed. I'll catch you around. Sorry again for my outburst."

"No need to apologise. I get it. You on shift tomorrow, or are you free?"

"I'm free. I actually have forty-eight hours off. Provided I don't get called in, of course."

"Great." He grabbed the door handle to return to the corridor. "In that case, I'll bring some beers around. I think we both need to remember how to relax a bit. This job is rewarding, but it sure isn't healthy when we take on the pains of others. Do yourself a favour and stop thinking about who you're responsible for. In fact, do whatever it takes to knock yourself out for eight hours, and then I'll pop round in the afternoon to chill. We'll have a barbecue, some beers, and some sun. That work for you?"

No, that didn't work for me.

What *would* work was returning here at ten a.m. tomorrow to be the physician to give the all clear to Sailor and take her home.

After all, we lived side by side. It wouldn't be a hassle to carpool.

I needed to see how she'd react stepping back into the scene of her crime.

Would she cope?

Would she freak out?

But...Colin was right.

She wasn't my responsibility—no matter the promise I'd made as a kid or the twinge in my heart as an adult—and I wasn't on shift. Besides, it already sounded as if Lily was abducting her for the time being.

She isn't mine to worry about.

A couple of beers to remind me to let shit go was definitely needed.

"You're on." I forced a smile. "See you there."

Three

Sailor

Home is Where the Pain is

"ARE YOU SURE YOU WANT TO DO this?"

I scowled at Lily as she asked the same question she'd asked a hundred times since she'd picked me up from the hospital and kindly driven me back to Ember Drive.

I went to speak and remembered the many guidelines the elderly doctor had advised before discharging me this morning. He'd suggested I stay for another day's observation, but I couldn't sleep, couldn't relax—constantly on high alert in case Alexander North popped by again.

I hated the fact that I was as wary about him as I was about Milton. That he'd been the catalyst for all my pain, and my body refused to forget that.

I'd refused to stay, but I had agreed not to use my voice for a week to let the swelling in my throat recede. My bruises would fade. My cuts would heal. My slight concussion would disappear on its own. What happened yesterday would be a distant memory in six to eight weeks.

However, that wasn't what the counsellor had said when she came to visit me as I awkwardly dressed to leave. She warned me of flashbacks and panic attacks, and I'd politely nodded along, all while convincing myself that I would be fine.

I'd survived.

He was locked up.

The end.

Luckily, Milton had tried to murder me on a Monday, which worked in my favour as I didn't have to be at the market until Saturday. That gave me four whole days to heal and figure out how to use enough concealer to hide my black eye and paint-by-numbers bruises.

Shutting off the engine of her silver Mercedes coupe, Lily turned to face me. "I know you can't talk, but I feel your annoyance, Sails."

She frowned and pointed a finger in my face. "I don't like this. I really, really don't like this. What if he comes back? What if you need someone to help you cook or go to the bathroom or—"

I slapped my good hand over her runaway mouth and smiled as best I could.

God, I didn't think not being able to speak would be such a pain, but it literally killed me having to stay silent. (And yes, I was aware of the irony that being killed had gotten me into this mess.)

Shaking my head, I dropped my hand and pointed at my inherited home.

Sitting on the grass-striped driveway, the red-brick garage full of Pop's tools welcomed me back. White jasmine vines draped off the slate roof, window boxes full of rainbow flowers, the gorgeous archway made of bent willow branches, the little fountain that attracted all the blackbirds and finches, the bird feeders, the Japanese maples, the lemon trees and feijoas, right to the huge hobbit-style gate leading to the secret garden of a backyard. The two-story house sat nestled in all of that. Softened by lichen and love, wrapped tightly with a white veranda with a swinging egg chair, and crowned by a front door with a stained-glass window showing a riot of frangipani and freesias.

This place wasn't like the house I'd grown up in with my parents across the country. That had been stark and sterile with no garden, no welcome, no soul. I'd found who I truly was ever since I'd moved in with Nana, and I'd never felt so safe or so comfortable...so yes.

I was sure I wanted to do this.

I *needed* to do this.

I wouldn't let Milton chase me from my happy place. No matter that my pulse skipped and adrenaline made me jittery at the thought of going inside.

Sighing heavily, Lily nodded as if she'd heard all my thoughts as we stared at the house. "I get it. You love it here. You feel safe here. But..."

I clucked my tongue and arched my eyebrow.

She smirked. Her dark brown hair caught the late morning sunshine, her fierce blue eyes like sapphire chips. She wore a navy power suit with white lapels and pocket trim, looking every inch the successful real estate agent. Next to her, I was the unnoticed skinny Minnie who preferred inappropriate jokes and comfy leggings.

I didn't always used to be that way.

I used to work in corporate.

I'd been an executive assistant to a publishing house editor. And as much as I loved to read the slush pile and help make other people's dreams come true, when Nana had admitted that she was past the point of living on her own and was deliberating moving into a home now that Pops was gone, I upped and quit and moved in.

My life had irrevocably changed.

For the better.

And Milton is not *going to take that away from me.*

With a huff, I opened the car door with my good hand and gingerly climbed out. Every bruise and injury seemed to hurt even worse today. The throbbing and stiffness almost crippled me as I hid my shuffling limp and strode as straight as I could up the garden path.

"Hold up, you stubborn woman." Lily scrambled after me, grabbing the overnight bag she'd brought to the hospital for me from the trunk. Locking the flashy car, she darted to catch up.

Cutting in front, she strode up to the front door.

I shook my head and pointed at the round portal leading to the backyard.

I didn't have a key.

But the spare was tucked under the lavender pot, courtesy of Jim. *He saved my life.*

If Jim and his dog hadn't heard me…

I shivered and pushed away such morbid thoughts.

How did you repay someone for saving your life?

Bake a cake? Buy him a new something or other? Get on my knees and tell him how grateful I was that I was still here?

"Ah, that's right." Lily nodded and hoisted my bag higher up her shoulder. "Ambulance ride while unconscious equals no key."

With a nod, I pushed open the hobbit gate on its well-oiled hinges and stepped into another world.

The back garden might look chaotic to some, but to me, I understood the madness within which Nana had planted. In the west, all the herbs for her essential oil pressing grew with wild chaos. In the east, all her vegetables. In the north, all the flowers she dried and designed into jewelry, and in the south, all the medicinal plants she turned into tinctures and ointments.

Not hers anymore.

Mine.

A swell of gratefulness filled me.

Memories of Nana teaching me how to use all her tools to turn petals into medicine and forage for nightly salads fresh from the soil echoed in every corner.

Despite her advanced age, she'd spent every day in the garden teaching me everything she knew. And with each lesson, I'd lost the drive to live in a city and run in the rat race. I'd become her assistant, selling her wares at the local artisan markets and natural healing shops.

Moving past me in her nude high heels, Lily nudged the lavender pot up and grabbed the key beneath.

That was another thing with a neighbourhood like this one.

Everyone knew the secret hiding places for keys and emergency items. I wouldn't have dreamed letting people in my old apartment block know where my spare key was, but here? It granted such peace knowing we all watched out for one another.

The back door creaked a little as Lily unlocked it and pushed it open.

The scents of drying lemongrass and oregano wafted from the farm-style kitchen.

The smell rocked me back on my heels.

The pain as I'd bashed into the counter.

The agony as he grabbed my hair and threw me into the dining table.

"You stupid cow, I told you not to look at him! I told you he's after what's mine, and what did you do? You smiled! I think it's time you had a lesson in how I expect you to act around other men. There are no other men, do you hear me?"

I flinched as his fist walloped against my cheekbone.

I stumbled as he cut off my air—

Not here.

Not real.

It's over.

I gasped as I forced myself to remember he wasn't here. That was yesterday. Today, he couldn't hurt me.

Today, he's in jail.

Dropping my bag by the back door, Lucy scaled the two short steps and grabbed me in a crushing hug on the lawn.

Her embrace hurt, but I returned it, all while trying to school my breathing. Trying so, so hard not to let Milton ruin this.

"I'll only ask one more time, Sails, and then...I'll trust that you know what you're doing." Pulling away, she cupped my tender shoulders and squeezed. "Are you absolutely *sure* you want to be here so soon? You don't have to sell. You don't have to move. Just...maybe give it a little time?" Her blue eyes softened. "Come have a few sleepovers with me like old times, alright? We can stay up late and watch swoony rom-coms. We can eat all the bad food and gossip about all the boys." She winced. "Oh, sorry. What on earth am I saying? Of course you don't want to watch rom-coms and gossip about boys. You probably want to stay single for the rest of your life after what he did. But if you stay single, what if you have an intruder? What if a pipe bursts? What if you have a gas leak? Living alone is dangerous, especially in a big old house like this. What if someone breaks in or a rapist is on the loose and—"

Laughing silently, I planted my hand over her mouth again.

She spoke far too much the moment she got anxious, whereas I tended to clam up.

That was why we worked so well. We'd met in high school. I wasn't exactly shy but preferred my own company. Meanwhile Lily, with her motormouth, couldn't seem to shut up the moment she got flustered.

Letting my hand fall, I went to speak. My throat spasmed. I just shook my head and mouthed, "*I'm sure.*"

She sagged and nodded. "Fine. Let's get you inside, then. I have a house appointment at three, but I'll stay until then. Afterward, I'll come back with easy-to-swallow soup and have a sleep over. No arguments."

I linked my arm with hers and smiled.

I gave her a thumbs up.

Together, we went inside.

Four

Zander

Appropriate Morality

CLUTCHING MY BEER BOTTLE, I TRIED TO look away but couldn't.

Down below, in Melody's overgrown wild back garden, Sailor sat alone at the wrought-iron café table for two. The metal used to be painted black, but the years had weathered it, and now rust crawled up the arms and legs.

Leaning against the window frame where I stood in my bedroom, I wished I was closer so I could see how she was coping.

From up here, she looked okay.

Her straight back and fierce hold on the book she was reading seemed normal enough but, at the same time, all wrong. She was too still, too tense.

Was she struggling being back so soon?

Had Jim put her furniture in its rightful place so she didn't see evidence of just how badly Milton had thrown her around the house?

Taking a swig of beer, I took my glasses off and rubbed at the indent left behind on my nose.

Guilt squeezed my insides.

After all my determination to leave things alone, I'd…done something.

Something that could get me into a lot of trouble.

Last night, after I'd come home from the hospital, I'd tried to do exactly what Colin told me to do. I ran on my treadmill to exhaust my body even though my mind kept racing. I had the hottest shower followed by the coldest, shocking my nervous system to reset. I even watched a show I didn't care about, hoping it would act like a sedative.

Yet at five a.m., I found myself sneaking out my back door, and trespassing onto someone else's property.

I broke the law.

Me! The guy who'd followed every rule and regulation and was proud of a lifetime of conscientious, appropriate morality had used her spare key and sneaked his way through every room. Melody's ghost followed me as I used my phone torch to check the house and ensure it was as neat and safe as possible.

But then I saw the blood.

Not much.

A few streaks on the kitchen bench.

A couple of droplets on the dining room floor.

I hadn't been prepared for the rush of fury; the crippling wash of *savagery*.

For the first time in my life, I understood what drove other men to murder. Good men. Men who gladly went to prison for executing their wives' offenders. Men who wouldn't touch a fly yet suddenly became experts in torture.

And so, I'd done the only logical thing.

I'd raided the cleaning products under the sink and scrubbed every surface and floor until I was sure Sailor's blood no longer tainted any of it.

I'd replaced the key as the sun shone on my illegal activities, then fallen into bed and crashed into nonsense dreams full of black clouds, blood, and powerlessness.

Colin had woken me at four in the afternoon by pressing an icy-cold, dew-dripping beer bottle against the back of my neck where I lay sprawled on my stomach, still in my black track pants and hoodie.

He'd laughed his ass off as I jolted upright, ordered me to get out of bed, then gone to start the barbecue while I took another shower, trying to rinse away the fog of bad sleep and the knowledge that I'd overstepped.

If Sailor knew I'd been in her house.

If she knew another man had trespassed when she already didn't feel safe.

Fuck.

"Thought I'd find you up here." Colin appeared on the threshold of my bedroom, nursing another beer. His baby-blue baseball cap, white t-shirt, and black jeans made him seem as if he was still in college and not a renowned doctor.

Tearing my gaze from Sailor, where she sat strangling her book, I forced a smile. "Just came to grab my spare prescription sunglasses. No idea what I did with the pair that lives downstairs."

Padding barefoot toward me, he ignored my messily made bed, black bedside tables, chest of drawers, and towers of medical texts and books. I'd renovated this room years ago, hiring two women who did local interior design to hang wallpaper that looked like concrete slabs and install wooden black-out blinds to take it from floral fifties to an industrial loft feel.

"I saw your glasses by the toaster." He smirked. "You should know by now you can't lie to me."

Slouching, I tossed back the rest of my beer. "Has anyone ever told you that you're a royal pain in the ass?"

"You do." He clinked his bottle against my empty one. "Daily." Looking down into my neighbour's messy garden, he studied Sailor for a moment too long. Finally, he said with kindness instead of scorn, "She's not looking so good."

I stiffened as I allowed myself to stare at her again.

She'd given up pretending to read and sat with her face buried in her hands. Her bandaged wrist bulky and awkward, her head bowed as if she was exhausted.

My heart fisted into a knot.

I couldn't keep looking at her. If I did, I'd do something stupid like go over there.

Forcing myself to move away from the window, I grabbed the case for my spare sunglasses on my dresser and strode in my flip-flops to the door. My black shorts and white tee allowed me to soak up as much vitamin D as possible seeing as I spent most of my life in a hospital. "It's understandable. She's brave to want to come back so soon, but it will take time before she feels safe again. You coming?" I arched my chin. "Those wings will be done by now. I'm assuming that's why you came to find me."

Abandoning his post by the window, Colin followed me down the stairs to the large foyer and open-plan living. I'd gotten rid of the paisley curtains and shagadelic carpet. I'd stripped off the busy wallpaper and refreshed the walls with off-white and grey.

I might've updated every inch of this place over the years, but I still got the feeling that my grandparents would be in the conservatory reading their magazines and newspapers, refusing to enter the digital age with iPads and interwebs.

"I came to find you as I *know* you." Colin shrugged and pushed past me. Swinging by the modern wood and marble kitchen, he snagged another beer from the fridge before stepping into the hexagonal conservatory and the deck beyond. "I know you're worried about her, just like you worried about your folks. You become personally invested in the lives of others and—"

"And you don't?" I grabbed another beer and joined him on the deck. The scents of charcoal-roasted chicken wings, garlic bread, and creamy potato salad accompanied the late afternoon perfectly. "I've seen you take work home all the time. You spent countless hours on that woman's leg last month, ensuring the knee joint was reinforced so she could keep jumping her horses."

"I did. But the difference between us is I like the puzzle of how to keep her doing something she loves, while you'd worry about her returning to a sport that made her lose her leg to begin with." Using the tongs, he loaded up a platter already towering with sausages, juicy steaks, and grilled corn on the cob. "It's fun for me to figure out ways for a new mechanism to work. Each patient is different with their needs and prosthetics." Grabbing a sausage, he bit into it and pointed the rest in my face. "The difference between us, Zan, is I don't worry about their mental health. I'm there to provide a service. A service I'm good at. And they wouldn't be getting the best of me if I constantly worried about their state of mind while adapting to their new way of life. That's not my job. My job is to gift that new way of life. The rest is up to them. See where I'm going with this?"

Scowling, I snagged a wing and sat heavily in the wooden deck chair I'd made with my gramps before he passed away. "You're being pretty heavy-handed, so yes. I see where you're going."

"Good." Finishing his mouthful, he dolloped a spoonful of potato salad onto a plate, tore off some garlic bread, and stacked a dangerously high mountain of wings before taking the seat beside me and tucking in. "Her mental health is not your responsibility. Her wounds were dealt with. Her overseeing physician will see her for a check-up. She has numbers to call if she's not coping. The only thing you should worry about is how long you should give her before asking her out for a drink."

I choked on my beer. "You what?"

He chuckled. "Oh, come on. You can't be that dense or believe I'm that blind." Biting off a hunk of bread, he said, "You've been sneaking peeks for years. You think you're fooling me, but you're only fooling yourself. You want her." Swallowing his large bite, he grinned. "And now she's finally single, so…how long are you going to wait to remind her that not all men are murderous assholes? That she lives next to one of the best guys I know and—"

"Quit talking while you're ahead." Leaping to my feet, I busied myself with loading a plate of food. I was grateful for my sunglasses— not only to block the sun but his far too piercing gaze. "I'm not interested in her in that way. I'm merely keeping an eye on her like her grandmother told me—"

"Yeah, yeah, *sure* you are. So this grandma of hers specifically told you to stand in a dark bedroom while she's in hers with her lights on? Did she tell you to freeze each time you see her by the letterbox? Maybe she also told you not to bring women here in case your neighbour sees you with someone else, and it breaks her itty-bitty heart?"

I groaned and sank back into my chair. "*One time* I asked to use your place. One time, Col."

"Because you wanted to fuck and not have your neighbour—"

"No, because I was too exhausted to drive anywhere, and she was tipsy. Your apartment was closer. Nothing happened that night."

"You're shitting me." He raised an eyebrow. "You went home with a super pretty girl from the bar, used my place with its bachelor vibes with a spa tub on the balcony, and *still* didn't score?" Leaning toward me, he scowled. "What's wrong with you?"

"Like I said. She was tipsy."

"Tipsy isn't drunk."

"It's still not right." I couldn't hold his eye contact or stop remembering how the woman in question had tried to instigate sex multiple times throughout the night. And each time, I'd politely but firmly turned her down.

By the time morning came around and she'd sobered up enough to make a rational decision, I'd frustrated her so much by doing the right thing she said I'd ruined her self-esteem, called me a tease, and left.

Which was fine.

Completely *totally* fine.

I didn't have time for a girlfriend.

I barely had time for a friend, and we both worked crazy hours, so our relationship came with built-in understanding.

I'd gone into this profession knowing full well I might struggle to balance love and career. I'd chosen it because I was great at what I did, got satisfaction from helping people, and had grown used to being on my own.

So what if I'd completely forgotten what it felt like to be touched by someone? So what if every release I had was by my hand and no one else's?

I was doing something worthwhile, which made up for the loneliness.

Not that I'm lonely.

Of course not.

I was twenty-nine, owned property with a mortgage covered by rent, inherited a house worth far more than I could ever afford, and most of my education had been paid off thanks to my parents' life insurance policy when they passed away.

I had no worries in my own life.

Which meant I had plenty of time to give it to other people who might not have as much as I did.

Flicking a look at the fence between my garden and Sailor's, he sniffed. "If you don't ask her out, I'll do it for you."

"You can't be serious."

His eyes hardened. "Deadly serious. I'm sick of you putting yourself last. If this is the only way to get you to think of yourself occasionally, then so be it."

"She was just strangled by her ex, you idiot. She's not exactly in the market for a hook-up."

"So don't be a hook up." He devoured a wing. "Be the guy you are. Support her while she's going through this rough patch. Be her friend first if that's what floats your boat. God knows you could use another one, seeing as I'm the only one who tolerates you."

"Get out of my house." I pointed at the gate with my beer. "You've overstayed your welcome."

He laughed. "Threats don't work when I know you don't mean them."

Sighing heavily, I dumped my plate on the wooden table between us. I tried to gather my thoughts so he wouldn't ruin my life. "Look, I appreciate your concern—"

"You're welcome. I figured I better worry about you, seeing as you worry about everyone else."

"But you have to promise me you won't go near her, alright? It's not my place, and it's sure as hell not yours."

He sat up and wiped his hands on a napkin. "Not your place? What the hell does that mean?"

"I mean it's not ethical. I'm a doctor, and she's a patient and—"

"She's not *your* patient. And even if she was, there's no law saying you can't date." He grinned. "That 'suggestion' was just some morality clause thrown in to prevent—"

"Predators from preying on injured people."

"So you're a predator now?"

"No, I'm—" I cut myself off with a groan. "I'm her neighbour. That's all."

"Didn't you say your grandmothers had dreams of marrying their kids off to each other?"

"They did, and look at how well that turned out. Melody and Rory's son ran as far away from them as possible, and my parents were childhood nemeses only to somehow defy all odds by getting married at eighteen and staying married."

"There're always the grandchildren then. That's you, by the way. I'm sure you'd make some ghosts very happy if you married the girl next door."

"Not gonna happen. And if you're not going to drop this subject, leave."

"How are your sisters, by the way?" Colin waggled his eyebrows, knowing full well my threats were useless. "Single?"

I relaxed slightly, grateful the topic of conversation no longer included me. "Jolie just had a bad breakup actually, and Christina doesn't want anything to do with the opposite sex after what her ex did to her, so you're shit out of luck."

"Why does it sound as if all the women in your life hate men?" He toasted me with a sausage. "You know, you should start repairing women's faith in our fair sex by proving to Miss Sailor Neighbour over there that you're—"

"Done with this." Standing, I loomed over him. "Pick another subject or forfeit the right to eat this insane amount of food and go home hungry."

Standing too, he clapped me on the shoulder. "Tell you what." A dangerous glint appeared in his blue eyes. "I'll drop all mention of you pining over the girl next door if you make up a plate for her and take it over there."

"You've lost your damn mind."

"No, I'm saving yours." He smirked and shoved me toward the table. "You won't relax if you don't see for yourself that she's coping being home. So…here's your excuse. You're only being a good neighbour. Take some food. Isn't that what everyone does around here anyway? Borrowing sugar and baking cakes and shit? I doubt she's cooked dinner, and this way, you have an excuse to see for yourself that she's gonna be okay. She doesn't need you worrying about her on your day off, and then we can get back to the program of drinking and relaxing. Fair?"

I had a sudden impulse to stalk inside the house and slam a door.

But a tantrum wouldn't get Dr Colin Marx off my case.

He was like a rottweiler with an intruder: he wouldn't let go until an arm fell off.

"Fine." I huffed. "But one of these days, I'm going to make you regret this."

"I look forward to it."

Five

Sailor

Silence is Sometimes Deafening

"OH, GOOD GOD, YOU GAVE ME SUCH a fright!"

Lily's high-pitched voice sailed through the open back door. I'd left it ajar to let the slowly setting sun spill inside, encouraging it to chase away the shadows and the memories.

Eighty-three-year-old Jim must've not only rearranged my fallen furniture but cleaned too. The scents of pine and lemon invaded every room, overshadowing any lingering smell of Milton's musky aftershave.

I made a mental note to bake Jim two cakes. No, *ten* cakes.

The fact that I couldn't smell Milton anymore, even in my bedroom, helped keep the awful flashbacks at bay.

Mostly.

I hadn't been prepared when I'd stepped into my bedroom and saw yesterday play out in crystal detail. How I'd been standing by the window thinking up a new hand lotion recipe, deep in thought, when my neighbour, Dr Alexander North, had strolled into his bedroom, glistening with water droplets, dressed only in a white towel.

I hadn't been looking.

It was pure coincidence I was standing there when he'd appeared.

Unfortunately, that was when Milton appeared too.

He'd caught me staring gobsmacked and cheeks on fire as Alexander padded toward his dresser. His hands went to the towel. It came undone. I squeaked and went to move, to give him some privacy. Only a fist yanked my head back so fast, I'd fallen to the carpet with one pull.

"So this is what you do all day when I'm at work? Fantasise about your neighbour fucking you?"

His spittle had covered my face.

I'd been too shocked to move.

And then black spots and agony robbed me of the ability to run as he punched me.

"Sorry, that wasn't my intention."

I froze as Alexander's voice spilled like the twilight into the kitchen where I stood, cutting through my memories and giving me something else to panic about.

"It's all good. I was just coming to hang with Sails. I didn't know she had company." Lily's voice held a hint of suspicion.

"She doesn't even know she has company. I just got here," Alexander replied. "I figured she might not have anything for dinner, so…"

"You're being a good neighbour and bringing supplies?" Lily lost all sounds of being wary. "Wow, that's incredibly nice of you. Come on. I'm sure she's not far away. That smells delicious, by the way. What's under the tinfoil? Barbecue?"

A crinkling sounded followed by a gruff, "My friend always cooks too much. We have enough for the entire neighbourhood."

"Well, that's handy as I'm sleeping over tonight, and I have to say, it smells too good to let Sails have all of it."

Alexander didn't reply.

I imagined him struggling with something to say. We'd never said much to each other, but I got the feeling he was rather set in his ways and didn't like many people.

Which I got.

He dealt with so many at his job. He held so many lives in his hands that when he came home, I could understand the need to be quiet and recharge rather than being chatty with the people who shared the same street.

Putting down my water glass, I padded with bare feet toward the back door. My jeans and white jumper ought to be too warm for the lovely summer evening, but I couldn't seem to equalize my temperature. Plus, long sleeves and pants hid a lot of what Milton had done.

I didn't know how I'd cope having a shower tonight and seeing all my bruises and cuts.

I forced myself to put on a brave face.

I'd come inside to get a glass of water.

Most of the afternoon, I'd sat in the garden reading, or at least *trying* to read.

I'd tried to stay inside after Lily left to deal with her open house, but the minute she'd gone, the walls had closed in, and claustrophobia clawed. Without her, I couldn't stop my mind from going to dark places, so the sun had become my babysitter.

I'm so glad she's back.

I was so lucky to have her.

She'd been such an angel this morning.

While I'd straightened out the remaining out-of-place things downstairs, she'd marched upstairs with a black bin liner and removed every single piece of clothing, toiletry items, and phone chargers that'd been Milton's.

He'd moved in a couple of months ago despite the little voice warning me not to agree. The sob story he'd fed me of his awful roommate who'd kicked him out with no notice ensured I'd said yes over my reservations. After all, we'd been together almost a year. It didn't matter that not all of that time had been happy. It was the next progression in our relationship.

And up until then, he hadn't done anything cruel.

Sure, he'd become a master at passive-aggressive comments. Sure, he criticised the fact that I'd turned into a 'flower child' and sold homemade wares at a local market instead of going into the city every day and working for people who sucked my soul dry. He didn't care that I kept my promise to Nana to do something I loved while also keeping her customers supplied. And sure, he called me lazy, thanks to my inheritance that ensured I was debt free and had savings in the bank that meant I could live off the interest comfortably for the rest of my days. The red flags were there but I'd been blind—

God, enough, Lor.

Shaking my head, I marched from the house and almost tripped down the two steps as Alexander froze on the bottom one. Our eyes lined up with his taller height. His vibrant green gaze snapped to my lips before shooting back up.

For a second, I couldn't catch my breath.

He was so close. *Too* close. Every instinct recognised him as someone who could hurt me even though he'd only ever been kind.

But he *had* hurt me. In a horribly unfortunate way.

Inhaling hard, he took a step backward and winced. "Sorry, I…I came by to give you this." He practically shoved the platter of delicious-smelling food into my hands.

I grabbed it automatically.

My pulse skyrocketed that he was so close.

"Drooling over him again, I see. How about I rip out your tongue next?"

I almost gagged on the viciousness of Milton's voice inside my head.

I swayed and clung to the platter, hoping to God I didn't drop it. *Get a grip.*

Another gush of adrenaline had sweat running down my spine.

No matter how much common sense I tried to cling to, my body drowned with terror it couldn't shake.

Squeezing the back of his neck, Alexander looked nothing like the self-assured doctor in the ER yesterday. Nerves collided in his gaze, and lines bracketed his mouth as if he wanted to be anywhere else but here. Then his eyes narrowed behind his glasses. "Sailor? Are you okay?"

I tripped backward.

Lily rushed up the steps and grabbed the plate from me before setting it down on the deck chair and wrapping her arm around my waist.

She managed to find twenty bruises to press on, but I sagged against her anyway.

My mind buzzed.

My heart raced.

Sweat broke out on my temples, and sickness rushed up my sore throat.

"Sailor—" Alexander reached for me.

"He's touched you, hasn't he? How many times has he fucked what's mine?"

Milton's red-splotched face replaced Alexander's kind concern, and I choked on a scream.

He wrenched back just as Lily pulled me against her. "She's fine. Just…it's a lot being back, you know?" She squinted against the setting sun. "She'll be okay, though. Won't you, Sails?"

I nodded quickly, hoping like hell I didn't offend him.

He'd done something so sweet in bringing food over, and all I could do was look at him like he'd been the one to strangle me. Remembering my manners and cursing my awful black eye, I dipped my chin and went to speak.

But only pain came out.

"No, no, don't try to talk." Alexander flinched in commiseration. "Just rest."

Lily hugged me tighter, making me grunt in pain. Her voice adopted the polish of her real estate training. "It was so nice of you to drop off food for Sails. Thank you so much, Dr North."

He scowled but didn't look at her. His eyes never left mine. "No need for titles. Call me Zander."

"Well, thanks for the dinner, Zander." Lily nudged me not so subtly toward the back door. "I'd welcome you to eat with us, but you said you have a friend waiting?"

I winced again at her not-so-subtle hint for him to leave.

I tried to speak. To apologise. To explain I wasn't afraid of him, even if my panic said I was.

But he shook his head and held his finger to his lips. "Don't talk, remember?"

My eyes locked on his mouth.

Heat scalded my cheeks for no reason whatsoever.

His shoulders tensed as the moment dragged uncomfortably. Clenching his jaw, he focused on the black and blue swelling of my cheek. "Before I go, are you sure you're alright? Do you need anything? Did you pick up a prescription for pain meds? What about Dr Klep? Did she give you her number in case you need to talk to someone?"

Something deflated inside me all while my fear kept stalking.

This man was a doctor.

He wasn't here because he wanted to raise our acquaintance from occasional hellos. He was here because he was fabulous at his job and took every patient seriously, even if I wasn't technically his patient.

Forcing a smile, I nodded.

I didn't try to speak this time and was actually grateful that I couldn't.

I had no doubt that I'd make a complete fool of myself trying to cover up my irrational fear, all while confused over the quick inflation of my heart followed by the rapid deflation of reality.

You are seriously messed up, Lor.

Lily gave me a look. A look I knew well and a look that would come with many, many questions once he'd gone.

For now, though, she had my back and held me through my trembles. "She's okay. I took her to get the prescribed pain relief, and I've ensured the card from Dr Klep is on the fridge if she needs it." She smiled sweetly. "You're amazing for going above and beyond. I can't believe you made a house call, but truly, it's not necessary. She's got me, and she's strong." She flashed me a smile. "She's got this."

With a terse nod, Zander backed up another step. "Glad to hear it. In that case, I'll get going. Like you said, my friend is waiting for me."

Another twinge caught me unaware, just as sharp and agonising as my fear of him.

Was his friend a woman?

I'd never seen him bring anyone home, and he lived alone, but that didn't mean he wasn't seeing someone.

My chest squeezed to say something.

Anything.

But with another lingering stare, he smiled, nodded, and marched through the gate without a backward glance.

Six

Zander

Zero Responsibilities

THREE A.M. AND SURPRISE, SURPRISE, I WAS awake again.

I'd never been the best sleeper, but these days? Sleep was utterly elusive. Especially thanks to the almost coma I'd enjoyed earlier today after some all-night deep cleaning in someone else's house.

Pacing my bedroom, I contemplated running around the neighbourhood to burn off the anxious energy percolating in my blood.

I had no reason to be anxious.

I'd had a good evening with Colin before he'd called an Uber at ten p.m. Sailor had survived her ordeal and had a good friend taking care of her.

My sisters had their own lives elsewhere.

I had no pets, no responsibilities.

I literally had no one relying on me or needing me, and that…that was the fucking problem.

Heading downstairs, I strode through the dark house and into the kitchen. I would never prescribe three a.m. drinking to insomniac patients, but right now, it was the only cure I could think of.

Grabbing the bottle of Johnny Walker from the top cupboard, I poured far too much into a heavy glass tumbler before taking my medicine to the living room. The moon was out. Its silver light streamed over potted plants and my flatscreen TV on the wall.

I'd drink my cure, force my mind to quieten, then go to bed.

Moving the reading chair closer to the bay window, I went to fall into it, but movement outside caught my attention.

I went instantly stiff as I searched for any intruders daring to mess with our street. The moon shone extra bright, not granting any shadows to hide in.

And then, I saw her.

The fence between us was lower at the front of our two matching properties, our street-facing gardens comically different. Hers had her grandparents' arches, bird feeders, and plants while mine had modern gravel pathways and trimmed hedges.

Our wraparound porches were twins with the intricate architraves and banisters. However, Sailor had painted hers a butterscotch yellow last year, while mine were stark black.

I hadn't bothered putting any furniture out front because as much as I enjoyed living on Ember Lane and had grown up with the families around here, I didn't want to talk to them every time I tried to relax. Sitting out front was a ripe invitation for old maid Josephine to ask about my lack of a love life or busybody Patricia to set me up with her long-suffering niece.

The back garden was my safe space, but it seemed Sailor preferred the front tonight.

Perhaps she wanted to moon bathe. Maybe she knew the chances of being dragged into conversation against her will wouldn't happen at three in the morning.

Either way, there she was.

Curled up on a gently swinging egg chair, hugging her knees and staring at the sky.

I didn't move.

I didn't dare.

I doubted she'd be able to see me with the moon's reflection on my windows, but I didn't want to interrupt whatever she was going through.

My chest tightened as the glimmer of tears tracked down her cheeks, visible even from here. She made no move to stop them from falling.

Every instinct snarled to go over there.

To assure her she was safe. That he couldn't touch her. That she wasn't alone.

But I wasn't a psychologist, and this was none of my business.

If she needed to talk to someone, it needed to be with a professional, and as handy as I was with a scalpel, I had absolutely no finesse when it came to mental health.

I'd once scarred my eldest sister so badly that I'd been banished from offering a shoulder to cry on. It wasn't my fault that she'd asked me to try to save her dead hamster, and I'd helpfully announced it was dead and I could perform an autopsy instead.

Our mother had pulled me aside and explained that Jolie needed me to offer words of comfort, not hack up dear ole' Harry the Hamster.

Ever since that incident, I'd done my utmost to avoid any kind of healing that involved talking, crying, and sympathy because I wasn't wired that way. My idea of helping was to do something about it, not just sit around and do nothing. Even though doing nothing was exactly what most people with trauma needed.

Silence in which to heal.

Quiet in which to hide.

Therefore, Sailor definitely didn't need me going over there and making things worse.

Tossing my entire drink down my throat, I stalked away from the window before I could make a terrible decision and scale the fence.

She's not my responsibility.

I kept repeating that as I took the stairs two at a time and threw myself face first into bed.

Seven

Sailor

An Awful Mess

THREE DAYS PASSED BEFORE I FINALLY HAD the courage to write Lily a note.

A note that said thank you for everything, but hovering over me and watching me like a mother hen was doing the opposite of what she hoped.

I appreciated her sleeping here, but it wasn't helping me move on—she was just giving me a crutch to avoid having to face what'd happened. When she went to work, the walls closed in. When she came back, I felt stifled.

I didn't know what I needed to get over Milton's attempted murder, but whatever it was...*I need to do it on my own.*

Reading the note, Lily clenched her teeth before nodding with understanding. We stood in the kitchen where I'd made her a fresh salad full of herbs and delicious things from the garden to take to work with her.

Friday had come around so fast, and despite my hope that I'd be healed and have my voice back to go to the market tomorrow, I'd already emailed the organiser and apologised that I wouldn't be at the usual spot.

I also didn't want to admit that the thought of leaving this house sent a clawing, crawling sensation through me. Which didn't make sense as Milton had hurt me here. In this very kitchen. He'd throttled me five metres away in the living room, yet it was outside that suddenly seemed monstrous.

The big, bad world held so many more men like Milton, and I was far too stupid to know which ones to trust and which ones to run far away from.

"Are you sure?" Lily asked. "I don't like the thought of you being here alone."

Taking the note back, I scribbled as quickly as I could, hoping she could read my loopy, messy handwriting. *I hope you're not offended,*

Lil, but…you can't live here forever, and I can't move on until I face it. So yes, I'm sure.

She scowled as she read upside down. Her power suit of choice today was a thin silver pinstripe with a white blouse and pearl drop earrings. With smoky eyes and soft pink lips, she looked gorgeous.

Not for the first time, I worried about the male sex.

How had none of them swept her off her feet yet?

Not that they hadn't tried.

She dated often and had numerous apps looking for love.

Unfortunately for her, she was successful in her own right, had a fancy car, saved every penny of her commission to buy some land to do her own development, and most likely terrified all the boys away with her ten-year and twenty-year life plan.

Compared to her, I was going nowhere.

I truly don't know what she sees in me.

"I get it. I do." She fussed with her sleek ponytail. "I just don't like it. How certain are we that he isn't going to come back and try to finish the job?"

Knowing better than to try to speak—thanks to my throat that only seemed to get worse instead of better—I headed to the knife block and yanked out the carving blade. I winked and slashed it through the air.

She smirked. "Be an awful mess if you decide to give him a few holes."

I shrugged and gave a thumbs up.

"Yeah, yeah, I know. It would be totally worth it." She smiled a little sadly. Her gaze slipped over me, no doubt taking in my white summer dress that skimmed the tops of my feet. It didn't have sleeves, so the bruises on my arms couldn't be hidden, but at least the huge purple splodges on my legs and torso were covered.

"Okay, I know you're far stronger than you look, and I respect that. Just…" She drew up her shoulders and snatched the salad bag and her satchel. "You'll text me throughout the day and keep me informed of how you're doing? And you promise to call me anytime—day or night—if you need me to come back. *Promise*?"

I nodded. Placing the knife back in the block, I went to her and squished her in a hug. My bruises tried to complain, but I shushed them. I tried to whisper but it came out like a frog's croak. "*I promise.*"

Patting my back, she gave me a quick kiss on the cheek. "Fine. I'll leave you to it. What do you have planned today? I know you're not going to the market tomorrow, so you don't have to make any last-minute orders."

I pointed at the garden anyway and mimed harvesting and pounding in a bowl.

"Well, have fun making all your potions. You really should be resting, but I know that suggestion will fall on deaf ears." She headed toward the back door. "I'm warning you, though, if you don't message me back within a reasonable timeframe, I'll assume the worst and come racing back here." She narrowed her eyes with a false glare. "So reply, Sailor Moon. Otherwise, I'll tell the police to drop by to check on you."

I laughed silently at the nickname.

Memories of us calling ourselves after the anime cartoon that played before high school every morning warmed the cold parts of me.

Back then, we'd both believed we had superpowers. I'd been Sailor Moon, and Lily had been Jupiter, thanks to my blonde and her dark hair. We'd been ordinary girls by day and powerful goddesses by night. To be honest, I'd still believed that...until *him.*

Anger bled through me.

Stop it.

Enough!

How dare Milton strip all my power? How dare I *let* him?

Time to get over this and move the hell on.

Shoving Lily toward the door, I smiled and shooed her onto the porch.

"I'm going. I'm going." With a huff, she gave me one last look, then followed the garden path to the gate and left me alone.

I winced as I caught my finger on the edge of the hot tin as I tipped it upright. I held my breath as the peach syrup upside-down cake plopped perfectly onto the flower-printed plate below.

Thank goodness it's not a disaster.

Tossing the tea towel aside, I ran my singed finger under the cold tap for a moment while eyeing up the dessert I'd made for Jim. Peaches were his favourite—according to the conversations he and Nana would share over the fence. Peach in anything. Cobblers, crumbles, biscuits, muffins.

I'd never been a baker until I'd moved in with Nana, but thanks to some immensely enjoyable days spent in the kitchen with her, I'd graduated from eating store bought prepackaged monstrosities to scrumptious delights from scratch.

Licking my lips—still tasting the sweetness of the peaches that I'd sliced and caramelised in brown sugar—I checked the plastic bag wrapped around my bandaged wrist and stacked the dishwasher with my dirty utensils.

I'd stayed busy all day despite my injuries nudging me to rest.

I'd cleaned, even though the house was still spotless from Jim and the neighbours. I'd harvested all the herbs and flowers that were ready and gone through the intricate process of starting the oil press to make a new tincture of peppermint and geranium. The oil worked well on headaches, and stocks were low for the natural pharmacy that I offered at the market.

Nana had called her little stall *From Soil to Soul,* and when I'd first started helping her, I'd thought it would bring in pocket change from her friends in the area.

I couldn't have been more wrong.

People travelled from all over to visit her. Far too many had her personal number for refills, and when I'd offered to put her concoctions online, orders came through day and night.

She often joked that she worked more hours at ninety than she did when she was nineteen, and I believed it. I was also endlessly grateful to have inherited her customers because if I hadn't, I honestly didn't know how I would've tamed my racing thoughts.

Every time the house cracked from expanding with the sun, I jumped. Each time a bird pecked at the windows demanding more seed, I flinched.

I hated being this wary, this afraid.

It isn't me.

And the sooner I was back to my carefree, happy place, the sooner I could move the hell on.

Throwing myself into work all day had been a saving grace, but now I'd done everything that needed to be done. I had a delicious smelling cake ready to be gifted, and the awful knowledge that I had to leave this little sanctuary to deliver it.

My pulse instantly skyrocketed.

Wooziness made me dizzy. I leaned against the kitchen counter, pressing fingertips to my temples and begging the lingering concussion to fade.

His house is literally next door.

You're safe.

You're fine.

"You're a slut, that's what you are! A motherfucking whore who's fucking the neighbour. What is it about him, huh? Never took you for a snob who prefers to open her legs for an asshole doctor instead of your devoted boyfriend!" Milton threw me across the living room, laughing as I crashed against the sofa and fell in the gap between the couch and the coffee table. Landing on me, he shoved my legs apart and fumbled at his belt. *"How about you spread them right now?"*

Gasping, I doubled over and clutched the sink.

Memories I hadn't dared recall unravelled in a sickening movie.

He hadn't just beaten me that day, he'd—

I collapsed to my knees.

"Come on then. Moan for me like you moan for him." His hips *pressed against mine, his zipper digging into me.* "Why are you crying? Moan!"

Burying my face into my hands, I shook my head. I didn't want to remember. I liked the foggy forgetfulness that protected me.

"Open your damn legs!" Milton ripped at my underwear. "How many times has he taken what's mine, huh? How many times have you been that asshole's slut?"

Falling onto my side, I buried my head in my arms and curled up. I'd almost died, thanks to Milton's jealousy over a man I'd barely said a hundred words to since I was born. I'd tried to tell him Alexander North meant nothing to me. He was just the grandson of my nana's best friend. Sure, I'd heard enough stories about him growing up that I felt like I knew him. Sure, he was sweet and wonderful, and Nana loved him just like he was her own, but we didn't have a relationship. We didn't even have a friendship.

I'd screamed all of that while Milton tore at my dress and knocked aside my arms as I fought him. But then his hands had gone to my throat, and he'd squeezed so terribly hard.

"I'm the last man you're ever going to have inside you, do you hear me?" His hiss wriggled like a snake as unconsciousness came for me—

Gasping through my sobs, I sat up and clutched my hair.

He didn't.

He didn't rape me.

The hospital did a test, and it showed no evidence of sexual activity. It'd been at least a week since we'd last been *willingly* intimate.

Jim must've stopped him before he...

God, Jim.

It was as if a switch flipped inside me.

My tears dried up. The memories stopped. Jim had saved my sanity and my life that day. The least I could give him was a cake. And tomorrow, I'd bake him something else. And the day after, and the day after. I would drown him in peach desserts all because he'd rescued me from a fate I would never have woken up from.

Sucking in a deep breath, I stood on wobbly legs and washed my face.

I didn't let a single thought enter my head as I grabbed some apricot-coloured cellophane that Nana used to make gift baskets and set the plate in the middle. Gathering up the sides, I twisted it into a tower, secured the top with a silver ribbon, attached the card I'd written that would never convey my level of gratitude, and strode bravely out the door.

I kept my chin high all the way to the back gate and rehearsed what I would say to Jim, but the moment I stepped into the front garden and looked toward the street, every accusation and agony that Milton had thrown at me screamed back into being.

"You spread them for your neighbour, why not for me?"

Alexander stood with his elbow resting on his letterbox, his emerald eyes covered with dark sunglasses, his black slacks and shirt extra dark in the sun. He'd rolled the sleeves to his elbows and his hair looked as if he'd ruffled it a few times, hinting at his exhaustion and the fact he'd probably just got back from the hospital.

I only ever saw him in jeans and shorts on his days off. All other times, he dressed professionally despite donning scrubs the moment he stepped into work.

"Caught you looking again. How many times have you perved on him, huh?" Milton's awful voice echoed in my ears.

Guilt spread like wildfire, despite the fact that I'd never done anything wrong. I always made a point to look away if I ever caught sight of Alexander in the window. Our houses were close enough that we could string a rope ladder across our bedrooms and climb through each other's window, but that didn't mean I'd ever strayed over the boundary of respect.

"I'm glad Mable is enjoying Evermore Care," Alexander said, smiling wearily at old Josephine. The woman looked as if she'd fly away in a gentle breeze and clung to her walking stick as an anchor, but her smile lit up her entire weathered face. "Thank you so much for recommending it, Zander dear, and for the personal letter you wrote ensuring she was shuffled up the waiting list. Poor Mable doesn't have long in this world, but at least her last few months will be comfy."

"Don't mention it." Opening his letterbox, he grabbed a few letters and shifted awkwardly on the spot. His body language screamed he couldn't wait to get inside and be alone, but the politeness instilled by his grandparents ensured he forced a wider smile and stayed right there talking to her. "How's Gary enjoying Alaska?"

Josephine grinned from ear to ear, her blue-rinsed hair twinkling in the sun. "Oh, he's fabulous. Adoring the wild North. Says he's enjoying his new position putting in something or other." Shuffling forward, she rested her hand on his arm. "He video called me, isn't that grand? Showed me his house and everything." She frowned. "But it's so sunny and warm that I think he might be pulling my leg. I thought Alaska was meant to be covered in snow?"

Alexander patted her hand on his arm. "They have summers like us, Jo. Very hot ones, I hear, with lots of bugs."

"Oh dear, I don't like bugs."

"Then I suggest you avoid Alaska in the summer." Squeezing her hand, his chin tipped up and he froze.

My cheeks broke into an inferno as he looked right at me. The tension from talking when he would rather be alone switched into even tighter knots. The envelopes in his hand crinkled as his fingers curled into a fist.

I stood there in my white summer dress, bruises on display, and the curses of the man who put them there screeching in my ears.

"How dare you look at him. How dare you think he could ever want someone like you!"

It took every ounce of courage not to run back the way I came.

How had this happened?

How had I *allowed* this to happen?

In one awful moment, Milton had ensured the world switched from a happy place full of nice people to a terrifying place full of danger. And the one man Nana had drilled into me who would always be there for me if I ever needed help was the reason it all happened.

Dropping my gaze, I held up the tower of cellophane to hide my face and darted like an idiotic mouse onto the street, past Alexander and Josephine, and straight to Jim's house.

I didn't stop until I practically bolted through his back door.

I trembled as the old man dressed in a plaid suit and wire-rimmed spectacles hauled himself out of his chair and lumbered to let me in.

And I threw myself into thanking him with fierce hugs, wordless gratitude, and a huge piece of peach upside-down cake. I also gave his dog Biscuit a million cuddles, so I didn't have to think about Alexander North, his wonderful care to young and old, and the fact that I didn't think I could ever make eye contact with him again.

Eight
Zander

Not My Place

MY HEART FISTED FOR THE HUNDREDTH TIME.

I couldn't get the image of Sailor scurrying across to Jim's house—with her arms full, eyes red from crying, and hair a mess—out of my head. Her white summer dress was perfectly appropriate for the hot weather we'd been having, but the splodges of blacks, purples, and greens down her arms and shoulders made my guts clench.

He'd hurt her so badly.

He'd put his hands on her in ways that should *never* be allowed.

And instead of joining Josephine and me in a light-hearted neighbourly conversation by the mailbox, she'd looked at me as if I was the one who'd hurt her.

The flash of fear in her eyes. The splash of shame on her cheeks. She'd hunched and bolted as far away from me as possible. Every instinct surged to chase. To follow her to Jim's door and ask her if everything was alright because it obviously wasn't.

But…

Ugh.

…not my place.

If the very notion of talking to another man after what one psychotic monster had done to her sent her scampering for the closest hidey-hole, then how the hell did I think I could help by forcing her to be in my vicinity?

She visited Jim.

That thought stopped me short.

She'd vanished into his house and not come out for an hour. Long enough for me to pace a polished line over my living room floorboards and look out my front window far more times than I wanted to admit.

I'd forgone a shower even though that was the only thing I'd dreamed of as I'd driven home after a long shift. I ignored my stomach rumbling for food. I cursed the scratchy anxiety in my blood as it grew and grew until I found myself reaching for my door handle only to yank my hand back and pace again.

Now it was seven p.m., and I hadn't seen any lights come on in her house.

What if she was alone in the dark and drowning in awful thoughts?

What if she wasn't coping?

Should I call Lily and tell her to go over there?

Would that be stepping over a line?

Should I go check on her?

"Goddammit, it's not my place!" Snatching my glasses off my nose, I rubbed my eyes. All the tiredness from working crushed me. All the worry about my neighbour felt endless.

I wished Lily would sense that her friend wasn't doing so well and pop over. At least someone would be there with her. Someone would be there to listen if she needed to talk or stop her from doing anything stupid if the memories got too bad.

Right, that's it.

Jerking my glasses back on, I stalked to my back door and wrenched it open.

I had to see for myself.

I have to know she's okay.

With a churning heart and balled fists, I cut through my manicured garden toward the three fence palings that'd come loose in my childhood and had slowly rotted ever since.

I'd sneaked through this secret entrance multiple times, going to visit Melody and steal a freshly baked cookie or two. I even hid at her place a few times when I'd been in my 'I hate my siblings' phase and couldn't stand my two sisters. I'd begged Melody to adopt me so I never had to share a home with two bickering girls again.

A rusty nail snagged on my shirt, tearing a hole in it as I squeezed through.

My gaze tracked through the wild garden that always reminded me of a picture I'd seen of a Roman hospital back in the day. The land surrounding the hospital had been planted with every known medicinal plant, allowing doctors to pop into the flower beds and grab what was needed right off the stem.

At least the kitchen light was on, showing bunches of drying herbs and pretty flower magnets on the oversized industrial fridge.

This house was as familiar to me as my own, yet now it felt like it'd been touched by evil.

If I'd done a better job of talking to Sailor over the years, I could've offered her to stay at mine for a while. She could've been close to everything she loved and able to make her concoctions for the market but have space from the actual place where he tried to kill her.

Melody's probably cursing me right about now.

Pushing my way through the final paling, I sucked in a breath and took a step toward the house. Then froze as my cell phone erupted with an obnoxiously shrill ring tone that I heard even in the deepest of sleeps.

Fuck.

Slipping the phone from my pocket, I cut off the racket and did my best to swallow my temper. "Dr North speaking."

"Dr North? I'm so sorry to do this after your already long day, but are you able to come back in? There's been a minibus versus an overloaded truck, and we need all hands on deck."

My shoulders slouched as I spotted Sailor sitting on the couch, facing away from me. Her hair was just as tangled as before. The TV wasn't on. The fact she sat there, all alone staring at nothing, ripped the knots in my guts into smithereens.

I couldn't tell if my concern came from the physician who'd seen her in the ER or as a not-friend-but-childhood-something.

Either way, I couldn't leave her like that, but…I had no choice.

Not my place, remember?

Exhaling hard, I squeezed back through the fence and headed toward my car. "Sure, I'll be right there."

Nine

Sailor

Walls Are Closing

THREE MORE DAYS PASSED AND THE WORLD kept closing in around me.

I hated that I couldn't stop it.

I hated that I hated myself for letting it happen. I *knew* this wasn't me. I knew this fear didn't belong to me. I knew that I was safe and had a good life and was lucky to *be me* and nothing should shake that foundation, yet…it was shaken.

No matter how many pep talks I gave myself, I couldn't seem to stop the clotting cloud sticking to my thoughts or the creeping depression each time I looked in the mirror and watched my bruises fade from purple-black to brown-green.

My throat finally started to heal, and I could whisper without too much pain. Lily kept popping by unannounced between her open houses and client appointments, which meant I walked around in a perpetual state of false cheer, just in case she surprised me, when all I wanted to do was sob in the corner.

A wise part of myself knew I needed to feel what I was feeling in order to free these blocked emotions inside me. I had to be kind to myself and acknowledge that right now, I was feeling hurt and weak and small, and the sooner I *allowed* myself to feel it, the sooner I could move on.

But the moment I tried to let myself sink into the grief of losing something I couldn't even name, another wall would shoot up and fortify the barrier I'd already put in place. It came with thoughts like 'You're being silly, you're fine.' 'Stop moping, you're alive.' 'Stop feeling sorry for yourself, so many others are worse off.'

And so, I stayed on that awful carousel of knowing I needed to grieve, all while being far too stubborn to think I needed to grieve anything.

The morning my voice came back just enough to speak to someone without choking, I called the police number that'd been assigned to my case. I listened as the officer told me every shred of information I wanted. Milton hadn't met bail and was currently in a prison a few states over awaiting trial. His family hadn't helped him, and none of his friends had stepped up, revealing by their actions exactly the type of person he was.

How I'd been so hoodwinked by him for so long added yet another layer of guilt and shame to my already overloaded sense of failure. I'd failed as a woman. I'd failed my nana. And most of all, I'd failed myself.

Argh, enough!

Stalking through the house, I balled my hands.

If my mind wasn't ready to process and my heart was stuck in some sort of emotional jail cell, I wouldn't sit around and wait for things to get better. I'd fight to get there as fast as possible, which meant staying busy. I'd already replenished all the stock required for the market this coming weekend. I had no more flowers or herbs to harvest, and the oil press didn't need me to hover.

I didn't want to go out in public. I wasn't ready to face a shopping mall or a coffee shop or even a local park. Therefore…I would renovate.

I slammed to a stop at the bottom of the stairs.

Renovate?

I'd dabbled with the idea of slowly turning Nana's house into my own but…now? Would that be a wise decision or be seen as a cry for help? Was I trying to paint the walls and erase the past of the house or myself?

Am I the doer-upper?

Wow, I'm driving myself crazy.

Marching up the stairs, the black-and-white photos of my grandparents crept up the wall beside me, revealing their first date at a dance hall, their wedding, their honeymoon, and my father in his bassinet. I'd grown so used to seeing them on the walls that I no longer saw them.

Wasn't that the thing about life? We became blind and complacent until something reminded us to pay attention?

Maybe a renovation was exactly what I needed? To reclaim myself just like I would finally claim this house as my own now that my loved ones were gone.

Heading into my bedroom that I'd shared with Milton for the past few months, familiar black ice oozed through me. My bed no longer looked safe with its mound of lacy pillows, the ancient wooden dresser by the wall, or the bedside tables with dusty Tiffany lamps.

None of those things were mine. I'd moved into Nana's guest room and hadn't minded that there'd been no room for my furniture.

After all, I'd only been renting previously, and most of my stuff was second-hand.

But now…the thought of never sleeping in here again and erasing the ghost of the man who'd tried to ruin me sounded like a *wonderful* idea.

With a bubble of hope in my heart, I headed down the corridor to Nana's bedroom. The large suite took up the front of the house. Her window wasn't directly in line with Alexander's bedroom, thanks to the building work she'd had done in the nineties when she'd stolen some room from the huge primary to make another bedroom for guests.

Alexander's bedroom hadn't been carved up and took up most of the front of his house. The matching curved bay window downstairs added a nicely rounded area to stand and admire the neatly tended street. Nana's dresser still sat with its doily table runner and her jars of handmade face creams. Her bed and its large rattan headboard in the shape of a blooming rose was an ode to her love of flowers but also to her last name.

A last name I shared.

Rose.

The sensation of trespassing on her memories niggled. I didn't want to desecrate her past or throw out her old life, but she'd been gone a while now, and…she no longer lived here. She'd begged me countless times as she was nearing the end to put my own stamp on her home.

I'd put off claiming this house as mine, but now that I'd lost my sense of self, what better way to get it back than by renovating every room in the hope of fixing myself too?

Fine, I'll do it.

A flash of fear filled me at the thought of visiting a hardware store.

But that was the beauty of this day and age. I didn't have to go out. I could order it all online and have it delivered.

Spinning on the ball of my foot, my salmon-pink dress fluttered as I headed back downstairs to where my laptop slept on the dining room table. I ignored the whispers in my mind that I was getting too comfortable with not leaving. Sooner or later, this mild case of agoraphobia would become too big to fight, but as I clicked on the local homeware store and made a list of everything I'd need, I felt a little calmer. A little more in control. And that feeling was so much better than my current spiral.

Ten

Zander

Overworked Equals Spying

I SAT NURSING MY FOURTH CUP OF coffee in the staffroom.

I'd completed two minor surgeries today and still had one to go. At least it was a simple keyhole on a forty-year-old man's knee. He'd suddenly taken up football as part of his goal to get fit and popped a ligament because he'd broken the cardinal rule of not preparing his not-used-to-exercise body before thinking he was the next David Beckham.

After that, I could go home and rest.

And spy on Sailor.

I scowled at my half-empty cup. Somehow, I'd gone from catching glimpses of her in the window to actively searching for her across the fence. I couldn't rest worrying about her over there on her own, especially seeing as she hadn't left her house in over a week.

She had food delivered, groceries delivered, and yesterday, a huge van had turned up with two men who'd unloaded boxes and paint buckets, hauling them around to the back deck.

I recognised the supplies as tools for a renovation, which made sense seeing as Sailor hadn't updated a single room of Melody's place. However, the fact that she'd jumped into the project right now? It worried me.

Groaning, I yanked my glasses off and buried my face in my hands.

Not your place, Zan. How many times do I need to say this!

I'd repeated that phrase so often that it'd become a fucking mantra at this point. Yet it didn't stop the incessant urge to check on her.

The way she ran away from me repeated in my mind. I didn't know what caused such a reaction, but I had no intention of making matters worse by going over there unwanted.

But what if she's spiralling?

What if no one helped her before it was too late and—

"Fuck it." Snatching my phone from my pocket, I logged into my home security cameras. Two days ago, I'd angled the cameras to stop recording my front and back door to record hers instead. I felt disgustingly seedy for pointing a video feed at Sailor's home, but not enough to stop myself.

I'd checked with the local police that her ex was still locked up, but I couldn't erase the concern that he'd get out soon and finish what he started.

Inputting the password, I sucked on my bottom lip as the feed refreshed and showed me her house etched in buttery yellow, thanks to the afternoon sun.

No movement. Nothing for the sensors to narrow in on.

Dammit, what are you doing?

If anyone caught me spying on her, I'd be in just as much trouble as Milton.

The door to the staffroom swung open as a nurse I'd seen around but hadn't spoken to shuffled in wearily. Her eyes lit up on the fresh coffee pot, and she gave me a smile that widened as she looked me up and down.

My stomach knotted. I couldn't spy on my neighbour with someone else in the room. Giving her a half smile back, I put my glasses on and went to log off.

Only...the cameras suddenly sensed motion and zoomed in automatically as Sailor stepped onto the back deck and tipped her face to the sky. Dressed in paint-splattered jeans and a grey t-shirt, she'd wrapped a flower-printed handkerchief around her head with her sandy blonde hair in a high ponytail.

Thanks to the high resolution of the camera—that'd cost a fortune but delivered exactly the quality I'd been promised—I could almost count the bruises marking her bare arms. Her black eye looked particularly dark, and the way she took a shuddering breath and shook out her hands as if forcing herself to shed some heavy emotion hinted that all my fears were warranted.

She's not okay.

"You're Dr North, right?"

Exhaling heavily, I clicked off my phone and looked up. The nurse smiled and sat across from me at the large round table, sipping her coffee. "Alexander North?"

"Zander," I corrected, then forced myself to grin. "And you are...?"

"Elisabeth. I'm usually in paediatrics but was sent to help in the ER."

"That reminds me." I glanced at my watch. "I better get back."

"Oh, okay." Her shoulders deflated.

I stood and looked down at her.

And felt nothing.

No reaction—visceral or sexual, friendly or interested. She was pretty with an empty wedding finger, yet I couldn't have cared less. With big dark eyes, sleek brown braid, and a muscular form that said she'd be sought after in the ER when manhandling unruly or unconscious patients, all I could see was my goddamn neighbour.

Her eyes lingered on mine, simmering with a familiar look.

I recognised her signals of interest and invitation. Reacting to that invitation might be exactly what the doctor ordered. I desperately needed to learn how to balance a love life as well as my career. But the thought of kissing this pretty girl, of getting to know her and falling into bed together…all I seemed to want was another.

Fuck, I have **got** *to get myself together.*

"Enjoy your break," I said softly.

Not waiting for her to reply, I headed toward the sink, washed my cup, placed it on the draining board, and slipped back into the chaos of healing.

Eight p.m. and I still hadn't gone home. My last routine surgery went well, but I'd been roped into helping with a few emergencies. I'd decided to stick around just in case anyone needed anything else so I didn't have the nightmare of being called back later.

Resting in the staffroom, trying to ignore the persistent hunger pains growling in my stomach, I turned on my phone and noticed the security camera app was still open.

I went to turn it off, but the feed zoomed in on Sailor sitting in the centre of her wild garden. Illuminated by the hundreds of fairy lights strung in the citrus trees ringing the flower beds, she looked part fairy herself. She held something in her hands, and every now and again, she swiped at her cheeks as if brushing away tears.

My chest grew tight.

I looked past her to the back door of her house, hoping Lily was around and would gather Sailor in a hug or at least offer an ear to share whatever worries were hurting her.

But no one appeared.

She was all alone, in the dark, crying.

And that's about as much as I can fucking take.

My hands curled around my phone. Anger splintered through me.

Logging out of the camera feed, I pocketed my phone and headed to Colin's office, where I stored my personal things while on shift. Grabbing my satchel and keys, I powered through the hospital, refusing to make eye contact with anyone. By sheer luck of the universe, I escaped into the muggy night without being dragged into another emergency.

My black Chrysler beeped as I cut across the car park and pressed the key fob. It roared to life as I threw myself inside and burned unprofessionally fast onto the street.

Every part of me tugged to go home. To sneak over the fence and be that shoulder Sailor needed to cry on. Screw all my previous failures with helping psychologically damaged people. She was hurting. She obviously hadn't reached out to Dr Klep. She hadn't confided in her best friend. And she ran away from me as her neighbour.

If I didn't know any better, I'd say she was hiding her true feelings. And the longer she got away with it and built a false façade, the harder it would be to shatter it.

Not gonna let you spiral, Sailor. Melody would never forgive me.

At the intersection where I usually turned left toward home, I flicked on my indicator and went right. A stupid plan unravelled in my head. A plan that meant I could help her without her knowing it was me. A plan where I became her confessional instead of the guy next door—or the doctor who'd seen her in such a broken state.

Careening into the large department store's car park, I locked up and headed inside.

It didn't take long to find what I was after.

I grabbed the first cell phone I came across. Nothing fancy. I just needed it to be able to send and receive messages. As a bonus, it came preloaded with a SIM card and data.

I paid cash.

If I was going to do this, I wanted nothing tying me to an irrational, crazy idea all because I'd made a vow to an old woman and only now decided to honour it.

I strangled my steering wheel the entire trip back; I pulled up outside my house with chaos churning through me. This felt wrong. This felt seedy.

Yet I couldn't seem to stop myself as I killed the engine and sat there in the night.

Ember Drive was quiet and hushed, people already in bed or preparing to. With suddenly shaking fingers, I tore open the cell phone box, booted up the new device, and put in a bunch of Xs as fake credentials to get it operational.

Scanning the prepaid SIM information, I went to save the number into my phone under her name, but froze.

What the fuck am I doing?

This was shady as hell…wasn't it?

I mean, I'd bought a burner phone so I could message her without her knowing it was me, all in the idiotic hope that she'd trust a faceless, nameless stranger after being almost beaten to death.

You're the dumbest fool alive.

Slamming my head back against the headrest, I groaned.

This was a new low.

I'd let every protective, nurturing part of me run wild.

I wasn't qualified to help Sailor get through this. I had absolutely no business meddling in her affairs, especially hidden behind a wall of invisibility.

And yet...

Removing my glasses, I scrubbed my face. I couldn't get the image of her crying—alone and in the dark—out of my mind. She looked so small. So lost. If Melody was here, she'd know what to do. She'd boss me around on how best to help. She wouldn't even *need* my help because Melody would know exactly what to say to her granddaughter and how to make her heal.

But she's not here anymore.

Guess you're doing this then.

Gritting my teeth, I typed the new number into my phone and saved it under LL.

LL for Little Lor.

Her nickname gifted by Rory, her grandfather, and a name I'd often heard dancing on the breeze as he played with her in the back garden.

Opening a new message on my own phone, I hovered my thumbs over the screen. It took far too long to figure out what to type. I deleted so many sentences with a scoff and a sneer. I wanted to tell her I knew she'd suffered. That I knew why she was crying, and she could talk to me.

But that would hint at who I was.

In the end, I settled for simple.

Simple or creepy, I could no longer tell.

I pressed send; the other phone buzzed with the message, waiting to be read.

Wiping it down on my shirt—fulfilling my destiny as some criminal mastermind who thought removing his fingerprints could pretend he wasn't stepping over a line—I climbed out of my car and walked warily to Sailor's letterbox.

It matched mine in every way.

Unlike the overhaul I'd done to my place, I'd left the letterbox alone. Our two properties shared a mirroring gingerbread house mailbox that our two grandmothers had made the first week they'd moved in.

I'd heard my gran tell the story a hundred times. How they'd sanded wood and hammered nails and took turns to paint rows of pretty flowers on the sloping roof. The pink-and-purple numbers had faded enough to require fresh paint multiple times over the years, and in the end, Rory had lacquered both of them so the sun and rain didn't destroy the legacy of two friends.

The back of my neck prickled as I placed the phone without the box or paperwork inside. It sat there like a black brick, sinister and judging me.

Glancing into her windows, I didn't spot Sailor watching, but that didn't mean she hadn't seen. I just hoped like hell my unethical attempt at helping didn't backfire colossally in my face.

Eleven

Sailor

Random Gifts

I BARELY WAITED TILL DAWN TO CLIMB back up the ladder and continue painting Nana's—now my—bedroom.

The entire house smelt like paint, and I wore almost as much as I'd put on the walls. The moment the homeware store delivered my online order, I'd shifted all the furniture out into my old bedroom, packed away Nana's things for Goodwill, and covered the gold and silver swirly carpet with old sheets. Once I'd finished painting upstairs, I'd decide on what flooring to install, but for now, I focused on the bits I could do on my own.

I'd watched a few YouTube videos on how to prep the walls and applied plaster to the holes where old paintings and pictures once hung, sanded down areas that needed smoothing, and washed high-traffic areas with sugar soap. I'd applied the primer yesterday and now needed sunglasses indoors because the walls were so blindingly white.

Today, I planned on putting the first layer of the topcoat on. Thanks to a Pinterest post, I'd chosen a soft dove grey for the walls. I'd even managed to track down the wallpaper they'd used of a misty lake with white herons standing on long legs in a steamy new day.

The entire vibe was calm and tranquil, and I couldn't wait to get the feature wall done so I could spray-paint Nana's rattan bed frame a glossy silver to complement the cool tones, then scroll online for a bedspread to match.

By the time lunchtime rolled around and my hunger made itself known, I padded downstairs in my old high school sneakers that were now splattered with grey and headed outside to grab a carrot, cucumber, and salad leaves. The sound of a van accelerating had me changing direction and going through the hobbit gate to the street.

Thanks to my new project, I'd been able to ignore my itchy discomfort and memories of Milton for most of the day. However, I had a moment in the back garden last night while holding a photo of Nana and Pops. It'd been taken on their fiftieth wedding anniversary

when they renewed their vows at a local garden centre, and Mary—
Alexander's grandmother and my nana's best friend—had arranged for
blossoms to be blown in a never-ending dance of pink and white as
Pops sashayed Nana in a dance.

The sheer romance and affection suffocated me in happiness and
sadness, and I'd stumbled outside, needing some fresh air.

If Lily had turned up while I cried my heart out at the thought of
never getting to experience a lifelong partnership and marriage like
they had, I would've choked back my tears and pretended I was fine. I
would've tossed the picture I hugged into the closest veggie patch and
hidden just how much Milton had broken me.

I would never be able to explain why I felt so sad.

Nothing had changed.

Not really.

Sure, I had a few bruises, but I was still alive. No one had taken
my home away or left me destitute. I was still financially stable and
young. Still had time to find 'the one'. Still had my health and
happiness.

Yet in that moment of grief when I gave in to that sticky darkness
inside me, I sobbed into the grass and was grateful no one saw me.

*You weren't going to think about anything other than the
renovation, remember?*

The sooner I could get back to work, the better.

Scanning the street for neighbours I didn't want to talk to, I
headed to my gingerbread letterbox to check today's mail. At the end
of my drive, I glanced at Alexander's home. His garage door was
down; the house looked hushed. He was either sleeping from a long
shift or wasn't home.

I didn't care to analyse why a coil of disappointment worked
through me, followed by the tightest knot of anxiety.

Urgency to get back inside where no one could see my cracks had
me flipping open my letterbox, grabbing the two letters inside, and
hightailing back to safety.

Stepping into the kitchen, I tossed the letters onto the kitchen
bench and scowled as something heavy clunked instead.

"What the...?" Plucking the top envelope off the bench, I sucked
in a breath at the cell phone tucked beneath it. Sleek and small, it
looked utterly lost and out of place.

Did someone mistakenly put it in my mail? Was someone looking
for it? Freaking out to have lost all their photos and data?

Picking it up, I tapped the screen.

It came to life without requiring a password or keycode. A
message bubble waited to be read. A flicker of hesitation shot through
me. I didn't want to invade someone's privacy, but if it meant I could

find the owner of the phone, then…it wouldn't be so bad to read.

Tapping on the bubble, I waited for it to load, then sat heavily in the dining room chair.

> You don't know me, but I'm here.
> If you need a faceless friend, you have one.

I almost dropped it.

Why did that feel so personal? Why did it feel as if the message was addressed to me?

I rolled my eyes.

Lily.

My anxiety popped into affection.

She had a habit of buying me random things. Books she'd read and thought I'd enjoy. Kitchen appliances that changed her life. And I did the same to her. I'd sent her headphones last month when she complained of her old ones hurting her ears and ordered a huge basket full of all her favourite foods when she earned a big commission.

It wasn't unusual for us to drop things into each other's boxes or backyards, little keepsakes that said we were thinking of each other.

Smiling, I fondled the phone. Not the most logical present she'd ever given me but also not the strangest. A tad odd that she hadn't left it in its packaging, but maybe she figured it wouldn't have fit.

Slipping my own phone from my back jeans pocket, I called Lily on speed dial.

She answered on the second ring. "Hey, Sails. What's up? You all good? Are you safe? Do you need me to come over? Tell me!"

Ignoring her not-so-subtle-freak-out, I asked in a croaky-healing whisper, "Did you sneakily put a phone into my letterbox this morning?"

"Huh?"

"Did you give me a phone?" I swallowed hard on the residue of pain.

Her tone switched from panicked to suspicious. "No, why?"

"I just found one in my mail and there's a message that's a bit odd."

"Odd as in it's Milton trying to scare you? Can prisoners find a way to deliver stuff? What name is on the receipt? Oh God, what if it's a bomb? Call the police, Sails. Report it!"

My heart thudded.

Maybe she's right.

Trying to stay calm, I forced my whisper to get as loud as my healing would allow. "It's not a bomb, Lils, and I doubt it's from him."

Swallowing hard, I shoved aside the other envelope, looking for any sign of a receipt or clue as to who dropped the phone off. "There's no receipt. It's literally just a phone all by itself. It didn't even come with a charger." My voice burned and cracked. Wow, it still hurt to talk this much. "Perhaps I'm overthinking it, and the message isn't for me? It could just have been found in the gutter and shoved in my letterbox for safe keeping?"

The tension I hadn't realised was building slowly disappeared. "That's it. It's fine. I guess someone found it and put it into the closest place they could." I rubbed my throat, trying to ease the lingering swelling.

"Are you sure? I dunno, Sails. I have a bad feeling about this. What if it *is* Milton? He might be trying to scare you. Do you think he has friends who would come and finish what he started? Maybe he's hired a hit on you and—"

"This isn't a movie, Lily. He was just a lazy, jealous jerk who thought violence made him the bigger person. That's all."

"I still think you should call the police. Tell you what, I'll do it. I'll call them right now. What was the name of the officer overseeing your case again?"

"Andrew something or other."

"Helpful." A rustling sounded in the background. "Found it. I took a photo of his business card. I'll call them and—"

"Wait, I think—"

"What did the message say? Tell me word for word. They'll want to know."

"I really think we might be overreacting."

"Just tell me. I'm going to write it down."

"Fine." Activating the strange phone again, I reread the message. "It says, you don't know me, but I'm here. If you need a faceless friend, you have one."

"It definitely sounds threat-like," she gasped. "Like…I'm watching you and I'm going to kill you?"

"How on earth did you get to that conclusion?"

"Friend could be code for murder. Like he's watching you to make sure you don't testify against him or something."

God, *testify?*

I hadn't even thought about that.

Sitting in court, reliving what he did. *Seeing* him.

My entire body broke into ice and shivers.

Before I could get myself together, Lily rushed, "Get off the phone and call the cops. You should be the one to tell them about this. I'm coming round right now. I'll be there by—"

"No, don't." With a trembling hand, I did my best to fight back the clawing panic attack brewing in the centre of my chest. I'd never had one before, but the creeping breathlessness, the tightness…it was either that or a heart attack. Breathing carefully through my nose, my scratchy voice almost stopped working. "D-Didn't you say you had that promising couple having a second viewing today?"

"Yes, but—"

"Then go there. Don't come here. I'm fine. Truly."

I'm not strong enough to hide from you right now.

Swallowing hard, I added with a forced laugh, "I'm busy painting, so stay away, do you hear me?"

"But—"

"No buts. I'll call you later." I hung up before she could argue.

My pulse skittered as I traded cell phones and ran my fingers over the unfamiliar one. The message glowed on the screen, demanding an answer.

It was either Milton tormenting me, a complete coincidence, or…someone was playing a very cruel and unnecessary joke.

All my panic switched into rage.

I grew angry.

I was probably leaping to ridiculous conclusions, but I found myself typing:

Who is this? I found this phone and would like to return it to its rightful owner.

I could just imagine the rolled eyes of the police investigating my future murder. *'Ah, yes, Sailor Rose? She replied to a message from a hitman hired to kill her, and we found her in teeny tiny pieces stuffed in a suitcase the following week.'*

Swooping to my feet, I fisted the phone and trembled with the urge to throw it away.

This was a mistake.

Fumbling for the side button, I went to turn it off, but it chimed with a new message.

Stupid, *idiotic* curiosity had me clicking on it even while common sense screamed not to be a statistic.

The message was to you. It's not a mistake. You're the rightful owner.

My pulse skyrocketed.

My fingers flew over the keys.

Who are you and why did you give me a phone?

So you have someone to talk to.

My heart rate grew faster and faster.

Why would I need someone to talk to?

A reply appeared instantly.

Just a feeling I have.

Who the hell is this? Milton? Is that you?

The phone vibrated in my hand.

Names don't matter.
But if you need to call me something, X will do.

My entire body turned to Jell-O.

X? That's not at all terrifying or weird. Who the hell are you? Is
Milton putting you up to this? What do you want?

Tears burned my eyes as I waited for a reply.
The phone chirped.

Just like names don't matter, it doesn't matter who I am. All
you need to know is, I will never hurt you. I will never threaten you
or put you in danger. And no, this isn't Milton, and no, he didn't put
me up to this. (Whoever he is.)

Oh my God, I was going to be sick. This was a prank. A sick, evil
prank by a sick, evil man who thought he could torment me.
I shivered as I replied:

I don't believe you.

I don't know what I can offer to give you peace of mind.
Tell me what you need, and I'll give it.

Tell me why you put this phone in my mailbox. How do you know me? What else do you know? Why are you doing this?

The soft chime of a new message had me holding my breath.

This isn't going like I planned. I didn't want to be so frank, but I think...I think that might be best. Ready?

I could barely type, I shuddered so much.

Tell me.

I saw you that night. Being hurt.

The tears burning my eyes finally broke the seal and tumbled down my cheeks. I sat down heavily.

How did you see? Why do you even care?

I grabbed a tissue from the crocheted holder in the centre of the table and blew my nose. By the time I'd soaked up my tears, the phone buzzed.

I heard the sirens and saw you being loaded into the ambulance. I felt sorry for you. And I care because I don't like seeing good people in pain.

You don't even know me.

You're right. I don't. And that's what makes me perfect.

I sniffed back fresh tears.

Perfect for what?

To talk to.

Why would I talk to a creep who left a phone in my letterbox all because he/she saw me being beaten?

Because that creep has promised to never hurt you. And if he can do anything to help you...then he'll do it.

So you're admitting you're a guy?

Damn, guess I just did.

And you live around my neighbourhood?

I didn't say that.

How did you see me being loaded into the ambulance then?

I was just passing through.

Right. Sure. Don't believe you.

My brain throbbed with questions. Huddling on the chair, I fired another message off before he could reply.

Is this Jim?

I didn't truly think X was eighty-three-year-old James McNab, but it might trip him up. If he knew Jim, then I might be able to narrow down who it was. I wouldn't put something like this past the residents on this street. A helpful Samaritan doing the right thing in a very shady way.

I have no idea who Jim is.

Sure, you don't.

You're ruining this, by the way.

I'm ruining it? Ruining what exactly? Your attempt at some creepy god-complex superhero attempt at....I don't even know what to call this.

Call it whatever you want.
You can call me your friend too if you'd like.

I have a friend. I don't need another.

Okay then, consider me your little secret.

My little secret?! Do you say that to all the girls you plan on murdering?

Murdering? What? I literally just said I would never hurt you.

Yet you're hiding behind a screen and asking me to keep you a secret.

If no one knows about me, then no one will know what we talk about.

And that was my limit.
Tossing the phone down, I reached for mine and called the police.

Twelve

Zander

Nobody's Perfect

WELL, THAT BLEW UP SPECTACULARLY IN MY *face*.

What the hell had I been *thinking?*

Putting a burner phone in her letterbox? Telling her to keep me as her dirty secret? Christ! No wonder she thought I was planning on murdering her!

Thank God, I'd paid cash for the phone and not put in any of my details. This could destroy my career. I could be arrested. Gran would be rolling around in her urn right about now, wondering why the fuck I'd done something so stupid!

She called the police.

If I wasn't so shit terrified, I would've been so damn proud of her.

I'd heard stories from Melody that Sailor had a sharp tongue, inappropriate sense of humour, and could give back as good as she got, but I'd never been on the receiving end of such a conversation. Whenever we'd talked, it'd never gone past the common pleasantries of strangers.

I hadn't been prepared for the kick in my gut as her replies vibrated in my palm. I'd been wrong that she was broken from what Milton did to her. She wasn't. She might be a little banged up and choking on things she didn't want to voice, but she wasn't broken, and that…that gave me decidedly mixed feelings.

I no longer just felt responsible for her but was also *intrigued* by her.

And that wasn't gonna work because I couldn't be intrigued.

I didn't have *time* to be intrigued. Intrigued led to…other feelings.

Feelings I'd done my best to convince myself were never there.

Feelings I definitely had no business feeling: that tightening in my chest. That rush of endorphins and surge of testosterone snarling with unpermitted possession.

For God's sake, I'd only had one conversation with the woman, and I was already contemplating going over there and telling her everything.

I'd always known I was a goody-two shoes. I'd never been able to lie or steal or break even the smallest of rules. But it wasn't just the well-behaved doctor inside me needing to confess what I'd done but the very real, suddenly very protective part of me that didn't want anyone else to know just how incredible she was.

Goddammit, this is bad.

Nursing my small icy glass of Johnny Walker, I watched from my living room window as the two police officers stepped out of Sailor's front door and headed toward their cruiser parked across her driveway.

At the last second, they cut down the footpath, onto my property, and rang my doorbell.

Christ, could this get any worse?

What gave me away?

How had they figured it was me so fast?

Should I call a lawyer?

Throwing the rest of my drink down my throat, I hoped like hell I didn't smell like alcohol at two o'clock in the afternoon. Raking my hands through unruly red hair, I straightened my glasses, smoothed my grey t-shirt, and strolled to the door as if I wasn't about to explode inside.

"Can I help you, officers?" I pinned a polite smile on my lips as I swung my door wide and employed every trick I'd ever been taught to hide my true feelings. I'd gotten enough practice delivering bad news in the waiting room. I'd learned how to block myself as a person and become nothing more than the stoic, compassionate doctor my patients needed.

I didn't move a muscle as the two officers, one man with receding brown hair and one with a beer belly, returned my smile and rested their hands on their hips. The bulk of their tool belts full of weapons and walkie-talkies made my mouth go dry.

"Do you know your neighbour Sailor Rose?" the balding one asked.

"Of course. Our grandparents were best friends. We've grown up together."

"Oh, so you know her well?" Beer Belly perked up.

"I wouldn't say that. We're acquaintances. Why, did something happen?"

Be cool. Be cool.

"Did you see a strange man drop a cell phone into her letterbox, either yesterday or today?"

I shrugged with as much innocence as possible. "I'm sorry, no. I work at the local hospital, and my shifts are long. I didn't get home until nine thirty last night and slept in for my shift later tonight." I grinned. "Unfortunately, I don't have time to do much else than work these days."

The older one smiled. "I'm aware of how hard you work. I've seen you in the ER. You're a great doctor. Always go above and beyond on the cases we bring in."

True appreciation made me stand a little straighter. "That means a lot. Thanks."

It would truly suck if this nice blue-collar worker arrested me.

They didn't speak for a while. My heart rate went berserk. Finally, Beer Belly said, "Well, if you see anyone who doesn't belong in the neighbourhood, please give us a call." He passed me a business card.

I took it with a frown. "Is Sailor okay? Did something happen?"

"Oh, nothing to worry about. Have a good day, Dr North."

I ignored the worrying pinch that they knew my name and did my best to convince myself it was because they knew me from the hospital. I'd even patched up a few of their fellow officers when arrests and callouts went bad.

They definitely didn't know my name because I'd bought a phone and pretended to be a masked vigilante desperately trying to get the damsel to talk to him.

"You too." I nodded. Retreating inside, I closed the door and watched them climb into their cruiser and drive away. The second they were gone, I took the stairs two at a time and sprinted to my bedroom window.

Sailor's bedroom was empty, just like it had been for a few days now. A glimpse of her in Melody's room—that'd been stripped of furniture and had gotten a new lick of paint—hinted she'd finally decided to claim the house as hers.

She balanced at the top of a ladder, adding paint to the corners of the ceiling.

My heart rate calmed a little.

At least she was okay.

At least my attempt at helping her hadn't backfired and made her worse.

Fuck.

This was a *good* thing. A great thing. She'd called the police because she was smart. She'd let them take the cell phone away, which meant I was safe from doing anything else immensely wrong.

She'd be okay without me.

She'd heal on her own.

After all, I'd already proven I had no experience with heart-to-hearts. I'd barely been able to keep my identity hidden on the first volley of messages.

I'd had to lie within the first few texts by telling her I saw her in the ambulance, which actually…wasn't *totally* a lie. I'd seen her in the ambulance, just being unloaded at the hospital, not loaded in the street.

But that's beside the point.

I'd stepped over a line.

And now that line had been reinforced.

I would forget all about my attempt at helping and leave her the hell alone.

"Fancy coming over for a beer tonight?" Colin asked, throwing me a look as we both took a twenty-minute break for lunch three days later in his office.

Finishing my chicken wrap, I tossed the wrapper into the trash and took a swig of sparkling water. "That could work. I was supposed to come in tomorrow, but the planned surgery has been pushed back."

"Good, it's a date." He finished his sesame beef salad and closed the container. "You're looking a bit more haggard than usual. Anything I should know about?"

Screwing on the bottle cap, I shook my head. "Nope."

"Said like a guilty criminal."

I smirked. "Guilty? What am I guilty of?"

"Oh, I dunno. Perving on your hot little neighbour?"

I dropped my bottle. Thank God the cap was on; otherwise, I'd be wearing most of it.

Colin burst out laughing. "No comment, hey? You've finally given in to your dirty little habit. Have you asked her out yet? Remember my threat? If you don't do it, I'll do it for you."

My cheeks erupted with fire. I'd never cursed being a redhead as much as I did at that moment. I'd been lucky to avoid the freckles decorating my sisters and most days my hair could be taken for deep auburn instead of anything on the crimson colour palette, but right now, my natural skin colouring gave me away.

Colin quit laughing as I choked. Literally choked on spit and deliberated bolting for the door.

"Wow, I…I'm kidding, Zan. No need to have a heart attack." Leaning over his desk, he looked genuinely concerned for my well-being. "Are you alright, man? I mean, I've seen you wound up before, but this…this is something else. Did you lose a patient or something?"

Groaning, I took off my glasses and tossed them on his desk. Digging my fingers in my tired eyes, I refused to look at him. "Just…it's been a long week, that's all."

"It's Tuesday."

"Is it?" I didn't look up. "Feels like an endless Monday, then."

"What's going on? Fess up."

Dropping my hand, I blinked back the stars I'd left on my eyesight and did my best to lie to a friend who was basically a savant in lie detection. "Nothing's going on."

My phone beeped.

I sat ramrod in my chair, not because the alert was for a patient or another work call but because I'd assigned that noise to one person. A person I didn't think I'd ever hear from again.

One second, I convinced myself I had no intention of reading it.

The next, I practically threw myself off my chair, fumbling for my phone from my back pocket.

Ignoring Colin, I swiped on the screen and clicked on the new message.

A secret, huh?

Full-body shakes had my thumbs punching the screen far too fast.

No one else has to know.

And you won't murder me?

If I was going to, wouldn't I have popped around by now? After all, you did call the police on me.

Shit!
Fuck!
Unsend. Unsend.
Too late.

How do you know I called the police?

Hanging my head, I deliberated how to dig myself out of this shit hole. I couldn't confess who I was. If she wanted me to be her secret, I'd be her goddamn secret. But I also couldn't admit that I watched her from my house far more often than was normal, legal, or acceptable.

Is your delay because you're trying to come up with a lie or confess the truth?

Goddamn, this girl.

This was going to end so very, very badly for me.

She was scarily smart and almost as perceptive as Colin.

And look how well I held my own around him.

Sweat rolled down my spine beneath my scrubs as I made one of the biggest mistakes of my life.

I have a camera in your house.

"You *what?*" Colin screeched, snatching my phone out of my hands and scrolling his way through the message thread.

Ah, Christ.

How had I not noticed him looming over me? What possessed me to say I had a camera in her house?

What am I doing?!!!!!

In one message, I'd gone from a creepy idiot who'd gifted her a cell phone to full-blown home invasion stalker.

Colin's face went white. His dark brown hair flopped over his forehead as he peered at the screen. "What the fuck is this, Zan? What—"

"Give it back." Leaping to my feet, I snatched the phone out of his hand. I hated that I was more desperate to read Sailor's reply than to assure my best friend that I wasn't crazy.

And this is where I call the police again.

Wait!

"Zander…you've got to start talking. Otherwise—"

"Give me two seconds."

Tapping back a reply, I hoped to every deity in the universe that I wasn't fucking up everything I'd worked so hard for.

I meant outside your house. I have a camera **outside** your house.

Not technically a lie.

And you think that's appropriate? What are you? Some kind of pervert?

No. I told you. I will never hurt you. I will never take advantage of you.

You just watch me instead.

"Zander…talk to me. Right now." Colin crossed his arms.

I didn't bother looking up.

She didn't reply.

Of course, she didn't fucking reply.

My pulse pounded in my ears as I waited and waited, and when the phone remained silent, I sucked in a huge breath and turned to face Colin.

As expected, his eyes glinted with fear for my mental health, all while anger rippled down his arms as if to punch me. "Tell me. Right now. What are you doing?"

This was why I never put myself out there. Why I focused on helping others with scalpels and surgeries. I was better when bound by textbooks and things I'd learned through repetition and study. The second I went off script, I messed up.

Gran always said I was too impulsive, too eager. Each time I'd tried to help a sick bird or attempted backyard medicine on a friend from school, I always made matters worse.

And this cannot get much worse.

"You have three seconds, or I'm admitting you to the psych ward on an involuntary hold."

Sinking back into my chair, I held my head in my hands and did what I always did around him. I blurted the truth because he always heard a lie.

"A week or so ago, I angled my home security cameras to face Sailor's house. She's not doing well. She's not talking to her friend and has no other support. I saw her crying one night in the garden and...I made a stupid decision to give her someone to talk to."

His tension bled out slowly. Moving behind his desk, he sat down and cupped his chin in his hand like a shrink charging me five hundred dollars an hour. "Go on."

"She's not talking to a psychologist—or at least not one I know of. I know they say it's easier for people to talk to strangers about this sort of thing. More so than with loved ones. Impartiality is helpful to voice all those tangled thoughts. So...I tried to be that person for her."

"Okay...that doesn't sound so bad." He dropped his hand. "Anything else?"

"She called the police."

He sucked in a breath. "She knew it was you?"

"No...but they knocked on my door—"

"Jesus, Zan—"

"But only to ask if I'd seen the man who dropped off the phone in her letterbox. I-I was careful. I thought she'd handed it over because she hadn't messaged me since, but it turns out…she kept it." And I hated the twitch in my chest because of that. "I-I bought it with cash and—"

"And you're using your own phone number to message her. Do you not watch any movies? They can track you that way."

That's it then.

I'm screwed.

"Oh." My head tipped down.

"I'm not going to lie to you, Zan. This could get very bad very, very quickly."

"It's already bad."

He nodded with a wince. "It kinda is." His lips pursed. "But you did it for the right reasons. And I'm actually rather proud of you."

I frowned. "What do you mean?"

"I mean, you've boxed yourself in with work for so long. You've never done something off script like this. I see what you're doing. You use work to keep yourself from getting messy, but I hate to tell you, mate, this is *way* messier than just asking her out for a drink like I suggested."

A strained chuckle fell out of me. "Yeah, I know."

"I wonder why she didn't hand the phone to the police?"

"No idea."

"If she does and they track your number, you'll probably lose your job."

"I know that too."

"Even if you stopped now, you're already in way over your head."

"I know. Wait." I stiffened. "*If* I stop now? Shouldn't you be telling me to cease all contact immediately?"

His gaze darted over mine, churning with thoughts. "Tell me why you're doing this. Is it because you feel responsible for her because you're a doctor and she's the bruised little granddaughter next door? Or…"

I didn't want to ask. "Or?"

"Are you perhaps waking up to the fact that you actually *like* this girl? That you've liked her for years. And not because you were told to by your gran but because you get that certain kind of feeling whenever you look at her."

"What certain kind of feeling?"

"If I have to describe it, then it isn't it."

"Why are you so annoying?" I crossed my arms. "I've never disliked you more than I do right now."

He chuckled. "Answer the question."

"Or what? Still threatening to put me in a straitjacket?"

"No, I'm trying to decide if I'll help you or not."

"Help me?" I shot to my feet. "You can't be serious. You should throw my phone in the river and tell me to stop destroying my career."

He stood too. Moving toward me, he clapped me on the shoulder. "Perhaps you won't destroy your career. Maybe this is you attempting to have a life. Finally."

"By stalking a vulnerable girl who almost died."

"Hey, nobody's perfect."

"This isn't a joke, Col."

He went serious. "No, it's not. And I won't lie to you that it could get out of hand and end in some serious legal complications, but…" He sighed. "*But* if you truly want her to heal and she has no one else, then…she needs you. And frankly, you need her. So I'm in. I have your back. I'll help you so you don't royally fuck this up, but my help does come with a time limit."

"What does that mean?"

"It means, I agree that it sounds as if she needs someone impartial to get over this initial hump of healing, but the second she's finding herself again, you have to tell her. Alright? You have to be honest that it's you behind the screen. Who knows, she might already be madly in love with you by then and think it's adorable."

"Or hate my guts so much that I have to move to Australia."

"That's a big possibility."

I groaned. "Fuck, this is a disaster."

"Welcome to the world of dating, my friend." Patting my cheek, he headed toward the door. "I have to go. A patient is waiting. But this conversation isn't over. See you tonight for that beer. Don't be late."

Thirteen

Sailor

Stars Don't Talk

I LIED.
To the police.
Lily.
Jim across the fence.
Even myself.

I lied that I'd destroyed the phone when the police came to take my statement.

I lied to Lily that they'd taken it in for testing.

And I lied to Jim when he asked if everything was okay when we were out pruning the rose bushes last night.

All of them had bought my lies, but I couldn't buy the ones I told myself.

I lay in bed for three nights, convincing myself that I would never reply to the crazy man who'd given me the phone again. It wasn't acceptable to hand-deliver a cell phone and tell me he could be my little secret. That was wrong. Very, *very* wrong.

And yet…

Whenever I woke in the dead of night, all alone and curled in the corner of my bedroom—so, so sure I'd heard a key in the front door and Milton was back to finish what he started—all I had to do was look at that small black phone, and I'd find the strength to get up and check all the doors without turning on all the lights.

I took it with me that first night as I opened all the cupboards and checked behind every door. I kept it in my pocket as I painted and stared at it for hours, unable to fall asleep.

He hadn't messaged again.

And the fact that he hadn't slowly grew from relief into frustration.

He was the one to barge into my life.

He was the one to frighten me with his faceless forwardness.

But he'd also done something I didn't think was possible.

He'd broken up the shadows, just a little, and I no longer felt so suffocated.

He's watching me.

I huddled on the couch, staring at the old square television that I still needed to replace. Nana had never been one for technology unless it benefited her *From Soil to Soul* business, and she'd never bothered to upgrade her TV for a flatscreen.

I watched most things on my tablet, so the huge ancient box flickered in the corner, fuzzy and snowy, dancing light around the living room.

Scrolling through the message thread, I tried to make sense of why I wasn't as bothered about the fact that he was watching me as I should have been. I didn't know him. He could be just as dangerous as Milton…worse even.

So why did I feel protected instead of threatened?

Why did I search all the nooks and crannies of my garden to find a camera—not to remove it—but to make sure he wasn't lying?

Ugh, this is ridiculous. You're ridiculous. Stop this nonsense right now.

His last message glowed on the screen.

I use it to make sure you're safe. That's all.

I'd lost track how many times I'd read it. Each time, I found myself losing the initial understandable reaction of feeling violated, heading toward the incomprehensible feeling of safety.

Tapping the screen to make the keyboard pop up, I hovered my thumbs in place.

Don't you dare.

I sighed and slouched.

No, I really shouldn't.

Glancing at the time, wincing that two a.m. had rolled around and I still wasn't in bed, I did the adult thing and turned off the screen. Hauling myself upright, I padded barefoot toward the stairs.

I was proud of myself.

I'd withheld against growing temptation to message him for another night.

A few more days and the feeling would pass. I could throw the phone away, and life would continue as normal.

But normal sucks right now.

Gritting my teeth, I changed direction.

I stepped over the carpet where Milton had almost raped me.

The thought of going to bed—even if it was in a newly painted bedroom on a mattress on the floor instead of the room I'd shared with him—wasn't inviting.

I knew I wouldn't sleep.

Milton's whispers teased on the edges of my mind. The scratchiness of my throat still tickled, and I didn't want another nightmare so soon after the last one.

Instead of wasting the evening, I stepped through the back door, off the deck, and onto the grass.

There, I sank into a cross-legged position and stared at the stars. The glowing fairy lights in the foliage acted like earthbound celestial balls, glimmering on leaves and petals. The yin-yang fountain in the corner for the blackbirds splashed lazily, and a dog a few houses down whined to be let back in after a late-night pee.

I'm safe.

I'm fine.

So why did my eyes suddenly ache and tears start pouring against my control?

Why did they drip off my chin as I stared at the stars, begging them to unravel and fix the mess inside me? For most of the day, I could pretend I was healing. But at this time of night, in this much honesty...I couldn't.

Burying my face in my hands, I gave in and cried for things I had no words for.

I didn't know how much time passed, but I started to shiver in my Sailor Moon t-shirt and night shorts. I needed to go inside and crawl beneath warm cozy blankets, but...I didn't want to move.

Perhaps I should sleep out here amongst the flowers and the insects. Maybe they'd watch over me and—

My phone buzzed quietly.

No, not my phone.

His.

I hate it when you cry in the moonlight.

For a second, all I could do was gawk at the words.

My head tipped up, my eyes darting in all the shadows.

H-He's watching me right now.

Another message vibrated.

Whoever made you cry will never touch you again. You have my word.

My fear switched to terror. Scooting onto my knees, I went to leap to my feet, but a third message buzzed.

> I'm only watching to keep you safe. I will never approach you. Never hurt you. You will never see me or have to pretend with me. I'm just here...with you.

Fresh tears glassed my eyesight.

I sagged back onto the lawn, cradling the phone. All the tangled mess inside me suddenly, *crazily* melted into…relief. It was the sweetest, sharpest relief that made no sense and made me fear for my sanity.

My thumbs stroked the screen. I wanted to reply but had no idea what to say. I wanted to know why he chose to protect me but didn't know if I'd like the answer.

My chin tipped down as exhaustion fell over me.

A fourth message vibrated, almost as if he sensed my unwillingness, eagerness…confusion.

> You can talk to me instead of the stars, you know. Unlike them, I can answer back.

Sighing heavily, I replied in a daze.

> Where are you? How can you see me?

What I really wanted to know was how close he was and how much danger I was in.

Once again, he heard what I didn't say and sent me exactly what I needed to hear.

> I'm far enough away that I can't reach you if you run into the house, but I'm close enough to stop anyone from reaching you if they try to hurt you.

> So you're watching me on camera?

> I have been. But right now...no.

Climbing to my feet, I walked slowly around the riot of blooms, herbs, and fruit trees. Every alcove and branch-filled nook looked empty, but I could feel his eyes on me wherever I went.

He didn't message me as I did a full circle of the garden. He stayed quiet as I resumed my cross-legged position in the centre of the lawn. But the moment I sucked in a big inhale and chose to accept this, no matter how stupid and crazy and wrong, my phone chirped quietly.

What can I say to make you trust that I will never lay a finger on you?

Rubbing at the lingering ache in my knee where Milton had kicked me, I replied:

You could tell me who you are?

But that would defeat the purpose I'm trying to achieve.

And what are you trying to achieve?

Honestly?

Always. In fact, if I'm going to talk to you—against better judgement and sanity—then every message you ever send me better be nothing but the truth. If you ever lie to me, I'll drop the phone off to the police, and they can deal with you.

You could've done that last time you called them. Why didn't you?

Honestly?

Truth goes both ways. Question is are you brave enough?

I glanced at the moon, chewing my bottom lip. God, why did this make me feel so seen, so vulnerable, so...torn open?

He was nothing but a ghost.

And I'd done my fair share of talking to ghosts lately with Nana and Pops leaving me. I'd often wished they'd reply.

Sitting a little taller, I typed:

I didn't give the police the phone because

I looked at the moon again, searching for words that could explain the strange comfort that came from having a lifeline to a faceless, nameless stranger. He wasn't completely human to me. He could be a guardian angel or protective warrior. In the wreckage of my mind after being at the mercy of a man I'd given my body, home, and trust to—whoever X was...he was *more*.

As long as he abided by his own rules of never approaching me, never hurting me, then he was already ten times the man Milton ever was.

My phone buzzed.

> If I said something wrong, forgive me. I'm not asking you to tell me your deepest, darkest fears, I'm just...I don't really know. I just want to help.

I deleted my unsent sentence and typed:

Do you go around helping everyone you see in pain?

> Because I vowed I'd never lie, my answer will sound pompous and contrite. But yes. Yes, I do. Or at least, I try to.

Why?

> Because we all need help at some time or another.

Who are you?

> New rule. No more asking who I am, what my name is, or any other personal details.

Why? So I don't recognise you on the street when you come to murder me?

> There you go with the murdering again.

Can you blame me? No one will understand why I'm messaging you back. Everyone will think I'm suffering a psychotic break for not handing this phone in to the police when I had the chance.

> And we're back to my question. Why didn't you?

I stared at the keyboard.

I chewed my bottom lip.

The fairy lights flickered while I sat under the moon in a puddle of absolute honesty that I'd done my best to shove away and ignore—not just since Milton had hurt me, but for most of my childhood. Sure,

I'd had a good upbringing where every physical need was met, but my parents hadn't been well-versed in delivering emotional needs.

Nana had been the only one to nurture me in that way.

But even with her, had I ever had a frank, unscripted, honest-to-God *brutal* conversation with someone?

Glancing at my screen again, I began to type with all the truth he demanded. Because that was the deal if we were doing this, and...I rather liked not having to censor myself. I didn't have to second-guess or pretend or worry. I could be the rawest, truest version of myself, and if he didn't like it, so what?

He's no one to me.

Why didn't I? I think it's because I like the idea of having you as my secret. Someone I've never met before and never want to. Someone who does bad things but hopefully for the right reasons. Someone who cares enough about a stranger to sit watching her at three in the morning when everyone else is in bed.

He didn't reply as quickly. But I waited and trusted, and eventually, my phone chirped with a new message.

You asked me what I'm hoping to achieve by talking to you? I want you to see what I do when I look at you. I want you to smile instead of cry. And I want to beat the ever-loving shit out of whoever put those bruises on you.

My stomach flipped upside down.

Not that I'm violent or that I'll ever hurt you. I shouldn't have said that.

I swiped at the drying tears on my cheeks and forced a half-smile.

I wish you could beat the ever-loving shit out of him too.

Truth?

We just agreed, didn't we?

> I know I just said I will never approach you and you will never know my name, but I really want to know yours. I can already tell the promise to never see you in person will drive me crazy.

My forced smile turned genuine as the faintest feeling of the old me perked up.

Come anywhere near me, and I'll ensure you can never help anyone else again.

> You couldn't have said better words to keep me away.

Good. Remember them.

> Give me a name.

What? Like you gave me a single letter? X isn't a name.

> It's the only one you're getting. Come on...I need something to call you by. Choose one. Anything.

My mind went blank as I stared at the sky. My eyes dropped to Alexander's roofline. No lights in his windows. No sign of him awake or Jim or Josephine or any of the other neighbours on Ember Drive.

I was all alone, yet for the first time in forever, I felt safe.

I also had no idea what name to give him. I didn't want to use my real name as whatever we were doing wasn't real. He was a ghost who could use a cell phone, and I was the human he watched from the other side.

I like that idea.

Peering at the flowers around the garden, I tried on names for size. Orchid, Peony, Daisy, or Lavender.

Nope...

Following the patch of pansies, my gaze snagged on the three fence palings that'd always hung loose and offered a passageway from this garden to the Norths' next door.

A memory exploded. A moment I'd completely forgotten.

Carefully adding purple to the mane of my unicorn in my Mythical Creatures colouring book, I gasped as a teenage boy wriggled through the fence.

"Oi!" I sat up from where I'd been lying on my stomach in the grass. "What are you doing?"

Alexander pushed up his black-framed glasses as his cheeks tinged red. "Oh, it's you. I didn't know you were visiting." His nose wrinkled. "How many years has it been, and you still look like a weed."

"Who're you calling a weed?"

"Oh wow, not any smarter too." He smirked. "You'd get on with my sisters."

I huffed and crossed my arms, my pencil digging into my side. "What are you doing sneaking about?"

"I smelled cookies." Shooting me a grin, he marched straight to the back deck as if his grandparents owned this house as well as next doors. "Melody won't mind if I steal a few."

"I do. Those are mine. She baked them for me!" I shot to my feet and dashed in front of him. "Go away."

Rocking backward on his heels so he didn't crash into me, he scowled and tugged my left pigtail. "Move out of the way, Lori."

"Lori?" My chin tipped even higher as I swatted his hand off my hair. "My name is Sailor. Not Lori." I stomped my foot for good measure.

"No, it's not. I hear Rory calling you Lori all the time.

"He says Little Lor, you dingbat, and he's the only one allowed to call me that."

He burst out laughing. "Dingbat?"

I fought a giggle. "Suits you."

"Yeah, well. Lori suits you more. Now out of my way, Lori, I have cookies to steal."

The past dissolved as I shook my head. How had I not remembered that? How many other interactions had I had with the boy next door and forgotten? And why did my chest squeeze just a little too tightly because I could no longer even think about Alexander without feeling the thwack of Milton's fist or the horror of his hands pawing between my legs.

"How many times have you fucked the neighbour while I've been gone—"

Swallowing hard, I shoved aside Milton's hiss and typed:

Lori. Call me Lori.

He replied quickly, as if he'd been watching me trip into my thoughts, waiting patiently, keeping me safe from monsters in the dark.

I've always liked the name Lori.

I yawned and lay on my back, feeling sleepy and floaty for the first time in far, far too long. I should go into the house and climb into bed like a normal person. But the balmy evening, soft grass, and twinkling stars promised to keep the nightmares at bay. Even my shivers subsided as if I'd shook from other things.

How long are you going to watch me?

You should go inside.

How long?

All night if you want.

Rolling onto my side, I went to type back. To thank him for saying exactly what I needed to hear but sleep pounced, the phone slipped out of my fingers, and I drifted into dreams of cookies, unicorns, and protective ghosts watching me from afar.

Fourteen

Zander

Painful Nicknames

I WAITED UNTIL I KNEW FOR SURE she was asleep. Until her legs twitched and her body went loose on the lawn. Only then did I slip from my bedroom where I'd been watching her, grabbed the grey sherpa blanket from my couch (that came in handy whenever I passed out from a long surgery), and slipped out the front door.

I was halfway to her house before I realised why I couldn't be seen on the street carrying a blanket, why I couldn't sneak through her gate at almost four in the morning, and why I couldn't go anywhere near her as Zander North.

Fuck.

My phone weighed a thousand pounds in my black pyjama pocket. Our second conversation and I no longer feared this would end badly for me, I knew it.

The expression that the way to a man's heart was through his stomach might work on some, but for me? The way into my heart was to let me care. To trust me enough to put your very life in my hands, and tonight, she'd done that.

She'd gone to sleep outside.

She'd trusted that I'd watch over her. She trusted a stranger with shady means of communication to guard her against all other men, including the one who'd covered her in bruises.

I wasn't just in trouble, I was fucked.

Gran had always said I fell quick and hard. Give me anything injured, and I became utterly obsessed with making it better again. I'd devote every waking moment, every penny and effort, and if whatever creature I was trying to help died? Good God, it broke me.

I should've remembered that before I gave her the phone.

I should've recalled all the heartbreak of my youth when I wasn't good enough to save a life.

And to make an already bad situation worse, she'd asked me to call her Lori.

A name *I'd* accidentally given her.

A name I'd used on the rare times she visited, secretly loving that it got under her skin.

Ugh, this was a terrible idea.

I'd agreed to watch her all night like an unemployed fool. At least I wasn't working tomorrow but still...what sort of idiot agreed to stand in the bushes and watch a girl sleep on the lawn when she should be safely behind lock and key?

What possessed her to reply to me? Why hadn't she used common sense and told me to take a flying leap off a cliff or buy herself a gun?

Hugging the blanket, I stalked to the side door of my garage and snuck inside. I didn't dare turn on the light and used my phone torch to locate the old motorcycle scarf that I used whenever I rode my Harley.

The sleek machine rested under its canvas cover, looking dejected in the middle of neatly organised shelves of tools and offcuts. I'd bought the motorbike the day I graduated. It'd been half a dare, half a rebellion.

I'd pledged my life to saving all those in need of saving, yet the weight of that pledge? It crushed me with responsibility. It'd driven me into rocky territory that made me test the boundaries of my own life. After a long day in surgery or an awful afternoon of losing a patient, revving my bike and zooming like a reckless idiot was the perfect antidote to the uber conservative, overly safe doctor in my waking life.

Yanking the cover off the bike, I ran my fingers over the chrome handlebars and inhaled the rich scent of metal and oil.

I hadn't ridden it in over three years.

Most days, when I drove home from the hospital, I could barely see straight from exhaustion. I'd also seen enough motorcycle accidents that the kamikaze asshole inside me was quite content to drive a safe Chrysler these days.

But for the first time in a while, the urge to fly through the night made me ache for freedom. Freedom to have a life, make mistakes, and not let down thousands of people by being human.

Dammit, enough already.

Sucking in a deep breath, I found my helmet and the half balaclava waiting where I'd placed them last. The white print of a skull's jaw on the black material looked a bit ghoulish in the glow of my torch. It would probably petrify her if she woke up.

Ah well, better than nothing.

Shoving the fabric over my head, I yanked it up until it covered just below my eyes then fisted the blanket and sneaked through the palings between our back gardens.

They creaked a little, but Sailor didn't move.

She didn't stir as I crept across the stepping stones and over the springy grass. She mumbled a little as I draped the blanket over her then sighed as I stole a cushion from the reading chair in the little pagoda in the west corner and tucked it beneath her head.

I shouldn't be here. I shouldn't have broken my vow not to go near her.

But...I couldn't help it.

The shadows under her eyes spoke of her exhaustion.

The pinched sorrow in her face.

How many sleepless nights had she suffered to pass out this hard? Was it the memories keeping her up or the nightmares?

I made a mental note to ask her next time she messaged me as X.

Next time?

I balled my hands and returned to the shadows.

Do you hear yourself?

There shouldn't *be* a next time. This time was dangerous enough. I knew I should stop.

I knew I should march over to her house tomorrow and tell her it was me all along. I needed to confess that I was lying through my teeth all while saying I'd always be truthful. I couldn't have her tell me anything too personal as X because when she found out it was me, the betrayal she'd feel would be catastrophic.

Damn, this is a mess.

With my chest too tight and nerves too stretched, I went to stand by the palings so I could sneak out quickly if she woke.

And that was where I stood as the stars slowly faded and the sky lazily lightened and dawn brought a new day.

How old are you?

I smirked at the message that was waiting for me when I finally had time to check my phone after a long morning in surgery two days later.

I'd let my guilt fester and argued with myself each time I glanced at her from my windows. At least I'd had enough self-control not to give in to the temptation of messaging her.

I still couldn't shake the fact that every time we spoke, I was betraying her.

But...I'd also given myself a get-out-of-jail free card.

I could message her if *she* messaged *me*.

If she reached out then—in my twisted logic—she'd accepted me as X *and* Zander, even if she didn't know it.

Plus, I said I'd watch out for her, so I owed her a reply just in case she needed me.

Remember your other rule?

I sagged a little in my chair.

Seeing as I did better with rules, I'd drawn up a tight little contract for myself.

I could message her whenever she messaged me, but I couldn't instigate. And I was allowed to keep this going for one month. After one month, if she was no better, it proved I sucked as a counsellor, and she needed to see a professional. That would also be the day I confessed it was me.

Sipping my coffee, I adjusted my glasses and replied.

I'm one hundred and two but don't worry, I can still beat up anyone who dares go near you uninvited.

Putting my phone down, I went to the communal fridge to grab the leftover pasta I'd made last night. It wasn't often I cooked but Sailor had groceries delivered again yesterday, and a pottle of spaghetti sauce had fallen out as she'd collected the bags while I'd gathered my mail.

I'd had a hankering, so went to the store to get my own, even though I'd hated that she stiffened when she saw me hop into my car.

I'd waved and tried to remember how to talk to her as Zander instead of X, just in case she said anything. But she scurried away in a rush.

I didn't get it.

Apart from a bit of teasing and name-calling growing up, I hadn't done anything to justify the mix of shame and fear in her blue eyes whenever she saw me.

If I was honest, it hurt.

No, it killed.

Especially because she seemed to like X—a faceless stranger she'd never met—over the man who'd been her neighbour her entire life.

What is it about me that's so offensive?

My phone vibrated across the table.

Somehow, I don't think that's the truth.
What happened to the promise of honesty?

I groaned and wedged my elbows on the table. Running my hands through my hair, I hung my head. I'd changed her contact from LL to Lori the same night I'd stood by her fence and watched her until dawn.

Unfortunately, thanks to that chosen nickname, I couldn't get the past out of my head. The memories of her as a scrawny girl with pigtails or that time she came to visit and ended up with chicken pox. She'd looked atrocious, all spotty and sick yet…I'd spent more time over at Melody's in those two weeks than I ever had, not so subtly trying to help her get better.

When Sailor and her parents had left, Melody hugged me so hard. She'd thanked me for taking such great care of her granddaughter then giggled that she couldn't wait for us to grow up and fulfil her and Mary's dream of marrying their offspring to each other.

I'd scoffed, stolen a brownie, and bolted.

I'd forgotten all about it by the time Sailor visited three years later.

Fine, I'm twenty-nine. And that's all the personal information you're getting.

I went to press send but stopped.

Whoops, close call.

She was good at this. Too good. And I knew my weaknesses when it came to outsmarting wily people. The more information I gave her, even tiny tidbits like my age, the more she'd start painting a picture of who I was.

She might one day look next door and put the pieces together.

Deleting my message, I retyped.

I'm thirty-four. Now stop asking personal questions.

Don't you want to know how old I am?

I already know. Your birthday is on the 9th of May. You're six years younger than me. Melody would bake you a lemon meringue cake each birthday with lemons from her own tree.

Let me guess, you're sixteen, and I'm breaking yet another law just by talking to you.

Ha ha. It would serve you right if I was. But really?
Do I look that young? That fragile?

I didn't know how we'd become this familiar with each other so fast.

What was it about a screen and a keyboard that allowed an ease to form that never seemed to be this simple in person?

I just thanked every star in the galaxy that she'd never known my number as Zander because, thanks to the stupid decision to use my own details, she was far too close to the truth already.

Nausea suddenly filled me at the thought of never talking to her this way again.

Fine. You look twenty-three.

Shit, unsend. *Unsend*!
Too late.
What was I thinking using her real age?

Have you been in my house?

Why would you ask that?

Because you broke your rule about coming near me and gave me a blanket in the garden the other night.

Shit.
My hands shook.

I couldn't leave you uncovered. It just wasn't possible.

I should follow through with my threat to make you regret coming near me.

Will you?

I should be freaked out that you were close enough to touch me.

But you're not?

I shouldn't admit this but no...I'm not.

I would never touch you without your consent. I merely sheltered you.

I don't know what this says about me but...I believe you. And thank you. And now, please answer my question. Have you broken another rule and been in my house? Because your answer about my age doesn't feel like a lucky guess. Have you been snooping in my paperwork?

"Goddammit, Zan, you suck so badly at this—"

"Uh-oh, muttering to yourself is the first sign of insanity." Colin chuckled as he barged through the door and filled the staff room with his blinding personality. Clipping over to me in his dress shoes, he eyed up my pasta, then swiped my phone straight out of my hand.

"Hey!" I stood, trying to snatch it back. Bracing against me, he curled himself over my phone and scrolled quickly through the text thread.

I snarled, "Do you mind?"

Tossing me the phone back, he smirked and headed to the coffee pot. "Just making sure you're not going to jail. Yet."

"Christ, don't even joke."

Pouring himself a cup, he sat down at the table and gave me a genuine smile. "How're you doing? Judging by her replies, she seems to have accepted her friendly neighbourhood stalker."

Sinking into my chair, I groaned at the ceiling. "If anyone is going to get me in trouble, it's you. Keep your damn voice down."

"You're right." Leaning forward, he dropped his voice to a conspiratorial whisper. "So...tell me. Is she already in love with you and ready to see the man behind the screen or are you still going along with this?"

"How on earth could she be in love with me? She doesn't even *know* me."

"She's known you her entire life, dickhead."

"You know what I mean. Him. X." I flicked a glance at the door and whispered, "Her friendly neighbourhood stalker."

Sipping his coffee, he eyed me. His smile fell a little as he no doubt noticed the sleep deprived lines making me look every bit of my lie of thirty-four. I scratched my clean-shaven jaw self-consciously. "What?"

He sighed heavily. "You're doing it again."

"Doing what?"

"Sacrificing your own health for another's. What have we talked about?" Pointing at me, he scolded. "Remember the oxygen mask rule? You can't help others unless you help yourself."

"Yeah, yeah."

"Don't yeah, yeah me." Dropping his palm on the table, the loud smack made both of us flinch. "I think it's good that you're connecting with her, but I also don't like that you're staying up all night watching her or sacrificing your own mental health by falling for this girl all while she falls for someone who isn't you."

"There's no falling involved. We're just…friends. Not even friends. I'm just helping."

"There's that word again, Zan. You and helping isn't a good mix. It's great when you're on the payroll and got your scrubs on but outside of this place?" He arched an eyebrow. "You need to have better balance."

I sighed.

I wanted to argue but…he was right.

Pinching the bridge of my nose, I nodded. "Fine."

Cupping his ear, he leaned into me. "I didn't hear you. What did you say?"

I chuckled. "I said I'll work on getting better balance, jackass."

"Good boy." Grabbing his empty cup, he headed toward the sink. "I'm hosting the monthly poker night at my place on Saturday. You'll be there, right?"

My watch erupted with an alarm, reminding me I needed to check on my patient in recovery. Following him from the staffroom, I nodded. "I'll be there."

"And you won't stand me up if your little damsel needs help?"

"Ah well, I can't promise that." I slapped him on the back. "After all, I'm providing a service."

"You could always bring her. Markus and Oscar are bringing their wives. They're planning on drinking cocktails on the balcony while we men gamble and drink beer."

"Somehow, I can't see that happening."

He sighed dramatically. "Not as X no. But as Zander…it could."

I flipped him the bird as I headed down the corridor.

Fifteen

Sailor

Haunted & Hunted

"GOODNIGHT, LILS. CONGRATULATIONS AGAIN!"

Lily gave me a wobbly wave as she headed down the drive to the Uber waiting on the street. She'd closed a deal on a million-dollar house yesterday. With the commission she'd earn, she had enough to buy the piece of land she'd been eyeing up ever since she decided to scrimp and save every penny to become a developer and not just a real estate agent.

She hiccupped and whisper-shouted, "The night is young. You sure you won't come with us into town? Steph and I will look after you. Find you a nice, respectful boy who will treat you right."

I laughed and went to close my front door. "Nah, you guys have fun. I've had enough drinking for one night."

Which is true.

We'd made mojitos with fresh mint and basil from the garden, plenty of crushed ice, and far, *far* too many shots. I was tipsy and while Lily had been here, it'd been fun, but now she was leaving, the house settled silent and empty around me.

In the shadows, the nightmares got ready to swarm.

Brushing down my jeans and blossom printed blouse, ignoring my still tender bruises, I needed her gone before I revealed just how badly I wasn't coping.

"Byeeee!" I waved as she slipped into the Uber. "Be safe."

"Talk to you tomorrow!" She slammed the door. I waited until her ride pulled away. Only once the taillights rounded the end of the street did I back up, lock up, and pad barefoot through the house.

I avoided the living room and refused to look at the carpet between the couch and the coffee table. Already, Milton's phantom fingers squeezed around my throat, stealing my newly healed voice and making me wish I hadn't drunk at all.

The house cracked as it cooled for the night.

I jumped so high, I bumped my toe on the skirting board.

"Ow, ow, *ow*." Hissing between my teeth, I stood in the spine of the home and did my best to remember only good times. Of Nana baking apple pies and Pops doing a jigsaw puzzle at the dining room table. Not Milton kicking me from room to room or his sick laughter as I bled from his punches.

It's in the past.

He's not here.

You're fine.

I should've been better by now.

But I had a horrible feeling I was getting worse.

The house creaked again.

A shadow caught the corner of my eye. A shadow that looked horribly like Milton stalking me from the living room.

Get out.

Now.

With a cry, I spun on my toes and bolted out the front door.

Without thinking, I ran down the street, not looking back, not able to think about anything but getting far, far away from...

He's not real.

It's in your head.

Calm the hell down.

Slowing at the end of the road, I eyed up the manicured pathway leading between two houses to the park beyond.

Before Milton covered me in pain and left me barely able to walk, I used to jog around Firefly Park most days. It was as familiar to me as my back garden, but right now...the dark alleyway seemed full of teeth and terror.

The alcohol in my blood made me stagger.

What am I doing?

Get a grip, Lor!

I shouldn't have left my house. I was tipsy and barefoot and an absolute *fool*.

My nerves snapped and I sprinted back home.

I ran so fast, I grazed the soles of my feet and hurled myself through the front door as if the entire street was populated with axe murderers.

Slamming the door, my hands rattled as I did up the lock and threw the deadbolt into position.

The house pressed around me, heavy and ominous.

My knees gave out.

Collapsing against the door, I had my first ever panic attack right there on the rug. My lungs seized, my heart skipped, and all I could do was roll into a little ball on the floor and cry.

I didn't know how to stop it.

I didn't know I was capable of being this weak.

It made no sense.

I was *fine*.

No one had threatened me. Nothing bad had happened, yet my entire nervous system acted as if Milton had beaten me all over again.

I'm alone.

I hated *so much* that I was alone.

But the thought of calling Lily and letting her see me like this? I couldn't.

I could never tell her how my thoughts were full of despair, or that I no longer knew how to be happy. I didn't want to be that person. Didn't want her to look at me and judge me because what the hell was I so sad about? I was alive. I had no worries. No hardships.

God!

My head stuffed with tears. The mojitos threatened to come back up.

I-I need...

I don't know.

I just needed something. *Someone.* A hug without needing to explain. A kind word without pity.

I huddled deeper into my ball. My cell phone fell out of my jeans pocket, clunking against the rug. My chest ached with pins and needles, and fresh fear filled me that perhaps this wasn't panic but a heart attack.

A shimmery figure glittered in my peripheral; I swore I heard Nana whisper, *"Call someone, Little Lor. Quickly now. Just in case."*

My entire body jittered as I reached for the fallen phone.

Fresh sobs choked me at the thought of what my neighbours would think if another ambulance pulled up outside my house for the second time this month.

"Never mind that," Nana's ghost cooed. *"You're spiralling, dear. Best let someone help—"*

Help.

Yes.

I needed help.

But not from anyone who knew me.

Snatching the phone that'd fallen out of my pocket, I laugh-sobbed as I caressed not my mobile but the one he'd given me.

A sign. A lifeline.

Hauling myself up, I reclined against the wall, brought my knees up, and typed with quaking fingers.

Tell me something random. Anything. Quickly.

Time ticked. My tears fell. A text message pinged.

> What's happened? Are you okay?

The level of caring in that one sentence. The fact I didn't have to hide to protect his feelings.

> No, I'm not okay. I'm having a panic attack. I think.

> List your symptoms. Right now.

> My heart is racing. My mind is too. I feel stupidly overwhelmed, like the world is closing in. Which is ridiculous as I have no right to feel this way. But I can't stop seeing the guy who hurt me.

> First, it definitely sounds like a panic attack. Second, you have every right to feel that way. I don't know what happened, but your bruises and black eye say something serious did.

> You probably think I'm being idiotic messaging a total stranger when I'm having a meltdown.

> I offered, remember? And I can't tell you how glad I am that you took me up on it. If it will help, tell me what happened. You can say as little or as much as you want. I'm good at keeping secrets.

I sniffed back my tears, my heart no longer colliding with my ribs. Taking a deep breath instead of the shallow pants that'd crippled me, I went to type but paused.

I hadn't told anyone.

Not even the psychiatrist who'd visited me before I was discharged.

How could I even contemplate telling someone I'd never met the most terrible thing that'd ever happened to me?

Do it.

What have you got to lose?

Maybe that was my problem. I'd blocked up all those memories by *not* talking. If I shared them, maybe they'd vanish with no more power over me.

I was blind and didn't see the signs until it was too late.

Exhaling hard, I added.

I look back now and have no idea why I agreed to let him move in with me. I hadn't felt attracted to him or affectionate with him for months. But I felt sorry for him, I guess. He was good at making me feel guilty.

Did he beat you often?

No, he only did it the once. He wasn't doing it to hurt me. He wanted to kill me.

Sucking in a deep breath, I typed the part I would never be able to say aloud.

He almost raped me on the living room carpet. If it hadn't been for my elderly neighbour and his dog, I would've died all while he violated me. But that's not even the part that haunts me. It's the reason he tried to rape me in the first place.

My shakes slowly calmed the longer I focused on texts instead of memories. Putting it in black and white stole its power. The weight of the house lightened. The oppressive terror vanished with every word.

X took a long time to write back. He took so long, worry tiptoed down my spine and reminded me all over again why I hadn't wanted to tell anyone.

I'm sorry. I shouldn't have shared that.

What was the reason? The reason he tried to rape and kill you?

I sat on the rug and saw a crossroads: tell this stranger the secret that kept tearing a hole inside me or choke on it for the rest of my life.

On the other side of me—not the neighbour who saved my life—lives the grandson of my nana's best friend. We've known each other most of our lives, but we've hardly ever spoken. Every now and again, I see him through his windows. I do my best to respect his privacy and look away, but the day Milton came home, I was looking into his place, my head in the clouds, thinking about work instead of watching. Unfortunately, I hadn't noticed my neighbour had come into view. He was in a towel. Milton thought I was gawking at him, and he got jealous. He accused me of cheating. He threw me down the stairs to teach me a lesson. He said he'd be the last person who would ever be inside me. I passed out with his fingers around my throat.

I stopped breathing as I reread what I wrote, my thumb hovering over the send button. Could I confess something like that? Could I risk *not* confessing?

My fingers shot over the keyboard again, adding to the long message:

That part was awful, don't get me wrong, but the real struggle is...I can no longer even look at my neighbour without feeling Milton strangling me. I feel guilty and ashamed like I truly did something terrible. The minute I see him, my entire system panics. All I can hear is Milton accusing me of cheating and how he's going to remind me that I belong to him and only him.

Chilled and eerily empty after my panic attack, I scanned my deepest, darkest truths. I deliberated deleting them all. I almost erased every sentence. But...just the act of writing it down had helped. The thought of sending them away, getting the thoughts as far from me as possible?

God, yes.

I pressed send.

And then, I waited.

And waited.

I waited so long, I climbed off the rug and went into the kitchen for a glass of water. Grabbing a mug from the cupboard, I held it under the tap as my chin tipped up and my eyes cut through the window to the dark garden beyond.

I screamed and dropped the cup. It clattered into the sink, spraying water everywhere.

Scrambling for my own phone, I went to call the police.

The burner phone chirped with an incoming message.

> It's just me. You're safe.

My heart drummed with adrenaline as I darted to the back door and checked the lock was in place. Returning to the kitchen window, I narrowed my tear-stinging eyes at the dark masked silhouette standing in the middle of my lawn.

Fumbling with the keyboard, I typed:

> What the hell are you doing here? I thought you said you'd never approach me? That's twice now. Stop breaking your word!

The blue glow of his screen sent garish light over the skull scarf covering his lower face. With the dark evening and the baseball hat pulled low over his forehead, I couldn't tell if his hair was dark brown or black, nor could I see past the blue shadows of his phone to guess his eye colour.

Dressed all in black, standing in chunky boots with his legs slightly apart, he looked every inch a murderer.

> Leave! Get the hell away from me.

His shoulders tensed as he read my message and replied.

My phone buzzed. It took all my willpower to look down. I didn't want to take my eyes off him, petrified he'd charge the house and break in.

What was I *thinking* telling him so much personal stuff?

You're an idiot! Such a stupid, moronic idiot!

> I know you won't believe me when I say this was not my plan. I had no intention of coming so close, and I definitely didn't want you to see me. But I couldn't help myself. I literally couldn't stop my feet from bringing me here.

His chin flicked up, his eyes cast in thick shadow from beneath his cap. He looked down again, his thumbs flying over his phone before mine beeped with another message.

> I'm not a violent man. In fact, you could safely say I'm the opposite. But reading your message? Knowing what he did to you? And why he did it?

He broke into a pace, stalking over the grass all while he typed with furious stabs of his thumbs. His every muscle looked tense and ready to snap.

> I want to kill him. I want to break him into tiny pieces and destroy him. I want to kill your neighbour for being the reason you got hurt. I want to kill myself for thinking I could help you when I'm in motherfucking awe of you.

He looked up, catching my stare through the window.

His screen glowed brighter, etching his eyes with icy light, highlighting sleepless shadows as if he slept about as well as I did.

He finished typing. My phone buzzed.

> Not only do you have every reason to feel the way you do but you're also so strong to still live in the house where it happened. I can't imagine what that must feel like, how talking to your neighbour must hurt.

New tears rolled softly as I read his message.

Catching his eyes again, he shrugged and cocked his head as if he truly was speechless.

The moment stretched.

Neither of us looked away.

Goosebumps covered my arms as he sighed and slouched, sending me another message.

> I know I shouldn't be here. I know I said I wouldn't. But...I can't leave. Not yet. You said you could tell me anything. Can I tell you something in return?

A shiver rolled down my spine as I swept my thumbs over the keyboard. I should tell him to go. I should be terrified. Yet having him here...? I couldn't explain the calmness slowly slipping over me, just like the blanket he'd given me the other night.

I didn't want to examine my feelings. I doubt I'd ever understand. Instead, I trusted in the safety he delivered and replied:

You know the worst part of me. It would help to know the worst part of you.

His shoulders hitched; his eyes dropped to his phone.

I have a complex where I find self-validation in helping others. I've never told anyone how bad that complex truly is. It's something I struggle with on a daily basis. It's an obsession. A visceral need. I can't control it most of the time, so...I guess I need to warn you.

My heart kicked.

Warn me about what?

I don't want this to end. I don't want you to stop messaging me, but I wouldn't be protecting you the way I said I would if I didn't tell you that the more you lean on me and the more you let me help you...the harder I'll find it to stay away.

I backed up from the window, clutching my phone.
I tried to get my fingers to behave and message him back. To demand a less cryptic reply. Only he vanished into the dark, leaving me staring at an empty garden.
A final message came through.

I'm not going to make this about me. This is about you. This is about you moving on, and I want you to tell me anything and everything that you feel or fear or do. I'll be watching over you, Lori. I'll behave and keep my distance. You won't see me again. You have my word.

I didn't know how I felt about that.
I couldn't unravel why his vow made me frustrated as well as relieved.
But...as I checked the locks for the fourth time and headed to bed, my thoughts were of another man and not the one who'd tried to kill me.
My eyes saw X instead of Milton.
And for the first time in a very long time, I slept.

Sixteen

Zander

Stalking is Bad, But Friends Make it Better

"I'M ONE HUNDRED PERCENT GOING TO JAIL." Throwing myself into the patient chair on the opposite side of Colin's desk, I snatched my glasses off and tossed them onto his paperwork. Digging my thumbs into my eyes, I groaned. "Do you think they'd let me practice medicine in prison? I mean…I'd be able to provide a better service in whatever hospital they have rather than being a laundry bitch or burning shit in the kitchen."

Colin laughed from where he stood by his filing cabinet. The folder in his hands was thick with paper, no doubt full of case notes for a specially designed prosthetic. "Should I say my goodbyes now, or are you just being dramatic?" Cutting across the room, he slapped the file on his desk and sat down.

His office had a prime position in the corner of the thirteenth floor. With two banks of windows, the sunlight streaming in bounced over three skeletons dangling from their racks, various diagrams on the wall on how tendons and ligaments operated, along with multiple drawers full of prosthetic pieces, ready to help his patients come to terms with what he called an upgrade in whatever limb or joint they'd lost.

To him, trading a blood-and-bone leg for a top-of-the-line titanium running blade *was* an upgrade. In all the years I'd worked with him, I'd never seen a patient leave his office in tears. Even the children came out bouncing with excitement at the thought of being part robot.

"You're a good man, Col." I grabbed my glasses and put them back on.

He smirked. "Wow, you truly are going to prison. You wouldn't give me random compliments if you weren't."

"I mean it. You're great at what you do. You say I'm addicted to helping, but you're just as bad." I pointed at the black metal chest on his desk. "How many lives have you saved with that toolbox?"

He frowned a little. Opening the lid, he pulled out a micro screwdriver for tiny fixings on fingers and knees. "About as many lives as you've saved in surgery I reckon."

"Think you can save mine?" I chuckled with black humour.

His blue eyes darkened. "You're legit starting to scare me." Tossing the screwdriver away, he headed to the door, closed it, locked it, then sat back down. "Talk to me, Zan. Tell me everything."

Tossing my head back, I glanced at the ceiling. He even had posters of animals up there with prosthetics. A giraffe with a bionic neck. An elephant with a metal trunk.

"Zander," he growled. "Spill or I'll steal your phone again and see for myself."

"She finally opened up to me. To X, I mean."

"I thought that was the whole point of this?"

"It was. It *is*. I just didn't expect it to hurt this bad."

"Hurt?"

I sighed and rubbed my chest. The same crush of agony from last night vised around my ribcage. The tightening of my heart had almost suffocated me when Sailor told me what Milton had done and why. Why she couldn't bear to be around me as Zander. Why she'd chosen to close herself off to all those she knew.

The second I'd read her message, I'd staggered from my house in a daze. My pulse pounded until it roared in my ears. Milton had almost raped and murdered her because of *me*.

By the time I'd looked up from reading her message a thousand times, I was standing in her garden.

"Alright, hand it over." Colin snapped his fingers. "Give me the phone. Right now."

Tipping my chin down, I gripped the armrests and confessed, "Apparently, Milton caught her looking into my bedroom. I was in a towel. He thought she was perving on me. He beat her black and blue, then attempted to rape her, all while strangling her to death."

Silence screeched between us.

Colin didn't speak.

Rubbing my mouth, I added, "It's why she doesn't say two words to me these days when at least before we'd share pleasantries. I found myself in her garden before I realised I was even walking over there." My voice thickened into a growl. "Every atom inside me wanted to grab her in a hug and hold her. To promise that he'd never lay another finger on her, but...I can't. I'm the link to all her nightmares. Not only is she living in a house where she was hurt but every time she sees me, she remembers why. No wonder she seems to be getting worse. *I'm* the one making it worse. It's my fault and—"

"Stop right there," Colin snapped. "None of this is your fault, and to say so is egotistical and robbing her of her justified trauma. Stop making this about you."

I swallowed hard and nodded. "I know that. I *told* her that. I ran before I could make things worse. But…I need to stop this, right? I need to never message her again because if she keeps sharing things with X only to find out it's me? I could truly do some damage."

I looked up, silently begging him for a solution even though I'd sat up most of the night trying to figure out a way to stop her from feeling this way and somehow find a way to help her as myself and not some faceless stalker.

I exhaled hard as Colin sat down, chewing the inside of his cheek, deep in contemplation.

I whispered, "I gave her the phone to help, but I think I'm making shit worse."

His eyes shot to mine. For a second, I thought he'd rat me out, but then he swooped from his chair and marched to a cabinet full of drawers.

Opening a few, he rummaged inside. Grabbing some boxes and bottles, he returned to his chair, then dumped the supplies on the table before me.

I scowled. "What's all this?"

"Tricks of the trade so she'll never know it's you." Crossing his arms, he shrugged. "I agree that she can never know. Not with her associating you with what happened. You're her trigger, Zan. And if she ever suspects she's sharing her darkest secrets with you, you're right, you could make shit a lot worse."

I groaned and raked my fingers through my hair. "Then I'll stop. Right now."

Almost as if she'd felt my decision on whatever strings linked us, my phone chirped in my pocket. The same chirp I'd assigned to her.

I stiffened.

Colin raised an eyebrow. "I'm guessing that's her by the way you've frozen." Arching his chin at me, he ordered, "Read it. What does it say?"

With jittery fingers, I shifted on the chair and fished my phone from my pocket. Swiping on the screen, I pursed my lips as her text appeared.

I don't know what it says about me, but…I'm not mad at you for appearing in my garden. I can't believe I'm going to admit this, but…I actually slept better than I have in a while, all because you were the last man I saw before going to sleep instead of the memories of what happened.

Groaning, I couldn't make eye contact with Colin as I read it aloud. By the time I repeated it to him, another chimed into my inbox.

I'm sick of feeling like this. This depression isn't me, and I refuse to let him take away my happiness. I haven't been outside in weeks because I'm afraid. I can't relax inside because I'm afraid. I need to start living again. If you're still offering to watch over me, I want to tell you everything. But in order to do that, I need your word that you won't judge me or pity me. No matter how honest I get.

Colin sucked in a breath as I relayed the second part of her message. I felt like I betrayed her all over again for sharing something so personal.

My shoulders slouched as exhaustion cloaked me.

Neither of us spoke.

Nodding once, accepting what he'd tell me—to refuse her request and cut all ties—I pressed my thumbs against the screen to tell her I couldn't do this anymore.

"Wait." He held up his hand and shook his head. "You can't."

I scowled. "Can't what?"

"Turn your back on her the moment she's agreed to accept your help."

"Are you forgetting the shitstorm this could cause?"

"I'm aware."

"If she finds out it's me—"

"We'll make sure she doesn't." Tossing me a box, he went cold as if preparing me to go into battle. "Black hair dye, a fake eyebrow piercing, and prescription-coloured contacts."

"Wait, what?" I wrinkled my nose. "What are you saying?"

"I'm saying I have plenty of cosmetics and stage-wear prosthetics. You're forgetting that's how I got into this field in the first place. Not only do I provide my patients with new mobility but also a new look if need be. Sometimes a new hair colour or eye colour is just the armour someone needs to wear while they adapt to their new normal. The different appearance tricks the brain into accepting the change far quicker than remembering who they used to be."

Standing, he came over to me and perched on the desk. "The dye lasts a single wash—it'll rinse out easily for your shifts at the hospital. I'm pretty sure I remember your eye prescription last time I broke your glasses by accident and you made me buy you a new pair, but if I got it wrong, help yourself. I have plenty more. I figure dark brown will hide your bright green. It would help if you see her with some stubble on your face and not clean-shaven, and you should probably walk differently. Wear clothes she'd never see you wear as Zander and—"

"Whoa, whoa, hold on." Swooping to my feet, I glowered at the box of hair dye. "You can't be serious? You're saying I shouldn't just keep messaging her but actually see her in *person*? Have you lost your damn mind? She'll see right through me!"

He smirked and crossed his arms. "Have you ever heard of the Clark Kent effect?"

I frowned. "What the hell is that?"

"The scientific description is: a disruption of facial recognition via the use of a disguise such as makeup, a beard, and/or glasses. Tweaking these markers is enough to hinder being recognised. It gives the person changing their appearance the ability to hide in plain sight."

"I'm not goddamn Superman."

"No, you're not. That's the point." He chuckled, enjoying my demise far too much. "You're about to *become* him." Waving a hand at me, he smirked. "Right now, you're Clark Kent. Slightly nerdy, slightly bashful. You even have his glasses, and your twitch of always touching them or pulling them off to rub your eyes is the epitome of you as Zander North."

"Did you just call me a nerd with a twitch?"

"It's a proven fact that humans only see what they wanna see. Soldiers in combat sometimes wear full-face hoods with no eyes or facial features because there's overwhelming evidence that shows people cannot spot fellow humans if they don't have eyes or a mouth to lock onto."

"I'm not going to war, Col. This is ridiculous." Pushing back the chair, I shifted to leave. "I'm done."

"You started this, man." He threw a small box of brown contacts at me. "You can't be done until she doesn't need your help anymore."

"I'm telling you, she'll know it's me the moment I'm stupid enough to go near her."

"Did she recognise you last night?"

My back tensed. "Well, no, but only because I wore a mask and a hat."

"Alright, keep wearing those but also rinse your hair and put the contacts in. I'm telling you, Zan, the one thing that comes to mind when I go to describe you to others is your stupidly green eyes and glasses. That and your carrot colouring."

I groaned. "You did not just call me a carrot. What are we? Back in freaking kindergarten?"

Grabbing all the boxes, he shoved them into my arms. "Not my fault you decided to help the very woman you shouldn't be around. You're in this now. You wanted to help? So help. And when she's smiling again, you can have X die a mysterious death and attempt to mend your relationship with her as Zander."

"We don't *have* a relationship."

"But I happen to know you want one."

I scoffed and strode toward the door. "You're sounding like Melody. She drove me nuts thinking I'd marry her granddaughter. She even confessed she and Gran put aside money for our wedding!"

He burst out laughing. "God, this just gets more and more idiotic the more you talk. Now, shoo. I have a patient coming in." He waved me out the door. "Remember, do the opposite of what you do as Zander. If you can do accents, it wouldn't hurt to put one on. And if she looks like she's starting to suspect, abort. It's best she's left wondering rather than finds evidence to prove that her lovesick neighbour has been pretending to be Superman." He chuckled. "You should start calling her Lois Lane."

I stumbled over the threshold.

Fuck, that was too close.

Lori and Lois?

Why did their damn names have to be so similar?

What the hell have I gotten myself into?

"Oh, you almost forgot your phone." Colin chucked my cell at me. I caught it, juggling a few of the boxes. "Better text her back before she thinks you're avoiding her. Who knows? Maybe she'll want you to come over tonight."

"I'm not going anywhere near her."

"Lying to me or yourself?" Sitting back at his desk, he opened the file he'd been working on when I first arrived with my troubles. "I won't say I told you so when you come to me and say you've met her face to face. It's inevitable with her willing to trust you and you needing to protect her." He caught my eyes, seriousness carving brackets around his mouth. "But mark my words, Zan, this will escalate before it gets better, so I hope you're ready. Now go away. I look forward to your next episode of A Day in the Lives of Zander North and Sailor Rose."

"You're a jackass." I closed the door on his laughter.

Seventeen

Sailor

Trespassing Guardians

MY HANDS WERE COVERED IN EXTRA VIRGIN olive oil, beeswax, gotu kola extract, orange blossom, and witch hazel by the time X replied four *excruciating* hours later.

He'd taken so long. I'd had second thoughts about what I'd written. I'd doubted and pouted and driven myself stupid, wondering if *I* was the one who'd stepped over a line when *he'd* been the one to drop a phone in my letterbox and barge his way into my life.

Wiping my hands clean, I made sure the empty crystal bottles couldn't blow off my counter, seeing as I had the kitchen window and door open, then snatched my phone off the dining room table.

> Sorry I couldn't text sooner. Had to deal with an emergency.

Wait. That's it?

I'd panicked all day about the level of neediness in my last message, and I only got a one-line response?

Oh my God, do you hear yourself?

He doesn't owe you a thing. He doesn't know you. You don't know him.

Maybe this wasn't healthy. I'd somehow latched onto the only person I felt safe and seen with—someone I didn't have to pretend to be okay with—and I'd made it mean far too much, far too quickly.

You're cut off starting this very second.

Slamming my phone down, I didn't reply.

I forced myself to go back to making Nana's special face cream, absolutely determined to go to the market this weekend and sell like usual. I'd let our *From Soil to Soul* customers down and the amount of internet orders that'd come in meant I had an entire suitcase of product to wrap and drop off at the post office.

My phone chimed again.

And then another little buzz.

Don't you dare.

I kept ladling the wonderful-smelling mixture into the cut crystal bottles I bought in bulk from a local glass-blower Nana had become friends with a decade ago.

My cell vibrated one last time before falling silent.

As the sun set, I finished the batch of face cream, printed off our special labels listing all the natural ingredients and contact details, then carefully put them in the storage room off the downstairs laundry to cool and solidify.

Every part of me wanted to lunge for my phone, but I forced myself to cook a quick pan-seared fish and head outside to harvest a fresh summer salad. I even made a gooey lava cake in a mug like Pops used to enjoy.

Nightfall had well and truly blanketed Ember Drive by the time I'd punished myself enough, got my head back on straight, and believed I was sane again.

I can talk to a masked stranger without getting weird. I know I can.

My silly heart fluttered as I grabbed my phone and turned off the kitchen lights. Thanks to what Milton had done, I'd stopped going into the living room, but I was being brave tonight.

It was just a couch. Just a coffee table. Just a carpet.

He was locked up. I was here.

No one is going to hurt me.

Throwing myself on the couch, I pulled my legs up, draped a blanket over my lap, and dared to open X's messages.

> I know it shouldn't, but it makes me happy to know you slept better because of me. And you can be mad at me for trespassing. I'm mad at myself for breaking my rules so soon into this. You have my word. I won't do it again.

My teeth ground together with annoyance.

If I *admitted* I'd liked him trespassing, why was he adamant that he'd never do it again?

I paused, assessing the swelling feelings inside me.

I smiled.

It'd been so long since I'd felt anything but out of control and lost. The faintest tinge of frustration felt good. It gave me back a spark, a flame, and I scrolled eagerly through the rest of his messages.

I'm not saying I can help with the depression you mentioned, but I'll try to give you back your happiness. Not sure how but...I'm always here to talk.

I scanned the next one.

If I were a doctor—which I'm not—I'd say you're suffering from rising agoraphobia because you can't trust open spaces, but you're also claustrophobic because the house is closing in on you. Talking about what sets you off might help, but you should also probably see someone with expertise in these conditions.

Why did he sound exactly like a doctor even after professing he wasn't one?

How about you start now? Talk to me as if every word you say gets deleted the second you type it. Give it a voice and then let it go.

Cradling my phone, I read and reread that last one.

The idea of whatever I said suddenly un-existing as soon as I said it was resoundingly enticing. Whoever X was, he was good at this. Good at giving me pathways out of the dark forest of my mind.

It's my turn to apologise for my late reply. I was busy making face cream for my business.

I sent it but immediately felt guilty.

That's a lie. I stayed busy because I didn't want to message you back.

My phone hummed in my palm a second later.

Why didn't you want to message me back?

Because I sounded like a clingy girlfriend demanding to know you won't judge or pity me. I don't like how weak I sounded.

Would it help to know it's physically impossible for me to pity you? I can't because I'm in awe of you.

There went my heart again.

What about judging me?

> The only thing I'm judging is myself and how much I'm fucking this up.

My heart flutters switched into full skipping rope hops.

What do you mean?

He took a few minutes as if gathering his thoughts.

> I'm going to take our vow of honesty at face value, okay? I guess this is me asking you not to judge me now.

I shivered and cuddled deeper in my blanket.

I won't.

> I think I made a mistake messaging you.

Every bubbly feeling crashed and burned.
Oh.
Tears pricked my eyes, revealing just how stupidly invested I was over a masked watcher who didn't have to cover me in a blanket the night he kept me safe, but did. A faceless stranger who knew more about what happened than Lily, my best friend.

I went to type a generic—'That's fine. Have a nice life'—but my phone buzzed.

> I can't stop thinking about you. I can't stop watching you. And I'm afraid that when you no longer need me, I'm going to need you, and I honestly don't know how this is gonna end for me.

The stinging tears from his previous message spilled down my cheeks. I'd never been a crier. I'd never been one to weep at movies or books or silly things like messages.

But lately…God.

Swiping the wetness off my face, I typed.

I should reply like a normal person and say we don't know each other. That what we're doing is absolutely ridiculous............

The more we talk, the more I don't want to stop.

You know you can trust me, right? No matter what? No matter what happens, I vow on my life, I will never **ever** hurt you.

Why does that feel like foreshadowing?

Probably because it is. Eventually, we'll have to stop. We can't be pen pals for the rest of our lives.

A short laugh escaped.

Oh, I don't know. I think pen pals are very underrated.

I used to have one as a kid, actually. My family signed me up to converse with some kid in China as some sort of global networking. It was fun. We still flick emails every now and again.

That's actually super cool. Does writing notes to flower fairies count as having a pen pal? I posted them by leaving them in the garden. My nana always said if we gave thanks to the flower folk, then the blooms would be brighter.

I can see you being a flower child as a kid.

And there you go again making me wonder if you've been in my house and snooped through the family photo albums.

If there are photos of you in there, don't tempt me.

I gasped. That message felt decidedly unsafe and entirely too...fun.

God, fun.

Just like frustration, I'd missed fun.

I missed the highs and excitement. The long-lost art of flirting.

Flirting?

Have you lost your mind? You don't know this man. How on earth can you think about flirting?

Especially after Milton. Especially after—

It was *because* of Milton that I even contemplated such a dalliance. Bracing my shoulders, I sucked up courage and threw myself into the first step toward freedom.

Tell me something, X.

His message was slightly slower, but I shivered when my phone pinged.

Tell you what, Lori?

Ugh, my heart reacted again. That silly skip. That buoyant little bubble.

Who would've thought a nickname given to me by Alexander North could make me melt?

Every muscle locked as Alexander exploded in my mind. His trim chest as he appeared in his bedroom in just a towel. The droplets rolling down his lean muscles. The blinding pain in my scalp as Milton yanked me backward by my hair.

Sucking in a breath, I shoved Alexander away and focused entirely on the skull-masked stranger who'd stood like an immortal guardian in my garden last night.

Do you watch me because you're some closeted vigilante trying to be Batman, or do you watch me because you like me?

This time, his message took a while. I'd probably freaked him out. I didn't send another one, dragging out whatever nerves he had.

Finally, my phone chirped.

I said I'd give you honesty, so...here's honesty. I've watched you for a while. I've watched you far more than I should admit. And you're right, it's not entirely for the reasons of protecting you.

How long?

That I can't answer.

Have you seen me naked?

His reply was instant, almost a knee-jerk reaction.

> No! God, no. I wouldn't. I look away if you ever get close to stripping.

He sent another one.

> Fuck, I really, really suck at this. I didn't mean anything by that. Look, I'll make the decision for both of us and say we should stop this. I've probably freaked you the hell out, and I'm sick to death that I even admitted something like that.

He sent a third one before I could reply.

> I'm sorry. You're safe. I won't contact you again. Goodnight, Lori.

My chest pinched at the thought of him following through with that promise. He couldn't take away something I didn't even know I needed.

Somehow, he'd made me feel seen without being pitied. Wanted without being terrified. Despite what'd happened, he still found me attractive. But he was gentle enough, *human* enough not to take something that didn't belong to him.

I found that…

God, I'm turned on.

I laughed out loud as I pressed my thighs together and marvelled that I could feel even the inklings of pleasure after Milton.

Yet another cloud dispersed from my soul, leaving me warm and toasty instead of cold and empty.

Stroking my thumbs over the screen, I bit my bottom lip.

I had two ways of playing this.

I could play the victim that I'd become. I could allow the percolating panic in my gut to make him a bad guy and twist every message from honest to creepy. Or…I could be guided by instinct, which said that despite his actions, he was a good guy. After all, what did I know? I'd lived with an asshole and never seen the signs. Could it be possible that I spoke to a saint hidden behind a mask?

> I keep saying this but…I truly don't know what it says about me when I admit…I like that you watch me.

> You sure you don't want to hand your phone into the police again?

> I rather like talking to you, so no.

You're unlike anything I expected.

You sound as if you're disappointed?

Disappointed?

He sent another one straight away.

I think you mean in big fucking trouble.

What sort of trouble?

I can't believe I'm going to say this. Even thinking about writing it makes me break out in a cold sweat.

You'll definitely have to tell me now.

I watch you because I find you drop-dead gorgeous, smart, brave, and... Damn, this honesty clause keeps biting me in the ass.

Go on.........

The real reason I watch you is because. Fuck, it sounds so cheesy. If it doesn't freak you out, it's going to make you laugh.

Try me.

I watch you because I have a crush on you. I think I always have. But now I'm ending this conversation before I say something else that gets me into trouble. I'm around if you need me. Message me if you're struggling. Sleep well.

I fell onto my side in a dramatic swoon.
He has a crush on me?
How long had it been since I'd heard that word? When I was fourteen at school? Why did it deliver the same delicious shivers and tingles as it did back then, knowing a boy liked me?
He said he was in trouble?
What about me?
How had this happened?
How did I stop it?
Did I even *want* to stop it?
Snuggling on the couch, I drew the blanket up to my shoulders

and shoved a cushion under my head.

I lay there in the soft light of the Tiffany lamp, rereading every message we exchanged.

And then, I fell asleep in the very spot where a man tried to kill me, all while thinking of the one helping me move on.

Eighteen

Zander

Barefoot & Masked

I WOKE TO SOMEONE SCREAMING.

The noise cut straight into my nightmares and yanked me from sleep so fast, my heart palpitated. Vertigo scrambled my eyesight as I got up too quick, sending me swaying sideways. I bashed my toe on the end of the bed as I bolted to my window.

Sailor!

Another scream. Her horror floated easily between our two houses, thanks to our open windows.

I didn't think.

Hauling on a pair of black tracksuit bottoms and fighting my way into a black t-shirt, I bolted down the stairs. Skidding through my conservatory, I went to fly off the deck, but common sense had me sprinting back into the house and snatching my motorcycle scarf and hat.

Yanking the balaclava over my head, I jammed my hat into place and brought the scarf as high as it would go to just below my eyes. My vision was fuzzy without my glasses, but not so bad that I couldn't beat the shit out of whoever was hurting Sailor.

Prying the palings apart, I fought my way through the fence. The loose screw snagged my t-shirt as I wriggled into her back garden. Barefoot and absolutely panicking, I charged onto her back deck and tried the door handle.

Locked.

Fuck.

Hurry.

Hurry!

Ducking to one knee, I found the lavender pot where Melody always kept the spare key. Shoving it into the lock, I swung the door open.

Moans and thrashing came from the living room.

My hands curled into fists. All my training as a doctor switched from saving a life to taking one. I knew what artery bled the most. I knew what bone to snap to cause the most pain.

He's dead.

Skidding into the living room, I flicked on the light, then snapped it off again.

Shit.

Shit!

This is bad.

So bad.

So very, *very* bad.

Sailor woke up, thanks to me blinding her with the overhead light. It took a second for her brain to work and another second to drink me in. Sweat glittered on her temples, her phone beside her where she'd fallen asleep, her legs tangled in the blanket I'd given her when she'd slept outside.

Our eyes met, and for a second, she didn't react.

And then, she exploded into action.

"No. Don't. *Help!*" Scrambling to the opposite end of the couch, she hunched into a ball and went to scream again.

I did the only logical thing I could do.

Throwing myself over the arm of the couch, I landed beside her and slapped my hand over her lips. With my other hand, I reached behind her and turned off the side lamp, suffocating the room in darkness.

Everything Colin had said echoed in my head.

The Clark Kent effect. The fact my face and hair were hidden but my bright green eyes were not. I had to stay in the dark. I had to act different, speak different. If I wanted any chance of her not recognising me, I needed the night to be my ally.

Squirming beneath my gag, her eyes bugged with terror. Her nails scratched at my wrist, leaving me with welts I would never be able to explain in the morning.

"It's me," I growled, keeping my voice as gravelly as I could, grateful I still had sleep tangled around my voice box. "It's—" *Do not say your real name.* "X." Backing away, I curled my fingers around her cheek. "I'll let you go, but you can't scream, alright? I don't think you want the police here, thanks to a nosy neighbour calling, do you?"

Never looking away from me, her face obscured by shadows, she nodded once.

Trusting her with my life—literally—I slowly pulled my palm away and moved to the opposite end of the sofa. Perching on the end, I kept as much distance between us as possible. Raising my hands, I made a show of surrendering before clasping them together between my spread legs.

She didn't say a word, watching me with an intensity that made me itch. "W-What are you doing here?" She touched her lips, rubbing where I'd touched her. "How did you get in?"

And this was the moment where I should come clean. I should give the truth instead of walking a bridge made of lies. It wasn't a bridge—it was a crocodile-filled chasm with the thinnest, breakable tightrope keeping me afloat.

One wrong answer and I'd destroy my career, her sanity, and whatever relationship we'd had over the years.

Clearing my throat and deliberately making my voice extra low, I said, "I know where you keep the spare key."

She frowned. "You know from watching me?"

"Yes." I rushed to add, "But don't change the location just because I know. It's handy for emergencies."

"And you thought barging into my house at two in the morning was an emergency?"

I scowled, focusing on the bruises still framing her black eye. "You were screaming."

"No, I—" She went to argue but then sucked in a breath. "Wait. I was?"

I almost said 'it woke me up' but that would be a sure clue to who I was. Thinking on my feet, cursing my exhausted brain, I lied, "I was walking past. I heard you."

She scoffed. "Yeah, okay." Sitting taller, she curled her bruise-mottled legs beneath her as she turned to face me. "You just happened to be strolling around the streets at this time." Leaning forward, she studied me. "Try again. No lies, remember?"

Nervousness had my fingers touching my mask, making sure it was still in place. I tugged my hat extra low, dropping my stare, hoping she couldn't see a damn thing in the dark.

Fucking hell.

I needed to figure out a way to get out of here before she saw right through me.

"I, eh…" I gulped. I wasn't cut out for this. I wasn't good at deception. I'd always cracked under pressure if Gran ever asked if I did something wrong. Most of the time, I confessed to all kinds of misdeeds, even if it was my two sisters' fault, just because I couldn't handle interrogation.

Panic fisted my heart; the truth burned my tongue.

I tugged the bottom of my scarf, a second away from yanking it off and telling her everything. Wouldn't it be better to tell her now? Before we got even deeper into whatever this was?

Had she felt the same tingly rush when I'd admitted I had a crush on her? Just the act of writing it down, after decades of denying it, had made it far too real. It fucking hurt to think of ruining that feeling, thanks to lies and deception.

You're the reason she's black and blue, remember? He beat her because of you.

"Do you want help removing that?" She raised an eyebrow at where I fiddled with my balaclava. "Why are you hiding? Does it really matter if I see your face?"

Removing my hands, words I hadn't even thought of spilled free. "I promised you the ability to share everything to a faceless stranger." I shrugged. "This is me faceless. I'll keep it on."

"And if I want you to lose the hat and mask?"

"Then I'll leave and message you later." I stood, noticing I was barefoot.

Fuck, how could I explain that?

Not only was I out for a walk at two in the morning but without shoes?

Goddammit.

Rolling my shoulders, I waited for her to figure out that my bedroom was one fence over and put a restraining order on me.

Turning to go, I muttered, "Now I know you're not in danger, I'm leaving."

Swooping to her feet, she said, "How do you know I'm not in danger?"

I glanced at her, making sure to keep my face shaded with the peak of my cap. "Like I said, I heard you screaming. I thought someone was murdering you. But it was just a nightmare. You should go to bed, Lori. And I do mean a *bed.* Don't sleep on the couch."

She hugged herself as if I'd said something wrong. "Y-You called me Lori."

I froze.

Had I slipped already?

Did X know that name or Zander?

She messaged you as X, you dumbass.

Breathing hard, I tried to get my anxiety under control. This was literally the worst thing I'd ever done, and I'd already burned through enough luck not being recognised.

"I have to go." I stepped toward the kitchen.

"Wait." She swayed toward me as her hand came up.

I stiffened. The nurturing aspect of my soul that got me into far too much strife reacted instantly. Shifting back to her, I almost—*almost* touched her again. My fingers burned to cup her elbow or grab her hand. To offer support and contact.

It took all my willpower to stay where I was.

Her gaze slid over me, taking in my black attire. Her eyes widened, fear glossing her stare.

The tops of my bare toes stung as she glared at them.

"Don't ask," I growled, adding more rocks to my voice. "I can't answer, and I don't want to lie."

Her eyebrows pinched together, but slowly, she nodded. "I wasn't looking at your feet, actually. I..." She swallowed hard and balled her hands. "I was looking at the carpet where you're standing."

My heart thundered against my ribs. My gaze dropped to the spot between the couch and the coffee table. Her little inhale of pain told me all I needed to know.

I didn't have to focus on changing my voice to a growl, it happened naturally. All those aggressive, possessive instincts that I'd always buried *roared* through me. "This is where he tried to kill you."

She flinched and rubbed her bare arms.

Her dress floated around her legs with soft grey and pink layers. The sleeveless bodice twinkled in the night with pink and silver threads in the shape of falling flower petals. Her sandy blonde hair floated around her shoulders in messy, sleepy curls, and the night softened her features until she looked like a dream.

A dream where I'd wake up any moment and she'd be gone.

A single tear glimmered in the dark, rolling to her chin.

And I didn't think.

Striding into her, I snatched her around her nape and waist and pressed her hard against me. The second her body collided with mine, I saw literal fucking stars.

Every synapse arrowed in on her. Every breath. Every heartbeat. I'd never felt anything like it with anyone. She felt so right. She fit so perfectly.

She struggled a little, and rationality tore through my mistake.

"Shit, I'm sorry." Untangling my hand in her hair at her nape, I gently pushed her away. "I didn't mean. I wasn't going to—"

With a soft cry, she threw herself against my chest. Her arms looped around my waist as she buried her face into my t-shirt.

I didn't move for a second.

I couldn't.

And then, chemical reaction overrode common sense. I enveloped her in the tightest hug I'd ever given. My fingers wove through her hair as I pressed her cheek to my heart. My spine curled to curve around her, sheltering her the best I could, all while my other arm fit snugly around her waist, pinning her in place.

She shuddered a little as if silently crying, but she didn't push me away. Didn't ask me to release her. We stood there, on the spot where she'd almost died, and didn't say a word.

My eyes closed as I rested my chin on the top of her head.

My heartbeat grew thick and loud, pounding through me.

I lost track of time. I didn't care how many minutes or hours passed. I had her in my arms. She was safe in my protection. I never wanted to let her go.

A shimmer of light danced on my peripheral as if someone's shadow passed by in the corridor. The old box TV suddenly turned on, spewing snow and hissing loudly.

Sailor jumped out of my embrace, pressing a hand to her chest. "Oh my God."

Snatching the remote off the coffee table, I turned it off. Partly because the noise was awful but also the light would be my downfall.

She blinked as I tossed the remote onto the couch and shifted toward the dining room. "I better go."

"You probably should. This house is haunted."

"Excuse me?"

She smiled. "By my nana. I think it was her who turned on the TV. Probably doesn't approve of me hugging a skull-masked stranger in the dead of night."

"She's wise, and you should probably follow her suggestion." I backed up slowly. "I hope I didn't scare you. That wasn't my intention when coming in here. I promise I won't—"

"I won't move the key." She dropped her eyes as if embarrassed. "I might second-guess this in the morning, but...I'm glad you were able to get in. You stopped a particularly awful nightmare." She shuddered as she looked at the carpet again. "I should know better than to fall asleep in here. It's where the memories are the worst."

My gaze dropped to the floor. "Are you sure you want to stay here? Maybe a change of scenery would—"

"Don't you start." All softness bled from her tone. Crossing her arms, she stood straight and brave. "I'm not letting him chase me out of my home. I'm happy here. Or at least I was. And I'll remember how to be again. Besides—" she shrugged "—there's a ghost looking over me. I'll be okay."

"And there's a stranger on the other end of a text message too." I smiled, not that she'd see it behind my mask. "Anytime."

"But you won't let me see your face?"

I shook my head with a sigh. "No, I won't."

"Ever?"

A prickle of despair worked its way down my spine. "One day, you'll know."

"You sound as if that will be a bad thing."

Bowing slightly, I ignored her fishing comment. "Goodnight, Lori."

She sucked in a breath. "I don't know why hearing you call me Lori makes my heart skip."

I stiffened. I'd grown used to her honesty on a screen, but to have it in person?

Shit, this couldn't be any worse for me.

I'd never cared for the games girls played. The secrets and flirting—saying one thing and meaning another. It was partly why I didn't date—that and my brutal work hours. I wanted straightforward and simple. If I pissed someone off, I'd rather know than be told otherwise. If I impressed her or made her happy, I'd like to see her reaction rather than her hiding it from me, thinking it made her weak.

Reaching for my glasses to nudge them up my nose, my hand stilled as I remembered...*I'm not wearing any.*

Colin's warning came back to mind that fiddling with my glasses was one of my biggest tells. I would have to be careful the next time I saw her.

Fuck, next time?

You barely coped this time.

Slowly dropping my arm, I whispered, "Go to bed. I'll message you in the morning."

Hugging herself, she held my stare for a long moment before smiling slightly. "Thank you, X. Thank you for not judging or pitying me."

"Always."

I slipped out the door, locked it, put the key back, then walked in the opposite direction to home, just in case she was watching out the window.

Nineteen

Sailor

Market & Mistakes

> IF I DIDN'T KNOW YOU, I'd say you were having a wonderful day. But because I'm the keeper of your secrets, tell me, little Lori. How are you really doing?

I grinned as I checked my messages during the only spare second I'd had all morning.

The market was extra hectic, the questions about my products constant, the testers very well used, and the smiles from familiar faces all the more friendly after being away for so long.

Despite the heat, I'd deliberately worn a long sleeve dark grey blouse and longed to trade my jeans for shorts, but at least most of my bruises had started to fade. A bit of concealer on my black eye and the green-brown tinge was covered.

Only a few personal friends of Jim's or those who lived on my street knew about what Milton had done, so I didn't have to field too many invasive questions about how I was doing.

Funny that I didn't mind X had asked.

Knowing he was out there, watching me...protecting me from afar made me feel bubbly and brave all at the same time.

It didn't matter that I'd had to fight a panic attack to be here.

The fact that I was here was all that mattered.

Four days ago, when I'd had my nightmare, X had freed something small and terrified inside me. Trapped in a dream where Milton murdered me again and again, I'd had no way out and no one to help. But then that dream had been smashed apart by a flash of blinding light. As my eyesight returned, I'd stared at a man dressed all in black with a mask and baseball cap.

The terror I'd felt had been an instinctual reaction. Every feminine part of me screamed to run, but then...he'd spoken.

His voice had reached deep, deep inside me where I was

thrashing and gasping on the carpet in my nightmare, and in one sentence, he yanked me back into living. Raspy and gravelly, he sounded absolutely delicious—almost as if he'd watched too many comic book heroes, layering his timbre with aggressive possession.

I wished I'd recorded him.

I wished I'd asked him to stay.

I couldn't describe the unfathomable feeling of safety I felt around him.

It didn't make sense. We didn't know anything about each other, but I couldn't ignore the blanket of relief he gave me.

After he'd gone, I'd retreated upstairs to bed, and in the morning, I'd woken to a message that tugged me further from depressive black clouds and straight into the first inklings of the true me.

The *happy* me.

> Today, the weather forecast is meant to be hot with a side of scorching. I recommend you don't fall asleep in the garden between the hours of nine and six lest you burn yourself to ashes. Never fear, though, if you ignore my advice, I will ensure I'm nearby with a hose to prevent you from bursting into flames.

I'd snickered.

What sort of text was that?

Wonderful?

Cheeky?

Sweet?

I'd replied something corny, and somehow, we'd traded equally oddball messages ever since.

Scrolling through the thread from yesterday, I smiled.

> Are you cooking your poor flowers again? All I can smell is floral perfume.

You're close enough to smell my concoctions, huh?

> I'm close enough that I can see you. Don't freak out, but...you look absolutely ravishing in that tee and shorts.

Are men still using the word ravishing these days?

> This one does. But I have been called a nerd before.

A nerd with a stalker personality. Could be kinky.

Careful, Lori. I know where you keep your spare key.

And you have my permission to use it.

Don't encourage me.

By the way, do you have a Sailor Moon fetish?

Eh, should I have?

You like what I'm wearing. It's a fifteen-year-old faded tee of Sailor Moon. And my shorts are part of a Sailor Moon set I had when I was fourteen. She was my idol growing up.

I remember her. A friend of mine had sisters who ate that show up. And you know what? You kinda look like her.

And that's not fair because I have no idea what you look like. Care to show me?

I'm grotesque, and you'd run away screaming. This is the first time I've been able to get close to a girl without scaring them off with my hideous face. Don't ruin it for me.

I thought we were always meant to be honest?

I am. I'm a troll. Best just enjoy my glittering personality and forget all about the boils I'm hiding under my mask.

One of these days, I'm going to count those boils.

As much as I'm enjoying this very un-arousing conversation, I have to go. Something just came up. Will you be okay on your own, or do I need to hire another stalker to keep you safe?

I don't want anyone else stalking me but you.

He hadn't replied.
Not long after, I'd heard Alexander's Chrysler leaving his garage,

his tyres squealing a little as he sped off—most likely heading toward the hospital and an emergency.

For the quickest second, I had a crazy notion that X was Alexander. That the reason he stayed in the dark and covered his face was because he didn't want me to know it was him.

But then another message had pinged and eradicated that stupid idea.

OPEN PHOTO.

I'd clicked on what X had sent, grinning at an image of myself. I stood exactly where I was with a soft smile on my lips and a wooden spoon in one hand, diligently mixing by the kitchen window as I combined jojoba, vanilla, and lemongrass into lip balm. My t-shirt print of Sailor Moon was faded, baggy, and hanging off one bruised shoulder, while my crescent moon shorts were a little too short.

I can't seem to tear myself away. Stop being so dazzling.

I really ought to have been offended. He'd not only violated my privacy, but taking photos of me as well?

Does he look at them when he's not watching me?

Did he think of me when he—

Stop right there.

Too late.

An image of him spread out on a bed, cock in hand, toned body on display, exploded through my mind. The only piece of clothing he wore was that damn mask, and I wanted to yank it off so I could see him biting his bottom lip as he self-pleasured.

You need professional help.

"Hey, Sails. Sails! Earth to Sailor Moon!"

I jumped high enough to fumble with my phone. It flew from my hands and clattered into the last few vials of essential oils.

"Oops. Sorry." Lily snickered. "I've been trying to get your attention for the past five minutes." She waved at a pretty young woman with an equally pretty daughter clutching at her jeans. "This lovely customer wants to know if you have anything that can help with eczema?"

I smiled at the shy girl before nodding at the mother. "I do, actually." Grabbing a particular tincture that Nana had spent years perfecting—thanks to her own battle with itchy, dry skin—I passed it to her. "This is medium strength, but I can make up a stronger batch if it's not enough. It's all natural with no side effects."

"Oh wow." The woman grinned. "That's so nice of you."

I left Lily to handle the sale, ever so grateful she'd agreed to help today. When I'd told her I was braving the big bad world and heading to the market, she'd cancelled her three open homes and insisted on being my honorary shopkeeper.

She'd tried to meet me at my place to help me load the endless boxes of face cream, night cream, lip balm, tinctures, essential oils, and other goods made from my garden into my pop's ancient Honda Civic, but I'd laughed her off and said she needed her beauty sleep and to meet me at the local showgrounds where the market was held.

I hadn't told her why I'd forbidden her from coming to my house.

I didn't want to admit that I'd gotten up at three a.m. knowing it would take me that long to pack the car, thanks to the trembles and panic that kept attacking me at the very thought of leaving. I couldn't pretend that I was okay, and I didn't want her seeing me like that.

I'd only had the strength to get through it because X had messaged around five in the morning.

Are you running away?

No, just trying to be normal and get back to routine.

And that includes packing your life into a car, why?

I'm going to the market. To sell my flower concoctions.

Ah, in that case. I know what I'll be doing today.

Before I could reply, he'd sent another one.

By the way, you're doing amazing. I know it isn't easy to fight your natural instinct to hide away, but you're incredible and strong, and I'll be watching you. You're safe.

I'd repeated his words over and over, especially when the tears stung, and the urge to throw up in the camellia bush latched around my throat. I wished he'd been with me as I'd finally driven away, fighting debilitating jitters all the way to the market.

Dawn had cast the showgrounds where the market was held in pink and gold by the time I'd received his next message.

> You got this. Fake it till you make it. You know I have your back if you're a little unstable. You can talk to me about anything.

And then, I'd been too busy to think, let alone be afraid.

Little by little, customer by customer, the agoraphobia that'd slowly been restricting my life loosened its claws and let me breathe.

Smiling at Lily as she laughed with the woman, I tapped my screen to bring up the keyboard.

Hello, Keeper of Secrets. Thanks for checking in on me. Are you here? Are you watching? You can come and say hello, if you're brave enough.

I laughed under my breath as I added:

I'm sure I have a cream for those boils you're so self-conscious about.

His reply came quickly.

> I'm rather attached to my pizza face. Thanks anyway. Is it condescending of me to say I'm proud of you?

Not condescending. Rather sweet.

> Is it stepping over a line if I tell you that the little pinafore you're wearing is driving me mad?

Glancing down at my apron, I ran my fingers over the logo Nana and Pops had designed so many years ago. They'd used a Tree of Life emblem with sparkling soil and flower blooms. The pink frills around the collar and hem gave it a cottage housewife vibe.

I'm beginning to think you have multiple fetishes where my clothes are concerned.

> I think you mean I have a you fetish.

I gasped.

A woman giggled in the milling crowd while customers moseyed up and down the grass aisle, buying homemade jams, jewellery, sweets, and bric-à-brac. Scanning the bustle, I tried to spot a man who might be X. A few strolled past. One even caught my eye and smiled, but his short height was all wrong. I had no idea what hair colour X had or his facial features, but I did know he was fairly tall.

My cheek had rested perfectly on his chest while he could prop his chin on my head.

I sighed, remembering the overwhelming comfort I'd found in his embrace.

Someone caught my attention in the distance.

Every droplet of carefree happiness evaporated beneath the memory of pain and strangulation.

Alexander North stood with another man and a beautiful auburn-haired woman not far away. While his friend inspected a homemade chopping board, Alexander glared at his phone, and the woman watched both men with a bemused smile on her face.

My own phone pinged.

Sorry, did I step over the line again? Note to self: don't use words like fetish or send photos of the woman you're technically stalking even though it's for all the right reasons.

Alexander's friend let out a loud laugh and handed over some money for the chopping board. Both men with the woman vanished into the crowd again.

Rubbing the back of my scalp where Milton had ripped my hair as he threw me onto my back for looking at Alexander, I did my best to forget the pain. I ignored the throb in my hip from his kick. The bruised ribs. The bite he'd left on my collarbone.

I'd been having such a good day. I'd been free for such a short while.

But thanks to seeing my neighbour, all I wanted to do was bolt home, lock every door, and never look at Alexander again.

My phone chirped.

What is it? What happened? You don't look so good.

Sighing heavily, I sat down on the large plastic box I'd used to transport my wares.

I just saw my neighbour. It gave me flashbacks.

His reply wasn't as fast, but it came eventually.

Want me to find him?
I can deliver every bruise you're wearing because of him.

No! Goodness, of course not! It's not his fault that Milton was a jealous asshole. My neighbour is actually very...

I stopped typing.

I didn't know how to describe Alexander.

A trickster when he was a kid. Obsessed with anything injured as a teen. Quiet, reserved, and slightly standoffish as an adult, all with a boyish habit of fiddling with his glasses as if he'd never gotten used to wearing them even though he'd had a pair since he was twelve.

Why on earth do I remember how old he was when he got glasses?

I knew why.

Because Nana had baked him a cake with a big pair of spectacles on it with the words 'Congratulations, you're a distinguished gentleman'. I'd overheard her talking to Pops how Alexander had been bullied at school for having four eyes, and she'd wanted to lift his spirits.

...he's a good person. It's not his fault. He'd take it so personally if he knew.

I'm sure he'd do whatever it took to wipe away those memories associated with him if he could.

Standing, I smoothed down my pinafore and made my way to Lily.

I have to go. I'm slacking while my friend works so hard. Talk to you later.

I threw myself into helping customers so I didn't give in to the urge to look for Alexander in the crowd, hoping like hell the feeling of helplessness and panic would vanish.

Twenty

Zander

Claws Come in All Shapes & Sizes

"THIS IS ALL YOUR FAULT," I GRUMBLED as Colin inspected his newly purchased chopping board. "I should never have agreed to come here with you. My plan was to covertly watch from a distance. Not shop where she could see me."

"Are you saying I took advantage of your sleep-deprived state at the hospital this morning and coerced you into doing something against your will?" He smirked. "Do you wish to make a formal complaint? Perhaps tell the girl you're crushing on that—"

"Quiet." I narrowed my eyes. "You said you'd hold your tongue."

If it hadn't been for my security cameras alerting me to Sailor packing her car like she did most weekends for the market, I wouldn't have known she was here. I'd logged in on a coffee break at five a.m., my cameras sending me a motion alert. I'd watched for a while, my chest swelling with pride at how brave she was. She'd also made my heart clench a few times as she sat on her doorstep and hugged her knees, swiping away tears and fighting back her panic.

I'd made a stupid comment to Col that I was going to watch her at the market after work, and he'd invited himself along.

"Did I? I don't remember saying that." He chuckled. "You're unfairly accusing me. I have every right to defend myself. What do you think, Christina? Did I do the friendly thing by dragging your older brother out of the hospital after a fifteen-hour stint to ensure he sees the sun and buys some homemade goodies, or did I overstep my boundaries?"

Christina—my sister who'd had a bad breakup and hated the fact that she'd recently turned twenty-eight—laughed under her breath. "Don't ask me. I'm not getting on Zan's bad side."

"But you're happy for me to take all the blame. Harsh."

Christina stared at him for a second too long. She tucked her long hair behind her ear.

"She's not interested, you fool," I muttered. "I've told you this."

Colin pouted. "Really?" He fluttered his eyelashes at my sister.

"You sure I can't tempt you back into the dating pool? I promise I don't bite."

"How do you know that *I* don't?" Christina crossed her arms.

Colin laughed out loud.

I didn't appreciate them flirting right in front of me. "Stop that. Both of you."

Colin fired back, "Only if you stop giving yourself blue balls by texting this woman."

"I said *quiet*," I hissed, looking over my shoulder, just in case someone—Sailor—heard.

"Say what?" Christina frowned. "You're seeing someone, Zan? I thought you'd chosen the monk lifestyle."

"He's definitely *watching* someone. Aren't you, Zander?" Colin winked. "He's very, *very* good at watching."

My fingers curled into a fist.

Would I be arrested if I punched my best friend's face in the middle of a busy market?

Christina looked back and forth between us. "I don't get it." Rolling her eyes, she shrugged. "And I don't wanna know. I'm off browsing. See ya."

"Call me!" Colin yelled after her. His gaze tracked her as she weaved around other people. It was his fault she'd joined us in the first place. He'd spotted her as we'd headed into the market and practically begged her to tag along.

"And you say I need to get laid," I huffed. "As your friend, I understand your interest in Christina. She's smart, funny, and sensible. But as her brother, I'm warning you…she isn't one-night stand material."

"Who said anything about a one-night stand?" He scratched his jaw where a five o'clock shadow had come in. We'd both pulled an all-nighter. I'd been in the ER, and he'd had a patient who'd developed difficulties after amputation surgery. "I'm looking for the same thing you are." He dropped a bit of his swagger. "I just want to have someone to care for and have them care about me, that's all."

As much as I appreciated him opening up to me—most likely running on exhaustion and craving the comfort of going home to someone—I had my own problems. With Christina gone, I could share them.

Shoving my phone in his face, I hissed, "She saw me. That's why this is all your fault. All the progress Sailor has made today, thanks to X, has taken a flying leap out the goddamn window because of me. That's how toxic I am to her. I should go over there right now and tell her who I am so I don't destroy her even more."

Colin skimmed my inbox, no doubt lingering on the slightly more suggestive messages. I still felt guilty for those.

"You need to stop talking about yourself from X's POV," he said. "If the lies come toppling down, you don't want her to have too many instances when you actively kept up the ruse. As long as you have a plausible reason for why you approached her this way, she can find a way to forgive you. But the more you back-stab yourself, the more explaining you'll have to do."

"Christ, this is getting completely out of hand."

"I agree." Grabbing my wrist, he dragged me through the crowd back the way we came. "Let's go see if we can fix it."

"Wait, what?" I yanked on his hold. "What are you doing?"

"Helping." His fingers dug into me, pressing on the faded welts left behind by Sailor's scratches when I'd slapped my hand over her screams.

Every time I thought about touching her, my body tightened in ways it shouldn't. For four days—as we texted as casual friends about nonsense with the occasional check in on her mental health—I'd fought the very real, very awful craving that was becoming far too insistent to deny.

I wanted her.

I didn't just want to protect her or keep her safe. I *wanted* her. In my arms. My bed. My heart.

And while X existed, I couldn't.

But while Zander existed, she would never talk to me the way she did with X.

It'd been a stroke of pure luck that I'd snapped a photo of her stirring her cauldron of whatever she'd been making when I'd been called into work yesterday. I knew she'd probably heard my car leaving, and if I stopped texting her as X the moment Zander left…that could connect a few dots that couldn't be connected.

I'd sent her a photo that was only ever meant to be for me. A photo of her by the window that I'd taken a few minutes before I'd been summoned to work. I'd hoped she was still there in that exact position—still stirring and staring into the garden. If she was, then she'd assume I'd just taken the pic and would never wonder.

I liked to think I'd been pretty clever and she'd bought it, but who the hell knew for sure?

With anxiety bubbling in my gut, I tried to untangle Colin's grip. "Let go of me." I managed to pry his fingers off just as we almost bashed into the long table with its white runner, neat little pyramids of bottles, and numerous postcards listing old-fashioned remedies for different ailments.

"Zander!" Lily beamed. "Lovely to see you out and about. And who's this?"

"This is Colin," Colin said with an idiotic bow. "I work with Zan."

"Oooo, another doctor. Be still my beating heart." Lily's laugh cut through the hum of passersby voices, whipping Sailor's head to face us. She moved in slow motion—her sandy blonde hair flicking over her shoulder, her blue eyes widening with fear, her lips parting with shock.

I had a prime position to see her hard-won happiness bleed into the shadows of the past.

Goddamn you, Colin.

Colin ignored that Sailor looked as if she'd bolt out of the tent and waved. "Hey, Sailor. How're things?" He reached across the display and held out his hand. "I've seen you around but never officially been introduced. I'm Colin Marx."

My throat mimicked the desert. My heart gave up and played dead in my chest.

I couldn't say a word as Sailor swallowed hard and moved to join us. The table kept us separated, but the soft scents of blossom, vanilla, and other fragrant flowers permeated the air.

Ever so slowly as if stealing herself, Sailor accepted Colin's handshake. "Hi, Dr Marx. You're right. I've seen you popping by to see Alexander a few times."

"Call me Colin, please." He arched his thumb at me. "And call that one Zan. It's better than that other mouthful."

Breaking the handshake, she forced a smile. "Not sure we're familiar enough for me to call him nicknames."

"Oh, I dunno." Colin winked. "I think you might be more familiar than you think."

I elbowed him in the gut. *Hard.*

Sailor flinched as if my 'friendly' punishment was more like a mortal blow.

My entire back prickled with the urge to leave and never come back. I hated seeing her eyes turn flat instead of sparkly. I hated the way her entire demeanour folded inward, making herself as small as possible.

My hands balled.

If I ever got near Milton, I'd definitely be done for murder.

I despised what he'd done to her. I hated seeing her this way when it wasn't her. I needed to rip him apart with every prehistoric beast inside me.

"So…what brings you guys to the market?" Lily asked, dragging my attention from Sailor. The moment I stopped looking at her, she tripped backward and rubbed her chest with the heel of her hand as if fighting a panic attack.

Unlike the night I'd heard her screaming, I couldn't grab her in a hug.

All I could do was get far away from her. To give her the space she needed because I represented all her worst moments.

"I, eh, I just remembered I..." Any believable lie flew out of my head. With a grunt, I pushed my glasses up my nose, turned around, and marched away from Sailor's stall as quickly as possible.

"Where are you?" I barked into my phone. "I'm waiting to drive you home, seeing as you made me your chauffeur."

"Oh, sorry! I'm already back at my place. Your sister kindly gave me a lift. You didn't tell me we lived so close to one another." Colin laughed. "Besides, I didn't know if you were sticking around to switch from Clark Kent to Superman."

My fingers tightened around my cell phone. "Can you drop the jokes, Col? Didn't you see how badly she reacted toward me? It's not a laughing matter." Sighing heavily, I hated that my stress made me snappy. "Sorry, man. I'm just...yeah, I'm struggling with this. I don't mean to take it out on you."

"You're fine. I like you grouchy. And...you're right." He sobered up. "It's not a laughing matter. I genuinely feel sorry for her and rightfully a little worried about how she's processing this, but I also think you're being an idiot for not showing her the type of man you are."

"What's that supposed to mean?"

"I mean, instead of X saving the day, you could've done something as Zander."

"Like what?"

"How about talking to her like a normal man instead of bumbling an excuse, then galloping off like a sixteen-year-old moron with a stiffy."

"I take my apology back. I honestly have no idea why I'm friends with you."

"For my wonderful wisdom of course. Go find her. Go help her take down her stall. Better yet, take her to dinner. She's managed to fight some of her issues by leaving her house. That's worthy of celebration. Give her a happy memory to cling to when the walls start closing in."

"If I took her to a restaurant as me, she'd have a panic attack right there at the table."

"But if you talk her through it and show her that you won't deliver the same pain she's feeling from whatever he did, then you can reverse all the damage and prove that you aren't a trigger for her.

You're innocent in all of this, and the sooner she realises that, the sooner you two can have your happily ever after."

"There won't be any happily ever afters."

"I'm going to make you eat those words in three to five years from now when you get married."

"I hate that you're so positive and believe in fairytales."

"Meh, what can I say? It's my superpower." He chuckled. "Now go. If you're still at the market, offer your services and help her pack everything up—if you can stay awake of course. Call me later and tell me how it went."

He hung up.

I looked past the still busy car park to the slowly emptying market. With my ass leaning against the hood of my Chrysler, I crossed my arms and peered down the aisles of the stalls still operating.

The market was winding down, but customers still darted into the showgrounds, scooping up end-of-day bargains.

I deliberated doing exactly what Colin suggested.

If I went to help, could I slowly teach her that all those phantom pains had nothing to do with me? I wasn't the one to almost kill her. But…she hadn't messaged me as X even though I'd texted her a few times to check in. She'd shut down on me, and it hurt to have her slam a door in my face when I'd gotten so used to having her respond.

Sighing heavily, I took off my glasses and rubbed my eyes.

I was too exhausted for rational thought.

With how cloudy my mind was, I'd end up calling her Lori and screwing everything up.

Best go home, crash for a bit, and then possibly sneak into her garden as X and—

You're not sneaking anywhere.

You're not allowed to go anywhere near her.

Texting is all you're allowed.

The softest meow wrenched my gaze to the gravel by my front wheel. The scruffiest orange kitten appeared, its whiskers bent and fur dull with mud.

With heartbreakingly bright green eyes, it looked up and screamed. Padding toward me, it wound its tiny body around my ankle. Its meows grew louder and more pitiful, begging as manically as it could.

Stealing my leg back, I ducked to my haunches and cupped its little head. Its fur was coarse and malnourished, his little skull terrifyingly fragile in my fingers.

Instead of running away petrified, the kitten tried to crawl into my hand. Its meows turned to caterwauls and every instinct inside me—

every urge I'd had as a kid and the calling I had as a doctor—instantly reacted.

Scooping the skeletal cat from the car park, I cradled him in both hands. Holding him up to my nose, I inspected his little face.

He tried to headbutt my chin, wriggling and squirming to get closer.

"You're definitely not afraid of me," I said softly. "Where did you come from?"

He screamed in response, trying to get free, not to leap down but to crawl higher up my arm toward my neck.

Holding him tight, I looked over the sea of parked cars. Had someone brought a litter here to sell? Had he escaped? We had a pretty big rainstorm the other night. Perhaps he got flushed from somewhere?

A woman walked by, her car keys jingling.

"Excuse me?" I held out the kitten. "You didn't happen to see anyone who this little guy could belong to, did you?"

The orange furball screamed again and tried to scramble up my arm.

She laughed. "I think he's saying he belongs to you." Scratching the top of his head, she winked. "Congratulations, you're now a cat dad."

Unlocking her car next to mine, she climbed in. With a quick wave, she drove away, leaving me standing with an unwanted patient.

I didn't have time for a pet—even though I would've adored to have another soul in the house. Each time I felt lonely enough to contemplate getting an animal, I always reminded myself that it wasn't fair with my long, erratic work hours.

The kitten stopped crying and pouted sadly as if hearing my thoughts and knowing he'd chosen the wrong pair of legs to beg at.

"It's okay, little guy. I'll help you. I just can't keep you."

He meowed and gave me sad little eyes.

"I'm not leaving you here, alright? You're gonna be okay."

His ears were a tad crusty, and his lack of body mass ensured I'd probably have to get some kitten formula.

Unlocking my car, I went to put him on the front seat but spotted Sailor and Lily in the distance. They carried a large plastic box between them. Lily said something, and Sailor managed to laugh.

Seeing Sailor responding to her friend eased the tightness of concern in my chest.

She's okay.

She wasn't alone and had someone she trusted.

She wasn't better or completely healed, but she would be okay for a little while.

Which was good because right now, someone else needed my

help.

Placing the little kitten on the leather seat, I closed the door and headed to the driver's side. First, I'd take him to the nearest vet for a quick check-up, pop to the store to get supplies, and then head home.

And when does sleep come into this?

I yawned as I drove out of the car park, checking on Sailor in my rearview mirror.

Sleep would have to wait for a little longer.

Twenty-One

Sailor

Pouncing Panic

I LAY IN THE DARK.

Arms crossed under my blankets.

Fingers pinching each arm hard enough to almost split the skin.

I couldn't move.

Could hardly breathe.

The stress of the market and the effort it took to stay sane for Lily and smile for my customers had drained me to the point of despair.

But this wasn't like the panic attack I'd had on the rug that first time.

This was far more stealthy. It'd waited until I'd had Thai takeout with Lily, put away all my merchandise, and bid her goodnight. It'd stalked me as I locked up, cleaned my teeth, and slipped into my bed on the floor of Nana's old bedroom.

The wallpaper shimmered with misty lakes and silver cranes; the faintest paint smell lingered in the air. I'd read for a bit and fallen asleep, but then I'd heard a noise.

A noise like boots on the stairs and the corridor landing creaking.

And that was it.

The panic pounced.

My system saturated with adrenaline and anxiety.

Tears gushed against my control. My breathing turned ragged. And no matter how many times I told myself to calm down, I just couldn't. Nothing worked. Nothing helped. The only thing stopping me from screaming into unconsciousness was my fingernails pinching each arm, giving me something to latch onto.

Pain.

Pain was good. Pain was *real*.

As long as I focused on that, I focused on reality and not the past.

I hated being alone.

I hated that I felt lonely.

The house pressed over me, stagnant and stifling, trapping me inside with the Goblin-Milton from my memories.

A moth fluttered too close, its dusty wings brushing against my cheek.

Swallowing a cry, I bolted upright and reached for the side lamp I'd placed on the floor beside my mattress. I still needed to spray-paint Nana's old bed frame. I needed to go shopping to buy some furniture, but the thought of going out again? Of being around people—no matter how kind and sweet—God, I *can't*.

Ugh, what's wrong with me?!

Why can't I move on from this?

Something thudded in the gloom.

I swear the doorknob of my bedroom jingled.

The moth swooped back over my eyesight.

With a cry, I snatched my gifted phone from the covers.

Are you awake?

I sent the message before I looked at the time.

One thirty in the morning.

Of course he wasn't awake. He had a job like a normal person. His professional occupation wasn't watching me for a living.

Of course he's in bed!

The house creaked again, shooting my heart rate into scary territory.

One of the closely growing trees scratched its branches against my window.

"Nana, if that's you...can you stop?" I panted into the darkness. "I'm not doing so well, and I really need my imagination to stop running wild."

The moth appeared again, drawn by my bedside lamp, but then it switched directions and landed on the blue glow of my cell phone screen.

Tucking away its wings, it perched on the edge as if replying to me.

Nodding, I accepted that Nana had heard my request even though the house cracked again, sending an ominous groan through the walls.

That's it.

My jitters and shivers had me writing another message.

Hopefully, X had his sound off, and I wouldn't wake him. Hopefully, he'd see this in the morning, and I would've survived the night on my own.

I know I probably did too much today with the market and dinner, but if I don't do those things, how can I expect to get better? The only problem is...I'm not okay now. I'm hearing things and seeing things, and I can't move or breathe or think. I hate that I can't just snap my fingers and be done with this. I hate that I know this is ridiculous, but the flight-or-fight inside me is still living in the past. I know you're asleep, and I'm so sorry for dumping this on you. It isn't your responsibility. And I don't want you to feel like I am. But I can't say this to anyone else, so...I'm saying it to you. I'm not okay. I hate those words. But they're true. Please delete this when you wake up. I'm sure I'll be fine come morning, but right now, I'm just going to use you as a lifeline, okay? I'm just going to keep typing nonsense so I can focus on other things.

I pressed send and immediately started a new text bubble.

I don't like mango. I don't know if I've ever told anyone that. I'm not keen on apricots, either. The smell gets me, and they're too sweet. When Nana used them in her creams, I'd feel sick from the smell. What else? I love this house. I always wished I could live here full-time when I was a kid instead of the cold, loveless home with my parents. I was wanted here. At my parents, I was an inconvenience. I might love this house, but it's treating me like I'm the inconvenience, just like my parents did. It keeps creaking and groaning. I really need to check that all the doors and windows are locked, but I can't move. I literally can't get out of bed, and oh my God, this is so stupid. I'm so sorry. I'll stop. I didn't mean to type such ridiculous things.

Sending one of the most idiotic messages of my life, I dropped my phone into the blankets and crossed my arms as tightly as I could. Squishing the life out of myself, I resumed my pinching, trembling with the need to snap out of this horrendous funk.

My phone chirped quietly.

I launched for it.

The next time you hear footsteps on the stairs, it's me, alright? Don't scream. Don't wake the neighbours. I'm coming over.

"What?"

I gasped and rushed to type back.

No! I mean, I don't expect you to do that. Stay in bed. Sleep! Ignore me. I'm fine.

We agreed no lies, Lori. Give me twenty minutes.

I blinked at my phone.

He couldn't be serious, could he? Did he live that close? Was that walking distance or twenty minutes by car?

Guilt crushed me at the thought of him driving across town just because I was having a mental breakdown.

Please don't. I feel so bad. Just talking to you has broken the panic. I'm okay now. Truly.

He didn't reply.

He didn't respond for five minutes, ten minutes, fifteen minutes.

And then the house inhaled and exhaled as if the back door had opened, letting in fresh air.

I froze under my blankets.

My ears rang from listening so intently. I quaked and rattled so hard my teeth chattered. The first heavy clomp of a boot on the stairs had me swallowing a scream and also wanting to burst into tears of relief.

One after another.

Step after step.

He walked slowly, methodically.

He reached the landing. The sound of his boots switched from heavy to soft.

I squeaked as his knuckles rapped on the door. "You have a choice, Lori. Either I can stay out here, and you can sleep knowing that I'm close by...or you can let me in, and we can talk face to face."

Swallowing so hard I almost choked on my tongue, I coughed, "Eh...you can come in."

The door handle pressed down. The only difference was, this time it was real and not my imagination. The door swung open just enough for him to slip inside before closing it again.

Glancing at the bare windows, he asked quietly, "Where are your curtains?"

"I...I took them down to paint. I haven't bought new ones yet."

Grunting an affirmative noise, he pointed at my bedside lamp on the floor. "I'm happy to stay for however long you want, but you have

152

to turn that off."

I frowned. "But then I can't see you."

His eyebrows rose. "That's the point."

Studying him, I took in the all-black attire, chunky boots, and skull-printed scarf/mask. He'd tugged it up so high, it brushed his bottom lashes. Something was different about him. Something I couldn't put my—

He's not wearing a hat.

I focused on his head and the strands falling roguishly over his forehead. His hair looked jet black with a glossy blue tinge. The ends were slightly damp.

"Did you just have a shower?" I asked quietly.

He stood tall as if about to deny it but then nodded with an exhale. "I did. Got in late from work."

"What do you do?"

He came a step closer. "Doesn't matter. Are you going to turn off the light?"

The panic loosened enough for me to sit on my knees. Peering at him, I focused on his eyes. A silver hoop pierced his left eyebrow, hinting he might have a rebellious streak. Did he have tattoos under all that black? His eyes gleamed a rich, deep brown. His forehead had no boils or pockmarks like he lied about, and judging by the beauty of his eyes and thick lashes, I'd say he was very handsome beneath his mask.

"I don't want to turn off the light," I whispered. "Do you mind if I leave it on?"

He sighed heavily. "Tell me why you want it on. Is your fear making you afraid of the dark or..." He splayed his hands. Strong, long fingers and nice square palms hinted he might be rebellious with an eyebrow piercing, but he didn't have a manual labour job. His hands were too perfect, too defined with tendons and ligaments that looked more suited to precision work.

"Or?" I couldn't take my eyes off him. The white skull printed over his mouth and chin drew me in. His refusal to show his face should ring loud warning bells, but I found it to be the opposite. Just like the reaction I'd had when he confessed he had a crush on me, I found my blood heating up in very different ways to the panic of before.

He has a crush on me.

The weight of that admittance seemed to swallow the entire room. My room.

A man I didn't know was in my bedroom at two in the morning.

And I'd never felt so safe.

What did that say about me?

Just how badly was I messed up, thanks to what Milton did?

Hugging myself, I lost whatever confidence I had.

This wasn't normal behaviour. I shouldn't put myself at risk like this. Perhaps I was trying to remember how to live by doing reckless things because this definitely counted as reckless.

"I need to keep the light on." I tipped up my chin. "Please."

His hand strayed to his face. For a second, it looked as if he reached for a pair of non-existent glasses but then he tugged his mask a little higher and nodded. "Fine."

Awkwardness fell between us. He shifted away from the bed, looking for a chair. He scowled, the soft lamp revealing the tired lines etching around his eyes.

He looked exhausted.

Guilt pounced all over again. "I woke you up, didn't I? You weren't getting home from work, after all. You were in bed, and I dragged you out here."

He stiffened. "It's fine. You needed me. I'm happy to be here." Swaying a little on his feet, he pinched the bridge of his nose.

Patting the empty spot beside me, I said, "Sit down before you fall."

He gave me a stern look with his chin tipped low and dark eyes glowing with dominion.

The slightest thrill worked through me.

"I'm fine over here," he grumbled, his voice extra gravelly.

Tugging the covers back, I forced a smile. "I won't be able to talk if I'm worried that you'll fall over any second. Sit...please."

He huffed. "So you're brave enough to boss about a masked man with no problem, but a creaking house gives you nightmares." He softened the rather harsh sentence with a low chuckle. "I'm not sure there's a word for that condition."

"Grateful. That's a word." I smiled the tiniest bit. "I'm grateful you're here. I'm grateful that you sacrificed your sleep for me. I'm grateful that you gave me someone to talk to."

He sucked in a breath and stepped toward me almost against his will.

I waited for him to say something, but he stayed silent. With jerky footfalls, he closed the distance between us, turned around, then bent his long legs to sit on the low mattress.

The bed sagged with his weight, and the covers pulled over my hips as he scooted backward and rested his shoulders against the wall. Looking behind him, he studied the crane wallpaper I'd installed.

The joins weren't perfect, but I was proud of my first attempt. I'd done it on my own and watched countless YouTube videos to get the paste mixture right.

"It's pretty." He dropped his stare again, his warm brown eyes

154

meeting mine. "You did a good job."

I frowned. "How do you know it's new?"

He twitched as if I'd caught him in something he didn't want to reveal before he grunted, "I saw the delivery of renovation supplies. It also smells freshly painted in here."

"I'm not used to the fact you know quite a lot about my life thanks to watching me when I know nothing about yours."

Reaching toward his feet still on the floor, he undid the buckles and laces of his boots before toeing them off and spreading his legs on top of my comforter. "How are you feeling? Was it a panic attack like before?"

I never took my eyes off him, studying the smooth skin of his forehead and the faintest lines feathering out from his gaze. He'd told me he was thirty-four. I didn't think that was a lie, judging by his half-appearance. "You know, one of these days, I won't let you change the subject."

He chuckled under his breath, his voice extra raspy. "One of these days, you won't want to talk about any subject with me."

"Perhaps." I nodded. "Or maybe I'll want to talk to you forever."

Skirting the topic once again, he ordered, "So…talk to me now. Tell me what happened."

Facing him, I sat a little taller. With our eyes locked, I searched for all the words that'd suffocated me before.

And found I was peacefully silent.

I wrinkled my nose and pulled back a little. "That's strange."

"What's strange?" His forehead furrowed; a few blue-black strands fell forward, catching on his eyebrow piercing.

"I'm not afraid anymore." The biggest yawn made me moan with exhaustion. "In fact, I can barely keep my eyes open."

He laughed softly and patted the bed. "Then lie down and try to sleep."

"But you're here."

"That's probably why your body isn't fighting sleep anymore. You have someone else to stand guard. Your system is ready to shut down and rest."

"But I didn't drag you over here to be my bodyguard."

"You didn't drag me, Lori, I came willingly. I'm glad you texted me, and I'm happy to be your bodyguard. I'm happy to be whatever you need." Hesitantly, he held out his arm. "Lie down."

Eyeing up the cradle he made with his open arm and body taking up most of my bed, I yawned again. I'd heard of tiredness that you just couldn't fight. I'd succumbed to it myself a few times recently, but I fought it all the same.

I didn't want to sleep while X was here.

I wanted to talk in person instead of via text.

I wanted to hear his rumbly, gravelly voice and hope I was cured by morning.

With a soft growl, he snaked his arm around my shoulders and tugged me slowly but firmly into him. My hand landed on his chest, not pushing him away but bracing myself all the same.

He froze. "I'm only trying to make you comfortable. That's all." He went to unwind his arm from around me, but I shook my head.

"Don't."

He sucked in a breath. Our eyes locked.

Ever so slowly, he gathered me even tighter against him. "Scoot down. Use me as your pillow."

Dropping my stare down his chest, I drank in the black hoodie he wore, wondering just how trim and perfect he was beneath it. His heartbeat thundered beneath my fingertips.

A frisson of power returned to me. The faintest re-awakening of my missing sexuality. Any ideas of femininity and desire had died the moment Milton strangled me.

I hated that I was the fairer sex.

I hated that I hadn't been able to fight back.

That I was smaller, lighter, and weaker than him.

But in that moment in X's protection, I liked that I fit perfectly against him. I liked the sensation of him looking out for me. I liked that I could surrender to him all because I knew he would keep me safe.

"Get some sleep, Lori," he purred, soft and hypnotic.

I yawned and scooted my way down his firm, toned body until my head rested on his lower belly.

Shifting me a little, he stole my pillow that I was no longer using and placed it behind his head. Angling himself so he wasn't sitting upright but wasn't fully lying down, he ran his fingers through my hair.

The first jolt of him touching my scalp where Milton had torn out chunks made me gasp.

He stopped immediately. "If there are places I shouldn't touch, just tell me. Don't suffer through it because you don't want to be honest."

Nodding, I forced myself to lose my sudden shyness and put my hand on his stomach.

His heartbeat pounded loud beneath my ear, and I smiled at another surge of power.

"You weren't lying when you said you have a crush on me," I whispered.

He laughed abruptly. "Am I shaking that much?"

"Your heart is racing."

His fingers feathered to my neck beneath my ear. Finger-mark bruises still collared me and I could barely touch that part of myself without suffering flashbacks, but X's touch was exquisitely soft. Endlessly gentle. Just a worshipping caress in the night.

I shivered as he pressed two fingertips to a pulse point there. He didn't speak for a moment. "I'd say yours is going just as fast."

Sifting his fingers through my hair again, he sucked in a breath. "Is this okay?"

My eyes closed, sinking into his petting. "Yes."

"You'll tell me if I do something that unsettles you?"

"I promise."

"In that case, close your eyes and let me restore your faith in men." He sniffed as if scowling beneath his mask. "Let me undo everything he did."

His fingers drifted like warm water droplets over my head, and I couldn't fight it anymore.

My eyes closed.

In a few seconds, I was asleep.

Twenty-Two

Zander

Nothing Like a Cat Gift

I WOKE TO MY ALARM BLARING ITS horrible foghorn alert, injecting me with an unhealthy amount of adrenaline.

Everything ached. My brain ached. My body ached. My cock throbbed with morning wood. I couldn't get my bearings. The light was all wrong. The scent far more floral than my usual clean laundry fragrance.

What the hell did I do last night?

"Oh my God!" a woman groaned. "What is that awful noise?"

I froze as last night exploded through me.

The kitten.

Sailor.

Her going to sleep on me.

I bolted upright, fighting to untangle my legs from hers and unthread my arm from beneath her shoulders. My fingers tingled with pins and needles, hinting I'd been sleeping wrapped around her for a while.

I'd been sleeping with Sailor.

Oh fuck!

Launching out of bed, my hands flew to my face.

My mask!

It'd fallen a little, clinging to the tip of my nose. Wrenching it up high enough to blind myself, I snatched my phone from where I'd placed it on the floor and killed the nasty alarm.

Six a.m.

I had surgery today. And I officially felt as if I'd been run over. Twelve times. By a train.

What with the kitten keeping me up, and then Sailor messaging me just as I'd gotten into bed, I was running on absolute dregs. Not to mention the fact that I'd put the blue-black rinse through my hair like Colin told me to, pinched a ridiculous fake piercing on my eyebrow, then fought my overwhelming dislike of wearing contacts to cover my bright green with muddy brown.

My parents tried to encourage me to use contacts after I got bullied at school for wearing glasses, but I'd never been able to put them in without causing myself serious harm. I didn't like the scratchy feeling. And I didn't like putting anything in my eyes—helpful or not.

Sailor sat up in bed. The covers slipped to her waist, revealing the same Sailor Moon t-shirt she'd worn when mixing her creams the other day. I'd found it sexy then, but now? Now, I found it horribly arousing. Especially with her hair tousled and eyes hooded.

Talking of eyes.

What if one of the coloured contacts had fallen out while I slept? What if she saw me in the light and saw past all the facial disguises that seemed utterly pointless but Colin seemed to think would trick all humans because we inherently sucked at *looking* at people.

"I-I have to go." Grateful that a lack of sleep coated my voice box with some serious gruff, I yanked on my boots and stumbled toward the door. "I'll see you later."

No, you won't.

This was the last time.

"I mean…I'll talk to you later. By text. I'll message you." Not daring to look in her direction, I yanked open her bedroom door and darted into the corridor.

"Hey, wait." Her feet thudded on the carpet, chasing.

"Go back to bed, Lori! I have to go." I didn't give her a chance to stop me. I'd never run so fast from a woman's bed before. Sprinting out of her house, I went left—toward the park and not my place—just in case she watched.

I was running short on time and hadn't factored in a dawn jog in my stupidly heavy motorcycle boots, but that was what happened to men who chose stalking for a hobby.

Cutting through the manicured alleyway between Yasmine and Terry's house, I raced through the familiar running track around the park and cut down another lane before doubling back and approaching my house from the opposite end of the street.

Panting hard with blisters already pinching my toes, I snuck into my own home like a criminal and slammed to a stop as a guest I'd forgotten about came barrelling from the kitchen.

The little pen I'd made up for him with random pieces of ply in the garage had been dismantled. The towel I'd left him to sleep on was destroyed. The cat litter and food bowls looked as if a level five hurricane had torn through them.

I groaned as the orange fur ball wound itself around my legs.

He meowed and meowed and *meowed* as if I'd been gone for a decade.

On any other day, any other morning, I would've gotten on the floor and played with him. I would've given him cuddles and fed him some more formula regardless that—according to the vet—he was old enough to eat on his own. It would be an absolute honour to ensure the little creature was emotionally cared for as well as physically.

But I had responsibilities.

I'd already been unprofessional by letting myself run on so few hours of sleep. I'd done what I could to keep Sailor safe, but I couldn't let taking care of her jeopardise the care I gave others.

"I'm so sorry to do this to you, little one, but you're going to have to go."

The kitten meowed again.

Snatching him from the floor, I cradled him in one arm while I fished my phone from my pocket with the other. While Colin's number rang and rang, I took the stairs two at a time and marched into the bathroom.

I put the kitten in the sink and gave him a few cotton balls to play with.

"Zan? This better be an emergency. I was having the best dream," Colin grumbled as he finally answered.

"Ah, shit. I'm sorry, Col. My bad. I'm being a terrible friend lately with all my stupid problems, but…I have a full day at the hospital today and somehow ended up with a rescue kitten that needs looking after. Can you do it?"

"You know I would, but allergies. I love the little critters, but my system sees them as weapons of mass destruction on my airways."

"Fuck, that's right." I remembered when a patient had spent an hour with him discussing a new hand prosthetic after losing hers in an unfortunate crushing accident. She must've had a cat at home, and just its fur on her jumper was enough to send Colin into a coughing, sneezing, runny-eye mess that lasted hours.

"Sorry I woke you. Go back to sleep." Hanging up on him, I went to call my sisters. But they both made a point of never having their phones on at night, and I couldn't wait for them to finish their Sunday sleep-ins.

"Now what do I do?" Catching my stare in the bathroom mirror, I scowled at my mask.

I'd forgotten I was wearing it.

Least that meant it was comfortable.

Pulling it over my head, I yanked off my hoodie and trousers and stood starkers on the bathmat.

And honestly…I didn't recognise myself.

My hair glossed with blue-black and my fake brown eyes soaked up all the light in the bathroom. Without my glasses or green eyes, without my red hair and clean-shaven jaw, I really struggled to see the man I'd inhabited for twenty-nine years.

Maybe Colin isn't bullshitting, after all.

The kitten batted a cotton ball toward me. It flew from his paw and floated to the tiles. He cocked his little head, his whiskers still bent and crooked.

I couldn't leave him alone in case my day turned into another endless shift from hell. He'd already proven he'd destroy my house if left unsupervised, and I couldn't take him to work in my briefcase.

What the hell am I going to do?

"Stay put." I bopped his tiny nose with my finger. He immediately tried to chin me, purring like a mini chainsaw.

I smiled despite myself. Tickling his neck, I pressed a kiss to his ginger head. His purring turned manic. He kept sliding in the sink, trying to climb out and launch into my arms.

"I just have to rinse this dye out, shave, and then I'll figure out what to do with you." Not trusting the kitten to stay where I commanded, I closed the bathroom door so he couldn't take off, then placed him on the bathmat. Immediately, he attacked my bare toes, his little tail whipping in stalk mode.

Laughing under my breath, I stepped into the shower and closed the glass door. While he hunted dead moths, I had the quickest wash and shave of my life, changed my hair back from X black to Zander red, cursed and winced as I plucked the nightmarish contacts out, and sighed in relief as I placed my glasses back on my nose.

I dressed in record time, even with a kitten attached to my shadow, and as the sun finally shone on Ember Drive and every house remained silent with their Sunday sleepers, I grabbed a spare box from my garage, placed an old towel in the bottom, and added the formula mix, feeding bottle, and food packets.

I hadn't thought this through, but I was out of options. For the first time in my life, I was going to be late, and I didn't have another second to waste. Dressed in black slacks and a silver shirt with dark grey tie, I shoved the kitten into the box and stalked over to Sailor's house.

With my back prickling with fear that she'd recognise me after spending the night cuddled in my arms, I rang the front doorbell.

And waited.

And waited.

Guilt swamped me for waking her up but worry for my patient made me tap my foot and check my watch. The kitten thought it was a great fucking game, trying to scramble out of his prison and bat at the flowers hanging in their wrought-iron baskets.

Another few minutes ticked past. I knocked again.

Shit, she's not coming.

I'll have to think of something else.

The door swung open just as I turned to leave.

I choked on every word I planned to say. I froze on her doorstep and cursed myself for thinking I could do this.

The arousal I'd felt all night with her in my arms detonated through me. The hard-on I'd woken with had barely gone down, and now it ached all over again.

My heart swelled, drawn to her so badly. I knew far too much about her now. I couldn't hide how in awe I was or treat her with indifference when I'd had the honour of protecting her.

She trusts me.

No, she trusts X, not you.

She hates you, remember?

"Alexander?" She recoiled back into the foyer, using the door as a shield between us. She'd thrown on an oversized pale pink jumper. It hung to mid-thigh, hiding what I knew she was wearing underneath: a faded Sailor Moon tee and scandalously short shorts.

I choked on a groan.

Having intimate knowledge of what she wore threatened to break me. I'd never seen her naked—if she ever got close to taking her clothes off, I always walked away from the window—but knowing what she'd slept in was somehow worse than knowing what she hid beneath everything.

I knew how warm she was when she dreamed.

I knew how she'd sigh softly if I moved or wriggled closer if I tried to shift away.

She was clingy in her sleep.

And the caregiver inside me fucking loved every minute of being her safety blanket.

However, all the warmth and trust I'd grown used to seeing in her eyes as X turned into stony coldness now I stood before her as her neighbour. "W-What are you doing here so early?"

The kitten meowed, answering for me while I forced my brain to remember words.

I hated the way she looked at me. It killed me to think that all she saw when she looked at me was pain and abuse and the man who'd tried to rape and murder her.

With my chest tight, I cleared my throat and held up the box. "I'm so sorry to do this, but I have an emergency and wondered if you could help?"

Her eyes dropped to the orange furball. "What kind of emergency?"

"I have to go to work, but I rescued this little guy yesterday. Can you watch him until I come back? I've brought everything he needs." I glanced at the box. "I've included the formula mix, but if you don't want to bother with it, he's old enough to eat on his own." I dared catch her eyes again. "I wouldn't ask if I had any other option."

A flash of pain cut across her face. "So I'm your last resort?"

"Yes. I mean. No. Eh ...I know this is a huge imposition, and I don't want to put you out."

Taking a hesitant step toward me, she peered at the kitten. A ghost of a smile tipped up her lips. "He's pretty cute."

"He's a rascal, but I think if you tire him out, he should sleep for the rest of the day. I'm sure he won't be a bother, and you won't have to cat sit again. I'll call the SPCA when I finish work and get him set up there."

"Oh, that's a bit sad." She pouted. "You can't keep him?"

"Not with my hours." I shrugged. "It's not that I don't want to. It just wouldn't be fair."

Sucking on her bottom lip, she hesitantly reached for the box.

My pulse skipped at her proximity.

"Okay...I guess I can watch him."

"You will? *Thank you*. I can't tell you how much I appreciate it."

She sniffed and tried smiling again. "I'm not planning on leaving the house today, so it might be nice to have some company."

I couldn't respond to that without revealing I knew far too much about why she wasn't leaving and why she needed company. To be honest, I liked the thought of her having a little creature in the house. Something she could talk to if the TV randomly turned on again or if memories decided to haunt her.

Taking a deep breath as if fortifying herself to come nearer, she squeaked a little as I shifted and handed her the box.

Our arms brushed.

Our faces came closer than they'd ever been.

All I wanted to do was grab her in a kiss.

I couldn't tear my eyes off her mouth.

I couldn't forget how happy she'd been to see me last night and how she leaned on me whenever she got scared.

I spoke before I could stop myself. "Sailor, I—"

"Didn't you say you were late?" Hefting the box-trapped kitten into her arms, she forced a smile. It came out a little strained, a little wobbly. "Go to work, Alexander. I've got this."

"Zander." I sighed. "Please call me Zan if you don't like Zander. No one has ever called me Alex."

She backpedalled, almost tripping on the rug in the foyer. "Okay, sorry. I, eh, I won't do it again. I didn't mean—"

"It's fine."

"Have a good day at work."

I squeezed my nape. My nervous fidget couldn't be ignored as I shifted my glasses higher up my nose. I backed up a step, giving her room. "If the cat gets to be too much, just call the hospital, and someone will contact me. I'll see if one of my sisters can pop by to take him."

"Okay." She refused to make eye contact, her entire body language screaming for me to leave.

Another wash of goosebumps coated me as my heart squeezed.

Her rejection shouldn't hurt, but it did.

Her refusal to get friendly broke me apart piece by piece.

She'd never once looked at X like that. Even when I'd broken into her house and found her on the couch, she'd traded her fear for relief the second she'd known it was me.

If I'd gone to her as Zander, she'd probably still be running.

A spike of jealousy joined in the mix of confusing feelings.

I was jealous.

Of X.

I was envious.

Of *myself.*

And that's my cue to get the hell out of here.

Walking down the two steps, I paused and said over my shoulder, "Thanks, Lo—" I coughed and cleared my throat. "Sailor."

Her eyebrows pinched. "What were you going to call me?"

I forced a chuckle. "What Rory used to call you. Lor. But I figured it might not be my place."

She drew herself up. "Look, Alex—I mean, Zander...I know we've practically grown up in each other's periphery, and our grandparents were best friends, and you're a great guy, and nothing would make the ghosts of our grans happier if we talked more and became more than just neighbours, but—"

"It's fine." I held up my hand. "I get it."

She nodded and fell quiet, but then she puffed out her chest and added, "I like you. I really do. I always have, if I'm honest. I like the boy you were, and the man you've become is super impressive, but...I just need...after what happened. I—"

"You don't have to—"

"Will you let me finish?" Frustration flashed in her stare.

I flushed. "Sorry. I...yes. Go ahead."

"I just wanted to say...I just need you to know..." She exhaled hard. Hugging the box, she kissed the kitten on his head as he hopped up to headbutt her chest. "All I'm trying to say is, it's not you, alright? I don't mean to be standoffish, and I would hate to make you uncomfortable. You shouldn't have to think I'm your last resort for help...that's all I'm saying." Her smile was tear-bright and brittle.

"I'm grateful for all you did for Nana and caring for me after my…"
She swallowed hard. "Accident. I'm lucky to have you as my
neighbour, and I hope I can be a good neighbour in return."

Unlike with X, who she'd sworn a vow of honesty with, she
spoke blatant lies today all because I'd acted like a nervous fool and
made her feel guilty.

Turning to face her, I balled my hands. "I'm not just your
neighbour, Sailor, I'm your friend. I always have been. Always will be.
And I like you too and completely understand it isn't easy for you at
the moment. I hate that I've imposed by asking you to cat sit. You
don't have to apologise to me. I get it. Probably more than you
realise."

She ducked her chin and held my stare for a second before
looking at the garden. "Don't work too hard."

Hearing the unspoken request for me to leave, I forced a smile.
"Thanks again for watching him."

As I walked away from her, my back broke out into full agonising
fire. I'd never felt such a complex recipe of shame and desire, guilt and
possession all in one thundering beat of my idiotic heart.

Marching out of her front garden, I beelined for my car.

I had to get away from her.

I couldn't do this.

Why did I think I could do this?

Her soft voice called after me. "Hey, Zander?"

I couldn't stop the rush of *blistering* hope. I spun in my dress
shoes and waited for her to tell me we could be friends, after all. That I
had a chance in hell of claiming her as mine instead of fucking
everything up the longer I deceived her as X.

"Yeah?"

She couldn't hold eye contact. Staring at the kitten, she asked
quietly, "What's his name?"

The fizzing and popping of hope left me dead on my feet. My
voice sounded a little flat, even to my ears. "He doesn't have one."

"You haven't named him?"

"You do it." Turning again, I left her property before I could do
something equally as moronic—like confess everything.

Twenty-Three

Sailor

I Have One Request

"HOW ABOUT PUMPKIN?"

The kitten pounced on the blue ribbon I'd borrowed from my nana's face cream decorations. Flipping upside down, he battered the ribbon with all four feet, his little claws flashing like teeny tiny daggers.

"Not pumpkin." I nibbled on my bottom lip, watching him like I had for hours. "What about Cheddar or Marmalade or Ginger or Rusty? Those are all very good orange cat names."

He attacked a dust mote, hissing as if he was a ferocious tiger and not the size of a hairball.

"None of those either, huh?" I lay on my stomach in the small snug off the living room. All morning, I'd been obsessed. I hadn't showered or dressed out of my nightclothes. The moment I'd taken the box off Zander and plonked it down in the living room, the kitten had stolen my every thought and terror.

I'd never had a pet before.

My parents weren't interested, and my grandparents kept saying they didn't want an animal in case they died and the poor thing was left behind. I'd tried telling them they could've had four pets by the time they were ready to perish but….deaf ears.

I'd always been secretly jealous of my friends with dogs or cats, and I'd been especially envious of Rosalee—a girl at school who had an aviary that took up the entire back garden thanks to her parents rehabbing wild birds. They kept the ones too badly broken to return to the wild and even rehabbed a penguin once.

"How about Penguin?" I giggled as the kitten darted into me, tumbling onto his side and rolling under my chest. Rolling off my elbows, I scooped him against my heart, utterly addicted to the purring rattle from his frail little body and the absolute wonderment that something so small could be so *alive*.

It made me want to cry because I wanted to be that effortlessly happy.

Then it made me mad because I had nothing stopping me from being that happy—if only I could let go of the past.

"So you like Penguin?" I sighed as the kitten wriggled closer and headbutted my chin. He smelled a little from living wherever he'd been before Zander rescued him. His whiskers looked as if he'd stuck his paw in a socket. And his ribcage was far too prominent.

But those eyes?

Good grief, they were heartstoppers.

Violently green and inquisitive and scarily intelligent. In fact, they reminded me of Zander's eyes.

I snickered. "You know…if you were a deep red instead of ginger, you'd match the man who rescued you rather perfectly. Both redheads. Both green-eyed charmers."

The cat meowed and yawned. He made no move to get out of my embrace, and I lay on the carpet with him, lulled into a drowsy daydream, thanks to his contented purring.

Soft images floated in my mind. Snippets of my childhood when Zander would rescue animals and do his best to fix them. Sometimes he was successful, and his parents would track down the owners who'd lost their pets, reuniting them with a happy ending. However, sometimes he wasn't, and he'd drop into a solemn solitude full of mourning.

He has such a good heart.

I smiled a little, grateful that men like him still existed.

"See! I knew you wanted to fuck him, you slut. That's it. I'm going to finish what I started."

I gasped and jerked out of my half-asleep state.

The house once again pressed over me, switching from protector to jailor.

"Get out of my head," I whisper-hissed, doing my best to forget Milton and his dangerous jealousy. "You're not real. You're in prison."

"I can still hurt you, slut. Go anywhere near him, and it'll be the last thing you ever do."

Breathing hard, I squeezed my eyes closed and focused on X. On his endless dark eyes and thick black hair. Even with his mask on, I could tell he was a good guy just from the way he guarded me in his arms. He'd cocooned me last night, and instead of having a panic attack at being spooned, I'd felt a level of peace I hadn't felt in ever so long.

When I'd woken an hour or so before his nasty alarm went off, I'd had no idea where I was. Whose arms were around me. Whose hips were pressed against my thighs. I'd waited to freak out, but the fear never came, and when he sighed contentedly in my ear and hugged me extra tight, I'd slipped my leg between his and wriggled even closer.

It'd felt so right.

We fit so perfectly.

I hate that he ran away so fast.

What would've happened if he'd woken up naturally and found me in his arms? Would he have rocked his morning erection against me? Would he have given in to the cravings of his crush?

I didn't know what it said about me, but if he had tried to kiss me, I would've kissed him back. I would've pulled his mask down and asked for his real name. And then I would've asked him to free me of the past, replace Milton as the last man who'd ever touched me, and shatter me apart with pleasure instead of pain.

Was that too forward?

"You're a slut. I keep telling you this!"

Ugh! Burying my face in the kitten's scratchy fur, I pushed Milton away again.

I wasn't a slut. I wasn't promiscuous. But I couldn't deny that I was insanely attracted to X. Something about him set my blood on fire, and it wasn't the mysterious appeal—although his mask truly did molten things to my insides. Ultimately, he felt familiar. Like I'd known him forever, and he would do whatever it took to keep me safe.

My phone pinged.

Oh my God, is that him?

My tiredness vanished.

The cat grumbled as I sat up on the rug and tucked him on my lap instead. My oversized jumper slung around my knees, making a perfect hammock for him.

Fumbling for my phone, I opened the text message.

> Sorry I had to run this morning. Did you manage to get back to sleep?

The kitten yawned and batted half-heartedly at my wrist.

I scratched his tiny head. "What should we do, little Penguin?"

He meowed softly.

"Should I tell him that I'm interested in him? That I want him to touch me again? Kiss me? Is that asking too much? What if he doesn't feel that way, and his crush is more of a hero-complex than liking me for me?"

Closing his eyes, Penguin ignored all my questions and snuggled back down.

Sucking on my bottom lip, I typed a reply.

Why did you have to leave so urgently?

Doesn't matter. I wish I was still there, though. I hate knowing you're on your own in that haunted house.

It's only haunted by Nana and my nightmares. Between both of them, I guess it's balanced. And I'm not alone, actually.

Was it wrong that I tingled with the thought of making him the tiniest bit jealous?

Oh? You've got company?

Of the feline variety.

I didn't know you had a cat.

I didn't until my neighbour begged me for a favour. To be honest, I think he's the one who's done me a favour.

How so? And how was it seeing him? Are you okay?

It wasn't easy, but I need to stop Milton from tainting a perfectly fine neighbourly relationship. My neighbour didn't do anything to me. I have to remember that.

You don't have to be nice to him if it's hurting you, though.

I know. But we have history with our families, and he's super sweet. The cat I'm looking after was a stray he rescued yesterday. He has a good heart.

Careful. I might get jealous.

"Ahh…" I glanced at Penguin. "Could this be a good moment?" Before I could figure out what to say, another message pinged.

By the way, I feel like I owe you an apology.

What for? Shouldn't that be the other way around? I'm sorry I dragged you over here so late.

> I meant what happened in the night. I passed out when I didn't mean to. I don't know how I ended up smothering you, but I hope you weren't afraid.

I wasn't afraid.

I panicked a little before adding.

In fact...I was going to ask you about that.

> Ask me what?

Do you have a girlfriend?

> You don't know me, but the fact that I admitted I have a crush on you and watch you rather obsessively is a pretty big indication that I'm unattached. I wouldn't be able to do those things if I was with someone. I'm not a cheater.

I have a crush on you too.

It took a while for him to respond as if he needed time to process. Finally, my phone vibrated.

> You probably shouldn't have told me that.

I told you because...the next time you come round, I was wondering if you might.....................Wow, this isn't easy to type.

> Type what?

What are you doing tonight? Would you like to come over and watch a movie with me? I can cook something? We can get to know each other and...you could stay over again?

This time, his reply was even longer and when it came, it splashed me with ice water.

> Unfortunately, I have to go away for a couple of days with work.

Tears burned my eyes, my emotions far too close to the surface. Probably unhealthily close to the surface.

Oh, no worries! That's fine. Completely understand. Of course you have other things to do.

Lori, don't do that.

Do what?

Lie.

I slouched.

You know, you should leave a girl with some dignity. Calling me out for lying when I say it's fine that you refused my offer of a date isn't very nice.

It's not that I don't want to say yes.

But you're saying no anyway.

Pained bravery made me send another text.

You call me out on my lie, so I guess that means you want me to be honest. Alright then...how about I'm totally, brutally honest in a way that petrifies me but what do I have to lose?

That's all I want. I just want you to heal and be happy. I don't mean to upset you in any way.

Oh God.
*Could you stop being so **nice**?*

Glancing at the ceiling and the drying seed heads and herbs that permeated almost every room in this house, I swallowed back fresh fear.

Penguin sensed my stress and nudged my hand.

"I really, really shouldn't say this. I *know* I shouldn't. If it was to any other person, there's no way I would, but…he's different. He's the one who took it upon himself to hear all my secrets. What's the point in keeping this one?"

The kitten scrambled off my lap and padded toward the kitchen.

My phone pinged but I focused on Penguin instead. I had to feed him again. I'd given him breakfast and my heart had melted when he'd sucked on the bottle, drinking down his formula like a dainty pussy cat, only to dive headfirst into a bowl of wet food and snarf up an entire packet with no manners whatsoever.

He's hungry again.

Zander would never forgive me if I didn't provide the best care possible to his little rescue.

Climbing to my feet, I followed him, loving the sway of his long tail and falling madly in love as he looked over his shoulder and meowed as if making sure I was following.

Scooping him from the floor, I placed him on the counter while I mixed him another bowl of formula. He didn't wait for the bottle this time, slurping it right from the saucer.

While he got a milk moustache, I pulled up the message thread.

what did you want to be honest about?

Leaning against the well-loved sink, I sighed as warm sunshine coated my shoulders from the window. I put every last shred of my self-worth on the line.

I can't speak for other women who lived through what I did, but for me? The physical abuse was the first hurdle to get over. But the thing with bruises and broken bones is, they heal. They heal rather fast and eventually you look in the mirror and there's no evidence of being hurt at all. The second part is the guilt and shame. I keep thinking it's my fault that he hurt me because I didn't see who he truly was. I was blind and let myself down, and I know it's not rational, but I still feel responsible—like I can't trust myself anymore because I didn't see the signs that had to be there. which leads me to the third thing.

I pressed send but didn't wait for his reply.

what happened that night stole away my self-worth and my sexuality. For a while, I hated my body for being so weak and unable to fight back, but...being in your arms last night reminded me I like being small because being comforted by someone bigger (who I trust) is the best feeling in the world. I didn't just feel protected last night, I felt cherished, and it's been a very, very long time since I felt that.

Which leads me to the fourth thing. I think the thing that's holding me back the most from healing is accepting who I was before. I'm tiny compared to most people. I'm not the bravest but I do like being with a man who treats me right. I suppose what I'm trying to say is, I like intimacy. I like sex. And for a very long time now, both those things have been tainted. I have a crush on you, and you have one on me. We both don't have expectations of where this is going, and I'll admit that I'm terribly attracted to you. This is so hard to write, but...I want you. Even if it's just one night. I want you to remind me how to let go and not be afraid of touch. I want to be free of these debilitating memories. So my totally brutally honest confession is...I want you to sleep with me.

Twenty-Four

Zander

Favour From Hell

"I'M FUCKED."

"Uh-oh. Now what?" Colin laughed in my ear as I made an emergency call to him. He wasn't working today, and I didn't want to risk this conversation in the staffroom where anyone might hear about my stalker-ish ways. I sat in my car in the car park, unable to stop the knotting of my gut or the rush of absolute bone-breaking lust to drive like a maniac back home and drag Sailor into bed.

"She asked me to sleep with her."

"She what?" He coughed and spluttered as if he'd just taken a mouthful of something. "She actually came out and said that?"

"She texted it, but yes. Those exact words. 'I want you to sleep with me.'"

He sniffed something non-committal as if weighing his words. "Keep in mind, I'm not a psychologist, but from my work with patients trying to be normal when they have to face a *new* normal, they sometimes have to go backward to go forward." He paused, then said quietly, "Do you know the full details of what happened that night? With a request for sex—to ask you to replace her ex—that means he must've—"

"Tried to rape her." I yanked off my glasses and threw them onto the passenger seat. "Yeah, he did."

"Well, shit. I'm sorry, man."

"Why the hell are you apologising to me for?"

"Because she's using you to heal."

"That's exactly what I signed up for." I groaned. "And I hate that I'm betraying her trust by talking to you about it."

"Hate to say it, but if you didn't offload to me, you'd be heading for your own issues. You take on too much, Zan. You take people's pain personally, and you need to learn how to stop that."

"I didn't call to discuss me. What do I do? How do I help her without making her worse?"

"I suppose you have to ask yourself how far you're willing to go."

"You're suggesting I do what she asks?"

"Only if you're happy to fuck her back to health, knowing that one day she might be done having a masked stranger give her an orgasm and be ready to move on. Because that's what this is. She's treating you as temporary. She's asked you for a favour that most of us would never have the guts to ask for, all because she doesn't think you're real. Not in the true sense of the word."

"So I cut all contact then? I let X disappear. I make her hate him?"

"You could try to cultivate those feelings she has toward you as Zander, not X."

"She'll never look at me the same way. I dropped off that kitten this morning, and she almost bolted down the street to get away from me." I sagged in the driver's seat, my head about to split open. "Plus, killing off X and making her respond to me as Zander would never work. What if I slip and give away the fact that I was X? The same guy who barged uninvited into her life, then left without a goodbye the moment she has the courage to ask for something she needs?" Agonising humour had me chuckling. "Do you know I'm actually jealous of him? I'm jealous of myself. I'm so fucking jealous, Col, that it's X who gets to comfort her and not me."

Colin sucked in a breath. His tone turned stark and serious. "You need to stop this. Right now. Not just for her sake but your own. You can't sleep with her. We both know you suck at casual sex. You catch feelings, Zan. And you're already in way too deep as it is."

"I know all of that. But I don't want to stop helping her just because I'm the one struggling." Hanging my head, I pinched the bridge of my nose, trying to rub away the indentations left behind by my glasses. "I love the fact that she's healing enough to want to start speeding up the process. I love that she's brave enough to even *want* sex after what happened. But just 'cause she didn't recognise me last night doesn't mean she won't when I'm goddamn inside her. That would be rape, right? She's given consent to a man who's not who she thinks he is."

"Technically, I suppose it might be, but if you think about it…almost all of us hide parts of ourselves during those first initial times. We're all insecure and make up stories. It's only when we're comfortable that we drop the act."

"This is different than me fibbing that I like wine on a date instead of beer. If I tell the truth and she hates me even more, I have to move to Australia, remember?"

"Yeah, there is that."

I laughed with every ache that'd slowly been suffocating me.

"Even if I was prepared to do it, how would I? What am I supposed to do? Get naked with her but keep my mask on?"

"Wait. I forgot to ask. You said you were with her last night?" His voice turned cagey. "Did you dye your hair and wear the contacts like I told you to?"

"I did. I even pinched on that hideous eyebrow piercing."

"Wow, you did? That was just for shits and giggles." He chuckled, injecting some much-needed light-hearted energy into this very heavy conversation. "Okay…so you were with her last night and she didn't recognise you. Interesting. Told you the Clark Kent effect was real."

"There's no way in hell I'd risk it without my mask."

"How long were you with her?"

"Four hours, I guess. Got there at two, left at six. But I crashed hard, Col. The second she fell asleep on me, I was out cold thanks to being awake for so long. I don't know if she sneaked a peek while I was unconscious. I have no idea how I ended up wrapped around her. Maybe I did something inappropriate in my exhausted state? Maybe I touched her? Can you molest someone in your dreams by accident?"

"I'd hardly call it molesting if she's asking you to sleep with her."

"This is so fucking bad." I groaned and let my head fall back on the headrest. "What do I type back?"

"Wait, you haven't written back yet? Jesus, way to give the poor girl a complex."

"You're not exactly helping! Just tell me what I should do."

He fell silent for a bit before huffing. "No idea. It's your call how far you're willing to go. There's a big difference between messaging her as X and sleeping with her as her hidden neighbour. Like you say, it could blow up big time. And I still think you shouldn't do it for your own mental health."

I trembled and clutched my steering wheel. "Exactly. There's no way I can do it. No way I can ever go that far."

"Then I guess you have your answer. Let her down as easy as you can. I hate to admit it but maybe you're right and you should end it."

Images of Sailor so freaking scared last night came to mind. All her rambling messages to distract herself from her fear. I didn't want her to live like that anymore. I wanted her to laugh and dance and be the flower fairy next door that always followed in Melody's footsteps.

"As much as I should, I can't walk away. I'll just…I need to figure out a way to keep things platonic."

"Good luck with that." He cleared his throat. "I'm about to head into the gym. I'll talk to you later."

"Thanks for helping with this, Colin. Truly."

"Meh, what are friends for? If one isn't used as an accessory to a stalker/identity crime at least once in their friendship, can they truly say they were friends?"

I managed a laugh before I hung up and stared at the messages from Sailor. I couldn't stop reading that last line: *So, my totally brutally honest confession is...I want you to sleep with me.*

The clinical part of my brain did its best to untangle the emotional part of my heart. If she was healing, it was natural to reclaim the parts of herself that were almost stolen. Sex was a part of her healing. I couldn't give it to her personally, but...I could help in another way.

The idea exploded without warning.

Don't be ridiculous.

You can't do that.

It could backfire so bad.

But not any worse than sleeping with her under a false identity.

Snatching my glasses, I shoved them back on so I could see without the typical fuzz, and then went online shopping.

With a groan, I slipped out of my car and stretched out the kinks in my spine.

Luckily, I'd finished my shift and had been free to go home. No emergencies. No overtime. I couldn't remember being as exhausted as I had been the past few weeks. All I wanted was an ice-cold beer, some takeout, and to crash into oblivion on my lounger on the back deck.

Only...I had to go and retrieve a cat from my neighbour. The same neighbour who asked me to sleep with her. I had to look her in the eyes and pretend I didn't know she was actively trying to move on. I had to lie to her face when all I wanted to do was drop to my knees and grant her every wish.

Moving toward her driveway, I clutched my car keys.

I...I needed a moment.

Ten minutes to get my head on straight and not look as run over as I felt before I reclaimed the kitten.

Striding toward my front door, I flinched as Sailor opened hers and waved.

She *waved.*

She approached me with the kitten in the crook of her arm, her eyes soft and tentatively happy instead of blank and strained.

She was absolutely beautiful in a linen dress with spaghetti straps. The off-white material kissed her bare feet and hugged all her slender curves. The cat watched me smugly as if knowing exactly where my mind had gone.

"Hi," she said softly.

I almost fell flat on my face.

My fingers strayed to my glasses, pushing them higher up my nose in case I was seeing things.

"Did you have a good day at work, Zander?"

I staggered a little. "Y-You're not calling me Alexander anymore."

Hefting the kitten a little higher, she attempted a smile, but it still came out like a grimace. "It was rude of me to keep calling you by a name you have never gone by, even if it is technically your name. I guess I was using it to keep distance between us."

I needed to wash my ears out.

What is happening?

After decades of avoiding me, why was she suddenly talking to me?

The back of my neck prickled. I raked a hand through my hair, needing to reboot my brain because she'd successfully short-circuited it. "Eh...it's fine."

You're a fool, Zander North.

Her smile became genuine as she looked at the orange puff ball in her arms. "I've fed him three times. He's a glutton. He's also made my pillow his bed and is a terrible helper in the kitchen, but he's freaking adorable."

I held out my hand. "Thanks so much for looking after him for the day. I'll take him back so you can get some rest."

"Oh." She tensed and stepped away. Her eyes flickered with tension as she dared look at me. "Are you still planning on dropping him off at the shelter?"

I nodded. "Not right now, seeing as it's Sunday night, but yes. Tomorrow, I'll take him. I have an afternoon shift so I can do it in the morning."

"Oh."

That word again. A sad little word full of unsaid things.

I dropped my hand slowly. "Is everything okay?"

Sniffing, she nodded and went to pass over the kitten. "Yes, of course. Um...I'll have to grab all the food you gave me. Oh, and I named him."

My hand went back up, ready to scoop the tiny cat. I stepped into her.

Goosebumps scattered down my arms, matching the flush hitting hers. I couldn't take my eyes off the fine hair on her forearms reacting the same way mine did.

What did that mean?

Goosebumps could be a fear response or reaction to pleasant stimuli.

Was she seeing past the pain of Milton and remembering who I truly was?

And why did that bring a spike of jealousy?

Fuck, I couldn't catch a break.

I was jealous of X when I was myself. And now I was jealous of myself because she was being nice to me over X.

You're seriously screwed up, you know that?

With a hitched breath, she closed the distance between us and placed the kitten into my hand. He was small enough to fit in just one palm. Our fingers brushed. She sucked in a breath.

Her eyelashes flashed wide as our gazes snagged and the entire street fell away.

Fireworks detonated in my bloodstream. Hellfire raced through my veins. I barely managed to stay standing as she gasped under her breath and wrenched her hand back, leaving me clutching the Cheeto-coloured kitten.

"Um, his name is Penguin," she said quietly, her voice wobbling as if she was near tears. "He had a long nap while I did some harvesting and housework, so he might be a bit bouncy later. I-I'll go get his food." She spun on her bare feet and went to fly back to her house.

I had no control as I reached out and snatched her wrist, wrenching her back to face me.

My fingers wrapped tight, not letting her go.

We both stopped breathing.

Her face filled with terror. My heart pounded with so many things.

But I couldn't seem to release her.

I couldn't stop my thumb from stroking over the bruises from another asshole's fingers. I couldn't prevent myself from stepping into her and drowning in her glittering blue eyes.

"W-What—?" With a feeble pull, she tried to get free.

With white noise roaring in my ears, my synapses no longer fired, and I couldn't unwind my fingers. "You're safe with me, Sailor. You have my absolute word, I will never *ever* hurt you."

"Then why are you holding me against my will?"

Her voice finally bypassed whatever caveman urges had rendered me useless. I let her go so fast, her arm swung to her side, and she stumbled backward.

"Sorry, I only meant..." Adjusting my glasses, I looked down at the kitten—Penguin—in my hand. He pouted. His little whiskers singed and twisted. His green eyes not nearly as vibrant as before.

He stared at Sailor like I did. Wanting something that wasn't his.

I pitied the little fellow.

But...just because I don't stand a chance doesn't mean—

"You know what?" Clearing my throat, I held out the cat. "I've had a really long day at the hospital. I'm going to crash early. Do you think you could look after him for one more night?"

Her eyes lit up far too quickly for her to hide the sudden spark of joy.

Joy.

Fucking hell.

My heart shattered into pieces and then reformed in two parts with a jagged line down the centre. It accepted its fate of being broken for the rest of my life because I only wanted this woman, and even if she got over the triggers I caused, she'd never forgive me for being X.

"You want me to keep him?" She stepped closer, her gaze locked on the cat. "I mean...I don't have any experience with animals. I might do something wrong."

"By the way he's looking at you, I think you did everything right."

"Really?" Her lips quirked in a self-conscious smile.

It was too soon to suggest she keep him. But as her fingers came out to scoop the kitten from my palm, rewarding me with an electrical shock that arched right to my toes, I hoped she'd adopt him. I hoped the kitten had come to me for this exact purpose—not to find a life with me but to fall madly in love with Sailor.

I know the feeling, little buddy.

The cat meowed as if it'd been separated from her for years before snuggling in the hollow spot of her collarbone. Sailor sighed heavily and closed her eyes, hugging him back.

The moment was so intimate, I squeezed the back of my neck and dropped my gaze.

The suggestion that he'd already found his forever home danced on my tongue, but I didn't want to scare her off. Plus...coming over to 'collect him' was a good excuse to see her again tomorrow.

"Why Penguin, by the way?" I cleared my throat, forcing myself to smile like a normal person and not a crazy fool.

For a second, she lost all fear of me and grinned. "I was throwing random words around, and he seemed to like it. I've already shortened it to Peng, though. The 'guin' is a bit of a mouthful."

"And what does Peng mean?"

"No idea. But he's Peng." Cradling him, she backstepped toward her front door. "I'll keep him overnight for you. I hope you get some sleep, Zander. You work too hard."

Before I could reply, she spun and darted back inside.

Twenty-Five

Sailor

Surprise in the Letterbox

> I TAKE BACK WHAT I SAID BEFORE. It's obviously made you uncomfortable and I'm sorry. Let's forget about it.

I sat on the floor in the snug where I'd been watching a TV show on my tablet with Peng fast asleep on my lap. I should go to bed. It was late, and I'd officially done nothing all day but play with my new addiction known as the kitten. I'd barely been able to cook dinner without burning my chicken fillets, thanks to Peng bouncing around my countertops and batting at all the drying herbs.

How embarrassing that I'd almost cried when I'd handed him back to Zander. How stupid could I be to become so attached in just a few hours? But having little Peng spend the night with me? Having him knead my hair and purr? All those things were fast becoming my favourite things in the world.

What am I going to do tomorrow when Zander comes to collect him?

How early would he pop around? Was I really going to let him take Peng to the shelter?

Are you really ready for a pet though? Something reliant on you for everything? Something that will restrict your travel and other freedoms?

I scoffed at myself.

I'd never liked to travel, and what other freedoms? I'd successfully ensured I had none, but with Peng I already felt braver about the world. The house cracking—as the old walls cooled from yet another hot summer day—didn't scare me nearly as much.

I didn't feel as if I was being watched.

I wasn't so afraid of being alone.

Peng's head suddenly shot up, his little ears pricked toward the living room where the old box TV rested by the wall. The snug off to the side held a beaten-up tan couch and a low coffee table where we used to have Monopoly nights and Pops tried to teach me chess. It'd always been one of my favourite rooms to sprawl and read or do a puzzle.

Milton had preferred the living room to watch his sports. In a way, the snug was untainted and the urge to rip out all the furniture and carpet in the living room had me itching for daylight to continue my renovation.

Peng hissed just as the box TV sprang on, hissing back with snow and white noise.

I didn't jump this time. I didn't scream or have a panic attack.

The TV wasn't Milton there to murder me.

It was the conduit from the woman I loved most in the world.

"Hey, Nana." I grinned and plucked Peng off my lap and held him out to the empty room. "Say hi to Peng."

The kitten stopped hissing and cocked his head as if hearing something otherworldly. They did say that was why cats were always favoured in folklore. The many myths hinting that they could sense ghosts and demons.

Stroking him, I murmured, "It's okay, little man, it's only Nana come to check on us."

The TV kept blaring. It might start on its own, but it never turned off by itself. Sighing, I climbed to my feet and carried my little ginger-ninja into the living room. His fur bristled, but he stopped growling.

I flicked the old switch dial. "There. Silence."

The curtains rustled with no breeze. Warmth filled me instead of ice. It felt like Nana was checking on me. That she approved of the new freeloader living in her home.

Kissing Peng on his head, I carried him into the kitchen for a final snack.

My cell phone pinged as I placed him on the counter and filled up a saucer with some more formula. Already he didn't feel as ribby. His fur not as coarse.

Leaving him to slurp up his fifth and final meal of the day, I returned to the snug and grabbed my phone off the floor.

> I didn't mean to leave it this long to reply. I'm sorry. That was cruel of me to leave you hanging on such a sensitive subject. I've tried to reply numerous times, but I keep failing on an appropriate response.

My heart kicked as I tapped the keyboard.

What response do you want to give me?

It doesn't matter what I want. But I will be honest and say I want **you.** I'd be a liar if I didn't. Falling asleep with you last night was one of the best experiences of my life, and we only hugged. I find you absolutely gorgeous, and of course I'd love to take you up on the offer, but...

But?

I'm not going to take advantage of you.

Even though I'm asking you to? Technically, I'm the one taking advantage of you.

As much as I want to, I can't, Lori. Not yet.

My chest squeezed as if he'd strapped me into a corset.

Not yet?

I mean. Shit. I didn't mean to type that last bit.

I'm happy with not yet. I can wait.

Before he could reply and deny that there was any chance between us, I changed the subject.

I'm thinking of adopting a stray kitten. Tell me why that's a bad idea and why I shouldn't do it.

I think that's a fabulous idea and you should definitely do it.

Gee, thanks for being the voice of reason.

I am being the voice of reason. I'd love a pet myself if I had the time.

You can come meet mine if you want? See if we're a suitable match? In fact, I'd love your opinion on whether I'm making the right choice. Maybe I'll make a terrible cat carer.

> You won't. He'll already be in love with you. And I can't tonight. I'm away, remember. I'll be gone for a few days.

Oh. Okay. Have a safe trip.

> I'll still be watching you.

On the cameras you installed in my garden?

> Yes.

What if I told you to take them down? That I don't want you watching me anymore?

> Then I'd respect your wishes and do what you asked.

I chewed the inside of my cheek.
Damn you, X. Damn you for being such a gentleman.
A stalker who was a gentleman. What an oxymoron.

Keep the cameras where they are. Message me tomorrow. Goodnight.

> Sweet dreams, Lori. Xx

Focusing on the two little kisses he'd sent, I accepted that was enough for now and went to retrieve my new best friend. And for the first time since coming back from the hospital, bruised and traumatised, I went to bed without panic, without memories, and slept with a tiny guardian on my pillow.

Grabbing the oblong box that'd been delivered into my gingerbread letterbox, I looked up just as Zander closed his front door and strolled toward me. Ten a.m. Far too early to claim the little beast who had captured my heart.

Dressed in dark jeans and a white t-shirt, he'd traded his everyday glasses for sunglasses and his rich red hair glittered with fire streaks under the already hot summer sunshine.

My heart skittered in a totally different panic than usual.

Strange that my fear where Zander was concerned now centred around wanting to keep Peng and not just the triggers Milton had instilled in me.

Hugging the box—another gift from Lily most likely because I didn't order it—I braced myself not to run and lock the door. "Good morning, Zander."

He gave me his typical reserved smile. Not able to see his eyes, I couldn't judge if he'd caught up on sleep or if running a stray cat to the shelter annoyed him.

"Morning, Sailor." He tipped his chin and stopped by my letterbox. His attention dropped to the package in my arms. One second, he stood loose with his hands by his sides. The next, he was as stiff as a tree with his fists clenched.

Wow...what?

A wash of anxiety cut through me.

I backed up a step. Even though he promised he'd never hurt me, it still didn't stop the fight-or-flight from kicking in.

"Maybe he'll take you like I did, slut. But you'd like that, wouldn't you? After all, you're begging masked men for a fuck. Why not let your nerdy neighbour have a turn?"

Trembling, I did my best to shut out Milton's horrible voice.

Zander swallowed hard and cleared his throat. "A present from someone?"

I frowned and looked at the box I clutched like a rubber ring, all while drowning in a sea of anxiety. "It'll probably be from Lily. We randomly send each other things now and again." I hefted it. "I haven't bought anything online for a while, so it has to be her."

It could be from X.

The tiny thought appeared and grew louder.

He'd dropped a phone into my letterbox. Would he send another parcel?

Curiosity itched to dash inside to check, but I stood my ground and prepared to deliver the speech I'd practiced in front of the bathroom mirror.

"Uh, Zander, I—"

"So, Sailor, I—"

We both laughed awkwardly as we spoke over one another.

"Sorry, you go." He unclenched his fist and waved politely. "What did you want to say?"

Standing as tall as I could, I forced out. "Do you mind if I keep Peng for another few days? I have a friend popping round to meet him. I...I might be interested in adopting him."

His smile didn't change, almost as if he knew this would happen. Had that been his evil plan all along? Was Peng a stray or some carefully planned gift?

Why would my neighbour give me a gift?

Because he knows you. He knows you're alone. He knows you're not coping. He's a doctor, and it's probably in the Healing Handbook. Isn't that why people have service dogs?

Shaking my inner thoughts away, I went to say something else, but Zander said quietly, "It means hot or goodlooking, by the way."

"What does?"

"Peng." He grinned. "Your new cat's name. I did a Google search to see if it meant anything. It means attractive or excellent in Chinese. So…he better grow out of the ugly kitten stage and become the most stunning orange cat on the street, or he's living a false identity."

"Oh!" I returned his smile. "Jeez, we can't have that. Lying about one's identity would alert the neighbourhood watch."

He flinched but covered it with another smirk. "And of course you can keep him. Keep him however long you want. He isn't mine." He leaned a little closer. "If I'm honest, I feel like he used me to get to you." He tugged off his sunglasses, pinning me with his violently green eyes. "Not that I blame him."

Once again, a tsunami of goosebumps covered me head to toe like they did yesterday. I hadn't been able to tell if it was fear or attraction yesterday, but today…I stumbled in shock to find my heart beat a little faster. My skin flushed a little hotter.

How had I never seen just how gorgeous he was?

If Peng meant attractive, well…Zander was peng with a capital P.

Oh my goodness, Lor, do you hear yourself?

How did my libido suddenly spring from death's door and now crushed on all the boys? What was I thinking, ogling Zander in that way?

For a quick second, I felt guilty.

What would X think?

But did it matter what he thought? We had no understanding. We weren't dating. We weren't even technically friends. And Zander had been in my life for well…all of it.

He didn't count.

He might not turn you down if you asked him for sex. X said no, remember?

My cheeks burned with embarrassment.

Backpedalling, I tripped, managed to somehow stay upright, then practically sprinted to my front door. "Sorry, forgot the oven is on. Byeeeee!"

Diving inside, I slammed the door and rested against it.

Peng came trotting toward me from the kitchen, his little meow curious and almost judgey.

"Don't look at me like that," I warned, scooping him up one-handed. My legs trembled a little as I plopped the kitten and the parcel on the dining room table. "*I* certainly wasn't looking at Zander like that."

Peng sniffed the box while I went to get some scissors.

I rubbed my chest as another wash of prickles infected my heart. I still felt guilty but, at the same time…a little less trapped.

For the first time since Milton beat me, I was able to look at Zander without feeling phantom kicks, punches to my face, or my hair ripped out. I saw him as his own person and not the catalyst for my attempted murder.

And…I was grateful.

I could ignore the part where he unwittingly made my system flare with need and the fact that my sexuality seemed to be waking up. I could also work on not shutting myself off so I could move on from this and be happy again.

"Any ideas what Lily could've sent?" I smirked as I placed the scissors on top of the box and snapped a photo with Peng still sniffing a corner.

Sending the pic to Lily, I typed.

You didn't have to send me anything. But thank you for being such a great bestie.

She called me almost instantly. "Hey, hey, how's my little moonbeam doing today?"

I laughed and tucked my phone on my shoulder so I could talk while slicing through the tape on the box. "I'm doing better, actually."

"You definitely sound better." She clucked her tongue. "However, I can't claim credit, because I didn't send you anything."

So it is from X…

Lily's voice echoed in my ear. "Please tell me why there's a manky-looking kitten on your table."

I scratched Peng under his chin. "Don't call my cat manky."

"Hold up. *Your* cat?"

Opening the parcel but not retrieving the item inside, I put down the scissors and sat in one of the chairs. "He's a rescue. Zander found him. He asked me to look after him when he had to go to work, and now…I'm thinking of adopting him." I sighed with aching affection as Peng jumped off the table and plopped into my lap with a purr.

"We literally spoke yesterday morning, yet so much has

happened." A crunch sounded as if Lily bit into something. "Tell me everything. And don't think I didn't hear you call your hot-as-sin neighbour Zander. You've never done that before. It's always been Alexander this and Alexander that. I always knew what you were doing."

I frowned. "What was I doing?"

"Keeping your distance."

"You're right. I told him that too. Yesterday, when he came to collect Peng to take him to the shelter, I apologised for using a name that he doesn't go by."

"Wait…you told him that you actively tried keeping distance between you?"

"Yep. Like I told you…progress. I don't want to live the way I have been anymore. I'm ready to heal. And it's all thanks to this magical little kitten."

"A kitten that you've called…what was it? Pang?"

"It's technically Penguin, but it's been shortened. He's going to grow up to be the biggest, most beautiful ginger cat on the block."

"Who are you and what did you do with my friend?"

"I'm the new and improved version."

"I like all versions. But I'm warning you, you better not get any more cats. You're single and live alone. I can see how this could escalate to you becoming the local weirdo with a million pussies."

Another giggle escaped, feeling so free, so like the old me. "Noted. No more pussies."

"You don't need more. You barely use the one you have now."

"Oh my God, Lily!" I burst out laughing, just like I used to when she made inappropriate jokes in class. "You can't talk. I bet yours is covered in cobwebs and has a haunted sign."

"Actually, it met someone with fixer-upper potential."

"*You met someone*?!" I sat up straight, scaring Peng a little. "Tell me everything, and stop talking about your lady parts in the third person. Where did you meet him? How? When? What's his name?"

"Jeez, hold the interrogation." She chuckled. "His name is Aubrey. We met at an open home. He's divorced and not looking for anything serious. But…he's a builder by trade, and we got talking about my development, and he offered to help draw up the plans I need to lodge with council so…"

"Oh wow. I feel like I'm about to be replaced as number one in your life."

"Never!" She giggled. "Never ever. You're stuck with me. Now, seeing as I didn't send you a gift, I'm curious. What is it? Who's it from? Have you opened it yet?"

Standing, I placed Peng back on the table and dragged the box a little closer. "Not yet. Should I see what's inside?"

"Tell me. Tell me."

My smile fell as common sense came rushing back.

If it is from X, do you really want her to know?

I couldn't tell her. He was the only thing I'd ever kept secret from her. If she asked me point-blank if I still talked to him, I'd fail at lying.

"Eh, you know what? I might open it later."

"You what?" she screeched dramatically. "No way. How can you wait to open a present? You truly are a weirdo. Open it. Maybe it's from your sexy neighbour. He might have been waiting this entire time for you to call him by his real name to finally ask you out."

I shivered. "Don't be ridiculous."

Zander's glowing green eyes shot to mind. The way he'd stiffened as he'd looked at the box in my arms. His sudden wariness followed by a smile that said so much and so little.

"If you don't open it, I'm going over there and doing it myself."

"Fine. Fine." I sighed heavily, hating that I'd backed myself into a corner. "Hang on." Pulling out layers of bubble wrap, I found a sleek black box at the bottom. Snagging it, I placed it on the tabletop, then fumbled one-handedly with the bronze clasp.

"What is it?"

"Patience, patience."

I flipped the lid open.

I squeaked and almost dropped my phone.

"Sails?" Lily asked. "Sails. What is it? Are you okay?"

"Uh, yeah…yeah, I'm okay." My heart skipped as I plucked the typed card sitting boldly on top of a sparkly silver dildo. It looked sleek and stylish but femininely erotic with ribbed lines all the way to the bottom.

Touching it hesitantly, I sucked in another breath at the coolness of it. Not silicone but something hard. Glass perhaps or crystal?

"You're scaring me, Sails. What is it? It's not something from Milton, is it?"

His name didn't hurt me like usual. Peng couldn't distract me as he batted at the bubble wrap I'd pulled from the box. The only thing I saw was the scripted lines on the note.

I can't be with you in the way you asked me to be, but I promised to help you heal. This is for you. To heal. Think of me when you use it. Love, X.

"Sailor, talk to me right now, woman!"

Slamming the box closed, I forced a laugh and did my best to lie. "Sorry, I was just reading the card. It's nothing, Lils. Just a gift basket with some care items. That's all."

"Care items?" Her voice bristled with suspicion. "Like what?"

"You know. Like face creams and bath bombs and stuff."

"What friend would send you something like that, knowing you make those for a living?"

Shit.

Why do I suck so badly at lying?

"Not a close one, obviously. Look, I have to go. I totally forgot I was steeping some cinnamon sticks for a new natural deodorant recipe. I can't leave them in too long. Bye!"

"Don't you dare hang up on me. Something is going on with you—"

"We'll catch up soon. I promise."

I hung up.

I collapsed back in my chair and ran my finger over the note.

"He bought me a dildo." I scowled at Peng. "The idiotic man bought me a sex toy, all because he refuses to have sex with me himself. I don't know if I should be offended or impressed that he figured out how to outsource the task."

Peng meowed and chinned the box.

Almost as if his ears were burning, my other phone pinged with a message from X.

> I saw on the camera that you spoke to your neighbour and retrieved a parcel from your letterbox. How did both of those things go?

"As if you don't know." I rolled my eyes, my thumbs hovering over the screen.

Seeing my neighbour was fine. I'm getting better each time we meet, but I don't know how I feel about what you bought me.

> It's the first time I've ordered something like that. Did I buy the wrong one? I can always send another.

No! No, don't do that. Don't send anything else. It's fine.

> Uh-oh. Fine isn't what I was going for. If it won't work for you, then tell me what you like, and I'll make sure to deliver it.

My heartbeat went crazy. Did he see what he wrote? The suggestiveness of such a message? The temptation to reply with less-than-innocent remarks itched my fingers.

Don't, Lor.

Don't you dare.

I sniffed.

Why shouldn't I?

If we were on such personal terms that he felt comfortable sending me a pleasure wand, well then…I was comfortable enough being honest with what I liked.

Pity that I'm not entirely sure.

"Then again, if I do go full truth, he might never see me again." I winced in Peng's direction. "What should I do, kitty cat?"

He meowed and nose bopped my phone, causing a couple of random letters to appear.

"Yeah, I think so too. He started this. He probably thinks I'm some timid wallflower who needs a big, strong man in the dark to protect her."

Peng gave me a wide-eyed look.

I scowled. "I mean…sure, at the moment, he's not wrong, but I wasn't always like this. Before Milton, I was pretty scandalous, you know? I like flirting. I like being adventurous. Doesn't matter that I've never found anyone to fully scratch my itch, if you know what I mean, but I think it's time I start remembering that I was brave enough to try, don't you?"

He yawned and sat down, licking his flank as if bored.

Sucking in a breath, I typed a message, freaked out, went to delete it, then pressed send.

You want to know what I like? Alright then. Under the banner of our honesty clause, I'll tell you. What do I like? I'm not sure, as I haven't found it yet. But I can tell you what I fantasise about. I like the thought of a man who can take charge but also take instruction. I like the thought of a man who knows how to use his fingers. I like the thought of feeling so safe that I'd have no problem surrendering to him. Think your sex toy can deliver that?

I shivered in my chair, my pulse hectic as X took his sweet time replying.

I jolted when my phone finally vibrated.

Why are these fantasies and not firsthand knowledge?

Oooo, you're really asking the tough questions today. You're determined to strip me down to the painful truth, aren't you?

Are you avoiding the question?

Nope. I'll tell you. I've told you everything else so far, what's a little more embarrassment? I only have fantasies because no one has ever delivered. Is that bold enough for you?

You're saying you've never had an orgasm with someone?

Nope. Never. I had hoped you'd be up for the challenge, but alas...you turned me down.

Lori...fuck. Are you trying to get me in trouble at work?

How am I getting you in trouble?

His reply took a while. Nerves crept down my spine. Perhaps I'd gone too far. This sort of talk wasn't right between two people who barely knew each other.

I still don't know his name, yet I'm confessing I've never had an orgasm with a man before.

Good grief, I really did need help.

Have you orgasmed by yourself at least?

His question caught me off guard. I'd wanted to know how he was struggling at work, but he'd directed the questioning back to me.

Sneaky, annoying man.

Yes, but it's not easy.

Will what I sent do the trick?

I'm not sure.

Would you try for me?

I froze.
I reread his message. Again and again.
And before I could move, he sent another.

> My dose of honesty for the day is...the thought of you using something I bought for you makes me insanely hard. I feel sick for even writing that. I feel as if I'm taking advantage of you when you're still healing. But...if you're up for it and it doesn't push you into dark places, I want you to use my gift and tell me how it goes. In as little or as much detail as you want.

Oh God.
My lungs stopped working as I forced trembling fingers to type.

> I'm surprised you didn't ask for video footage. You like cameras, after all.

> Are you insinuating that I have a camera in your bedroom?

> Wait, do you?

> What? Of course not!

I smirked, enjoying making him uncomfortable for a change. Before he could reply, I committed to making him squirm.

> Do you want to?

Radio silence.
No reply.
No phone chirp.
Before, his silence would've set my panic off, wondering if I'd gone too far or stepped over too many lines. But he'd erased those lines the moment he bought me a dildo.
Turning off the screen, I scooped up my kitten, the sparkly erotic toy, and strolled into the garden.
If he liked watching me so much, so be it.
I'd put on a show for him in the only place he could watch.

Twenty-Six

Zander

She's Going to Kill Me

I STOOD IN AN EMPTY PRIVATE WARD, glaring at my phone as Sailor triggered my camera sensors.

Still dressed in her linen shift from this morning, she gleamed like a fallen star in the sun as she placed Peng down and made a delicious, blatant display of stretching. In her left hand, something extremely phallus-like glimmered with silver. It looked almost identical to the image I'd chosen online.

It'd taken me ages to settle on that one: heavy glass designed to be classy and pleasurable—according to the website. I'd looked at a terrifying range of silicone penises and devices with vibrating rabbit ticklers, pearl beads, and a thousand different settings.

Thanks to working in the medical industry, I'd heard one too many stories of silicone allergies. However, if Sailor found it hard to reach that critical point, perhaps I should've gotten her something that stimulated everything all at once at an intensity that would leave her screaming.

Do you hear yourself?

These were not usual thoughts of a man who didn't even have a girlfriend. I'd also never confess that I'd almost had a wet dream last night. I'd been the one to use that glass toy on her. She'd definitely found that pinnacle, and I'd woken just as the first ripples of release quaked through me. There'd been nothing I could do to stop it, and I'd flushed with guilt that I'd gotten off to fantasies of my neighbour—the girl who had no idea how I felt about her.

"Fuck's sake, stop it."

Cursing my hard-on that she'd caused with her messages, I glowered at my phone as the cameras recorded her lifting her arms over her head. She arched her back, hinting she wasn't wearing a bra. The thin material of her dress clung to her in ways that should be illegal. Gathering her long sandy-blonde hair into a ponytail, she rolled her neck, then trailed her hands down her body, using the toy to torment me.

The damn dildo followed her curves, touching everything I wanted to.

"Christ, you're going to kill me," I groaned.

Even if an earthquake hit the hospital, I wouldn't be able to move. I couldn't look away as she bent over, grabbed the hem of her long dress, and hoisted it up to her thighs. Rolling the excess material, she didn't stop until she somehow turned the floor-length skirt into something scandalously short.

Her long, lean legs flashed far too bare. The fading bruises were still visible, thanks to her pale skin. Peng wound himself around her ankle, and she smiled so freely, so prettily, she sucker-punched me right in the heart.

Staggering against the wall, I could only watch as she sat down cross-legged on the grass and looked around the flower beds and fruit trees as if searching for a glint of a camera lens.

And then, she leaned back until she sprawled in the soft greenery. She arched her back as if someone ran their fingertips along her cleavage. And held up the glass phallus as if she was going to use it.

She wouldn't.

Would she?

Not there.

Not in broad daylight.

Slowly, sensually, she dropped her fingertips to her upper thigh where she'd rucked her skirt high enough to flash her pink underwear.

Lust exploded through me.

Longing clenched my middle as she dragged the glass toy down and down her body.

Jesus Christ.

A growl escaped me as a gush of overwhelming possession erupted.

For a second, she blinded me with black desire.

Then drowned me in animalistic rage.

Anyone could see her.

Sure, her fences were high, and her garden was overgrown, but what the hell was she *thinking?*

Gritting my teeth, I closed the camera footage and accessed our message thread.

Stop that immediately.

Splitting my screen into two functions, one window with the text bubble and the other with the video feed, I wanted to punch something.

I wanted to break every speed limit to go to her. To leap the fence. To pounce on her. To be the one and only man who ever brought her to an orgasm.

A vicious throb arrowed right between my legs as images of touching her, fingering her, licking her—

"Fuck, Sailor. You have no idea what you're doing to me."

On the video footage, she paused. Dropping the dildo onto her lower belly, she held up her phone with both hands, shielding her face from the sun with it.

My own phone vibrated.

Come and make me.

I almost buckled in half with how hot and hard and *agonising* my entire body became.

How had everything turned sexual? Come? Yes, please. Make her come? God, it'd be an honour.

"Get a grip, Zan."

This wasn't rational behaviour. Sailor had never been like this. Perhaps she'd finally snapped, and what I was watching was a woman having a breakdown, not a woman reclaiming her sexuality.

I should call Dr Klep and have her make a house call.

A little voice in the back of my head hissed that all of that could be true but…I had no authority to say what Sailor had been like before. Despite our family's fondness for each other, we'd hardly ever spoken. There'd always been a wall of politeness between us.

I might've seen her grow up, but I didn't know a thing about her. I didn't know her favourite food or favourite TV show or even how someone as brave and sweet and gorgeous as her had ended up with a murdering bastard like Milton.

My phone buzzed again.

Are you really away for work?

I sighed in relief as she slowly sat up, removed the dildo from her stomach, and tucked her hair behind her ears in a familiar, innocent gesture.

Peng immediately crawled all over her, sliding off her bare legs and no doubt leaving little claw marks amongst her bruises.

I groaned and yanked my glasses off.

Digging my fingers into my eyes, I cursed myself to hell. I'd told her X was away to put distance between my schedule and my alter ego. I needed her to keep seeing us as two separate people because after her thawing toward me in person, it only added to my terror that she'd one day look at me, see straight through the disguise, and call the police.

Christ, if she ever called the police on me again?

I wouldn't just be done for stalking; I'd be done for sexual harassment and lewd behaviour. Our texts would be all the evidence they'd need to send me straight to jail.

I am, and I'm not comfortable with you putting yourself in danger. I know you're mad at me, but please, go back inside or at least lower your dress.

On the video, she stood, placed the dildo inside on the kitchen bench, then headed toward the veggie patch. Peng bounced alongside her as she unhitched her dress, and let it cascade to her ankles.

Every inch of me clenched.

I somehow found watching her cover up just as erotic as watching her expose herself. Maybe more so because it seemed so...intimate. She'd done that for me. She'd listened and obeyed and I should *not* have this reaction.

I was not that type of guy.

I didn't get off on bossing women around, outside or inside the bedroom. I wanted a partnership, a friendship, a forever after. Yet...the mere idea of having her drop to her knees because I asked her to?

I bit my fist and whacked the back of my head against the wall.

She is your neighbour.

She is suffering from trauma.

She is not kneeling for anyone.

Dropping to her haunches by a spinach plant, she plucked off a few leaves. She laughed a little as Peng leaped into the overgrown beds, attacking a row of beans strung up with string. Already those two were inseparable. I couldn't picture her without him now.

My fingers shook as I texted her again.

It seems my role as your protector has been taken by something orange and fluffy.

She continued to fill a small basket with greenery and a couple of carrots before standing upright. Sighing, she pulled her phone from a dress pocket and scanned my last message.

She didn't move for a while, then glanced around the garden, most likely still searching for my cameras. At least those weren't on her property. I hadn't technically broken any law with them. Then again, some rule probably stated a neighbour couldn't use his own security system to spy on someone else.

She let Peng run amok in her veggie garden as she tapped her phone.

Mine finally chirped.

He's definitely keeping the nightmares at bay. Have a good work trip. Thanks for the gift.

Dumping her phone in her harvesting basket, she marched up the two steps of her back deck.

I blinked at her cool tone.

My heart twisted. I'd handled that wrong, didn't I? Had I made her self-conscious? What was I supposed to do? Leave my shift and go over there? Haul her over my shoulder and carry her to bed—to hell with her mental health and all the consequences?

No way.

I was doing this for her, not for me.

I'd bought her a masturbation aid so she could reclaim the pieces she said she needed to claim by *herself.* No man required. It wasn't up to me to give that back to her. She had to take it back for herself.

So why did I feel so wretched?

Why did an icy emptiness creep through me as all signs of the sexy tease who'd lain in the grass stiffened into shyness as she darted inside?

I wished I had a camera in her kitchen.

I wished I had audio to make sure she was okay.

I wished I could go over there, but I'd doubled down on my lie that I was away and now had to keep my distance.

"Shit. Shit. *Shit.*"

Turning off my phone, I jammed my glasses back into place and stalked from the ward.

Eleven p.m.

Another long day from hell thanks to a couple of emergencies and a surgery complication by the trainee anaesthetist. Luckily, it'd all been handled, but now I was exhausted and in desperate need of a shower, food, and sleep.

At least I'd sent X on a trip, so I wouldn't have to go over to Sailor's house in the middle of the night like the last time I'd pulled a long stint.

And if she has another nightmare?

What are you going to do? Not go?

Scratching my five o'clock shadow that'd grown in, I pushed that question away. Obviously, I wouldn't be able to leave her alone if she had another setback. I'd go to her and make up some excuse of coming home early, but right now, as Zander, I was free from responsibilities.

So why, *why*, did my feet change direction and head toward Sailor's front door instead of mine? Why did I knock when most people would be in bed?

I stood with my heart drumming, waiting for her to open the door.

I forced my exhausted brain to come up with an excuse as to why I'd found myself on her doorstep. I'd ask about Peng. I'd discuss the bloody weather if it came down to it. I just had to see her in person after her performance in the garden and cold shoulder via text.

Two minutes passed and her door remained stubbornly closed. Checking my phone to make sure she hadn't messaged me as X, I knocked again.

And waited.

And waited.

And when it became awkward and weird—especially to anyone peering at me behind their curtains—I turned, jammed my hands into my slacks pockets, and stalked back to my place.

Twenty-Seven

Sailor

Imprisoned by Orgasms

FUNNY HOW HUMANS WERE WIRED.

For most of the day, I almost felt like my normal self. I made a nice summery dinner with a fresh garden salad and chicken kiev from the freezer. I used some scrap material from my market stall decorations and sewed a few toys for Peng to wallop around the house.

I surfed online for concepts of a country-inspired but modern living room to prepare for the next stage of my renovation. I even managed to turn off all the lights and walk up the stairs like a normal person instead of bolting up them like I was escaping the realms of hell.

I'd heard someone knock on the front door around eleven, but I'd already curled up in bed and the shadows slowly switched from soft and harmonious to sharp and murderous.

I didn't want to go back into that slippery depressive place, so I stayed put.

Besides, the only person who would visit this late—without just sneaking inside because he knew where I kept my spare key—was Zander, and...I wasn't really in the mood to make small talk with him.

If I was honest, I was depleted and low, and every part of me ached as if I'd attempted too much, believed I was cured too soon, and now I needed to recharge away from masked guardians and considerate doctors.

Peng snuffled in his sleep on my pillow.

Lowering my e-book reader, I sighed in the gloom.

I'd deliberately left my bedside lamp off, reading by the light of my backlit e-ink. I didn't want the shadows to torment me, but they did anyway. The typical end-of-day cracking and creaking as the house cooled down seemed extra loud, interrupting my ability to concentrate on a single sentence.

God, what had I been thinking earlier today?

I'd been far too coy and crass—hoisting up my dress like that and waving that dildo around.

My cheeks burned in shame. I'd pushed myself to my limit and wouldn't have gone any further. Thank goodness X texted at the perfect time because I was seconds away from stopping anyway. At least it looked like I obeyed him instead of ran out of courage. I might be craving reckless things to get over the weakness inside me, but I drew the line at masturbating in full daylight in Nana's garden.

I shivered at the thought of what I must've looked like on his cameras. Had I turned him on? Annoyed him? Angered him? He hadn't texted me back, and I hadn't wanted to reach out.

I didn't want to tell him that I was thinking of obeying his other request.

I want you to use my gift and tell me how it goes. In as little or as much detail as you want.

Lowering my e-book, I glanced at the glass toy resting beside me. I'd washed and disinfected it, and it'd been resting on my covers like a tombstone for hours, waiting for me to get up the courage to see if I could eradicate Milton's monstrosity.

Turning my head, I looked at Peng, fast asleep on my pillow.

He looked so comfy and cosy, I didn't have the heart to move him from the room, but…I also didn't think I would be able to attempt an orgasm with him close by. Just the thought of touching myself in that way when the last person to touch me had tried to kill me made my lungs grow tight and pulse skyrocket.

Forget it.

It didn't have to be tonight.

I could wait.

I don't have to—

Gritting my teeth, I stopped those thoughts.

Sure, I could put it off. Sure, I didn't need to do it, but I knew in the depth of my soul this was the first trigger I had to overcome. This wasn't about pleasure. It was drastic medicine in order to reclaim myself.

With a heavy exhale, I slipped from the bed and snatched the glass dildo.

I used to have my own toy until Milton found it and threw it out. He actually cried when I asked him why he'd thrown away something that belonged to me—going full-on with the dramatics, claiming it challenged his masculinity if I self-pleasured, and it was up to him to give me all my orgasms.

Not that he'd ever given me one.

After his tears, I'd attempted to be understanding and open to trying. Hoping we could communicate a little more and find a way to patch up the holes beginning to show in our relationship.

However, my resentment slowly grew as the lacklustre sex we did have turned more and more one-sided. His half-hearted attempts at making me finish had me recoiling so much, I faked a release just to get him off me.

Once again, shame pounced.

I felt stupidly to blame for the slow breakdown of our relationship even though I knew in my heart no one should have to put up with the passive-aggressive narcissistic behaviour like he'd trapped me with. He'd wrapped his words and mood swings around me so well that I couldn't see he was boiling me alive until the water was too hot and he strangled me.

Enough!

Let's get this over with.

Shoving my shoulders back, I padded in my blue satin nightdress into the room that used to be mine. My bed sat in a puddle of starlight, encased by all of Nana's old furniture that I'd moved in here while painting hers.

Wriggling past her dresser and clambering over a few boxes of her belongings that I needed to donate to Goodwill, I slipped into bed, pulled the covers up to my chin, and clutched the dildo.

You can do this.

Don't think.

Don't let your mind get in the way.

A teeny tiny orgasm and you'll be free.

Nodding along to my peptalk, I slowly hitched up my nightgown and wriggled deeper into the bed.

My breathing ratcheted as I spread my legs, angled the toy X bought me, and cursed the tears that welled, spilled, and rolled hotly down my cheeks.

Twenty-Eight

Zander

Stranger Danger

I BOLTED UPRIGHT IN BED.

Blinking in the dark, I froze. What woke me? What had I heard? Adrenaline ensured I was ready to fight an intruder or leap from a burning building.

Fumbling with my bedside light, I scanned the industrial loft feel of my bedroom. Nothing had fallen. Sailor wasn't screaming. No wind or rain or thunder.

So what?

Something howled, tiny and miserable.

"What on earth?"

Slipping from my sheets, I plucked my glasses from the table and padded in my boxer-briefs downstairs.

I didn't bother turning on any lights, knowing the corners to avoid and managing to get to the back door in the conservatory without stubbing a toe. The howling came again, interspersed with a sad little meow.

Unlocking the door, I swung it wide and peered into the cloud-covered garden. No starlight or moonlight. Everything was hazy with mist.

Something warm and tiny bumped against my bare ankle, wrenching my gaze down.

"Penguin?" Bending over, I scooped him from the deck and held him up. "How did you get out here?"

He meowed again, his eyes dull and tail tucked.

He looked lost and alone and—

Panic shot through me.

Sailor.

"What happened to Sailor, Peng?" Holding him tight in one hand, I glowered at him as if he could tell me everything. "Where is she?"

He meowed and hung his head.

"Is she in danger?" Clutching him close, I bolted over the grass to the fence palings.

Then froze.

If I went over there as Zander—in my boxer shorts, no less—I might do more harm than good if she was having another nightmare.

But if I took the time to go as X…could I afford the ten minutes?

Fuck it, no time for hair dye and contacts.

Peng squirmed and meowed as if he agreed with me.

Racing back the way I came, I scaled the deck steps, and careened into the kitchen where I grabbed my motorcycle scarf and black baseball cap. Dumping Peng on the sideboard where my keys and mail lived, I quickly yanked both on, left my glasses on the countertop, raided the laundry rack holding a pair of black sweats and a t-shirt, and dressed as fast as I could.

Once decent and disguised, I scooped up the little kitten and ran out of my house without locking up.

The fence palings tried to snag me again. Peng whimpered as I squished him a little too hard. I raced over Sailor's lawn then plopped him onto his tiny paws to push up the lavender pot, claim the spare key, and unlock her back door.

Nothing.

No scream.

No cries.

Where is she?

My legs ached to chase through every room and find her, but I couldn't leave Peng outside. Replacing the key back under the pot, I grabbed the kitten and dumped him on the floor in the dining room. The kitchen window was open, hinting that was his escape route.

Closing it, I spied a saucer with some leftover food and shoved it under his nose. "Eat. I'll come check on you once I know your mistress is okay."

Leaving him to munch, I marched through the house, as familiar with this floorplan as I was with my own.

I didn't find her on the bottom level.

Taking the stairs two at a time, I charged down the corridor and into Melody's old bedroom. I'd almost slipped the last time I was here and praised Sailor's wallpaper choice. It'd modernised the room a lot from the pale lemon lace that Melody had favoured.

But the door was open.

The bed empty.

My heart went berserk.

"Sailor?"

Where the hell is she?

Striding back the way I came, I arrowed to the bathroom across the hall.

Just as empty.

"Sai—"

Fuck.

X knows her as Lori, you idiot!

"Lori?"

No reply.

"Answer me. It's Z—eh, X."

Wow, you're on a roll tonight.

Swinging open the study door, I peered through the shadows of stacked furniture looking like abandoned soldiers in the dark. The only other door was Sailor's old bedroom.

With my heart in my mouth, I swung the door open and peered into the blackness.

A sniffle made my chest clench.

Shoving my way past a dresser and almost tripping over a tower of boxes, I managed to navigate the room enough to reach the bed tucked up against the wall. The window where I used to watch her let in just enough light to find her buried beneath a mountain of covers.

She stiffened into a tight ball as I slowly sat on the edge of the mattress.

She trembled so hard the entire framework shuddered as I tugged part of the sheets away, revealing her sodden, tear-streaked face.

A dagger cut right through my vital organs.

"Hey…it's okay. I'm here. You're safe."

I didn't know if she was still trapped in whatever nightmare made her cry or she still held a grudge toward me for buying her a dildo, but she curled up even tighter and buried her face in her pillow.

I had no idea what I should do.

Comfort her?

Leave her?

Am I making this worse or better?

I could ask, but I doubted she'd give me an honest answer. I just had to hope we had enough of a connection and trust that I wasn't severely messing her up.

Forgive me if I'm doing this wrong…

Pushing her toward the window, leaving some space on this side of the bed, I brushed off the grass stuck to my bare feet, then swung myself into horizontal position behind her. The second I wound my arm around her middle and tugged her into me—spooning her like we had the other night—she went terribly quiet.

"It's just me," I whispered into her ear, pressing the softest kiss on her cheek. My mask absorbed the kiss, pissing me off that I couldn't taste her skin. "Just me."

It took a while.

It took an eternity.

But slowly, the stone in her bones thawed, and she unravelled her tiny ball just enough for me to scoot her a little closer and hug her a little tighter.

"X?" Her voice hitched with silent tears. "W-What are you doing here? I thought you were away for work."

All kinds of lies came to mind: I was let off early. I came back quicker than I planned.

I couldn't say any of them.

All I could say was the truth. "I missed you."

She sniffed and shook her head. "But...how did you know I needed you? I haven't been outside tonight. You don't have cameras inside." She groaned as fresh tears wobbled her voice. "*Please* tell me you didn't lie and truly do have cameras inside."

"I don't." I kissed her hairline. "I would never."

"Then how?"

This question I did have to lie about. And I had no idea how to be convincing. "I came to check on you. Your cat was caterwauling. I figured you hadn't locked him outside on purpose, so something might be wrong." Nuzzling her neck, I breathed, "I used your key to get in. But I can go if you want. Now that I know you're okay."

Sucking in a breath, she stiffened again.

I waited a few seconds before whispering, "You're not okay...are you?"

She turned to stone again before finally shaking her head. "No...no, I don't think I am."

Wrapping my arms even tighter around her, I didn't care I might be bruising something. I needed her to feel the sincerity of my feelings. The truth of just how hard I'd fallen, even if she had no idea who I was. "Do you want to talk about it?"

She scoffed with a sob. "Not really."

"That's fine, you don't have—"

"I tried the gift you bought me."

It was my turn to freeze. I didn't say a word, just in case I interrupted whatever she needed to say. Resting my chin on her head, I claimed one of her hands under the blanket and brought it to her stomach. Running my thumb over her knuckles, I just waited.

"I...I've never been good at that sort of thing." Tears escaped and poured freely. "That's not true. I used to be able to...you know. But when Milton found my vibrator and said it undermined him as a man, he forbade me from ever doing it again."

My jaw clenched.

I had a few choice words to say about that bastard, but I held my tongue.

"I don't know what's wrong with me. I don't know how I didn't see the type of man he was before it was too late. I don't know how I allowed him to chip me away, piece by piece. And I don't know how to glue myself back together again." Her tears cut her off.

Nuzzling behind her ear, I cursed my damn mask as I kissed her fluttering pulse point and waited.

"I thought I'd made a significant improvement today. I was happy for the first time in ever so long. Peng has done wonders for my mental health. Just having something to talk to, to be with...I wasn't aware how much I needed that, but..." She shifted in my arms, not trying to get away but to slot even closer against me.

I made space for her.

Dropping my legs a little, I slid her back until my hips were firmly lodged against her ass.

I wasn't hard—how could I be when the woman I wanted was in tears because another man had hurt her?—but I wasn't shy about letting her feel me.

Feel our size difference. Our power imbalance.

And then I loosened my arms, telling her without words that she could escape if she wanted to. That I held her this fiercely because I wanted to protect her, not dominate her, and every single moment of this was her choice.

Exhaling with a watery breath, she clutched my hand and tugged me. I understood her request and returned to squeezing the hell out of her.

With her trapped in my embrace, she spoke again, hitched and hesitantly. "I used your gift. It was hard at first. So hard to get past those memories. But then it got a little easier, and I thought...okay, maybe I'm not as broken as I feared. But the minute I got anywhere near potentially coming, I...I—" Her voice shattered into sobs.

Her grief tore me apart.

Rocking her, I pressed my forehead against her shoulder and held her while she broke.

I didn't know how much time passed, but eventually, her sobs turned to hiccups and the doctor in me wanted to grab her a glass of water to rehydrate and perhaps some antacids for the churning in her stomach, but she hooked her foot around my ankle, ensuring I couldn't go anywhere without some serious untangling.

"X..."

I sighed heavily. "Yeah?"

"Why are you here?"

I had no strength left to fake anything. "Because I hate that you're hurting, and I can't make it better."

There's no pill I can prescribe.

No surgery I can perform.

Only time and that made my skills as a healer utterly useless.

She went quiet, but not the quiet I'd grown used to. This one was prickly and poised with anticipation.

"What?" I whispered against her nape. "What is it?"

"You could, you know…at least try."

"Try what?"

"To make me better."

My eyes flashed wide. "Anything. Tell me what you need, and I'll do it."

The second I said it, I saw her trap.

Damn, I walked right into that one, didn't I?

Her hips arched backward, rocking against me.

Immediately, I went to shift away, but she moved with me.

"I know this is super forward of me and wrong on so many levels," she whispered. "I know I'm being manipulative and owe you a thousand apologies. We don't know each other. I don't know your real name. I don't know where you live or what you do or why you truly approached me, but I do know I can't do this on my own. And I can't move on until I claim my body as mine again. You were kind enough to be there for me and I'm weak enough to ask for something you're not willing to give. But only because I'm so *sick* of feeling him punch and kick me whenever I look at certain people. I hate feeling this lost, this broken. My bruises are fading, but the walls are only getting higher."

I clung to her. "I'm so sorry."

"Sorry enough to help?"

I groaned and buried my face in her hair. "You're determined to kill me, Lori."

Her hips rocked again, waking up the parts of me that were ready and very, *very* willing to serve.

"Do you find me attractive?" she asked on a shaky breath.

I laughed torturedly. "Do you really have to ask that question?"

"If you find me attractive and admit you have the same crush, then…why did you turn me down when I asked you to sleep with me?"

My teeth ground together. I didn't have to fake my growl to cover my usual baritone—it was a thousand percent real. "Because I refuse to take advantage of you."

"But isn't it *me* taking advantage of *you*? Like I said in our messages, aren't I the one asking you to do this? Aren't I the one in the wrong? Do you…" She trembled; fresh tears wobbled her voice. "D-Do you think I'm a slut?"

I reacted before I could think.

Pushing her away from me, I grabbed her chin and pinned her on her back. I didn't know where such a move came from. I hadn't meant to do it. But she gasped as her eyes popped wide, then shuddered as I shifted on top of her. With my spare hand, I hitched her higher up the bed and slipped between her spread legs, trapping her beneath me.

For a heartbeat, I feared I'd gone too far. This wasn't me. This wasn't who she *needed* me to be. But then her eyes melted into molten, scorching blue.

I couldn't stop staring at her.

With my free hand, I made sure my mask still covered my nose and mouth.

At least the room was dark. My hat had stayed low over my brow. She wouldn't be able to tell my hair or eye colour.

Hopefully.

"If he was the one who called you a slut, he's a motherfucking asshole. You aren't. I've never thought that. Not for a single moment."

She tried to nod, forcing my fingers harder against her cheeks.

Pulling my hand away, tingles sparked from touching her. "Sorry...I didn't mean—"

"It's fine." She attempted a tragic smile. "I'm not afraid of you."

"I'm glad." My gaze fell to her mouth. To her perfect lips. Her perfect, kissable, delicious lips.

All the blood in my body arrowed between my legs, leaving me with the intelligence of a rock.

Shifting, I attempted to get off her, but she placed her hands on my lower back. Her soft touch kept me from going anywhere.

Our eyes met.

The room, the night, the world all bled away like watercolour illusions.

We didn't speak for so long, but our hearts thundered to the same chaos. Finally, *finally*, she studied my mask and whispered a single word.

One word that undid me.

One word that made me hers.

One word that ensured I gave in.

"Please..."

Twenty-Nine

Sailor

Mask Fetish Unlocked

I HATED MYSELF FOR PUSHING HIM TO DO something he didn't want to do.

I did my best to take my pleading back.

To be strong enough to do this on my own and stop using someone for my own gain.

But…I couldn't.

For the first time in my life, I really, truly, *desperately* needed someone. Not sexually. Not physically. But in all the ways he made me feel: protected, cherished, *seen*. Every fractured piece. Every distorted part. He saw all of me, yet he didn't judge me or pity me or shame me.

I ought to be petrified.

A man in a mask and baseball cap pinned me to my bed and glowered at me with such intensity, I felt his stare in my soul.

Yet all I felt was safe. So *exquisitely* safe.

I had no more tears. No more self-doubt or hate or guilt.

I hummed and burned, and even if he said no to helping me, I might, just might, be able to achieve a happy ending on my own if he left me with more memories like this one.

When he hugged me from behind, I'd felt so sheltered.

When he flipped me onto my back and grabbed my chin, I felt so bare, so open, so *wanted.*

He gave off such a caring, secretive vibe with the occasional explosion of dominating masculinity.

It scrambled my senses, set fire to my system, and left me shaky and achy and…

"*Please,*" I whispered again, staring at the painted skull covering where his lips would be. The toothy grimace only added to the dynamic that I was the weak one while he was the one in my control.

He willingly gave me every power over him without speaking. I saw it in the way he watched me and felt it in the way he touched me. He told me, loud and proud, that his crush for me was real, that *this* was real, and everything else didn't matter.

Tugging one of my arms from under the covers, I reached for his mask.

I managed to tug it enough to reveal a part of his nose before his fingers locked around my wrist and pulled my hand away.

He shook his head just once.

He clucked his tongue.

He doused me with gasoline and struck a match that made fire erupt and heat burn and all I wanted to do was kiss him.

"If you won't sleep with me...kiss me?" I flicked my stare from his mask to his eyes, once again asking for something I shouldn't. "Kiss me and you can go."

With a snarl, he rolled off me and pulled his mask back into position. "You're definitely trying to kill me." Propping himself up with his elbow, he supported his head and stared at me. "And nice try, but I won't remove my mask."

"Ah, yes." I nodded seriously. "The boils."

He chuckled quietly. "Exactly."

Lying on his hip and facing me, he ran his fingertip feather-soft over my bottom lip. "I need you to know that I'm not denying you because I don't want you. I do. I want you way too fucking much. It's taking every ounce of willpower not to take you but...I'm trying to do the right thing and the right thing is..." He bit back a groan-snarl. "The right thing is not giving in to you even though that's all I want to do." Narrowing his eyes, he added, "I'm not going to kiss you, and I can't sleep with you, but...okay."

The world stopped spinning.

"Okay?" My heart almost leaped out of my chest.

Bending over me, he rubbed his masked nose against mine. The darkness in my room only granted shadowy features even this close. If I hadn't seen him before with my bedside light on, I wouldn't have known he had black hair under his hat or the richest, kindest brown eyes.

"Okay...I'll help you."

My leaping heart suddenly played dead. "H-How?"

Trailing his fingers from my mouth, he traced them along my throat, between my cleavage, and slowly down my belly.

His eyebrow rose as he felt the silky satin of my nightgown. "I thought you were more of a t-shirt and shorts to bed kinda girl."

I stretched under his petting, fully invested in the sparkling, tingling sensation he left me with. "A nightgown is easier access than shorts." I was so breathless, I sounded as if I'd run ten laps of the park.

He laughed again, low and rich. "You're right, it is."

His shoulder dropped as he lowered his hand from my lower belly and gathered up the fabric by my hip. Neither of us spoke as he hitched the hem up my shins, my knees, my thighs…

When most of it puddled on my stomach, he traced his fingers along the paper-thin skin of my lower belly.

I hissed and jerked, the sensitivity too hot, too sinful, too *much.*

"You sure you want me to do this?" His voice sounded like a beast, thick and croaky.

I didn't trust myself to be able to talk without giving away just how sure I was. A flush of hot wetness had me cringing. What if my need turned him off? What if I wasn't supposed to be this turned on by the local neighbourhood stalker?

He'll judge me—

I stopped that thought immediately.

He'd never judged me. Not once. That was why I'd gotten this far. Why he'd successfully allowed me to take back the smallest part of myself.

"We don't have to," he murmured, his fingers stroking fire over my exposed hip. "But if you want to, you have to tell me. Otherwise, this ends and I leave."

Trembling, I went to cup his cheek, but he reared back, his eyes wide.

"You can't take my mask off. That rule hasn't changed."

Lowering my arm, I nodded. "I wasn't going to. I just wanted to touch you."

"This isn't about me." His fingers sketched a little closer. "This is about you. Say the word and I'll do my best to give you an orgasm. I'm a little rusty and not saying I'm very skilled with my fingers, but…" His voice shaded with a tease. "You did say you like a man who takes instruction."

I flushed.

Lowering his masked mouth to my ear, he whispered, "So am I doing this? Yes or no, Lori."

I shivered at the nickname. At the separation it gave me between Sailor Rose, abuse survivor, and this new me rising from the ashes.

Licking my suddenly dry lips, I nodded. "Yes."

He didn't make me ask again.

His fingers navigated right to my clit.

My spine arched right off the bed as his hand cupped me, hot and steady, letting me get used to his possession.

"You can either teach me what you like, or you can retreat inward and focus on healing. Either way, I'm here." His voice hitched as his middle finger stroked my entrance. He didn't comment on my slickness or say anything to embarrass me. He merely held my stare, swallowed a growl, and torturously, slowly inserted that finger inside me.

I arched off the bed again. My blood heated, my bones trembled. No one had ever looked at me so intently all while touching me so intimately.

With just one finger, he blew me apart.

Unable to hold his stare while he systemically shattered my body into pieces, I closed my eyes and focused on his touch.

He didn't rush.

He savoured.

His heavy, harsh breathing sent goosebumps darting over me as he pressed his thumb against my clit and just held it there. I moaned as he hooked his finger inside me, pressing against that inner spot, making me clench.

I waited for him to speak.

I hated that I didn't really want him to. I didn't want to have to cringe with self-consciousness. I didn't want to fight to focus on his touch. I wanted him to remain with me but distant—here but far enough away that I could be swept away and hopefully find a way to come for myself, not for him.

Without a word—almost as if he'd heard my silent request—he feathered a second finger inside me. A soft cry escaped me as his thumb finally moved on my clit, just the barest rub, firm with pressure. He didn't tickle or bruise, he somehow knew the perfect press.

The longer he touched me, the less effort it took to concentrate. With every hook and flutter of his fingers, my mind turned darker and softer, and all that mattered was a release.

My hands clutched at the blankets as he shifted closer and pressed his erection against my hip, letting me feel I wasn't the only one burning. With a soft growl, he withdrew his fingers before pushing them back inside me.

Not rough, not cruel…worshipping and claiming and absolutely delicious.

And still, he didn't speak.

I lost track of time as he set a rhythm with his fingers, slow and languid to start, his thumb keeping constant pressure on my clit. He built me up and up. I felt heavier and heavier. Hotter and hotter.

And when I reached for his arm and felt his muscles contract and the steady thrusting motion of his wrist, I lost it.

My legs fell wider. My teeth clamped onto my bottom lip.

I *wanted*.

More and more and *more*.

I forgot why this was so hard for me. Why being touched had become so terrifying. All that mattered was the searing fire he cultivated inside me, slowly adding more and more fuel until my body clutched around his touch, and I cried out as his wrist angled deeper.

I clung to his bicep as his pace increased. His touch went deeper. His thumb pressed harder.

Up and up and up, he pushed me.

Quietly, firmly, wonderfully.

I couldn't stay still any longer.

I shivered and squirmed, fighting with him, needing to come, all while terrified of it.

His leg hooked over mine, keeping me pinned.

And then he inserted a third finger.

His pace lost its sweetness. His hand moved with the motions of fucking.

He didn't coax me anymore. He shoved me up the mountain, forcing me to tighten, to spiral, to spark. The telltale drawing up of my womb, the hot, delicious cramps that turned into a delicious knot just waiting to explode.

I was so close.

So, *so* close to detonation.

"Please…" I moaned, needing a final push.

His fingers drove deep, deep inside me, unapologetically possessive.

Sudden pain wrenched over my scalp from Milton pulling my hair out. My jaw ached from his punch. My shoulder blades and spine and ribs and wrists and legs. His every kick and throw repeated in horrifying precision. Discomfort and despair added awful layers to my rabidly popping pleasure. A cyclone of the past and the present howled through me, doing its best to blow away the future I needed to claim.

No.

Don't.

He's not here.

You're safe.

My forehead furrowed as I clung to happiness, not agony. I willed my body to remember the peace X gave me all while exterminating the memories of Milton.

It didn't work.

Pain built and built.

The crack of my cheekbone, the burn of my hip, the throb of my knee—

Fight-or-flight kicked in.

Adrenaline and terror and—

No!

The tingling coils of my orgasm dissolved. Milton cackled in my mind. All I could see was his sneering face. His taunts calling me a slut. His punches decorating me with bruises.

It happened again.

I hadn't been able to get past this part on my own.

I'd forced myself through it.

I'd screamed in resentment as that bastard prevented me from coming. I'd touched myself all while sobbing in defeat and failure because I'd let a monster into my life. It'd made me feel sick to my stomach—like I violated myself. He'd stolen my freedom, self-worth, and power and left me with frustration, irritation and bone-deep shame that I would always be tainted. Always be the stupid girl who trusted the wrong person. Always be the broken survivor who could no longer touch her own body.

"It's okay," X murmured, pressing his mask-covered lips to my cheek. "You're with me. No one else."

His fingers kept stroking me, tugging me back from the black nightmares. With each rock, he eradicated another pain, soothed another strike, deleted another kick.

Fresh tears streamed down my cheek that he was so patient, so understanding.

He touched me so worshippingly, all while reminding me that he did this for *me*. He touched me because I'd practically forced him to. He serviced me like someone I'd bribed or hired—obeying me despite his own reservations.

Guilt swarmed.

New shame drowned me.

I was so selfish. So greedy. Just as narcissistic as Milton.

It can't just be about me.

I can't use him like this.

My right hand dropped from his arm. Angling my hips a little, I put a little space between us and wrapped my fingers around his throbbing hard-on.

He went instantly, fatally still.

His breathing came fast and shallow, his fingers twitching inside me.

"S—Lori." He exhaled with a heart-clenching grunt. "Stop."

He shifted as if to prevent me from touching him, but I clamped my legs closed and kept his wrist trapped. "It's not fair for me to ask you to give me a release and not return the favour."

Stupid tears rolled hotly down my cheeks.

Every cell throbbed with hotter frustration as my impossible orgasm flew higher out of reach. What was the point? This was a waste of time. Milton stalked my thoughts, pacing on the outskirts of my mind, keeping me imprisoned in a cage of my own making.

"I can't come," I muttered almost coldly. Rocking my hand up and down, I focused on his climax instead. "But you can."

I'd almost gotten there.

I appreciated his attempt, but…I couldn't scale that wall just yet. *I'm not ready.*

I don't know if I'll ever be ready.

"You *can* come. If I'm doing it wrong, talk to me," he groaned. "Tell me what you like."

"Forget about me." My voice caught with frustrated tears. I clutched his rock-hard length. "Let me—"

"No." Removing his fingers, he clamped them hot and damp around my wrist and jerked my touch off him. In the same motion, he flung up the covers over his head and shot down the mattress.

I gasped as he settled between my legs, his face directly above my exposed pussy.

Grabbing the blankets, I looked down and, good God, I'd never had a mask fetish. I'd never had any kind of fetish, but seeing X between my legs—dressed all in black with a skull covering half his face and his baseball cap a little skewed, all the tingles and clenches he'd conjured returned in a wave of delirium.

His left hand went to his mask, his eyes flashing black. "You asked me to make you come and I never leave a job half done. You can trust me. I will never hurt you. And you can leave at any time. But…" His voice turned husky with gravel. "While I have you like this, while I can smell your need, and see your desire, I'm going to keep going. I'm not going to stop, and I'm going to enjoy every moment of licking you."

Holding my stare, he inserted two fingers back inside me.

My mouth fell open.

My arms trembled holding the covers up.

"However…in order for me to use my tongue, I have to lower my mask which means you have to drop the blankets. If I feel you lift them. If you try to look at me. If you attempt to stop me because you're feeling guilty that you're not returning the favour or that I'm not extremely, *desperately* willing to do this for you, then I'm leaving and not coming back."

Cold water doused me.

I tried to close my legs, but he pressed my thigh with his free hand and kept me wide.

"Do we have a deal or not?" He dropped his blazing stare to where his fingers vanished inside me. "Because my mouth is watering, and I either need to taste you or run as far away from you as possible." He groaned and squeezed his eyes closed. "And I just realised everything I said might terrify you, so if I've scared you and you want this to end, just give me the word and I'm gone, Lori. You don't ever have to see me again. We never have to discuss this or—"

"I trust you." I dropped the blanket.

I did my best not to worry about him being able to breathe under there or how he'd overheat or how a strange man was closer to my core than any other man had been. Milton had never gone down on me, and my other two boyfriends had never asked.

I couldn't stop shaking with a mixture of terror and torment.

My cheeks burned with fire. I'd never been so embarrassed or so turned on.

And when he shifted and his head lowered beneath the covers, I squeaked in shock, then screamed in ecstasy as his tongue licked hard and long up my seam.

He didn't build me slowly like before.

He didn't give me time to get used to the slippery sensation or give any space for my thoughts to ruin this.

I had no thoughts.

I was empty.

His fingers thrust inside me as his tongue licked again, driving from my centre to my clit.

I didn't stand a chance.

I whimpered and squirmed and begged for him to stop or lick harder.

He nuzzled me.

Devoured me.

And then, he bit me.

I shattered.

A guttural groan escaped as I threw my head back and surfed waves of rapture. The clenches came in frenzied crashes of ravishment, over and over and *over* again.

All those months of being denied. All those years of never finding true pleasure.

It demolished me into fragments, breaking me apart in all directions like a starburst.

I was blind and deaf and free. So *deliciously* free.

The bed rocked as X removed his fingers and licked me.

I shivered with oversensitivity. It almost hurt with how hyper aware I was, but I didn't stop him. I let him taste me, tongue me. I let him do whatever he wanted because he'd given me something I didn't think I'd have the courage to claim, and somehow, by giving me back myself, he'd claimed me for his own.

I moaned as his lick went deeper, penetrating me in ways that felt so much more intimate than fingers. I clenched around him. His guttural groan from beneath the covers almost, *almost*, made me come again.

I'd never had two in a row.

And a selfish part wanted him to try.

But I also couldn't bring myself to ask, so I lay there and let myself be devoured and—

He tore himself off me.

Breathing hard, he rearranged his mask and popped up from beneath the blankets. Without a word, he pushed my drunken shoulder and rolled me onto my side. I had no strength left and went where he wanted but my voice cracked with worry. "W-Why did you stop?"

With a powerful, possessive arm, he scooped me around the middle and drew me against him. His hard cock throbbed as he rocked into me, his breath coming in heavy, shuddering gusts. "I stopped because if I didn't, I'm either going to come all over your sheets or take you up on the offer to fuck you."

A lightning bolt of need arched through me. "You can…" I whispered. "I'd like you to."

"Fucking hell." Burrowing his masked face into the crook of my neck, he exhaled hard. "You have no idea how much willpower it's costing me not to plunge inside you right now." He arched his hips against my ass, grinding his throbbing length against me. "I'm seconds away from coming, Lori. A single touch and—"

"Then let me."

Reaching behind, I fumbled for him.

I grazed his length. I went to grip—

He snatched my wrist and pulled me away. Panting into my ear, he growled. "You touch me, and you'll destroy me. Do you understand?" Taking a heavy breath, he added, "This was about you. Not me. Keep your hands to yourself."

I laughed quietly, shocked that I felt happy after the memories trying to break me. "Okay, no hands. How about my mouth, then?" I rocked backward. "Let me return the favour."

His snarl cut right through his mask and arrowed into my heart. "You give me your mouth, and you won't be getting out of this bed until you've been fucked five different ways and can barely walk."

I moaned. Loudly.

I'd never been talked to that way.

Never felt the bolt of heat knowing how much he needed me.

Twisting in his arms, I tried to face him. To tug down his trousers and give him what he gave me.

But he clamped his arm around my waist and linked his still slick fingers with mine. Pressing our linked grip to my pounding heart, he grunted, "I'm going to go now."

"No, wait—"

"You're going to go to sleep, and no nightmares will find you—"

"X, don't—"

"I'm going to taste you on my lips all night." Kissing me through his mask, he untangled his wet fingers from mine.

I tried to hold on, but the lubrication meant he slipped easily from my grasp. "Message me in the morning, alright?"

The bed shifted as he slid off the side and stood.

I went to face him.

To leap on my knees and throw my arms around him, but his hand pressed on my shoulder, keeping me facing away. "Don't get up. Don't look back. Or this will always remain a one-time deal, okay?" His hand withdrew from my shoulder, fading into the dark.

I froze. My mind whirled. "You're saying this can happen again?"

I trembled, waiting for his reply.

I waited and waited until I couldn't wait anymore.

I rolled over.

But he was gone.

Thirty

Zander

Illegal Activities

I JERKED AWAKE.

Thick cotton wool coated my thoughts followed by the worst kind of agony between my legs. Swallowing a groan, I went to move, but my entire body throbbed as if I'd been beaten.

Digging my fingers into my eyes, I did my best to rub away the fog in my head, clutching at the reasons why I'd be in so much pain—

Sailor.

I went down on Sailor.

She came on my fingers.

I froze.

Fuck, was I still at her house?

I smelled her.

Everywhere.

Bolting upright, I blinked as a bedroom manifested around me. My shoulders sagged in relief as I recognised my faux concrete wall and no-nonsense furniture.

Huh, so I actually had the strength to come home.

I hadn't given in when I'd stood by the fence for an hour, cursing myself for leaving and buckling with crippling desire to return.

No wonder I felt as if I'd been beaten last night.

I had been.

By morality and sin.

I'd gone to war over right and wrong, and I'd been *so* fucking close to marching back to her, yanking off that seductive silky nightgown, and thrusting myself deep, *deep* inside her.

How I'd managed to stagger home with a hard-on from hell I didn't know.

How I'd had the self-control to stay in bed and not crawl my way back to her proved I was a goddamn saint because I'd never faced such temptation before. Never been so close to putting my own needs above someone else's, and even now, I hated that I hadn't done it.

That I hadn't said 'fuck it' and taken her up on the invitation to return the favour.

All I wanted was to come.

In her.

On her.

I'd almost repainted her fence with how much I needed her and the only reason I'd had enough willpower to leave had been my cursed red hair and green eyes.

If I'd gone prepared as X.

If I'd hidden my eyes beneath brown and rinsed black through my blazing strands, I didn't think I'd be in my own bed, alone, aching, aching, *aching* with unshed cum.

I'd be in her bed. In *her*. I would've done exactly what I threatened and taken her five different ways all before the sun rose and probably made things a shit ton worse because she would've seen me. She would've torn off my mask, and I would've let her. I would've ripped it off so I could kiss her.

And then she would've realised that the man driving himself inside her with all the finesse of an unhinged beast was her lying, scheming, stalking neighbour and called the police. She'd tell them that the man who'd eaten her out had been me all along, and I'd be in jail right about now.

Fuck.

My life would be ruined and my career over.

And I wouldn't even care because I would've had the best goddamn orgasm of my life.

"Shit, this is bad."

So very, *very* bad.

This wasn't me.

I wasn't impulsive or reckless.

In my right mind, I would *never* jeopardise everything I'd worked so hard to achieve. Never put my patients on the line. Never risk my ability to help others all because I couldn't help myself.

You know you can't see her again, right?

Throwing myself back down, I swallowed a snarl.

Her taste coated my tongue. Her sweet scent was thick in my nose.

Rationality told me to snap out of it but the monster inside me roared to be selfish for a change. I'd felt like a fucking hero last night as she'd shattered around my fingers. I'd been the best doctor in the world, curing her through pleasure and trust.

Trust?

Ha!

I'd destroyed any chance of her trusting me the moment I created a false persona and spied on her.

"Christ, what have I done?"

All my life, I'd grown up with the girl next door, been told by our grandmothers that our marriage was already destined, and been too pig-headed and focused on work to see what was staring me right in the fucking face.

They were right.

Sailor was mine.

She'd *always* been mine.

And now I'd royally fucked up because she'd never accept me after this. Never forgive me. Never trust me.

I might as well move to Australia because what was the point in staying?

I've already lost her.

Cursing every idiotic move I'd ever made, I threw myself out of bed and staggered into my bathroom.

A cloud of her sweet arousal intoxicated me. She covered every inch of my fingers and jaw. I swallowed my groan as my mouth watered. The pain between my legs grew feverish.

I needed to come so fucking badly.

My erection hadn't gone down, the ache only getting worse the longer I tortured myself with memories.

Sailor's smell sucker-punched me all over again, and I reached my limit. Tearing my clothes off, I tripped into the shower and wrenched the water on.

It wasn't even hot before I gripped my cock and squeezed.

Fantasy-Sailor's fingers replaced my own.

I pictured her before me, licking her lips before dropping to her knees and sucking me.

My left hand slapped against the tiles.

My heart exploded.

I pumped with ruthless, punishing jerks.

It only took five.

Five painful pulls before I cried out as the hottest, sharpest release blew apart my body, splattering white all over my black tiles. My knees almost gave way as I sucked in a tattered breath and quaked through the final shudders.

Trembling, I tipped my face into the falling spray.

I might not be haunted by an orgasm anymore, but she definitely haunted me.

I couldn't get her out of my damn mind or my stupid heart.

"I did something most likely illegal last night," I hissed quietly into my phone.

"Let me guess. You performed coitus on your neighbour, all while wearing a mask," Colin snickered. "I hope you used protection, Superman."

I bared my teeth and rubbed harder at the chrome of my motorbike.

Luckily, I had a day off today and just like I'd reached my limit and needed an orgasm to think straight, I needed to go for a highly ill-advised, stupidly reckless drive on my most prized death machine.

Falling for Sailor was not good for my physical or mental health. I'd taken care of the physical pain this morning and now I was going to flush my mind and try to figure out how to free myself from the web of crime I'd found myself in.

"I didn't sleep with her."

"But you did *something* to her."

Flicking a look at Sailor's place, I whispered, "I made her come."

"With your cock?"

"With my fingers." I cleared my throat. "And tongue."

"Well, well…who knew you could perform cunnilingus with a mask on."

"Can you stop using the correct terminology for everything? This is serious."

"And that's why I'm using the proper descriptions. I'm taking this *very* seriously." His laughter switched to his doctor tone. "Tell me, Dr North. Seeing as you're using me as your unofficial therapist, what do you think I should do with this information? Or better yet, what sort of prescription would you like me to administer now that you're fucked?"

Throwing the buffing cloth onto the black leather seat of my bike, I clenched my jaw. "I don't know why I bothered calling you."

"Oh, I know. I know." He chuckled. "It's because you have no one else, and the mess of this arrangement is doing your head in. Your OCD at fixing things and being the good guy is now knotted with messy things and being the bad guy."

Leaning against the bike, grateful I'd splashed out for a heavy-duty kickstand, I sighed and rubbed the indents on my nose from my glasses. "I should tell her, right? I mean…she'll probably be able to guess. Surely, there's some sort of sixth sense that kicks in that knows which people you've been intimate with."

"I keep telling you, man, that Clark Kent effect is real. I reckon she wouldn't even know it was you if you took your mask off. With the dark hair, brown eyes, and no glasses…you're incognito."

"And I think you're batshit crazy."

"I think if anyone is crazy in this friendship, it's you."

Glancing at Sailor's house, I stiffened as she appeared on her garden path. In her arms, Peng lounged like a jaguar lolling on a tree branch, his little legs dangling on either side of her forearm.

He gave me a 'I know what you did last night' glower, all while Sailor smiled shyly in my direction.

Every part of me clenched.

"I gotta go." I pressed the hang up button before Colin could reply.

Slipping my phone into the back pocket of my jeans, I stopped slouching and went to her. I froze on my second step, glancing at my motorcycle boots. I hadn't worn them in forever, yet I'd put them on when I went around as X. Would she recognise them? Just how observant was she?

Her smile faltered as she noticed me coming toward her. Waving, she hightailed it to her letterbox. Checking it for mail, she looked a little disappointed to find nothing.

Had she hoped to find another gift from X? Perhaps the dildo hadn't been that bad, after all.

What else could I send her? What other little keepsakes would help her heal day by day?

You're done with that, remember?

You're never allowed to see her again—let alone make her come, got it?

I cursed myself all over again for hinting that a second time was possible. I'd practically promised I'd stick something else inside her, all in order to make an escape without begging her to put me out of my misery.

Getting the vibe she didn't really want to talk to me, I headed back to my bike and continued polishing it. Not that the Harley needed much TLC. I'd always looked after it and with its life of semi-retirement, it looked almost as good as the day I rolled it off the forecourt.

The back of my neck prickled.

My spine snapped straight beneath my white t-shirt as Sailor crossed onto my driveway and stopped behind me.

Whirling to face her, I scratched at my chin where I'd freshly shaved this morning. "Sailor." I forced the brightest, nerdiest smile I could manage. "What are you up to on this fine day?"

Her half smile turned genuine as Peng swiped at a strand of her hair that had come loose from her ponytail. She wore yet another faded tee with sparkling stars and flowers, along with holey jeans that just begged me to tear a bigger hole and take her over my bike.

Fuck's sake...stop it.

"I, eh...I wanted to say I'm sorry I didn't answer the door last night. I was already in bed and…I didn't want to get up."

If it was X she spoke to, those lies would've been truths.

She probably didn't get up because her fear had pounced again, and walking through an empty dark house would've sent her spiralling into another panic attack.

But Zander shouldn't know that.

So I accepted her explanation with a shrug. "No worries. I was just checking on the kitten."

It was getting harder and harder to keep the two versions of Sailor in my mind. The Lori X knew seemed so much braver than this Sailor Rose who could barely meet her neighbour's stare.

I'd watched her on my cameras as she'd hitched up her skirt in the garden. I'd felt the power of her climax as she shattered on my tongue.

I didn't know which was the real version of her: the feisty survivor trying to remember how to live or the demure granddaughter of my gran's best friend.

Either way…I was stupidly in love with both of them.

"Yeah, about the kitten." She smiled again, but it looked brittle. "I…I think…I'm, eh—"

Crossing my arms, I clutched my polishing rag to avoid snatching her into a hug. I hated seeing her so wary. I wanted her in my arms again. I wanted her on her back, and my tongue—

Clearing my throat, I arched an eyebrow. "Let me guess." I tried to add a mixture of compassion, humour, and understanding into my voice, but somehow sounded like a stuck-up know-it-all instead. "You want to keep him?"

She flinched.

Peng reacted to her wince with a horrified look. Scrambling higher in her arms, he tried to embrace her neck and head-bopped her chin.

Whatever magic that tiny feline possessed instantly made her lose her tension. I caught a glimpse of the girl only X saw.

Her blue eyes glimmered like the summer sky, and she kissed Peng's head before looking up. "I still don't know if I'm any good at providing for an animal, but I can't imagine giving him up. He's helped me so much."

Reaching out before I could stop myself, I scratched Peng under his jaw. "He was yours the moment I found him."

The kitten purred like a freight train.

Sailor turned to stone.

I froze to match, realising how close my hand was to her cheek.

"Shit, sorry." Backing up, I shoved my hand in my jeans pocket. "I didn't mean to make you uncomfortable."

She sighed heavily, frustration etching her voice. "It's not you, Zander. It's me."

"Ah yes, the tried and true 'let 'em down easy' line." Holding the rag to my heart, I laughed gently. "Does this mean you're breaking up with me?"

Her eyes rounded. "Breaking up with you? We've never been together."

Way to make a joke that makes her super uncomfortable, you fool.

What I should do was laugh it off and pretend I hadn't been so stupid. What I did was double down like an idiot. "Ah, so you admit you forgot the vow you made to me when you were seven?"

"I-I did what now?"

Buffing my wing mirrors so I had something to do, I forced another laugh. "I think your dad had done something to irk you. You stormed out of Melody's house and pouted on the lawn. I'd been roped into helping her make a few more flower beds for some pocket money."

My mind filled with images of Sailor back then. Her sandy hair cut into a bob, her daisy-print dress slightly big for her gangly frame. "You said you hated all boys. I think I called out that I was a boy and didn't appreciate being lumped in with the rest. And you said that I was the one exception. I was an exception because I was nice to your nana. I was the only one you would tolerate from now on, so that made me yours, and no one else could have me."

I caught her eyes with another chuckle. "In my thirteen-year-old brain, I just assumed that meant we were dating. I've been waiting for you ever since."

Wow, you're the biggest moron alive.

Her mouth fell wide. "Please tell me you haven't. That didn't happen, surely—"

"Oh, it happened. But no." I shrugged, pretending the memory didn't make my heart skip. Funny how our childhood never really affected me. I'd always been aware of her. I'd crushed on her every now and again, but she'd just been the occasional guest next door. But these days, those memories had taken on a weight, a premonition. "Don't worry, Sailor, I haven't been saving myself all these years."

She looked at the ground, hugging Peng extra close as if I'd hurt her feelings somehow.

And you just keep digging that grave.

I was trying to make her like me as Zander, not push her deeper into X's arms.

Once again, jealousy spiked.

Was she thinking about him? Was last night permanently etched on her mind, replaying repeatedly like it was in mine?

"Anyway…" I dropped to my haunches and polished the chrome exhaust pipe. "I get that you're uncomfortable around me, and it's fine." The sun cast a halo around her. "I hope you have a great day. It's gonna be another hot one. Don't roast yourself in the garden. Otherwise, Melody will tell me off."

She frowned. Her head cocked as if thinking something important. But then she shook her head and clutched little Penguin close. "Are you going for a ride?"

Keeping my attention on the bike, I nodded. "I am. It's been a while."

She eyed my shiny black death machine. "I didn't even know you had a motorbike."

As much as I wanted to hang out with her and talk, I didn't have the capacity to keep my feelings hidden or hide how much it hurt that she still saw me as the trigger to Milton's abuse.

It wasn't her fault.

I didn't blame her.

But after last night, my stupid heart was fragile.

Tossing the rag into the plastic box of mechanical supplies, I grabbed my helmet. Matte black with a blackout visor—I'd almost had a local graffiti artist paint a matching skull on the front and back, so it looked as if I looked both ways in traffic. The skull matched my riding scarf.

Out of habit, I reached for the spare skull balaclava at the bottom of the box, then froze.

What the fuck are you doing?

You can't wear that.

She'd know immediately who I was.

My pulse skyrocketed. My palms turned sweaty.

Keeping my back to her, I went to shove the helmet over my damning red hair and muttered, "I hope the noise doesn't annoy you too much. I'll keep the revs to a minimum on Ember Drive."

I felt her staring at my back, granting another gush of goosebumps. "I still don't understand how you can ride something so dangerous when you're a doctor and probably see countless accidents."

Lowering my helmet, I turned to face her.

She petted Peng, her gaze bouncing from me to the bike and back again. "Is it safe?"

I shrugged. "What do you call safe? Is this as safe as a car? Absolutely not. Is it safer than swimming with a crocodile? Yes, I'd say so."

"But isn't it reckless to ride something you know might hurt you or even possibly kill you?"

"Gotta be a little reckless sometimes, I guess."

She sniffed. "You're not usually reckless?"

Our eyes locked, and I strode far too close to that line again. Words I hadn't censored fell from my lips. "Oh, I'm reckless all the damn time lately, but at least this hobby won't destroy me as badly as that little habit will."

Slamming my helmet on, I slung a leg over my bike. "Have a good day, L—Sailor." Cranking my key, the splutter of the combustion followed by the thunderous roar made me shiver with freedom.

Ah yes, I needed this.

I really, *really* needed this.

"Wait." Sailor cut in front of my bike, holding Peng who definitely didn't appreciate the racket like I did.

For a second, I panicked that I'd said something to give away my identity, but then she looked me dead in the eyes and said, "Take me with you."

Thirty-One

Sailor

Flirting With Freedom

WHAT THE HELL AM I doing?
What possessed me to ask that?

I held a squirming kitten and fought every instinct telling me to get away from Zander before Milton found me flirting with the neighbour, but all I could think about was that motorbike. The roar of it. The freedom of it.

With one snarl of that engine, whatever vixen lived inside me woke up, yanked on her riding leathers, and flung herself on the back of Zander's bike.

All I wanted to do was clutch him close, say fuck off to the past and the man who'd hurt me, and tell my kind, slightly nerdy neighbour to go as fast as dangerous lightning.

He scowled, his helmet cutting his face in half.

For a second, I saw X.

I saw the same faint lines around his eyes. The same possessive, protective stare.

My heart skipped and tripped. It wasn't the first time I'd wondered, but…with the full sunshine gilding Zander's vibrant green eyes and pale skin marking him a natural redhead, he looked nothing like the black-haired man who'd appeared in my bedroom just because he'd heard me scream.

X brooded.

Zander smiled reservedly.

X protected me all while possessing me.

Zander flinched if I got too close and fumbled with his glasses.

The two men might have similar eyes—if one wasn't rich brown and the other sparkling emerald—but they couldn't have been more different in personality. I could never imagine Zander pinning me on my back or going down on me. I couldn't imagine X blushing like Zander did when he'd touched Peng and realised how close we were.

The fear I had toward my neighbour was slowly melting away

thanks to X's help, but I could still hear the slurs of Goblin-Milton in my head.

All of that doesn't mean you're ready to gallivant around the streets on the back of a damn bike!

Peng meowed as he tried to get away from the snarling machine.

Zander killed the engine with a flick of the key and braced his legs on either side of the bike. Tugging his helmet off, the shock of fire-red hair tumbled over his forehead, making him seem so much younger than he was.

In that moment, I couldn't see him as a doctor. He returned to the gawky teenager in the garden that day when Dad had broken my heart. He'd promised to take me to a local waterpark for weeks and weeks but then said he couldn't be bothered.

If it'd just been that one time, I would've been okay. I was old enough to know that sometimes things didn't work out. But his broken promises had become habit, and I knew better than to get my hopes up all while hating myself that I still did.

Zander was right that I'd been hurt that day. Hurt and well and truly over boys. Maybe that was why I'd let Milton into my life? Because I'd never felt connected to him. Therefore, he could never hurt me?

Emotionally at least.

I hugged Peng a little closer as I recalled Zander's earnestness back then. How he'd steal my nana's baking and laugh at her terrible jokes. He'd always be there, rain or shine, to do any chore she asked of him.

I blinked as all the pieces suddenly slammed together.

He's always been a great guy.

How could I ever feel such terror when I looked at him? I'd literally never seen him hurt the tiniest bug, let alone me.

X had freed my body last night with the best orgasm I'd ever had.

And I had a feeling Zander could free the pieces that I'd lost well before Milton ever came on the scene by racing me through the sky.

"Stay right there," I ordered. "I'm just going to set Peng up at my place."

"No, wait." His hand came up, already encased in a leather glove. "Sailor, stop—"

I didn't obey.

Bolting up the garden path, I charged inside and deposited Peng in the kitchen where his litter tray and food bowls were. "I won't be long, little Penguin. Just…Nana will look out for you. I'm sorry to leave you alone, but…I really need to do this."

Grabbing an old canvas jacket that I used in the garden on bitter winter days, I locked up and sprinted back to Zander's side.

He blinked as if I'd made him speechless. "You weren't kidding. You truly want to come?"

That word.

Come.

The way he said it sounded so similar to how X had growled it last night. Heavy and thick, an innocent word turned into something sinfully erotic.

My pulse picked up as I narrowed my eyes.

Sunlight blinded me as I studied Zander all over again.

I tried to picture him with a baseball cap and mask on—of him hugging me or slipping down my body to stick his tongue between my legs.

And I couldn't.

"Lucky for you then, huh? You let one finger fuck you last night, and now you're riding another one today. See? You **are** *a slut."*

I shuddered at the memory of Milton throwing me onto the coffee table and laughing as I fell, bleeding and bruised, onto the carpet. All my carefree hope that I was healing screeched to a halt.

Everything turned dark.

Shadows crept over the sunshine.

Tears stung my eyes, and my fingers stroked the fading lacerations on my wrist, left behind from fighting for my life.

I didn't notice Zander swinging his leg off his bike.

I didn't function as a person as he came close, yanked off his gloves, then cupped my cheek with a gentle hand.

I shuddered at the contact.

I swayed backward to run.

But then his thumb swept through the tears tracking slowly, and with the softest smile, he stepped into me. "You're safe. He's not here." His strong, lean arms wrapped around me, loose and open but providing a protective wall between me and the past.

Everything hit me all at once.

The urge to scream and hide.

The desire to sob and crumple.

The nonsensical homecoming and familiarity.

X had shattered me apart last night and given me back my sexuality. But as Zander stepped a little closer and his arms tightened a little harder, I shattered in my soul.

My head fell forward and landed on his chest.

His voice rumbled with words I couldn't understand, and his boots collided with my paint-splattered sneakers. His embrace switched from tentative to smothering. He gathered me up and sheltered me with every bone in his body.

And I didn't panic.

I sagged with relief and gratefulness.

I let him hold me all while silent tears swelled and spilled, purging my mind and heart from yet another layer of hell.

He never moved or spoke, giving me all the time I needed to break, reform, and find my feet again.

Finally, when I felt a little saner, and Milton no longer yelled obscenities in my mind, I pulled away.

He let me go instantly.

Taking a step back, he pushed his glasses higher up his nose and stuck both hands in his back pockets as if preventing himself from reaching for me.

He didn't speak, but our eyes sought each other, and something happened.

A web of true friendship. A connection that'd always been there.

Zander had always been there in the background. A nuisance, a distraction, a crush.

I froze.

That's right…I-I had a crush on him.

I'd been fourteen or so.

I'd overheard Nana and her best-friend Mary giggling that their dastardly plan to finally hear wedding bells between the Norths and the Roses was working.

I'd torn my eyes away from watching Zander in the garden and asked what they meant. Both women had broken into obnoxiously loud laughter, pointing at Zander where he pressure washed the bird bath, then at me blushing because I'd been spying.

With the sun hitting the water droplets and the mist dancing rainbows all around him, Zander transformed from the annoying boy next door into something far, far more interesting. He'd been twenty then and already on the path to becoming a doctor. I'd felt woefully young when we'd gone for that visit.

My heart had fluttered as he'd looked over his shoulder, almost as if he sensed me gawking at him. He'd waved just once and given me a crooked half-smile. With his glasses sliding down his nose and his shocking red hair, I'd blushed ten times worse and darted to my room.

I'd dreamed of kissing him that night, and when I woke, I suffered a full-blown crush.

Only to have that crush obliterated when I confessed to my mother that if Nana and Mary had already picked out my husband, did that mean I could marry him straight away instead of finishing school?

"I know it's hard to stop thinking about him, but…he's gone," Zander whispered gently. "He can't touch you again."

His voice sliced through my thoughts. I blinked. Forcing myself to be as honest in person as I was by text to X, I shrugged. "I wasn't thinking about Milton, actually." I caught his emerald stare. "I was thinking about you."

His eyebrows flew up. "Me?"

"When you were twenty and I was fourteen."

He scowled. "Did I piss you off like I usually did?"

"No." I hugged myself. "You were sweet."

"Uh-oh." He smirked. "So that was around the time you enemy-zoned me?"

My mouth dropped open. "Excuse me?"

He laughed, but it held a sharpness that hinted he wasn't as carefree as he portrayed. "At the start of that visit, you were the same as always—shy but friendly enough." He pushed his glasses up again. "But by the end, you barely looked at me." He shrugged. "I figured you'd finally decided I'd stolen too many cookies and no longer wanted to talk to me."

I sucked in a breath.

All I wanted to do was brush aside this strange conversation—a conversation that I'd started—and pretend the past didn't matter.

But...the past *did* matter.

And if I had any hope of getting over Milton's abuse, I needed to clear the air with Zander.

Bracing myself, I confessed, "I couldn't look at you because I was afraid I'd ruin your chances of getting your doctorate if we hung out."

"Wait, *what*?" His eyes widened, then narrowed with confusion. "How could you have ruined my chances? You were fourteen—"

"Exactly." I nodded, my cheeks heating. "I'd overheard Nana and your gran giggling like buffoons about our wedding day and figured, if my future was already planned, then why did I have to bother with school?" I swallowed hard, forcing myself to stay truthful. "I asked my mother if I could just marry you earlier and skip the rest of my exams. I *hated* exams and figured you were a better alternative to those nightmarish things. She told me if I ever went near you with our age differences—regardless of what our silly grans were planning—you'd get into serious trouble. I avoided you because I didn't want to be the reason you didn't achieve your dreams." I shuddered dramatically. "In fact, I couldn't make eye contact with you after that, thanks to the fear of messing things up for you. I guess...I guess it became a habit. A habit I didn't really see forming until it was too late." I exhaled with a soft laugh. "Funny, I never stopped to think why I've always gone out of my way to keep my distance from you. Looking back, it stems from that moment: that teenage fear that I was bad for you and better keep my distance—even though it doesn't make much sense now."

For a second, he didn't say a word. Glowering at his house,

probably seeing us as naïve children, he dropped his chin and shook his head.

A low chuckle escaped him. "This is just ridiculous." Looking up, he caught my stare and smirked. "So...you've never actually hated me? Back then or now?"

My nose wrinkled. "Why would I hate you? I barely knew you."

"You didn't know me, yet you would've married me over taking exams?" His smile grew. "I don't know if I should be honoured or concerned that you'd rather suffer a lifetime with me over the momentary pain of a test."

"Concerned definitely." I rolled my eyes, grateful for his teasing. "Back then, I would've done anything to avoid two hours of exam hell. I'm a terrible person admitting I'd rather have been a child bride instead."

His voice thickened. "Oh, I dunno, I think being married to you might've been the single best thing to ever happen to me."

My heart stopped beating. I had no idea what to say.

His eyes widened as if realising what he said. Coughing into his hand, he backpedalled. "I mean...I just...I know the pain of exams. I've taken far too many in my life and if I knew how many I'd have to take in this career path, I might've been persuaded to get hitched instead."

My heart resumed its flustered strumming. "It's stupid how the past can affect the present."

He laughed, but he couldn't hide the sudden strain on his face. "I've been having the same thoughts lately."

"You have?"

His eyes softened. "I wonder where we'd be if I'd had the guts to ask you out when you moved in with Melody. If that one question might've set events in motion that meant Milton would never have touched you."

My mouth fell open. "You sound pretty sure of yourself that I would've said yes."

"Would you?" He pinned me to the spot, his eyebrows drawing together. "If I asked you now...would you say yes?"

"I—" Licking my lips, I struggled to speak like a normal person. My courage failed me; I fired a question back instead. "Are you saying you *still* want to ask me out?"

He scoffed as if I'd said something stupid. "You weren't the only one hearing our grandparents planning our future, you know. Back then, I wanted them to stop their silly games, but now...now I wonder."

"Wonder what?"

"If they saw something between us that we were too young to see ourselves."

Once again, he stole all my words.

"Anyway." He cleared his throat. "At least I finally know why you barely said hi to me from that day forward. I responded by actively staying out of your way. I figured you despised me and if I'm honest...it kinda hurt not knowing why."

I flinched as I fell back through time.

After that day, Zander hadn't been at Nana's so often. For a couple of visits—when I came on my own as my parents couldn't be bothered—I'd waited to catch sight of him, only to be disappointed. Nana told me he was a diligent student and working very hard to manifest his dreams.

I'd been happy for him but also...lonely.

Tucking away decades' worth of yearning, I forced myself to joke. "It all makes sense now."

"What does?"

"Those excuses your gran gave—that you were busy studying and couldn't have dinner with us or you were at the library cramming...that was you avoiding me."

"Some of them were, yeah." Crossing his arms, his frown turned into a genuine smile. Not reserved. Not polite. A full-blown happy smile that made my heart shiver off its layer of dust and flutter again. "But mostly, I was doing you the favour of avoiding my terrible company."

"Ever a gentleman, even then." I returned his smile, stiffening as Milton's slurs echoed.

"See? You were a slut even at fourteen. He knew it. Everyone knew it."

His face fell. "I'm the opposite of that word. Especially at the moment."

Not liking the dark look in his eyes, I dug my fingernails into my palms and ignored the phantom pain from Milton's fists telling me to get away from him. I even managed to take a step closer. I needed to take away the sudden sadness on his handsome face. For some strange reason, I felt responsible. As if his sudden discomfort was my fault. "Know what I think?"

His gorgeous eyes met mine, his glasses catching the sun. He searched me as if he'd lost something infinitely precious and still couldn't find it. Sucking in a heavy inhale, he breathed, "What do you think?"

"I think Melody and Mary are entirely to blame for our many misunderstandings, and it's up to us to set the record straight."

"T-The record?"

My chest squeezed at his minor stutter. At his obvious wariness and curse of shyness. His cheeks tinged pink, which gave me just enough confidence not to be afraid anymore. Not to be afraid of *him.*

Holding out my hand, I embraced enough courage to smile and wait for him to shake. "Hi, I'm Sailor Melody Rose. I prefer flowers over people most days. I don't like apricots or working for someone. I could technically be called lazy because I learned from the best that life happens in the moments where we do nothing. I've recently adopted a cat who has become my entire world, and my house is haunted by the very same woman who tried to set us up as kids. I also suffered from a mistake that cost me a lot of physical and emotional pain, and because I recently made a vow of honesty with someone, I'm going to be honest with you and say I'm sick of living in the past and want to step into the future. So..."

Reaching for his wrist, I brought his hand up and threaded my fingers with his. Shaking our combined grip, I smiled at the dazed look on his face. "Can we start again? No more misunderstandings. No more secrets. No more avoiding each other. Friends?"

He choked and cleared his throat. "You made a vow of honesty?"

"I did, and it's been surprisingly healing."

"Who did you make the vow with?" His tone thickened just a little.

A prickle darted down my spine.

Was he jealous?

Surely not.

"Just a friend." I squinted in the sun. "Go on...if we're to be friends too, you need to introduce yourself."

Sighing, he tightened his fingers around mine. His eyebrows knitted together with a flash of frustration. "Okay then. Nice to meet you, Sailor Melody Rose. I'm Zander North. I don't have a middle name. I don't like loud music. I suck at sleeping. Oh, and I'm a workaholic." His hand stopped moving, but he didn't release me.

We stood there, our palms and fingers linked, locked in a stare that neither of us could break.

I forgot about Milton.

I felt no pain.

The past couldn't find me as I drowned in a sea of green from his eyes.

For the first time, stirrings of belief that I would be alright grew bright.

This would pass.

I would be happy again.

Starting with doing something brand new.

Tugging my hand from his, I stepped toward his bike. "Take me for a ride, Zander North. I have a sudden urge to fly."

Thirty-Two

Zander

Let's Be Friends

I'D DIED AND WOKEN UP IN A different universe.

It was the only explanation for why Sailor's arms were wrapped around my waist, her thighs pressed against mine, her heart drumming through her canvas jacket and my leather bomber.

I hadn't said a word as I'd fetched her a spare helmet from my garage, then slung my leg over my bike and ignited the engine. She'd stayed equally silent as she shoved the helmet on her head, then clambered up behind me.

I'd suffered a full-body quake as she'd hesitantly leaned forward and asked if it was okay to hold me.

She was asking permission to touch me?

I'd had to clench my teeth until they cracked to prevent telling her she'd touched me in far more ways last night. The imprint of her fingers around my cock burned with deception.

Nausea splashed up my throat for lying to her face. I could barely handle those lies when she ran away from me. How could I hope to keep them now that she actively tried to be my friend?

No more secrets, she'd said.

Yet I kept the biggest one of all.

I'd often cursed our grandmothers for meddling with our lives. But now I felt as if they'd cursed *me*. That if I hadn't grown up hearing their whispered scheming about me marrying the girl next door, I wouldn't have been drawn to her against my will. She would've just been any other girl.

So why did I feel like she was the *only* girl?

Shaking away those thoughts and focusing on the road, I cranked the engine a little more now we were away from suburbia and heading to rural farmland.

I didn't check over my shoulder to see if she was okay with going fast.

I already knew she needed what I did.

She was healing and healing sometimes required ripping off scabs and tearing off bandages that'd become too restricting.

Bending low, I added speed until we flew, just like she requested.

"You okay?" I held her elbow, granting support while she staggered a little from climbing off my bike.

She nodded and wrenched the helmet off, leaving her hair crackling with static.

I couldn't take my eyes off her.

The late afternoon sunshine turned her hair into spun gold and her eyes brighter than the clear summer's sky.

Giving me a sated almost sensual smile, she nodded and sighed heavily. "That was...I have no words." Passing back my helmet, she shrugged. "Thank you, Zander. I didn't know how much I needed that."

Placing both helmets on the leather seat of my bike, I fought the urge to fidget with my glasses. But then I gave in because I wasn't pretending to be X, and I really, really needed to do something with my hands.

Taking my glasses off, I polished the lens with my t-shirt. "I'm glad you enjoyed it."

"Are you going out again sometime?"

Returning my glasses to my nose, I nodded. "Probably. I have a big week coming up, so I'll most likely need to blow off some steam. Why? Did you want to join me?"

She shuffled on the spot. "Would that be okay? I mean...if you want to be on your own, then—"

"You can come."

Her eyes narrowed on that word, sending me right back to last night when she'd come on my tongue. I didn't know if she recognised my voice or if memories of Milton made that word a trigger, but...I made a mental note not to say it anymore.

My stomach rumbled embarrassingly loud.

Sailor smirked. "I'm guessing you're as hungry as I am. I better let you go." Swaying toward her house, she bit her bottom lip. "Thanks again. For today, I mean."

Ice water splashed down my spine. I didn't want her to go. I wanted to invite her round. Have dinner with her. Kiss her without a mask on and—

"Have a good day at work tomorrow." She waved and headed up her garden path.

My window of opportunity closed far too quickly.

Clearing my throat, I dashed forward and grunted, "If you're not doing anything tonight, did you want to…" I waved at my house like an idiot. "Come round?"

You said that word again.

"I mean, pop round? For food."

Smooth, Zan. Real smooth.

She froze and wrung her hands. "Oh, um…" Her gaze shot to my renovated home. Excuses flickered in her stare; the fear she was slowly working through swallowed her back into the shadows. "Um, it's not that I don't want to. I'm just…really tired. Rain check?"

"Of course. You're still healing. Sorry, I…I wasn't thinking."

"No, I'm the one who should apologise—"

"Don't be ridiculous. I shouldn't have asked." Forcing a smile, I locked my bike, grabbed the two helmets, and stalked toward my garage. I couldn't be around her while my emotions were stupidly close to the surface. I wanted to call her out on her lies, but I also had no right.

She didn't want to hang out with me in a house on our own because no matter the freedom of today, I still represented all her hurts. I was still the reason she wore so many bruises. Why did I think she'd be over that? What egotistical asshole believed that, in one afternoon, he could erase all her trauma and expect to neck with her on his couch?

So what if we'd ridden together?

Flown together?

That was in public.

Outside.

And that was as far as she was willing to go with me.

"Have a good night, Sailor." I vanished into the garage and closed the door.

I sat nursing a beer while watching shit TV.

I'd cooked a vegetable burrito and chased it down with a bag of corn chips. I now contemplated going to bed at eight p.m., all so I could stop thinking about what my neighbour and her cat were doing.

It wasn't often that I felt lonely.

I worked too much to even contemplate the word.

But tonight…Christ, I *ached* with it.

I wasn't just jealous of X anymore; I was jealous of a tiny orange puff ball called Peng.

You could install a camera in her kitchen…that way, you can at least watch if you can't be with her.

Groaning, I tossed my glasses onto the couch and rubbed my eyes.

No way.

I wouldn't step over that line.

Even if I sat in my empty house like a loner, fighting every instinct to go next door, I wouldn't spy on her just because I needed her.

My phone buzzed beside me.

I snatched it up far too quickly.

I know you're probably going to say you're out of town or too busy or you'll come up with another million excuses after what we did last night, but...I baked you a cake to say thanks and...I want you to come over.

"Fucking hell, this just keeps getting worse."

Tossing my head back against the couch, I groaned at the ceiling. There had to be a word for this irony.

As Zander, I wanted nothing more than an invitation to spend time with her. As X, I should turn down her offer and disappear.

I wanted so badly to say yes but rationality gave me all the reasons I should say no.

The faintest whiff of chocolate slipped through my open living room window, tormenting me with unwinnable temptation.

If it will help you make the right decision, I didn't know what you liked so I went with a foolproof gooey lava cake. I've just lifted it out of the oven so...if you want a piece, it needs to be enjoyed now. I'll also throw in a scoop of ice cream—your choice of vanilla, rockyroad, or butterscotch.

My fingers typed without any input from my brain.

I literally had no willpower, summoned against my better judgement and hypnotised by an evening with her instead of being alone.

I'll be there in fifteen.

Thirty-Three

Sailor

You Have a Choice

I SENSED HIM BEFORE I SAW him.

Peng did too. His little ears sprang up and he scrambled off the couch, tearing toward the back door as if his long-lost littermate had returned.

Huh, that's strange.

Peng hadn't met X yet. Why did he react so—

Wait, they met briefly last night.

X had said he'd heard Peng crying outside, and that was why he came to check on me. I assumed he'd brought the cat in with him because all the windows were closed and the kitten safely tucked inside when I woke from my post-orgasm glow.

The quietest knock rapped on the back door as I padded barefoot into the kitchen. The dense sugary smell of chocolate permeated every inch, overshadowing the usual scents of thyme and oregano.

Brushing down my blue jumper that I'd shrugged into after getting a chill, I second-guessed my inappropriately short Sailor Moon night shorts. The tiny crescent moons seemed juvenile and far too young for the type of behaviour I hoped X would be open to indulging in once I'd fed him my thank-you cake.

I smirked.

Apparently, I was making a habit of thanking men with baked goods. Jim had enjoyed his peach upside-down cake so much, he'd begged me to make another, and I had every intention of making something for Zander after he let me tag along on the back of his bike today.

He'd gone fast but not petrifyingly stupid.

The fields had zipped past in a blur of patchwork green, all while fresh air blew away the shadows in my mind. I felt windswept and suntanned, and after a nice long shower and a cuddle with my best-friend, Peng, I floated with freedom I hadn't felt in well…ever.

You should've accepted his invitation to hang out at his house.

I stiffened, recalling the way my instincts flared with warning.

I liked Zander. I might even be at the point of admitting I'd always had a crush on him, but the thought of being alone with him...at night.

I couldn't.

It would prove Milton's judgment and jealousy were founded. That every kick and punch he'd given me had been justified because I did fancy my saintly neighbour, after all.

No.

It was too big a step, too soon.

I was getting better, but...I wasn't at the point of being alone with Zander despite every piece of me desperately ready to be alone with X.

It didn't make sense.

I shouldn't be afraid of spending a quiet evening with the guy I'd known all my life, yet be so turned on at the thought of making out with a masked stalker who refused to tell me his name.

You're messed up.

And you **will** *behave yourself.*

I chewed on the inside of my cheek as I forbade any ideas of throwing myself into X's arms.

Just because we'd shared a moment last night—just because he'd shattered me apart with his fingers and tongue—didn't mean we were an item or that he'd want to do it again.

With my cheeks pink and heart rabbiting, I opened the door and leaned against it.

Our gaze instantly met, locked, and held.

He stood cloaked in darkness. Black tee, black jeans, black boots. The boots looked similar to the ones Zander wore when we went riding, but that was where the similarities ended. X's glossy blue-black hair caught the glow of my outside fairy lights. The glint of silver through his eyebrow seemed a little out of place and his balled hands spoke of a thread of violence that Zander would never have.

Zander would give his shirt to anyone who needed it.

X would most likely make them work for it to prove they deserved it.

My stomach soared and dived, leaving me a little breathless. "You know...this is the fourth time you've been in my house and the first to actually be invited."

His dark brown eyes crinkled as he smiled, his mouth hidden beneath the familiar mocking skull mask. "I apologise. Next time I hear you screaming, I'll use the doorbell."

I stood taller, feeling better than I had in so long.

I could no longer tell if it was thanks to X teaching me how to let go or Zander proving I was stronger than I looked. Either way, both men had been the catalyst to finally guiding me out of the dark.

"You can *come* anytime you want." I grinned, shocked at my blatant flirting.

He staggered a little, then his eyebrows came down, shadowing his rich dark eyes. "Careful, Lori. I'm like one of those vampires who need an invitation into a house. Grant me the right to *come* whenever I want, and you won't be able to keep me out."

"I was hoping you'd say that." Leaning outside, I grabbed his wrist and jerked him over the threshold. He tripped against me, sending us crashing against the doorframe.

I sucked in a breath as one of his hands went to my hip to steady me and the other slammed above my head to stop us from tumbling over.

He stopped breathing. His eyes searched mine. His chin tipped lower, and for a second, I had the stupid idea he was going to kiss me.

But then the moment was gone, and he shoved himself away.

Peng meowed, sending X almost tripping again. Backpedalling to avoid stepping on my tiny orange soulmate, he scowled and grabbed Peng from the floor. "Both of you are trying to kill me, I swear."

Peng immediately began purring, trying to claw his way out of X's hold to rub himself all over the skull mask.

I'd heard some animals were affectionate to everyone, but the way he stared at X spoke of full-blown love, not just first attraction besottedness.

"He really seems to like you," I murmured, heading toward the cooling cake dripping with gooey fudge.

"I seem to have that effect on animals," he muttered, trying to extract himself from the forced loving Peng delivered.

"Oh?" I cut two big pieces of cake and put them into flower-printed bowls. "Vanilla, rockyroad, or butterscotch?"

"Uh, vanilla. Thanks."

I couldn't contain my smile as I headed to the freezer and took out the tub of ice cream. If he wasn't wearing a mask and I knew his name, this would be any other night with any other couple. This was normal. Nice. Addictive.

Ladling a generous scoop into both bowls, I giggled as Peng clawed his way up X's t-shirt and snuggled into his neck.

X squirmed as Peng headbutted his chin.

I laughed. "I think he might be telling me he'd prefer to be adopted by you. Either that or you've smuggled in some catnip."

He chuckled, sending a wash of goosebumps over me. "He's just happy. Aren't you, Penguin? Finally found your forever person."

The spoons I'd grabbed from the drawer clanked against the

bowls as I dropped them.

Spinning to face him, my heart took off at a dead sprint. "Zander?"

I had front-row seats to his reaction.

With smooth, unhurried motions, he reached up, plucked the kitten from where he'd made a home for himself on his shoulder, and held him out to me. Our fingers brushed as he plopped Peng into my hands, then backed up and leaned against the table. Crossing his arms, he cocked his head. "Zander?" His voice thickened with extra gruff. "Who's that?"

I frowned, searching him, not entirely convinced. "He's my neighbour."

He nodded slowly. "The one who's the reason your jealous psychopathic ex hurt you?"

"It wasn't his fault, but yes."

"The geeky one with carrot hair and glasses?"

Indignation swelled in me. "Don't call him a carrot, and he's not a geek. The glasses suit him."

His eyes crinkled again as if he was smiling. "Sorry, I didn't realise you two were so close."

Taking a step toward him, I searched his brown stare, wishing I could see his face. "You called Peng Penguin. I haven't told you that was his original name." I racked my memory, needing to go over our message thread. "At least, I don't think I did."

"You did." He nodded. "Otherwise, how would I know?"

"My question exactly."

He chuckled softly, sounding as if he didn't mind being interrogated and had nothing to stress over. "Do you want me to go? Am I making you uncomfortable?"

I reared back. "Go? No...I—" I glanced at the cake and melting ice cream. I'd ruined a perfectly fine evening by trying to figure out his identity. I grasped at straws all because I'd had an incredible day with Zander, and guilt chewed me for liking a stranger in a mask as well as my kind-hearted neighbour.

Despite Milton claiming I was a slut, I wasn't. I was wired to love and be committed to one person at a time. X had been there for me from the start, but so had Zander. He'd been there when I first woke up in the hospital. He'd given me a notepad to write with and told Lily to come get me.

Who did I owe the most loyalty to? The man who'd made me come alive again or the man who'd kept me alive in the first place?

"L-Let's eat in the living room."

"Sure." Grabbing both bowls, X headed toward the lounge where I'd set up my tablet to watch something on Netflix. I'd even strung a few fairy lights on the hanging hexagon-shaped shelves that Pops had made Nana. The potted plants gathered dust above, watching our every move.

Peng bounced behind us, leaping onto the coffee table and trying to get into the bowls as X placed them down.

"Oh no, you don't." Scooping the wriggly kitten up, I plopped him beside me and tried to distract him with an ugly snake thing I'd sewn.

X sat slowly, keeping distance between us.

Memories of the last time we'd sat on this couch came thick and fast. He'd planted his hand over my mouth to stop me from screaming. He'd shown me he was trustworthy by letting me go, then hugging me when the memories became too much.

My tension bled out the longer I studied him. He did a good job of hiding his nerves but couldn't quite delete them as he shifted a little and clasped his hands between his legs, a slight bounce of his knee belying his calmness.

He's nervous like I am.

"What's your real name?" I asked softly, passing him one of the bowls.

He took it and stared into the sugary mess. "I think I told you the last time I was on this couch that I didn't want to lie to you." He looked up, his brown eyes glittering with soft light. "I can't answer that, and I really don't want to lie."

"Okay then, how was your day?" I scooped up a spoonful of cake and shivered at the perfect combination of ice and heat, vanilla and chocolate.

X just kept holding the bowl as if he was a beggar waiting for someone to toss some coins into it. "It was good actually." His eyebrow rose as he twisted to look at me. "How was yours?"

I took another bite and went to tell him about the wind in my hair and the feeling of flying on Zander's bike, but…something stopped me. I'd been on the receiving end of jealousy, and as much as I didn't think X would beat me for being with Zander, I didn't want to hurt him.

If he had any feelings for me. If his crush was real…I couldn't tell him I'd found pleasure with another man. What sort of person would that make me?

Just because you haven't told him doesn't mean it didn't happen.

Had I cheated on X today by feeling so happy with Zander?

Could you cheat on someone you weren't officially dating?

Sighing heavily, I slouched back and poked half-heartedly at my dessert.

This was turning out to be a disaster.

The clink of his bowl hitting the coffee table drew my eyes back to his.

Ever so slowly, he shifted to face me and hooked his left leg onto the couch while his right boot remained firmly on the carpet.

I didn't care that he hadn't taken his shoes off.

I planned to rip everything out of this room tomorrow and begin painting. The carpet would be the first thing to go so I'd never have to look at the spot where Milton strangled me again.

Reclining against the armrest, he just watched me.

His eyes so deep, so intense, his entire demeanour crackling with power and possession.

I couldn't handle the way he stared. And I definitely couldn't handle the feelings he invoked.

Grabbing his bowl from the table, I shoved it back into his hands. "Eat. I made it for you. To say thanks for helping me last night." I couldn't stop speaking now that stress had gathered. I did what Lily did and blurted everything. "You unlocked the cage I've been trapped in. You took away his power, and I'll always be grateful for that. I'll always be so thankful you messaged me that day. I don't know how I'll ever be able to repay you, but I'd like to try and—"

"Lori." Swooping forward, he pressed his finger against my lips. "Hush."

I blinked and shivered.

The world fell away as our eyes locked. I forgot about cakes and gratitude. All I wanted was a repeat of last night. I wanted to give him the same level of pleasure he gave me. I wanted him to know that I might never know his name, but I would always, *always* remember him.

His finger fell from my lips, his breath catching.

A split-second decision had me snatching his bowl from his hand and tossing it back onto the coffee table.

He reared against the armrest with a scowl. "What are you—"

I didn't let him finish. Gathering all my fledging strength, I crawled directly on top of him.

He went deathly still. His hands gripped the couch as his body turned to stone. "W-What are you doing?"

Peng jumped off the settee as my knee went between X's legs and I planted one hand on his chest. Fighting my trembles, I reached for his mask.

"Lori, don't—" He tried to scoot backward but the armrest trapped him.

He shook his head.

I went to pull.

His hand snapped up and locked around my wrist. "Stop."

My eyes flashed to his. "You can't eat with it on."

He sucked in a breath. "I'm not hungry."

"But I baked you a cake."

"And I'm grateful. I'll eat it when I go home. If you allow me to have a piece to takeaway, of course."

I huffed. "I'm not a restaurant, you know."

"And I didn't expect you to bake me a thank-you."

My heart pounded far too fast. "How could I not? What you did felt...amazing." My cheeks burned as I forced myself to stay honest. "No one has ever...I mean, I've never had someone..." I swallowed hard. "That was my first time."

"I know," he said softly, full of gravel and gruff. "You told me no one has ever made you come."

I blushed. "Well, yes that too. But I meant..." I couldn't look at him. I focused on the toothy snarl of the skull. "No one has ever gone down on me."

His eyebrows shot up, his piercing twinkling silver in the lowlight. "You're kidding me."

My cheeks went into full blush.

"How...how is that possible?" he whisper-growled. "Fuck, if you were mine, I'd dine on you every night."

My gaze snapped to his. Prickly heat crackled over my skin.

Cupping my cheek with his free hand, he ran his thumb over my bottom lip. His gaze transfixed on my mouth. "Your taste is..." He glanced at the chocolate cake with an erotic huff. "A thousand times better than the sweetest dessert. You taste like the flowers you're always cooking—like the best kind of nectar." He chuckle-snarled. "To know I'm the only one who's sampled you in that way? To know no one else has licked you, tasted your cum, or heard you cry out in ecstasy is a *very* bad thing for me."

"W-Why?" I swallowed hard. "Why is it bad?"

"Because that stupid crush I have on you is blowing completely out of control."

He successfully set my heart on fire.

Groaning, he tipped his head back as if exhausted by the thick, sexual tension arching between us. "You have no idea how hard this is for me."

"I think I probably have some idea how hard you are." I forced myself to grin. "Probably about how wet I—"

"Fucking hell." He squeezed his eyes closed and shook his head. "You can't say things like that."

"Why?"

"Because it makes me want to keep you, and...I can't."

I froze solid, hovering over him. "Who says you can't?"

What am I saying?

His forehead furrowed. He ignored my question with a snarl. "I thought I could do this, but I'm so far out of my depth, I'm drowning." He laughed coldly. "And you know what the worst part is? I know I should get up right now and walk out that door, but all I can think about is how you invited me here for cake yet all I want to eat is *you*."

My stomach flipped. I tried to pull his mask again. "I can be on the menu."

Wow, who are you right now?

His chin tipped down, his eyes blazing a hellish black.

My fingers clung to the bottom of his mask, refusing to let go even as his hand tightened around my wrist.

"You wouldn't offer if you knew who I truly am."

I shivered. "Then tell me who you are, and I'll be the judge."

His eyes flickered over mine, searching me as deeply as Zander did this morning when I asked to go on his bike. "Not tonight."

"Why?"

"Because I'm feeling super fucking selfish and don't want to leave. And once I tell you, you won't want anything to do with me, and the thought of going back to an empty house without you kills me."

Both of us stopped breathing.

He tried to push me off him with a groan. "What am I saying? Jesus, just ignore me. I have no idea what I'm doing anymore." He forced a laugh. "I'm overtired. Overworked. Mentally insane. Take your pick. You're obviously doing better. You don't need me anymore. I'm gonna go and—"

"X." Shoving him back down with my palm on his chest, I searched his gaze. I recognised the telltale signs of panic. I'd felt them myself so often the past month. The fact that he suffered too—that my masked guardian who'd given everything and asked for nothing—felt the same out of control anxiety I did made me feel so ashamed.

"Let me go." He squirmed to get free but didn't manhandle me, careful even now not to use physical force against me. "Lori—"

"Tell me who you truly are."

Freezing beneath me, he grunted. "I told you, not tonight."

Barely breathing, I shifted just enough so my knee pressed against the crotch of his black jeans. It could've been taken as a threat, but it switched into a beg the moment I rubbed my knee against his thick length.

He jerked as if I'd electrocuted him. "Lori...you have to stop."

Licking my lips, I looked at the skull over his mouth. "I'll stop if you take off your mask."

He shook his head, his dark eyes flashing. "I can't."

"Why?"

"I told you." His other hand that clutched the couch came up and gently unwound my fingers from the material of his scarf. I couldn't fight him as he pried my grip open, then captured both my wrists and held me almost levitating over him.

I let him hold my weight.

My gaze danced from his eyes to his mask and back again.

He started to shake the longer he held me up, and I allowed that same vixen who'd jumped on the back of Zander's bike to be stupidly brave. Dropping my hips, I kicked my legs out and sprawled on top of him.

A guttural groan escaped him as my core pressed to his cock. My softness to his hardness. Energy zinged between us, binding us together with a volt of need.

The part of his face I could see etched with torment. "You're determined to give me a heart attack tonight."

"Not if you answer three questions."

He quirked his pierced eyebrow, his fingers lashing around my wrists. "What three questions?"

I balled my hands where they lay on his chest between us. "I don't need to know your name or where you live or who you truly are. All I need to know is if I'm safe to—"

"Of *course* you're safe. I might keep my identity secret, but I would never—"

"X...be quiet."

He huffed but fell silent.

"What I was going to say is...if I'm safe to let my crush become more, too."

His dark brown eyes flared, full of hunger.

"Question number one." I licked my lips and forced my voice not to turn breathless with how much I wanted him. How much his surrender turned me on all while knowing he had the power to throw me across the room if he wanted.

He was stronger than Milton, bigger than Milton, yet he was better than him in every way because he would *never* use that strength against me. He'd rather let me trap him on the couch and submit to my torturing than do anything to make me afraid.

"Have you told anyone about me?"

He stilled. "Why do you want to know that?"

"Just answer me. Yes or no?"

He shifted a little, arching his hips and pressing against me.

We both sucked in a shaky breath.

Finally, he nodded. "Yes. I've told someone about you."

"Everything? Including the hidden identity?"

"Yes."

"And what do they think about this...arrangement of ours?"

"He thinks I'm in way over my head because I've never been good at keeping my feelings in check, and he knows exactly how I feel about you."

"How do you feel about me?"

"Next question."

I laughed under my breath. "If you keep avoiding that one, I'll start thinking you're in love with me."

He groaned. "Can't you leave a man with a little self-respect?"

"Not while I'm trying to determine the type of man he is without knowing his name or appearance."

"Would it help if I said you're similar to the friend I told? That you both drive me crazy because I can never lie, and you're far too smart for your own good?"

I preened. "I think I'd get along with whoever this person is."

"Between the two of you, you're definitely driving me into an early grave."

"Okay, second question." I kissed his nose, the cotton of his mask fuzzy against my lips. "Why did you decide to help me? Why go out of your way to put up with my nightmares, my panic attacks, and all the other baggage I've been dragging around? And don't give me a generic reply because we both know what you're doing is not normal. You're not getting anything in return and—"

"Who says I'm not getting anything in return?" He arched his hips again, deliberately scorching me with his erection.

My heart rate skipped and tripped.

Clearing his throat, he said softly, "I think I've already told you that I'm borderline obsessive about helping people. It gives me purpose. It—"

"Yes but why? *Why* do you have to help? Doesn't it cost you to care so much about others?"

"It does, but...I've always been wired that way." His voice lowered to a gravelly whisper. "I was born with it. I've always been fascinated with blood and organs and how bones—" He cut himself off, searching my face. "I sound like a serial killer. No wonder you just tensed."

I forced a laugh. "It's fine. Continue."

He sighed. "I just mean I like knowing how things work. One of my favourite toys as a kid was a plastic skeleton that my dad bought me one Christmas where you build the ribcage with all the organs and then snap on muscle, skin, and clothes." His vision focused on the past. "When my dad got sick, I tried to figure out what went wrong so I could fix him. I was so sure I would be able to, but when I lost him, I had my first taste of powerlessness. I think that's why I had to help you." He focused on me again. "After what that bastard did to you, you felt that same powerlessness, and…I know the feeling. I feel it too often when I lose a patient and—" His eyes shot wide. "I mean—"

"So you're a doctor? I thought you sounded like one in your messages—"

"No, I'm a, eh, I'm a vet. I meant animal patient." He scrambled higher up the armrest, giving up when I kept him pinned. His eyes crinkled with a mask-hidden smirk. "Why else do you think your cat loves me so much? He can sense that I help his kind."

"Crap, Peng." Glancing around the living room, I panicked that we'd squashed the poor kitten. "Where is that ginger furball?"

Hearing his name, Peng trotted from the kitchen, licking his lips from enjoying a snack.

"There you are, you little rascal."

Sitting primly on the living room threshold, he washed his paws.

"Seeing as you won't release me until you've finished your inquisition, what's your third question so I can go?" X grumbled, dragging my attention back to him.

I fumbled for something to ask. I didn't really have three questions. I'd just wanted to talk. To see if we could hold a conversation in person as easily as we could via text.

A small part of me hoped the chemistry we shared would fade the longer we spoke. I needed something to stop my heart from dancing around him because I wasn't ready for my crush to become something more. I definitely wasn't prepared to develop feelings for a masked stranger all while the crush from my teenage days returned for my handsome neighbour.

I needed time.

I needed to be alone for a while so I could be whole by myself and not because a man patched up the holes I couldn't.

But…X had successfully thrown me into a whirlpool of confusion.

"Um…third question." I pursed my lips, thinking. "You said you live alone. Would you take me to your house sometime?"

He stiffened. "No."

"Never?"

"Never is a long word."

"I've thought of a better question."

"Four wasn't in our contract."

I smiled. "Neither was three. But I asked anyway." Stretching over him, I brushed my lips against his ear. "My fourth question is…if you won't let me feed you cake as a thank you…can I do something else instead?"

His muscles turned to granite. "I told you, you don't have to thank—"

"I get the feeling you're not good at accepting appreciation."

"It's not that, it's just—"

"Tell me, X, does anyone look after you as well as you look after everyone else?"

He added a layer of ice to his granite. "No. I mean, yes. I mean—"

"How long has it been since someone did for you what you did for me last night?"

He groaned, long and low and deep. "Lori...you've got to stop. I'm begging you."

"Do you know the acronym of fear?"

His eyebrows shot up. "What?"

I grinned at how he struggled with my subject change. "I stumbled on a psychology website one night when I couldn't sleep. I was searching for ways to break out of my terror, and it said fear can be broken into an acronym. Fantasised Experiences Appearing Real." I rolled my eyes. "Of course, Milton was very much real and despite my fading bruises, I will carry the scars of that night for the rest of my life. However...everything else? The cracking of the walls as they cool. The shadows I see out the corner of my eye. The anxiety I feel about him coming back or being hurt again...those aren't real. Those are simply echoes of the past and as long as I learn to let go and not let my panic consume me...they can't hurt me."

"W-What are you saying?"

"I'm saying, I respect your decision not to sleep with me. And I'll always be grateful that you broke my self-imposed barrier over being able to climax. But...just like you have to help others, I have to repay that help. Call it good manners or the polite thing to do, but I need to thank you, X, and so...you have two choices."

He sucked in a heavy breath. "What two choices?"

"I took advantage of you the other night. It was manipulative and I still feel bad. So...you either eat the cake, or I give you an orgasm. How you accept my gratitude is entirely your choice. But you're not leaving until this debt is settled."

Thirty-Four

Zander

Self-Control Only Goes So Far

I WASN'T JUST GOING TO HELL. I was there.

I had literally everything I had ever wanted. I had the woman I'd spied on for years offering to make me come. I had the girl I'd crushed on since I was a boy wanting to *know* me.

And the only reason she was in my arms was because everything I'd told her was a lie.

A lie just waiting to blow up my life and leave me in pieces.

God, *no one* had ever asked to take care of me.

Not my family.

Not my sisters.

I was the one who called to check in on them.

I was the one who booked the funerals for our grandparents and handled the estate. I was the one my grandparents made the executor because, all my life, I'd gone out of my way to prove I was dependable, trustworthy, and could fix any problem—medically or otherwise, even though I was a fraud some days.

Like I told Lori, I'd been born wanting to save lives, but it'd taken losing my dad to turn that calling into OCD. I still felt guilty, even now. Still believed if I'd been older or read more textbooks or had a little more time, I could've become the doctor he needed to survive.

When he died, I promised myself I would never let anyone down again.

I'd gotten so good at keeping that promise that no one asked about the toll it took on me.

Fuck, *I* hadn't even noticed.

Until her.

Until I'd sat in my empty house tonight, staring at my single plate, sinking beneath a crush of loneliness that came with decades of denial. I'd given Sailor a ride today because she needed it, and I'd let her go because she couldn't be around me without bad memories, but those couple of hours we'd spent together without a mask, without my lies, had successfully cracked my façade and left me with a yearning that felt like a goddamn dagger in my gut.

And now this motherfucking alter ego had everything I ever wanted.

A skull-masked wannabe Superman got the girl, which was exactly how all those comic books went. Clark Kent never got the girl. He got to stand by while Lois Lane threw herself at the version of himself he wished he could be.

Hot anger roared through me.

Frustration that I hadn't had the balls to reach out and take what I wanted when I had the chance. If I'd asked Sailor out the day she'd moved in with Melody, perhaps she would never have been hurt by Milton, and I would've been able to let down my guard to let her care for me.

She wouldn't have turned down my invitation tonight or be so blatantly brave toward a stranger in a mask. Her forwardness toward X and her fear of me as Zander absolutely butchered me. Would she be this willing with other men when X vanished from her life? Fuck, the thought of her being this free with someone else didn't just butcher me, it *slaughtered* me.

I-I don't know how much longer I can keep up this act.

"Your thoughts are very loud, but you're not speaking," Sailor murmured, her wrists so delicate and fragile in my hold.

I flexed my fingers, testing her. She didn't look afraid. She didn't fight to escape or show any signs that me holding her sent her into dark places. If Zander held her like this, she'd be screaming, and *fuck* that hurt.

Christ, it *broke* me.

Because I wanted so, so badly to accept what she was offering. I wanted to be a selfish asshole. I wanted to demand her to get on her knees and make me come.

But I couldn't.

Because I wasn't that guy.

I'd *never* been that guy.

But tonight, I desperately wanted to be different.

But if I was, I'd ruin any chance of winning her when the mask came off and my glasses went back on and *fuck*!

In a burst of rage, I swooped to my feet and swung her off me.

Keeping her wrists trapped, I bent with her, depositing her on the couch with her hands bound by mine. She sucked in a breath as my face loomed over hers. So close. Too close. It would be so easy to kiss her. Just a drop of my chin and—

You're wearing a mask.

Fuck, I had to get out of here.

Letting her go, I kicked the coffee table out of the way and raked both hands through my hair. The clunk of my boot against wood and the clank of spoons in bowls made her flinch.

And for the first time in my life, I didn't have the capacity to check in with her. I had no strength to sit beside her, wrap her in a nurturing hug, and beg for her forgiveness.

I-I'm done.

Dropping my hands, I marched toward the kitchen.

Peng meowed where he sat having a bath.

That damn cat had almost gotten me discovered tonight. When she'd called me Zander, my heart literally stopped. And I did mean literally. Only pure terror defibbed it again.

How I'd managed to stay still and not buckle to the floor was a testament to all those days I'd lost the battle helping someone and had to put on a stoic façade to give the news to the families I'd failed.

My pulse still hadn't calmed down.

I kept waiting for her to say she knew it was me all along.

My slip about losing patients, then lying that I was a vet. The fact that Peng recognised me as the guy who rescued him? Christ, he was as bad as his mistress in wanting to show his gratitude. I could barely claw the creature off me.

I mean...come on!

She was smart, wasn't she?

Had she guessed who I was and played me right back, or was Colin correct in that different eye and hair colour truly could trick a person into believing what was right before their very nose?

What did I have to do to make her guess?

Because if she guessed and still wanted me, then all my problems disappeared.

I could stay here.

I could be with her.

I'd know once and for all that I wouldn't lose her if I came clean, but no way could I take that risk on my own. No way was I brave enough to tear off my mask and reveal who I was without knowing if she'd accept me first.

I didn't want to move to Australia.

But I didn't want to lose her more.

Sailor tapped my shoulder.

I spun around, cursing the damn kitten for not getting out of the way and my own mind for tangling with thoughts. "What?" I barked.

She rocked backward on her heels. "D-Did I say something wrong?"

Any other night, I would apologise. I would be the gentleman, the guardian—the friendly neighbourhood stalker who'd signed up to take on all her pain so she could breathe a little easier.

But I was goddamn suffocating and no longer had the capacity to breathe for myself, let alone her. "I'm sorry, but...I have to go. I-I can't do this anymore."

Colour bled out of her face. "No, don't leave. I didn't mean to pressure you. I just...I loved being with you last night and-and I wanted to—"

"I get it." I stepped over Peng and entered the kitchen. "I enjoyed it too. But it's best we stop before either of us gets hurt."

Sailor chased, cutting in front of me and whacking her palm on my chest. "Please, don't go." Tears welled in her eyes.

Ah, fuck.

My shoulders slouched.

All my self-directed rage sizzled out as if her tears were a bucket of water on a forest fire. Taking a step into her, I grabbed her around her nape and pressed her against me like I had the first time I'd broken in and found her screaming from a nightmare.

She stiffened as I wrapped my arms around her and embraced her close.

Sighing heavily, I pressed my mask-covered lips to her hair. "I'm sorry for upsetting you. I didn't mean to explode like that. That isn't me. I'm not that guy. I think...I think you're drawing out a lot of suppressed emotions, and I have no right to take them out on you." Kissing her through my mask, I pulled back and cupped her cheeks. "I didn't mean to scare you, Lori. Like I've said countless times, I will *never* hurt you, even if I'm in a bit of a mood."

A single tear streaked her porcelain skin.

I rubbed it with my thumb. "Forgive me?"

Her fingers wrapped hesitantly around my wrists, burning me with electrical currents.

"Forgiven." Sniffing, she gave a watery smile. "But you're only proving my point that you've done whatever it takes to help me, but you haven't let *me* help *you*." Fierce determination filled her pretty face. "I wouldn't be a good friend if I let you walk out like this. You're the one hurting tonight, X. Not me. What will it take to let me take care of you?"

I went to pull away.

She dug her fingernails into my wrists. Her gaze dropped to my mask and her lips quirked into a sad little smile. "What would it take to let me kiss you, just once?"

My body flatlined.

My heart went berserk.

Highly inappropriate humour made me reply, "General anaesthesia would probably do the trick."

She didn't respond for a second, but then a soft laugh escaped. "You're saying if I found some chloroform and knocked you out, I could have my wicked way with you?"

Rolling my wrists to remove her grip, I shrugged. "I wouldn't be able to say no, would I?"

"Alright." She let me go and crossed her arms with a nod. "Nana taught me how to make a few sleeping tinctures. It might take a few hours to kick in, but if you drank an entire vial, you would be drowsy enough for me to take advantage."

I sagged against the doorframe between the living room and kitchen. "It wouldn't be taking advantage, believe me."

"Then why don't you let me help?" Her gaze dropped to my jeans where my erection hadn't gone down despite the mess of my heart. "Why are you being so stubborn about this?" She stomped her foot adorably, reminding me of a younger version of her when I'd called her Lori and pulled her pigtails.

God, even those memories hurt.

"How about you box up my dessert, and I'll go? I'll accept your thank-you in the form of sugar."

"Unfortunately, that choice is no longer available." She pouted. "The ice cream has melted and ruined it."

Arching my chin at the rest of the cake on the countertop, I smirked. "No problem. I'll just have a piece of that instead."

"Tell you what…" She moved toward the cake in question and picked up the knife she'd used to slice two pieces. "I'll serve you another *if* you eat it here."

I sighed heavily and pointed at my mask. "And we've circled back to the fact that I can't eat and I'm not taking this off."

"I agree, that is an issue. But I think I've figured out a solution to that little problem."

My eyebrows knitted together, the squeeze-on fake piercing tugging uncomfortably. "You have? How?"

Flashing me a smile, she tossed the knife back down. "Wait there." Darting from the kitchen, she headed toward the back of the house where the laundry matched the floorplan of my place. Unlike mine, where I'd installed a drying rack that came down from the ceiling and tucked away all the machines in slim-line cupboards, Sailor's was cramped with bamboo shelving holding copious amounts of creams and concoctions thanks to Melody's business.

She came back with something colourful in her hand.

I eyed her suspiciously as she dropped the item on the countertop. "Ta-da!"

Plucking the black silk ribbon, I hefted the surprisingly heavy eye mask. A motif of a butterfly with its two wings spread out to cover someone's eyes glimmered with iridescent purples, blues, and blacks. "I'm confused."

Taking it from me, she rubbed the thick padding. "Nana imported a bunch of these to sell with her essential oil blends. The interior is filled with absorbent micro beads that hold the scent of lavender for sleeping or peppermint for headaches. It also entirely blocks out light and vision. You can't see a damn thing with it on."

I stiffened. "Y-You're suggesting to blindfold yourself?"

"I am." She swung the eye mask around on its silk ribbons. "With the way the beads mould, I swear I won't be able to see anything. I'll wear it the entire time you eat. I promise I won't remove it until you say I can. Once you've enjoyed your thank-you gift, you don't have to rush away. We can talk or listen to music or...make out."

And there it was.

My limit.

I finally found the point where I turned into an asshole.

Snatching the eye mask, I stepped into her personal space. "Turn around."

She swallowed hard, her blue gaze flaring before she nodded and obeyed.

Reaching around her, I positioned the butterfly wings above her nose and rasped, "Hold it over your eyes."

Without a word, she did as she was told, gently pressing the beads to form a barrier over her sight. Once she found a comfortable shape, I tied a knot at the back of her head. My hands shook as I spun her around to face me. She swayed a little; my fingers dug into her shoulders, keeping her still.

Vestiges of the doctor who would never put someone's mental health at risk for his own gain had to ask, "Are you okay? Is this alright? You sure this isn't too much, too soon?"

Licking her lips—her tongue driving me motherfucking crazy—she nodded. "I'm okay. I trust you."

I caught her chin and held her all while my heart pounded so fast my blood turned to ash. "You really shouldn't."

She trembled a little and placed a hand over my thundering heart. "I know you won't hurt me."

"Not intentionally, no."

"And it's because of that honesty that I know you won't hurt me, even *un*intentionally."

I nudged her nose with mine. "It's inevitable if we keep doing this." My mask blocked our skin from touching. Fear about removing it clenched my gut. What if she could see? What if this was a ruse and I was falling for it, all because I couldn't fight her anymore?

"I should walk out that door and never see you again," I grunted, grazing my mouth over hers, the cotton keeping us chaste.

"You could…" She sucked in a breath at how close I was. "But I'd really rather you stayed."

"Because you think there's a debt between us?"

"Because you helped me, and I want to help you."

Help.

God that word could mean so much.

My head swam. My self-control quickly eroded with every chug of my pulse. With her willingly blinded and surrendered and trusting and *mine*…the pieces of me that clung to right and wrong, good over bad, cracked, broke, and shattered.

"I'm sorry," I breathed just as my hands locked around her hips and marched her backward.

She squeaked as I manhandled her to the wall beside the fridge. "Sorry for what?"

I fought my quaking as I yanked my mask down, cupped her cheeks, and trapped her with my body. "For this."

And then, I lowered my head, tipped up her chin, and kissed her.

The second my lips claimed hers, the box TV in the living room turned on, hissing with static and snow. Peng meowed. The curtains fluttered. And a bolt of lightning shot from my heart to Sailor's.

We both groaned.

Her hands flew up to fist in my hair.

Mine shifted to the back of her head, cradling her so I could kiss her as hard as I wanted.

I didn't stop to make sure she was okay.

I *couldn't* stop.

The protective part of me drowned beneath a possessive asshole who wasn't satisfied with a simple kiss.

It wasn't enough.

It would never be enough because I wanted goddamn *everything.*

Licking the seam of her lips, I plunged my tongue into her chocolate-flavoured mouth.

Sagging against me, she yanked my hair, demanding harder.

I delivered.

We became as unhinged as the other, our heads dancing, tongues knotting, lips wide, and breath ragged.

My hands dropped from her nape to her waist.

Not breaking the kiss, I shoved her up the wall and groaned as she wrapped her legs around my hips, connecting us, punishing us.

Grinding against her, the kiss turned demonic as we fought a war of lust, tripping straight into violence with every lash of our tongues.

I lost myself to her, to her kiss, to her power.

My hips surged up, rocking, needing.

The release I'd given myself roared back into agony. It burned through me, deleting all rationality, turning me inhuman.

I couldn't do it anymore.

Couldn't fight *instinct* anymore.

Gathering her into my arms, I carried her into the living room. Wrenching my mouth from hers, I kicked away the coffee table, dumped her unceremoniously on the couch, then blanketed her with my body.

The TV kept hissing, the cat stopped meowing, and the breeze that shouldn't exist rippled over my arms.

I fell on her and kissed her with years of pent-up longing, decades of agonising desire, and lifetimes of denial.

And she kissed me back.

Lick for lick, bite for bite.

Our teeth clacked. Our noses bumped. I'd never kissed someone this deeply or madly before.

And I didn't want to stop.

I want more.

Keeping one hand on her waist pinning her to the couch, I used my other to stroke down her body. She arched and quivered as my fingers drew a path of fire between us.

I had no capacity to ask for permission.

I'd gone past the point of sanity.

My fingers found her flat stomach; they burrowed down the front of her tantalising short shorts. My eyes flared wide as I found hot wetness instead of underwear. Angling my wrist, I plunged my tongue into her mouth just as I plunged a finger into her pussy.

She went bowstring tight beneath me. Quivering, gasping.

I had just enough brain cells to grunt against her lips, "Tell me to stop, and I stop."

With a savage little cry, she scratched her fingernails over my scalp and jerked me back to her mouth again. Her legs flopped wide in blatant invitation, the tightness of her shorts trying to cut off the circulation to my hand as I added a second finger and rode her.

I didn't go slow like last time.

I'd learned what she liked.

I'd gone to school in the dark of her bedroom and understood that a girl like Sailor—a girl who'd been hurt and lived alone and spent most of her life being responsible for her own well-being—couldn't find pleasure if she had time to think about it.

Her worries had snuck in that night. Her whirling mind had been loud enough for me to hear her fears of what she should and shouldn't do. How she should behave versus letting go.

Milton had tried to kill everything about this woman from her strength to her self-worth, and I had no intention of letting her second-guess her own power.

Kissing her as hard as I could, I pressed my thumb against her clit and thrust.

She screamed into my mouth then turned into a creature I could barely hold without being seriously mauled. Her teeth clamped onto my bottom lip as I thrust inside her.

She clutched my arm, feeling every muscle I used to penetrate her again and again.

Last night, she'd fought a long journey to reach that pinnacle of falling.

Tonight, she started coming before I'd had my fill.

Wait...

Moving my bulk, I went to pull her shorts down so I could taste her again. Only her fingers locked in my hair and dragged me back.

She kissed me like a hellcat, forcing me to give up my attempt at licking her.

I settled for my hand instead.

The blindfold stopped me from seeing the shock and unravelling of her orgasm in her eyes. Her mouth opened wide beneath mine, and I took full advantage as her core went tight around my fingers, then detonated outward with waves of powerful clenches.

Her moans turned to whimpers the longer her release lasted until finally she shuddered, hiccupped, and pulled away from our kiss. "Stop, I'm...it's too sensitive."

My fingers stilled immediately. My thumb released the pressure on her clit.

She melted into a puddle beneath me on the couch, sweat misting her face, a single droplet glittering in the hollow of her collarbone.

Bending my head, I licked and nipped my way down her throat, coating her in goosebumps until I reached that salty drop and claimed it for my own.

Neither of us spoke.

I didn't think we could converse in words anymore.

The longer we lay there, sweaty and sex-crazed, the more I noticed I was paralysed from the waist down. The blood-burning, nerve-slicing, bone-crippling need to come hijacked my ability to move.

Shit.

Stretching beneath me, growing drowsy from her climax, Sailor stupidly brushed against my throbbing cock.

I made a noise I wasn't proud of. Something tortured and dying, guttural and animalistic.

She froze.

Her hand went to the eye mask as if to tear it off.

I fumbled for my skull scarf, trying to wrench it over my mouth and nose, but…she sucked in a breath and lowered her hand, staying blindfolded.

Sinking her teeth into her bottom lip, she wriggled a little beneath me. "That's two debts I owe you now."

Her leg shifted, pressing against my cock again.

My teeth snapped together. My body burned with catastrophic agony.

Forcing myself to override the paralysing torment in my lower half, I swung my legs off the couch and sat up. My head swam. I clutched my temples, instantly regretting that decision because all I could smell was Sailor on my fingers. All I could see was her glistening desire.

My stomach clenched. My thighs hardened. My cock threatened to come without any other stimulation.

"I, uh…" My voice resembled a canyon after a landslide. "I have to go."

"No!" Snapping upright, she fumbled for me. Readjusting her illegally short shorts, she kneeled beside me and traced her fingers from my face down my chest.

Her lips were wet from our kiss, and her breath came in short little pants.

With her eyes blindfolded, she looked far too young, far too innocent for the sort of thoughts colliding in my sickly savage brain.

"Consider the debt cleared, Lori." I clamped a hand on her shoulder, preventing her from coming closer. "I took the gift I wanted. Having you unravel for me is the best kind of thank you. And I, *ughhhh*—"

All the air in my body gushed out as her hand slid down my t-shirt-covered belly and found my overheated erection.

"Ah, fuck." My eyesight went black. My legs went numb. I couldn't do a damn thing to stop her from unbuckling my belt, unzipping my jeans, and sneaking her tiny hand into my boxer-briefs.

The second her fingers found me, I thrust into her palm and made a pitiful noise. Not quite a grunt, not quite a groan. A beg really. A motherfucking beg to cure me before I died of heart failure right there on her couch.

Her fingers wrapped tighter around me, her thumb pressing against the top of my slick crown.

I had precisely two point two seconds to do the right thing.

With a shaking hand that barely functioned, I grabbed her around the wrist and stopped her first jerk.

"*Wait*," I strangled.

She shook her head, her blonde hair messy, the blindfold cutting around her head with a band of black silk. "Let me take care of you. I can hear how much pain you're in."

"I-I'm fine." Pulling her arm, I tried to be gentle all while fighting the highly aggressive beast within. The beast who wanted to wrap his fingers around hers and teach her how I liked it.

How to squeeze me. Pump me. Make me come.

"I can't." With a burst of strength, I tore her fingers off me and pushed her back. "I'm sorry for manhandling you so roughly, but I really can't let you—"

"Yes, you can. I want to. Can't you see I'm not doing this out of obligation, X. I *want to*." With a frustrated curse, she fell back over me, her hand blindly searching for my cock. It arrowed straight up, begging her to find it. Having her sightless and eager, knowing she couldn't see me or the state she'd put me in?

Fuck, it made me want to fist her hair and guide her face to my lap. To guide her to the part of me she seemed to need and surrender every shred of power I had left directly into her deliciously hot mouth.

But as much as I feared I would have an aneurysm if I didn't come soon, I couldn't do that to her. I couldn't be that selfish because when the day came that she found out it was me hiding behind this mask, I would never be able to look at her again.

The guilt would eat me alive.

Grabbing her chin between my arousal-coated fingers, I held her firm. "I'm going to go." With my other hand, I tried to tuck myself away.

Every nudge against my swollen flesh hurt.

Shit, it hurt.

Her fingers lashed out and found me, making me sag and stiffen at the same time. She tranquilised me. With a single touch, she shackled me to that couch, and all my good intentions flew out the goddamn window.

"Just once, okay? I just...if I can't see you, I want to hear you." She shrugged sadly. "I just want to take care of you the way you took care of me. It's not affecting my mental health. I'm fully here with you, aware and willing and happy. I'm *happy*, X. I feel powerful and sexy, and I really, really want to do this for you." Sucking in a breath, she stopped breaking me and crucified me instead. "Please?"

I couldn't speak.

I merely let go and leaned back.

With a heavy groan, I spread my legs and let my head fall.

Her lips tipped into a sinful smile, the butterfly mask over her eyes keeping her blind as she scooted a little closer on her knees and fisted me hesitantly. "That's more like it."

I chuckled-coughed-choked.

And then I cried out like a pubescent teen as her fingers looped tighter, somehow finding the perfect pressure.

My eyes rolled back in my head. "I'm telling you now, I'm going to severely embarrass myself."

"As long as it feels good for you, I don't care."

"Everything about you feels good," I whispered, my tongue almost slurring as if I was drunk. "After tasting you yesterday, I had no choice but to service myself. You were in my nose, my mouth, my heart."

My voice cut off as she stroked me, long and slow.

It was torturous.

Forcing words to form, I added, "I came in a few strokes. So it's really *me* who should be thanking *you*." I groaned mid-sentence, my breath coming fast and shallow as she pumped me again. "I haven't felt a release that explosive in a really long time."

"Do you think this one will be better than that one?"

"Uh-huh." I nodded, unable to speak like a normal person. "Y-You're going to break me. I can...*Christ*—" I suffered a full-body spasm. "I can already feel it."

"Good." Her hand pulsed, squeezing around me as she pressed down then came back up.

I almost passed out.

My hands balled into fists by my thighs. My legs turned to stone. My heart smoked with speed. And all I could focus on was what she did to me. The way her thumb swirled at the top and pressed down. The way her fingers gripped and jerked.

I lost track of time and space and sanity as she returned the favour by shoving me up a rocky, agonising hill and held me poised and panting at the top.

"S—Lori." My teeth pulled back as I snarled at the ceiling. "Fuck, please—"

Her hand came down, grinding to my base.

I lost it.

I didn't just come, I ruptured.

Supernova pain quaked between my legs and shot along every nerve ending of my cock. My stomach cramped. My bones broke. I snarled as the first ripple exploded, followed by another and another and *another*.

Ribbons of white spurted up my black t-shirt as she followed my body's natural rhythm and milked me. She didn't stop and when the end came with a blanket of sensitivity and sweetest agony, I snatched her wrist and stilled her. "Enough. I..." I sucked in a shallow breath. "I-I'm done."

With a sultry smile, she let me go and held up her fingers. "Tell me, X...do I need to wash my hand? I can't see after all."

A shocked chuckle interrupted my attempt at catching air. Translucent liquid roped between her fingers, marking her completely as mine.

Without a word, I tucked myself away, buckled and zipped, then threaded my fingers with hers. Her wet ones merged with my dry ones, combining our arousal. Sifting my other hand through her hair, careful not to undo her blindfold, I tugged her close and kissed her.

Our lips pressed, parted, and joined.

Our tongues hunted, found, and tangled.

We kissed with our palms joined and fingers knotted, and I'd never been so at peace or so fucking broken.

I wasn't just falling for this girl.

I'd fallen.

And I was petrified of losing something I'd never had.

This was the last time.

You can't do this again.

Breaking the kiss, I nudged her to recline against the armrest and stood on shaky legs. Peng instantly trotted toward me, his mangled whiskers bristling with judgement.

I gave him a glower not to interfere, then bent over Sailor and pressed a lingering kiss on her forehead. "Keep the blindfold on until you hear the door close."

She tried to grab me, but I swooped back too fast. "Don't go yet. You don't have to rush off."

"Believe me. I do." I rubbed at my aching chest. "If I don't leave now, I'll never go."

Her breath hitched. "See? You can't say things like that and then vanish."

I didn't reply.

The heavy footfalls of my boots gave away my exit and her shoulders sagged. "At least take the cake with you. If you don't, I'll door-knock every house in this town until I find you."

With her threat biting holes in my soul, I stole the cake, opened the back door, and disappeared into the night.

Thirty-Five

Sailor

Build Your Wings

"HERE. OLD MAN ROGER WAS SELLING his garden ornaments again. The second I saw this, I knew I had to buy it for you."

Looking up from where I replenished the stock of vanilla and coconut lip balm on my market table, I grinned at Lily. She'd had two open homes this morning so hadn't been able to be my helper until noon. But then she'd arrived in a fluster and instead of letting her trade her prim blazer for country pinafore, I'd marched her out of my stall and told her to go find some lunch and calm down.

"I told you to eat, not buy me gifts." I accepted the yellow-tissue-wrapped object, thinking of someone else who had a habit of gifting me things. Someone I'd barely heard from in four days. Someone who'd gone from being open and honest, to closed and monosyllabic in his messages.

Scooting between the two tables laden with homemade creams and essential oil blends, Lily joined me beneath the square tent that offered shade but no reprieve from the hot afternoon sun. "I did eat, but then I saw this and couldn't help myself."

I spoke my thoughts before I censored them. "You sound like someone else who gives without thinking."

"Oh?" She winked. "Do tell. Is it that mystery person who gave you a care parcel of things you make yourself? Because you still haven't spilled what you're hiding by the way, and don't think for a moment I believe you."

I blushed and fumbled with the tissue paper. "I have no idea what you're talking about."

"You know *exactly* what I'm talking about." Slipping her blazer off and trading it for an apron, she looked about as hot as I was. She eyed me with a familiar smirk. "In fact, you look much better these days, and it's not just because your bruises are almost gone."

I glanced at my arms.

She was right. My injuries had faded enough to look as if my skin was dirty not beaten. It'd allowed me to skip the jeans and jumper, and I'd chosen to wear a black linen dress that hinted at my skinny curves before skimming to my jewelled bronze sandals. The lingering greens and browns on my arms could be mistaken for soil smudges from working in the garden which worked with my business name, so I made no move to cover up.

Undoing the cellotape on the present Lily gave me, I pretended to be far too focused to talk.

Coming here this morning hadn't been easy.

Dealing with the first early-bird customers on my own had scratched at my still-there panic. But as the sun slowly crept higher in the sky and stragglers turned to crowds and familiar sellers all waved and shared hellos, I managed to embrace yet another piece of myself that I'd lost.

Everything was getting better. However, I hadn't heard from X today, and his disappearance made every part of my stupid body ache. He hadn't been the one to bruise me, but my God, he'd left wounds thanks to his kindness, consideration, and insane skills at making me come apart.

Somehow, he'd become important to me. Incredibly important and for him to just cease communication after what we'd done the other night?

It hurt even worse than being strangled.

Is he in the crowd?

Is he close by?

My fingers itched to message him, but I forced myself to focus and unwrapped Lily's gift. A wooden plaque, meant to hang on a garden fence, appeared beneath the final layer of tissue paper. The hand carved angel wings in the corners added a cute border to the words in the centre.

FIRST YOU JUMP OFF THE CLIFF AND THEN YOU
BUILD YOUR WINGS ON THE WAY DOWN.
Ray Bradbury

"Oh wow…" Tears pricked my eyes. "Ah, Lils, it's—"

"I know, isn't it perfect!" She bounced toward me and wrapped her arms around my waist. "It's exactly how I feel every time you smile and move on with your life." Her hands landed on my shoulder blades as if groping for non-existent wings. "I'm so proud of you, Sailor Moon. So in awe of you that you never let him win. Seeing you renovate that house to become yours? Seeing you continue running your business? Seeing you smile again? Ahh!" She kissed my cheek and whirled me around, making a few customers waiting to be served laugh. "I love you, girl. You jumped off that fear-filled cliff by going back to the very same house he hurt you in and you've been rebuilding your wings ever since. You're one feather away from soaring to the stars!"

I hugged her back. "It's only because I have you that I can be so brave."

And him.

Because of X, I'd healed far, far quicker than I would have, and as grateful as I was for my best-friend, my thriving business, and the freshly painted living room that I'd spent the past three days turning white, my heart panged with loss.

"Thank you so much, Lily. I absolutely love it. I'm going to hang it on the deck where I can see it out the kitchen window."

Letting me go, she glanced at the short line that'd formed. "I know we have to get to work, and now isn't the time to gossip, but...I really do want to know what's been going on with you. And don't say there isn't something because we both know there is, and I'm going to get it out of you, one way or another."

I sagged in mock defeat. "Fine. We're overdue a catch-up, anyway. I'll permit you to try to pry my secrets out of me."

"That's my girl." Tying on her apron, she said, "Fancy a movie on Monday night? I have a few evening open homes tomorrow, but we could go for dinner on Monday. Perhaps a quick drink, then hit the moving pictures?"

"Sure, sounds good."

With a wink, she turned to serve the young man bouncing a toddler on his hip. "What can I help you with today?"

I really ought to move beside her and take the next in line, but I hadn't been able to settle all morning. Taking Lily's amazing plaque to the back of the tent where we kept our personal items, I placed it carefully beside my petty change wallet and whipped my burner phone out.

Are you watching me today, or are you busy with the life you refuse to tell me about?

I pursed my lips and stared at my message. I didn't like my tone. It almost sounded passive-aggressive and that wasn't me. I'd been on the receiving end of that nonsense with Milton and never wanted to dish it out to others.

Ignore that. I didn't mean it. I'm just. In the rules of staying honest, I guess I'm a little sad that I've barely heard from you these past few days. I hate that you're the one who's completely in charge of this relationship. I have no way to stop you from fading away, just like I had no way of stopping you from barging into my life. I want to be mad about that, but...you taught me how to claim my life back, so I can't be. Not really. I'm glad you let me take care of you the other night. You always warned me this was temporary. I just didn't think it would hurt so much to say goodbye to someone who I never knew his name.

Sending the message, rubbing my cheeks to make sure Lily wouldn't see my tears, I turned off the phone and went back to work.

I sat in my pop's old car on my driveway, staring at the house that was slowly becoming mine. I'd made another online order for renovation supplies, and thanks to Pinterest, I'd found a few images of bright and airy living rooms that blended modern farm with cosy chic.

I'd already had the Salvation Army collect the furniture from the living room, so now Peng and I spent our evenings on cushions on the floor. Once I'd finished painting, I'd rip up the carpet and polish the floorboards.

The late afternoon sun promised a perfect balmy evening to spend reading in the garden or going for a swim in the local lake, but all I wanted was for a masked villain with a hero complex to appear uninvited in my house and kiss me.

Sighing heavily, I unbuckled and went to climb out of my car, but my phone finally pinged.

The chime I'd been waiting for all day.

My cheeks heated with how fast I launched myself at the passenger seat and snatched my handbag. Ripping my phone out, I pulled up the message thread.

I had to work, I'm so sorry, but I checked in on you using the video feed that the local fairgrounds have on their website. Your stall looked busy, and I'm glad you had your friend to help. I know I've been unfair the past few days.

> If I have to be honest, which I suppose I have to, thanks to that stupid clause, I wasn't prepared for how much this would affect me and...I'm not doing so good. No one has ever asked to take care of me before. I didn't think I needed anyone.
> But then you came along.

I kept scrolling, searching for more.
He couldn't end the message there.
What the hell?

You're speaking as if you've made up your mind never to see me again.

I held my breath, sitting in my car like a weirdo in front of my house. I pleaded with everything that he'd respond and—

> I didn't want to do this so soon, and I feel like I'm letting you down, but...I can't be your watcher anymore, Lori. You're healing. You'll be fine without me. I contacted you to help you breathe again, but now you're somehow stealing all my air.
> It's best for both of us to end this.

And if I don't want to end it?

> You're on the mend. I'm no longer needed.

But what about you? What do **you** need?

> It doesn't matter what I need. This was never about me. I'll keep watch in the distance and if you fumble, I'll make sure to send help your way, but you won't see me again.

So you're going to outsource my healing to someone else?

My teeth ground together as I added:

Don't you think that's a bit pompous? To think I'd even want your help after you've decided to break up with me without talking face to face?

No, we don't know that. How about you tell me who you are and let me decide. Just tell me the truth. Are you a convict? Did you do something bad in a past life? Do you have twenty children from ten marriages? What? Why are you so convinced that I won't accept you if I know who you are?

Goodbye, Lori.

A small cry escaped me as the final message glowed like a death sentence.

Tears tracked silently down my cheeks, half from anger, half from loss.

I wanted to message him back, begging him, threatening him, but in the end, I sent nothing at all.

On Monday, after attacking my house with sandpaper and paintbrushes all morning, I took a break to check the mail. I hated that my heart skittered with hope that X would've sent me another gift. That he'd message me and admit he wanted me. He'd tell me his name. He'd confess he wanted to be with me as much as I wanted to be with him, and we'd ride off into the sunset together.

But that was fiction and this was reality, and the fact was…I hadn't slept last night. I'd lived in twitchy anxiety, listening to my house cool, feeling the presence of my nana even though the TV didn't turn on.

I'd scolded her for that.

I'd sat in the dark with my wonderful kitten purring on my lap and told a ghost off, all because she'd turned the TV on the second X had kissed me. The curtains had fluttered, and the house seemed to sigh with relief as if it'd been holding its breath just waiting for that kiss.

I didn't appreciate her playing games with me or making it seem as if X had her approval from across the grave. He was a stranger. A liar by his own admission of non-admission.

I'd even blindfolded myself to make him feel safe, yet he hadn't let down his guard. He'd refused to sleep with me. I'd practically had to force him to let me take care of the agonising need in his voice.

Feeling him come had done something irrevocable to me. It'd

been the first time I'd felt true power over a man—not because I held his most vulnerable part but because of the way he'd surrendered to me. For a few precious moments, he'd given every piece of himself to me, and now he'd taken those pieces back and left me with nothing.

No face to remember.

No name to whisper.

He'd appeared like a ghost and vanished like one, and I flatly refused to be haunted by him any longer.

Stomping to the letterbox, I wrenched up the roof of the gingerbread house and scowled inside. A glint of flower-printed porcelain made me want to scream.

"Screw you, X. *Screw you*."

With anger-shaking hands, I scooped out my washed plate that used to hold a chocolate cake. A Post-it Note stuck to it.

THIS WAS DELICIOUS BUT NOT AS DELICIOUS
AS YOU. I KNOW I'VE MADE YOU HATE ME,
AND I HAVE NO RIGHT TO SAY THIS, BUT...
I CAN'T GET YOU OUT OF MY MIND. YOU DON'T
NEED ME ANYMORE AND, JUST AS I SUSPECTED,
I NEED YOU WITH EVERY FIBRE OF MY BEING.
I'M SORRY. FORGIVE ME. BE SAFE AND HAPPY.
X

"Everything okay?"

I jumped a foot and clutched the plate to my chest. "Zander." Squinting in the sun, I blinked back stinging tears. "Yes…yes, I'm fine. A-Are you?"

His face looked drawn and fatigued, his black-framed glasses ringing eyes full of sleepless shadows. Even his tall frame looked a little thinner and washed out as if he hadn't had a proper meal in weeks.

That reminds me. I still need to bake him a cake for giving me Peng.

"Not really." He shrugged. "But that's life."

"Is there anything I can help with?" Stepping toward him, I did my best to put aside my grief and anger over X. I also braced myself against Milton's awful voice, daring him to call me a slut for caring about Zander's well-being.

He was hurting for some reason. And I was his friend who should help.

I prepared to suffer through the phantom pain of my hair being ripped out or my body being kicked, but...nothing happened.

The only ache I felt was the one for my childhood friend who looked utterly exhausted.

"That's kind but no." He forced a smile, his eyes tightening as he looked at the plate in my arms. "I better let you go inside." His car pinged as it cooled down, hinting he'd just returned from work. With a sigh, he turned to walk up the pathway to his front door.

"Wait." My heart pinched at the thought of him leaving. I didn't like seeing him like this. So low, so...*un-him.* "Are you truly okay?"

His smile widened but didn't reach his eyes. "Of course. I should be the one asking you that." He cocked his head. "How are you doing with everything? Honestly?"

Honestly.

That word again.

I'd been brutally truthful with X, and while it'd been healing, it'd also left a wound inside me with his disappearance. Could I be brave enough to open myself that wide again? Did I have the strength to scare another man off with the truth?

Zander can't disappear.

I knew where he lived. I knew his name, his birthday, his star sign, and numerous other random facts that might not be true now that he was an adult. I knew more than I should about him as a teenage boy. I knew he didn't like breakfast and preferred older people to kids his own age. I knew he used to read a lot because I'd observed him devour book after book by torchlight when his grandparents thought he was asleep in bed.

I used to watch him from my window as I did the same, reading covertly when I'd been told to go to sleep. He never knew we shared a nightly ritual of reading together, but it was one of my favourite memories of coming here for visits.

So...tell him. Be his friend. He looks like he could use one.

"What books were you reading? When you were younger?"

"Excuse me?" He scowled as if utterly confused.

Stepping closer, I drank him in, my skin tingling with heat. "I used to read with you...by torchlight. You never knew that we had the same habit of not going to bed when we were told. I read fantasies and romance. I got pretty good at hiding my book and faking sleep if I heard anyone walk outside my bedroom. You did the same."

He balled his hands. "You watched me?"

"Hard not to when I had a crush on you."

He sagged and swiped a hand through his hair. He looked as if he'd say something. His jaw worked; his green eyes glowed. Tripping sideways, he took a step toward his house as if he needed to get away from me, but then he turned and marched in my direction.

The explosiveness of his steps. The almost angry look in his eyes. Self-preservation overrode common sense, and I reeled backward.

Goblin-Milton hissed in my ear. *"You're a tease, and teases get fucked, slut."*

I gasped and almost dropped the plate.

He wrenched to a stop, his gaze flaring. "Shit." Ripping his glasses off, he pinched the bridge of his nose and let out a heavy exhale. "Sorry. I didn't mean to scare you. I just—"

"I-It's fine. I'm fine." Breathing hard, I forced myself to stop being so stupid. "It's not you. Like I said, it's—"

"Go inside, Sailor," he snapped, putting his glasses back on. "Enough, okay? You don't have to make small talk with me. I don't expect you to be friendly with me. We're good." Lowering his chin, he watched me with terribly sad eyes. "I'm good with just being your neighbour, so stop forcing yourself to care about me when it's only making it harder for you to be around me."

A stabbing pain appeared right between my ribs. I hated seeing him so tired, so sad. I didn't know what he'd gone through at work or why he hurt, but...I felt responsible. He'd seen me jumping around him and watched me flee each time he approached me. He probably thought I hated his guts when nothing could be further from the truth.

Hugging the plate, I sucked in a breath and blurted, "I saw you...the day Milton attacked me. I didn't mean to look through your window, but I did, and he accused me of having an affair, and well...you know what he did." My voice turned wobbly. "I know you would never do anything to hurt me. I know that right to my soul. I know because I've seen you grow, and heard enough stories about you from Nana to know you're the best guy ever...I'm just...I'm having a hard time telling my nervous system that."

He couldn't look at me, keeping his gaze locked on the ground. "You don't have to tell me—"

"I do. I think...I think I've been quite blind the past few years and only just realising that you've been there all along. I know I've been cold to you and if I'm honest—which I'm doing my best to be—it was partly because Milton always made me feel uncomfortable if I spoke to you, but also because...I think...deep down...I knew I'd made a mistake. That I was looking for a way out the moment I started dating him and didn't know how to get free."

His eyes shot up. His throat flexed as he swallowed hard. "I would've gotten you out if you'd just told me. I would've done anything if it meant he didn't hurt you."

Tears stung. "I know you would've, and that's what kills me. I hate that I keep flinching around you. I'm getting better. So much better. I no longer feel the pain of what he did, and I can ignore what he said the more time I spend with you, but sometimes…I still fumble."

Going to him, I hid my flinch as he stepped away from me. "I just…I'm telling you this so you know it's not you I'm afraid of. It's the triggers from the past but they *are* fading, and I *am* getting better, and I want to be friends with you. I wasn't lying about that. Going for a ride with you helped me so much, and I hate seeing you so down."

You're doing what you did with X.

I was forcing my help onto a man who didn't want it. Begging him to let me care when all he wanted to do was get away from me.

That stabbing pain came again. I laughed at my stupidity. "Forget it. I didn't mean to come on so strong. It's super egotistical to think you're down because of me. You've probably had a shitty day at work, and it has nothing to do with—"

"Thank you." He cut me off with half a smile. "Knowing what Milton did to you? It helps. I'm grateful you told me."

I held his stare. "And I'm grateful you're helping those triggers fade away."

Awareness crackled between us the longer we stood there.

My heart skipped for all new reasons. I was *attracted* to him. Drawn to him. And I didn't understand how my body could crave his as if I'd already been in his arms and been kissed by his lips when we'd hardly ever spoken.

Shaking my head, doing my best to get rid of the uncanny sensation of déjà vu, I plastered on a bright smile. "Did you just get back from work?" I eyed the car keys clutched in his hand and the black satchel slung over his shoulder.

Nodding, he raked his fingers through fire-dark hair. "Yeah, it's been a week from hell. Barely stepped out of the hospital since Tuesday."

"You do look ready to pass out."

He sighed and squeezed his nape. "That's exactly what I plan on doing the second I go inside."

"Good plan." Awkwardness settled between us.

"Crime and autobiographies," he muttered.

"What?"

"The books I read. That and the occasional thriller."

"Can't say they're my cup of tea."

"I knew, by the way." He hitched up his satchel. "I saw your torch too. I just…didn't know you could see me."

I had no idea what to say. We'd crossed the bridge of neighbours to friends but hadn't established subjects we were familiar with.

The awkwardness stretched.

Tripping backward, I blurted, "I better go—"

"How's Peng—?"

We spoke at the same time.

Our eyes caught.

We laughed in a stumbling, endearing kind of way.

"Sorry." He bowed his chin. "You go."

"He's fine." I smiled. "Being the cutest little terror. Put his paw in my latest batch of lemongrass body butter, so I hope no one finds a cat hair in their cosmetics."

"Uh-oh." He grinned while stifling a yawn. "Tell him to practice better health and safety if he's going to help in the kitchen."

I laughed softly. "I will."

Clutching the strap of his satchel, he glanced at the plate I kept squeezing. "Is that some sort of shield for talking to me or…?"

Holding it away from me, I flinched at the neon yellow Post-it and ripped it off before Zander could read X's note.

Zander narrowed his eyes as I scrunched the paper and stuffed it into my paint-splattered pocket. "Nah, just someone I used to know giving me back what's mine."

He nodded slowly, his green gaze darkening. "Sounds pretty final."

"Oh, it is." I arched my chin. "Some things don't last, you know?"

He winced. "Yeah, life sucks that way."

We shared a stare again, the ghosts of our parents and grandparents thick between us. Funny that although I knew his family history, I hadn't stopped to think how similar we were in that respect. I was a true orphan in this world. I literally had no one alive who shared my DNA but him…he had two sisters.

"How're Christina and Jolie?" I asked, doing my best to be a better neighbour and friend. "Do they still live a few suburbs over?"

He half-smiled, tiredness making him sway. "They're good. Sworn off men, but that doesn't stop my friend Colin from flirting."

"I think swearing off men is contagious around here." I laughed a little too loudly.

He flinched again. "After what Milton did to you, I think you're wise to avoid my sex."

I let him think it was Milton I meant.

He yawned and shook his head as if to wake himself up.

You're keeping the poor guy up. He's dead on his feet and probably performed countless surgeries.

He didn't need me keeping him from bed.

A bubble of anxiety had me asking, "Do you have anyone to cook you a meal tonight? You look like you might fall asleep on the stove if you attempt to make anything."

His eyebrows shot up. Pushing his glasses back into position, he frowned. "Y-You're asking if I have anyone who takes care of me?"

"Of course." Taking another step toward him, I noticed how he took one back.

He'd always been very aware of others, and I'd just told him how I felt around him, thanks to Milton. It made sense to keep his distance. And the fact that he did so, even in his almost comatose state, made my heart swell with gratefulness. "Look, I'm done renovating for the day and have enough greens from the garden to make a huge salad. I was going to cook some roast veggies and either chicken drumsticks or garlic butter cod. I can bring you a plate if you want? You could have a shower and relax while I cook? I shouldn't be too long. Then you can go to bed and—"

"Seriously?" He staggered.

I reached out to grab him, but he backpedalled as if I was the one with the history of hitting people, not my ex.

I froze.

He coughed and ran his hand over his mouth, scratching at his five o'clock shadow that'd grown in after a long day at work. "That is…" Shaking his head, he shrugged as if I'd stripped him of all his strength. "That's so nice of you."

Why did that single sentence rip out my heart?

Why did he look as if I was the first to ever offer him a home-cooked meal when I knew all the old ladies on this street adored him? Surely, some of them would've dropped off a casserole at some point?

No…

Whenever I'd seen Zander talking to Josephine or Beverley, he was the one doing something for them. Fixing their lawnmower or teaching them how to buy groceries online.

In fact…had I ever seen anyone do something for him in return?

Would he even accept the gesture if someone did?

All my life, I'd thought he was a little standoffish and remote, but now…now, I saw a man far too willing to hide his true self in order to look after others.

I couldn't stop my feet from closing the distance between us. I might have lost X to his obsessive need to help people, but I wouldn't lose Zander too.

I touched his arm.

He hissed as if my fingers burned him.

His emerald gaze snapped to mine, his breath coming quicker. "I-I don't expect you to, Sailor. Honestly, I can order a takeaway and—"

"Don't even think about it. I'm happy to take care of you." Pulling away, I headed toward my house. "Go get clean and relax. I'll be over in thirty minutes."

Thirty-Six

Zander

Dreams Do Come True

I WOKE WITH A BANG.

Launching off the couch where I'd crashed the second I stepped through my door, I looked at my clock. "Ah, shit!"

Two hours.

How had I crashed for two fucking hours?

Sailor!

Had she been round like she said she would?

Had I missed her?

No.

No, no, *no...*

How could I have passed out? I hadn't meant to. I'd dumped my keys and satchel, then grabbed a beer and sat on the couch. I'd watched the clock tick its minutes away. After a week of countless surgeries, two stints in the emergency room, one lost patient, three urgent requests from fellow doctors, and countless horrible nights missing the hell out of Sailor, I was one breath away from telling everyone to fuck off.

Even Colin hadn't been able to make me laugh when I'd gone to see him a few days ago and shared the chocolate cake.

He'd asked for details of why I'd earned such a reward.

And for once, I didn't tell him.

What happened between Sailor and me that night was no one's business. It wasn't just a shared release. It wasn't the fact that I'd fallen so hard for her without even going past third base. It was the fact that I'd gone to third base all while lying to her face, and the handjob she'd given me had been the best sexual experience of my life because it was *her.*

She'd trusted me to be blindfolded.

Trusted me to touch her in the very same place where her ex almost murdered her.

So no, I didn't tell him.

And yes, he'd eaten most of the cake.

And when I'd written the Post-it Note and put her plate into her letterbox at four this morning when I'd been called back into work, I'd almost convinced myself I was doing the right thing.

X had to go.

Not because I feared I'd do psychological damage to Sailor anymore—she was too strong for that—but because it was psychologically damaging me. I wanted desperately to tell her who I was, but at the same time, I would rather let her go than have her hate me for the rest of her life.

But she offered to cook for you.

As Zander.

She'd touched me and hadn't recoiled.

I had no idea what that meant.

I didn't know if she'd truly healed or was just putting on a brave face because I looked like I'd been mauled by a pack of wolves and left for dead.

She probably only offered out of decency. Out of neighbourly generosity. Not because she felt anything for me.

But it didn't fucking matter, did it? Because I'd fallen asleep and not heard her knock. Now, she probably thought I didn't appreciate her and would never offer to check in on me again.

Christ, I'm a fool.

Staggering through the house, I headed to the kitchen to rustle something up that resembled a half-healthy dinner before passing out. Taking my glasses off, I rubbed my exhausted eyes before placing them back on and...slamming to a stop.

On my countertop sat the very same plate that she'd given X full of chocolate cake. Only this time, it held a crisp salad, big pile of roasted potatoes, and three perfectly chargrilled drumsticks.

A note sat tucked beneath it.

Hi Zander,

I hope you don't mind that I let myself in. I tried the front door but got no answer, and I figured you'd probably fallen asleep. Luckily, I know where Mary used to keep her spare key to the conservatory (I remember you painting that cute flowerpot for her). I didn't want to wake you, and I promise I didn't snoop. I love what you've done with the place, by the way. You'll have to give me a tour so I can get ideas for my renovation. Anyway, hope the meal isn't too cold when you wake.

Have a good rest. Sailor.

And just like I'd reached my limit in her kitchen the other night and kissed her like a drowning man, I reached another limit standing in mine.

She was going to kill me, one kindness at a time.

And I was happy to dig out my grave if it meant I got to keep her.

Yanking my phone from my back pocket, I went to message her.

To say just how much this meant to me. That she literally couldn't have done a nicer thing. That she was the first and only to make me a meal and I wanted to get on my knees and show her how grateful I was.

I didn't just want to bed this girl.

I want to goddamn marry her.

The windchimes Gran had strung up decades ago in the conservatory suddenly swung and sang.

I froze.

That's spooky as hell.

They couldn't sing as no windows were open. No wind of any kind.

So how...?

Goosebumps shot down my spine as one of the potted ferns rustled as if someone had brushed past.

Sailor had said her place was haunted.

I'd seen it firsthand with that damn TV turning on all the time, but I hadn't felt the presence of the dead here before. But now...now it felt as if all the people I'd lost were crowded by the back door, pushing their noses to the glass, and watching me have a quarter life crisis about how much I wanted the girl I'd been betrothed to as a six-year-old boy just because his grandmother had a best-friend who dreamed of becoming family.

Ignoring the nosy ghosts, I focused on my phone.

I can't thank you enough for the food. And for telling me why it's hard to be around me. I know you're still healing and this is probably far too soon but...would you like to have a drink with—

What the fuck are you doing?

I choked and deleted the text with a panicking thumb.

Holy shit, that was close!

I couldn't text her.

My number was registered as X in her phone.

Christ, how could I forget that?

A cold sweat broke out at the thought of what would've happened if I'd sent that message. She would've known instantly. All my lies would've come tumbling down and...

Maybe this was the way it was meant to go?

Maybe we could figure a way around all my lies and shady stalking behaviour?

Or she sells her house and runs away.

Bracing both hands on either side of the plate, I sighed heavily.

God, this is such a mess.

I'd gotten rid of X.

I no longer seemed to freak her out as Zander.

Instead of revealing my lies, I could just bury them as deep as every other skeleton in my closet and pretend he never existed.

I could resume my protective watching as her neighbour and not her stalker.

This...this could be a *good* thing.

And as long as I never made a mistake like the one I almost did, she would never have to know.

I could attempt to make her like me without the mask.

This could be *real.*

Hope bolted through me.

Before I could stop myself, I grabbed my keys, shot out the door, and headed to buy a second burner phone, all so I could message her as Zander instead of her stalker.

Thirty-Seven

Sailor

Movies Aren't Fun

"SAILS? OH MY GOD, I CAN'T believe I'm about to do this, but...I have to stand you up."

I jammed my phone between my ear and shoulder, paying for my bucket of popcorn and cola. "We're doing great at this, aren't we?" I laughed. "First, we both forgot we'd planned to go to dinner and the movies tonight and then when we remember and agree to just do the movie, you have the audacity to stand me up."

"I know. I know. I'm a terrible friend." Lily groaned, long and dramatic. "I have no excuse for forgetting dinner but then on the way to join you at the movies, the office called. There's an issue with one of the house contracts, and I need to go solve it because the buyer is panicking and the seller is threatening to call his lawyer to stop the sale, and...yeah, it's gonna be a long night."

"It's fine." Moving out of the line, I juggled my drink, food, and phone, and headed deeper into the cinema complex. "Super sorry to hear about the issues."

"Can we do the flick another night?" She moaned again. "I feel so bad. I'm also gutted I'm going to miss out on all your gossip."

"Honestly, I have no gossip, and I'm actually already here. I just found my seat and have an unhealthy amount of popcorn to eat by myself so I'm good."

"Argh, that just makes me feel extra guilty! If this wasn't a huge commission, I'd tell them to shove it. It's a Monday night. Who works at eight o'clock on a Monday night?"

"You do because you're on track to retire when you're forty, so go. Make that moolah. We'll talk later and—"

"Sails, hang on. Are you...are you doing okay being out at night on your own? I know how hard the market was for you to begin with. I can't believe I invited you out and then bailed when you're finally ready to start socialising again."

I warmed with affection for my best friend. "Honestly, Lils, I'm good. I won't lie that driving here wasn't all that easy and being hemmed in with the ticket line pushed a few buttons but…each time I put myself out there is another step out of the jail he tried to put me in. I'm growing my wings, remember?"

"You're so brave, and I'm so proud of you."

"And I'll be proud of you when you make those millions and shout me a trip to Bali."

"Done. That's definitely happening."

"Alright then. Go work hard. I'm fine. I'm gonna watch this, and then I'll spoil it for you because you know that's how I roll."

"I still curse you for spoiling that Sailor Moon episode all these years later."

"You're welcome." I laughed. "Okay gotta go. Credits are starting. Byeeeee." I hung up and quickly turned my phone on silent despite the fact that people still drifted into the cinema and the movie hadn't started yet.

I wasn't really one to go to the movies on my own. And if I'd known Lily wouldn't be coming, no way would I have fought through my mini panic attack at going into public at night, but now that I was here…oh well.

I was safe.

I was around lots of people who I could scream for help if needed.

I'd been brave enough to get here, and…to be honest, it was kinda fun. I'd never done anything like this, even before Milton tried to murder me. It felt healing in a way. A date by myself. Self-care and all that.

I'm fine.

Completely fine.

*See? This is **totally** good for me.*

My phone vibrated just as I went to tuck it into my bag.

I hated that my heart rate spiked, thinking it might be X.

After he cut contact, I'd torn out the SIM from the burner phone and put it into mine, cloning the messages and number thanks to dual SIM slots. I refused to carry two phones for the rest of my life, especially if he'd never message me again.

Swiping my inbox open, I stiffened.

Unknown Number:

Thank you so much for dinner. It was perfect. I can't believe you offered to feed me, and I wasn't awake to say thanks in person. Sorry about that.

I slouched in my velour-covered chair.
Well, it definitely wasn't X.

I'm assuming this is Zander?

He replied instantly, and I saved his number into my contacts. My address book flashed up with X's number, seeing as the two letters were at the end of the alphabet. Why did I have to crush on two men with uncommon letters? Why couldn't one of them have started with a D or an S instead of being almost side by side?

It is. I can't believe we've never exchanged numbers.

I agree. Don't take this the wrong way. I'm happy to be able to chat, but...how did you get my number? I don't remember sharing?

It took him a minute or two to reply.

It was in one of Gran's old notebooks.

Luckily, you didn't throw it out.

I agree.

The conversation reached a natural end; I didn't know if I should reply or not. I'd made him dinner. He'd thanked me. There wasn't much else to say, despite the rising bubbly feelings inside me.

The theatre suddenly plunged into darkness. People hushed each other as the movie started.

One second, I was fine.

The next, that awful, prickly, *horrible* fear tiptoed down my spine with icy fingers.

My pulse kicked up, drenching my system with adrenaline.

The music system blasted with its 'Dolby Surround Sound' experience, making me jolt like an idiot in my seat.

Oh no.

My eyes flew to the exit.

Fight-or-flight gushed through my limbs, making me desperate to run.

Breathe.

Just breathe.

The person next to me kicked my ankle as they shifted to get comfortable.

The urge to hit them and scream almost made me hyperventilate.

You're fine.

It's all in your head.

You're safe.

My legs bunched to stand. I peered down the long row of chairs. I'd have to brush past countless people and run the risk of being touched by a stranger.

Get out.

Go!

I breathed faster, harder.

No, please don't.

Not here.

Not now.

Swallowing hard against the bitter bite of panic, I closed out the message with Zander and opened the one with X.

I stared at his name.

I closed my eyes and breathed through the wash of debilitating terror. How could I think I was safe in this crowd? I wasn't safe. I was alone. And being alone was the exact opposite of what I needed.

I need Peng.

Why did I leave him to come here?

Why did I think I was ready for this?

I needed his warm little body in my arms.

I needed X to wrap me in a hug and protect me from—

"You're such a slut. I saw what you two did on that couch. No wonder you got rid of it so fast. You're a whore trying to get rid of the evidence."

Dropping my phone onto my lap, I clamped my hands over my ears trying to drown out Goblin-Milton's voice. But then the movie started with bright flashing lights and crazy booming music, and my system threatened to explode in all directions.

Something blasted on the screen, delivering shock value and making a few of the audience giggle-scream.

My system didn't just dabble with a panic attack, it went full blown.

Dry mouth, broken lungs, stinging tears.

Biting my bottom lip hard enough to draw blood, I forced my trembling hands to grab my phone.

The last time I'd had a panic attack, focusing on something else had helped. Talking about nonsense. Trusting someone on the other end to catch me.

Sipping breaths between my hyperventilating state, I texted as fast as I could.

I know you've decided to cut all contact, and I respect your choice not to see me again, but you appointed yourself as my protector and I need you right now. I'm not okay. I'm terrified I'm going to embarrass myself by screaming or fainting so even if you don't read this, I'm just going to pretend you are.

I pressed send, hoping against hell he hadn't blocked me.
The message delivered.
I didn't wait for him to reply before sending another one, distracting myself, using him like I did that night when I'd been jumping out of my skin.

Lily and I planned on coming to the movies tonight. But she had to cancel last minute, so I'm here alone. I thought I was better. I actually thought it could be kinda fun, but now I'm drowning and all I want to do is run. But the movie has started, and the crowd is thick, and I don't have the courage to brush past people in case they touch me.

Tears rolled down my cheeks as I typed faster and faster.

I miss my cat. Can you believe that? I miss him so, so much. I know I'd be fine if he was in my arms. Why am I not over this? Why am I weak enough to have flashbacks like this? It doesn't even make sense. Milton never hurt me at the movies. I have no reason for panicking when nothing bad happened here. God, I'm so stupid! I wasn't even abused like other women. It just happened that one time!

My heart stopped flying and turned to palpitations instead. My entire body jittered and shuddered. The words on the screen melted with my tears.

Closing my eyes and holding the armrest of my chair, I focused on my breathing.

My phone vibrated in my lap.

I snatched it up.

Hey, Sailor? Are you free to talk? Can I call you?

I quaked as panic set fire to my limbs. Why had Zander messaged me instead of X? I didn't want him right now. I didn't need an exhausted doctor with a heart so sweet sugar ran in his veins. I needed a masked stalker who grabbed me with no apology and kissed me with exquisite possession.

Another text flashed.

Please, Sailor? It's urgent. I need to talk to you.

I glared at my phone, daring, hoping, *begging* X to message.
And nothing.
I could barely see straight anymore.
My sniffles became too strong to choke down.
I needed to go somewhere I could huddle into a ball and sob.
But I couldn't shed the guilt of leaving Zander hanging. What if he was dealing with his own stuff? What if whatever had hurt him today was hurting him now and he'd reached out for my help?

Using my last remaining strength, I sent a generic reply, hiding how badly I unravelled.

Sorry, Zander. I'm at the movies. I can't call. I hope you're okay.

And that was it for my courage.
Closing Zander's message, I opened X's thread again.

If you're reading this and happen to be anywhere near the cinema tonight, I think...I think I might need help.

I pressed send.
Then lost myself to panic.

Thirty-Eight

Zander

Breaking Every Limit

"IS THAT LILY? WHAT MOVIE theatre were you planning on going to with Sailor tonight?"

Lily cleared her throat. "Um, usually the polite etiquette when calling someone out of the blue is, 'Hello, this is…'"

My fingers locked around my phone as I straddled my bike and prepared to fly out my garage. "Hello, this is Zander. Tell me where I can find Sailor."

"What? Why? Has something happened?"

"What theatre, Lily?!"

"Um…uh, we'd agreed to go to the new complex just out of town. We said the eight fifteen showing of—"

I hung up, shoved my phone into my jeans pocket, then jammed the helmet on my head.

Gunning the engine, I roared out of the garage so fast I could've run over nosy Patricia and not known. Leaning into the corners, I drove far too fast, leaving a wake of deafening noise.

I'd dealt with all kinds of pressure in my profession. I'd learned how to compartmentalise emotion versus action and sometimes did my best work if something unforeseen happened in surgery.

But this was different.

This was *her*.

And I felt completely fucking helpless.

I second-guessed everything.

I should've replied as X when she messaged me asking for help.

I should've told her who I was so she felt safe to confide in Zander.

I should've done so goddamn many things, and now she was breaking on her own, and I wasn't there, and fuck, I felt so responsible.

Streetlamps blurred past.

The bike vibrated beneath me.

I focused on one thing and one thing only, and that was finding Sailor before it was too late.

Thirty-Nine

Sailor

Car Parks Are Dangerous

I STUMBLED OUT OF THE CINEMA and staggered against the wall.

The huge car park held an ocean of vehicles but no people. Everyone was still inside, transfixed by loud, flashy movies, leaving me all alone in the dark.

I barely remembered how I'd managed to make my way down the row or trip my way through the foyer. A few moviegoers had given me side-eyes. One girl had even reached for me, clearly concerned, but I'd broken into a run and exploded through the double doors to freedom.

My car was out there somewhere.

Clouds covered the stars, threatening rain.

I felt very, very alone.

My phone had rung three times with Lily's number, but I'd ignored them. I couldn't pretend I was okay. I didn't want her feeling bad that this was too much for me, too soon. I couldn't have her feeling responsible for ditching when I completely understood work had to come first. For any ordinary person, that would've been fine.

But I'm not normal.

I'm—

"Hey, pretty lady! You waiting for someone?"

I froze into a chunk of ice as I looked through my tears and focused on a fairly tall man with a mop of dirty-blond hair. His saggy jeans and graffiti-designed t-shirt hinted he was in his late teens, but the sketchy look in his eyes and slight twitch to his fingers suggested he had habits of the adult variety.

Panic added another very unhelpful dose of jitters and breathlessness. Fighting the urge to bend over and clutch my knees, I didn't reply. My shoulder bumped along the wall as I half leaned on it for support and half ran toward the car park.

I needed to find Pop's car.

I couldn't drive in this state, but at least I'd be somewhere familiar. I could curl up on the back seat and let this idiotic episode pass.

My phone rang again.

I ignored it.

"Hey, if you're not using your phone, can I borrow it?" The guy fell into pace with me, grinning with stained teeth. "I need to call a friend to pick me up."

My already overloaded system fritzed.

My palpitating heart made me lightheaded.

A scream lived permanently on my tongue.

I shook my head, unable to speak. Fresh tears rolled down my cheeks as I headed down the first row of parked cars. I alternated between power walking and pathetically weaving, my knees like water and lungs like ash.

"Oi, where're you going in such a hurry?" He jogged to my side, grinning in a way that sent my instincts screeching.

Go back to the theatre.

Now!

Spinning on my heel, the cute slip-ons I'd worn to match my cutoff jeans and flower-print blouse didn't have enough grip to run fast.

I skidded a little.

He reached out and grabbed my elbow.

White-hot, *blazing* terror.

I yanked away from him, baring my teeth like a cornered animal. "D-Don't touch me!"

Holding up his hands, he scowled. "Jeez, calm down."

"Leave me alone."

"That's not very nice." He pouted and kept pace with me as I made my way, breathless and almost blind with terror, back toward the bright lights of the theatre. "You should say thank you. I just stopped you from falling."

"Go away."

He huffed and crossed his arms. "See, now that was just rude. I think you owe me an apology."

Keep going.

Stop talking.

Just run.

Sucking in a deep lungful of air, I broke into a sprint.

His hand lashed out and grabbed my wrist, stopping me dead.

Two things happened.

One, my panic switched from debilitating to hyper focused—the urge to protect myself brought a wave of power and ruthlessness.

Two, that awful fight-or-flight that'd crippled my system finally had an outlet. He'd stopped my flight so that left fight.

I'll kill him.

Balling my hands, I swung.

He ducked my flailing fist and laughed. "Want to do this the hard way, huh?" His eyes narrowed to slits. "Okay then. Give me your phone and wallet, and I won't hurt you."

I screamed.

His hand clamped over my mouth, his fingers smelling like Doritos and cigarettes. "Jeez, you don't learn, do you?" Wrapping his other arm around my shoulders, he hauled me backward, deeper into the car park, away from the bright lights and beckoning doors of the cinema.

No!

My feet scrambled for purchase.

My heart flew too fast to stay in my ribcage.

I lost it.

I turned into something inhuman as I cracked my head back, smashing into his nose. The phantom pain when Milton had ripped out a handful of my hair was instantly replaced by the nasty crunch of his cartilage.

He screeched and tripped backward, taking me with him.

I fell on top of him, my back to his front, his arm shifting from my shoulders to my neck. I gagged as he added pressure.

All those flashbacks of Milton strangling me.

All those nightmares where he'd done it again and again and again.

I'd been too hurt to fight back that day. Too bruised and beaten to prevent him from taking my life. James McNab wasn't around to save me with a cast-iron frying pan. No one could hear my struggles.

It's up to me.

It's always been up to me.

Scratching his arm over my throat, I gouged his flesh.

He cried out and wriggled beneath me. His arm loosened just enough for me to squirm a little lower. With a scream that'd choked me for months, I brought my elbow careening down...right between his legs.

Hard.

As hard as I could.

He *howled.*

Jack-knifing sideways, he kicked me off him and cupped himself. My phone lay with a cracked screen on the ground. Snatching it, I crawled out of grabbing distance and tried to stagger to my feet.

Only my legs didn't want to work.

Spluttering a thousand curses, the guy rolled to face me. Fumbling for my ankle with one hand, he protected himself with the other. "All I wanted was your phone and cash. But now you hurt me so…you're getting hurt right back."

I screamed again, kicking him in the jaw.

A roar of a motorbike drowned out his shout of pain, a bright spotlight careening into the car park and tearing toward the theatre in the distance.

"*Help!*" I yelled just as the creep managed to grab my calf and stop me from climbing to my feet.

The driver had his visor down, obscuring his face, but his head turned to face me. For a second, he looked as if he'd crash his bike. The front wheel wobbled and the engine coughed.

And then, he cut down the row of cars with a burst of growling speed.

The guy let me go, scrambling to his feet and cupping where I'd elbowed him. He hobble-ran away, but the motorcycle rider snarled to a stop, killed the engine, then launched himself after him.

The thief didn't stand a chance.

The motorbike rider grabbed him around the scruff of his t-shirt, wrenched him backward, then ploughed a fist into his face.

The thief screamed as blood spurted from his nose.

Just like I'd lost myself to instinct and rage, the rider did too. He punched the guy again and again. Ploughing him backward with each pummel until he bounced off a car and dropped to his knees.

Bowing over his legs, the thief cupped his head and begged, "Stop! I didn't do nuffin! I'll report you. Stop!"

The rider either didn't hear him or didn't care. His booted foot swung back and collided with the creep's ribcage, sending him sprawling on the ground.

Seeing one stranger beat up another finally cut through my panic.

Swaying to my feet, I went to where the guy kicked the thief again and hesitantly touched his shoulder.

The rider swung around, his visor reflecting me and the stormy clouds above.

Unable to see his face, I hoped—based on his help—that he could be trusted. "You can stop now. I-I'm okay." Holding up my cracked phone, I added, "I'll call the police. If you hurt him anymore, you might get into trouble."

The stranger's chest rose and fell beneath his leather jacket and dark jeans. His body seemed familiar. His scent tugging at memories skipping just out of reach.

The longer we stood there, the more my pulse calmed. He felt safe. Protective. I sucked in a sigh of relief. The only one who'd acted like that kind of sedative on my system was X, but…he never replied.

Checking my phone, I skimmed the notifications.

Nope, he hadn't texted back.

My gaze snagged on the bike. On the polished chrome and sleek lines.

Wait, I know that bike.

My eyes snapped back to the rider.

He made a noise in the back of his throat, then reached up and tore his helmet off.

I tripped backward as deep red hair and glowing green eyes appeared. "Z-Zander?"

Without a word, he stepped close and grabbed me. His hand went to the back of my neck like X did. His other fisted my hip and tugged me into him, crashing our bodies together and holding tight. His arms snaked around me in the tightest embrace.

I couldn't decide who trembled harder.

Neither of us spoke as he pressed his face into my hair and sucked in a tattered breath.

The thief scrambled to his feet and took off running. With a curse, Zander let me go and chased.

The creep didn't get far. With one strike of his helmet across the guy's shoulders, Zander ensured the thief fell forward, landing chin first on the ground.

I couldn't get my bearings.

Zander was the one who beat him up?

Zander willingly hurt someone after a lifetime of saving people?

"I-I don't understand." Rubbing my chest where my heart switched from fire to ice, I tripped toward him and shook my head. "How are you here?"

"Give me a sec." Fisting his phone, Zander called the police and muttered details to the operator while pacing around the guy who'd given up and sat in a dejected ball by his feet.

He refused to look at me until he finished. Once he'd hung up, he flexed his hands with a wince, a streak of blood and faint bruises staining his knuckles.

The thief whimpered as Zander glowered at him.

The night gathered thick around us.

I wanted to ask so many things.

Why had he defended me?

Where had he come from?

How was this *possible*?

But then he captured my hand and dragged me away from the creep on the ground. Once we were far enough away, he squeezed my fingers and let me go reluctantly. "Are you okay?"

Rubbing my hand from his tingly touch, I nodded. "Yes." I frowned, vacant from panic and feeling a little floaty. "Actually, I feel rather good."

"*Good?*" His eyebrows shot to his hairline, and for a second, I pictured a silver piercing. The way his eyes widened then narrowed reminded me so much of X, my brain tried to splice the two men together.

"Now, I'm the one who doesn't understand." He cocked his head. "Are you sure he didn't hurt you?"

Looking past him to the creep on the ground, I shrugged. "He tried."

"And...you feel good about that?"

"Yes." I crossed my arms, nodding with more bravery than I felt. "I fought back this time. It felt very good to do that."

His eyes darkened, reminding me all over again of another man with brown eyes. Eyes shaped so similar. Lashes just as thick.

Aghh, will you stop?

They are not the same person!

Apart from the height and a few mannerisms, Zander wasn't like X at all. Not to mention his hair and eye colour—

He attacked that guy for you.

He'd come to my rescue just like X had on those nights I'd needed him.

He knew where I was...

I froze.

Could it be him?

You told both you were at the movies.

But I couldn't remember ever giving the name of the cinema because I'd been drowning in panic like an idiot. *That's why X isn't here. That's why he—*

He's not here because he said you'd never see him again...remember?

I swayed.

"Sailor?" Zander stepped into me, his green gaze darting over mine as if worried I was about to pass out. "Are you alright? Do you need to sit down?"

I stumbled away, my heart resuming its panicked flurry. I couldn't get my bearings. Couldn't stop the yearning for one man all while another had saved me.

Anger rose, wanting to strike at all these annoying, confusing, *stupid* feelings.

I wanted to fight again.

I rather liked fighting back. I'd held my own despite my size difference. Perhaps I'd enrol in a self-defence course and take my rage out on the very man who'd stalked me, then abandoned me.

Cupping my shoulders with gentle fingers, Zander studied me. "Speak to me, Sailor. You're scaring me a little. Are you sure you're okay?"

My skin burned where he touched me, delivering the same prickly electricity that X gave.

My gaze caught on his mouth.

My stomach clenched.

If he *was* X, would he kiss me the same as he did in my kitchen? Would he shove me against a car and devour me just like he'd trapped me against the wall and worshipped me?

Kiss him and find out.

The thought blazed like a comet.

I flinched at the thought of being so bold.

My eyes fell on his mouth again—

But the flashing lights of a police cruiser pulled into the car park.

And Zander tripped away without another word.

Forty

Zander

Bruised Knuckles Were Worth It

"THANK YOU, DR NORTH, MISS ROSE. We'll be in touch if we require more information."

I nodded at the two police officers who'd arrested Chad Harris and taken our statements. They'd eyed Chad's bruises and peered at me, noticing my sore hands, but Sailor had jumped in and taken most of the blame.

I would've happily admitted I'd beaten him up and barely managed to stop myself from killing him, but it was probably a good thing she'd stopped me.

A doctor with a criminal record was not ideal.

Luckily, one of the officers recognised me from an evening when I'd stitched up his hand in the ER. I vaguely remembered him being stabbed by a housewife with a steak knife.

Apparently, the eighteen-year-old who'd tried to rob Sailor had formed a nasty habit for methamphetamines and had been targeting single theatre goers for a while.

I'd barely looked at Sailor while we went through the process of explaining. I withheld information on how I'd found her and claimed I'd been in the right place at the right time. I'd ignored the throbbing in my knuckles from ploughing my fists into his face and didn't worry about the day after tomorrow when I had to be back in surgery. Hopefully, the swelling would've gone down by then, and I could use my hands for complicated cutting and stitching. If not…I'd have to reschedule.

Colin is going to have a field day with this.

Lost in my thoughts as the police officers nodded politely at Sailor, I didn't move until the flashing lights of their cruiser drove away, taking Chad Harris with them.

Silence fell over the car park.

Faint thunder rumbled on the horizon, the atmosphere dense with the promise of summer rain.

I needed to get Sailor home before we got drenched. I needed to figure out a believable lie as to why I was here and how badly Lily would blow my cover when she told Sailor that I'd called with rude demands to know where she was.

I'd done a lot of unexplainable things tonight, but if I'd been just two minutes later…Christ, I couldn't think about what might've happened.

But there I went…thinking about it.

About the way Sailor had been on the ground, crawling away from a guy intent on hurting her. Yet another motherfucking *asshole* who thought they could hurt her. My chest seized. I staggered backward, landing against a car.

"Zander?" Sailor rushed to my side, her hand landing on my arm braced across my chest. "Are you okay? Did you get hurt?"

Her concern for me. Her caring for me. It was too much. I couldn't do it.

My knees threatened to buckle.

Who was I kidding that I could keep X a secret for the rest of my life? I'd crack. I'd never been good at hiding stuff and my cover was most likely blown anyway, but…the way she watched me? The soft gratefulness in her blue eyes. The utmost trust on her pretty pixie face. It was so different to her initial reaction. Before the police arrived, she'd looked almost angry with me. Her gaze locked on my mouth as if she was about to either punch me or kiss me.

She looked so worn out, so fragile.

It fucking killed me that I hadn't messaged her back as X. That I'd left her alone and afraid after promising to always be there for her.

But if I'd come as X…

My chin dropped as pain I'd never felt before carved through me.

The more interactions I had with her as X, the deeper my lies went. She'd never forgive me for touching her in disguise. For taking advantage of her like so many other pricks had tried.

I should never have gone around that night for cake and orgasms.

I should never have touched her so intimately. At least then she wouldn't feel so betrayed.

Swallowing the grief haunting my heart, I cleared my throat and focused on getting Sailor home. At least on Ember Drive, I could watch her through my window and ensure no one else tried to harm her.

"I'm—" I cleared my throat and stood straight.

She dropped her hand and took a careful step back, wariness once again appearing in her stare.

I ignored how much that gutted me. "I'm assuming you drove here?"

She frowned a little that I hadn't answered her question of how I was. "I did." Looking over her shoulder, she forced herself to stand taller. "It's parked over there somewhere."

I should offer to walk her to Rory's ancient Honda Civic. Hell, I should offer to buy her an up-to-date safe vehicle that wasn't as old as her, but all I could say was, "Come for a ride with me?"

Wait, what?

What the fuck are you doing?

She gasped, her eyes flaring wide. "What? Right now?" Glancing at the sky where the clouds pressed heavy and black, she wrinkled her nose. "It's about to pour down."

"I don't care."

You've lost it.

Well and truly lost it.

Stiffening, she searched my face.

I shoved my glasses up my nose and let her look. I doubted she'd see any evidence of X—despite me coming instead of him. Sure, I'd embraced violence and relished in beating the shit out of Chad Harris, but that was over and knowing how close I'd come to losing her?

Fuck, I'd never felt more like me—like the lonely doctor who'd convinced himself he didn't need anyone, only to realise that was the biggest lie of all.

One of the streetlights illuminating a row of cars suddenly blacked out.

It reminded me of her TV randomly turning on the moment I kissed her as X.

Goosebumps darted down my spine. She rubbed her arms, suffering the same curse.

I chuckled under my breath, forcing myself to stay honest and talk even though it hurt. "Ever get the feeling we're not just being haunted by our grandmother's ghosts but that they're still playing matchmaker?"

She snorted. "I thought it was just me."

"Nope." I smiled, fighting the insane urge to brush aside her hair that'd stuck to her bottom lip. "The windchimes in my conservatory started singing when I noticed the dinner you cooked for me."

"That's not that strange—"

"All the windows were closed. There wasn't a breath of wind."

"Oh. Yes, that's a little odd."

Finding courage from the desperate place inside me—the last-ditch attempt at making her like me instead of fear me—I stepped forward and cupped her cheek. I'd touched her far more intimately as X. I knew how she sounded and tasted and what she liked in bed, but being allowed to touch her like this as Zander? Being allowed to be this close without her flinching in panic? It blew anything else apart.

She sucked in a breath.

I froze, second-guessing everything but unable to let her go. "Are you okay, Sails?"

She flinched as I said the nickname I'd heard Lily use. With a soft sigh, she pressed her cheek deeper into my hold instead of away. "I am. Thanks to you."

"You would've won if I hadn't turned up. You did some serious damage." I forced a chuckle. "I doubt he'll be spawning kids anytime soon with the way he hobbled into the police car."

"Is it wrong that I enjoyed hurting him? I never got to fight back with Milton. It almost felt cathartic to do it now."

"Not at all." I ran my thumb over her perfect cheekbone before dropping my hand. "I think you needed to let that out. To be—"

"Violent?"

"Not necessarily. Just...you needed to realise you *are* strong enough to protect yourself. You don't need me or anyone else."

"Does it make me weak if I admit that I *do* need someone? That I *like* needing someone? That I want someone to need me in return?"

Wincing against the answering agony inside me, I headed toward my bike. "I think that just makes you human." Grabbing the spare helmet that I'd brought just in case, I went to her and gently placed the black protection over her sandy-blonde hair. "We're not meant to be loners, Lori. Everyone needs someone."

She froze.

Her eyes danced over my face.

Did I say something wrong? Had I pushed her too far?

I racked my brain, but after the exhaustion from long work hours, the terror I'd felt at her messages, and horror at finding her being hurt...I had nothing left.

Speaking through the gravel in my throat, I asked, "So will you? Come for a ride with me? I can take you home and grab your car tomorrow."

Her gaze searched mine. Too long. So long.

Finally, she gave a tight little smile and reached up to adjust the helmet. "Okay."

One little word spoken with bite.

My heart sank.

I'd fucked up.

I didn't know how, but I'd given her another hint, and I had no idea how to stop all of my lies unravelling.

Forty-One

Sailor

Storms and Secrets

I'D DANCED IN THE RAIN BEFORE when I was young.
I'd spun in a summer storm with my face tipped to the sky and caught fat raindrops on my tongue. Nana had said the rain could wash away all my worries, and she was right.

But this?

Nothing could compare to this.

There weren't words.

This was…flying through a waterfall. Swimming through a falling river. Racing through a water world with raindrops cascading, mechanical thunder rumbling, and the strongest, warmest protector charting a course through all my nightmares.

Zander leaned into the corner, taking me with him as I hugged him from behind. The snarl of the engine overshadowed the grumble of thunder above as we plummeted down rain-slick roads and past black-shrouded trees.

I tipped my head back and shivered as water splashed on my face. Both of us were soaked, but I wasn't cold. Zander kept me warm with his scalding body heat, all while thrilling, addictive adrenaline made my heart flutter.

As we roared through the wet night, the storm didn't just wash away my worries, I felt *reborn*.

This was what I needed.

This was what I'd been craving.

Not recklessness, not danger.

Connection.

Connection between me and the elements, earth and rain and stars.

And I shared this magical experience with someone who'd always been there…waiting.

An avalanche of affection had me squeezing Zander's waist.

The fact that he'd called me Lori repeated in my mind.

That one word had stopped me dead. The image of X had spliced with Zander, and for a second, I was *positive* he'd been lying to me all along.

But then I recalled all the times in our youth when Zander had called me Lori. I'd been the one to give that nickname to X to use, but that name had always belonged to Zander.

So...who was real?

The stalker who thought it was my real name or the boy next door who'd come up with it?

I wanted to ask him point-blank.

But the longer we flew together, the less it really mattered.

The less I worried because...it *didn't* matter.

Not really.

Both men were incredible.

Both men were kind.

And I'd been incredibly lucky to know each of them.

I hugged him again, feeling carefree and amazingly light.

He stiffened.

His back muscles flexed as he tried to look over his shoulder, but then he straightened and kept his eyes on the road.

His wrist shifted, adding another snarl of speed.

I closed my eyes as the world turned into a liquid blur. I felt like I could spread my wings and soar. I wasn't rebuilding them. I now had a million feathers and the newfound strength to fly.

Zander's gloved fingers suddenly touched mine.

Driving one-handed, he pressed my hand against his stomach, sharing so much with a single touch that words could never express. Spreading my fingers, I gasped as he threaded his gloved ones with mine. Together, we curled our combined grip into a fist. His belly tightened where I touched him as if that simple hand hold affected him as much as it affected me.

I shivered as he squeezed me.

I struggled to let him go as he resumed driving with both hands.

And as he shot us up a hill toward the rain-drenched clouds, pure happiness found me.

Not tainted by should dos and should nots.

Not ruined by racing thoughts or doubts.

In that moment, I was entirely present, awake, alive, and with *him.*

The growl of the motorbike seemed extra vicious as we weaved our way through twisty, sleepy suburbia and turned onto Ember Drive.

The slow speed after our fast fly seemed as if we'd become a snail after soaring like a hawk.

The rain still fell but not as heavy, the droplets kissing my skin instead of smacking me. With careful skill, Zander turned onto his driveway, bringing us home to the two houses that sat side by side with their matchmaking, meddling ghosts.

His garage door was still up, his trust in our neighbours evident with how safe our street was.

He killed the engine, leaving my ears ringing in the rain.

Neither of us moved.

I knew I had to stop hugging him but the thought of breaking that warm connection hurt more than it should.

I'd been blind for so long.

I'd been wrapped up in my own tragic tale and forgotten to pay attention to the boy next door. The boy Nana had always said was mine.

He called me Lori...

With a creak of wet clothes, Zander kicked the stand down and sat upright.

I pulled my arms away and scrambled off the back. No longer plastered to him, an instant chill soaked into me.

I needed to find Peng and apologise. I craved a warm shower and a cosy bed and a skull-masked stalker to tuck me in and hold me tight.

My heart panged with guilt that even though tonight had made me trip from crush to full-blown attraction toward Zander, I still had feelings for X.

Selfishly, I *wanted* them to be the same person because then I wouldn't have to say goodbye to either of them.

I struggled with my helmet as Zander swung his leg off the bike, wrenched his off, then helped me with mine.

Rain glittered in his fire-dark hair as he placed both helmets on the leather seat. The quiet ping of splashing droplets sung around us. The lenses of his glasses had water streaks and his grey t-shirt under his unzipped jacket was sopping wet, clinging to every crease of his toned chest.

Studying Zander as he stood in the rain, I narrowed my eyes and imagined him with a mask cutting his handsome face in half. I tried to remove his glasses and paint his fire strands blue black...but I couldn't.

All I could see was a slightly nerdy, extremely handsome doctor with a heart made of twenty-four karat gold.

My chest ached with fresh pangs.

I couldn't imagine him kissing me with pent-up passion like X had.

I couldn't picture him cursing under his breath as I made him come.

He didn't seem the type to be that…aggressive in bed.

He'd be sweet and gentle and soft and—

You could seduce him to find out…

I froze.

If I got Zander naked, perhaps I could tell by his size and shape—

You were blindfolded. You never saw X naked…

My shoulders sagged.

I needed to go to sleep before I did something crazy like pounce on my neighbour all because I thought he had a fake identity.

"Thanks for the ride," I said softly, backing up a step. "Don't worry about my car. I can get Lily to drop me off in the morning to collect it."

Without a word, he wrenched off his leather gloves and tossed them onto the handlebars. Glancing at his house, he captured my fingers, threaded his with mine like he had on the bike, then tugged me up the drive.

I gasped.

Wait. Is he taking me back to his place?

Had he read my mind and shared my crazy idea?

A part of me braced to stop him—the part so used to overthinking and living in fear. But then the vixen who'd decided she liked to swing a punch and fly on the back of a motorbike chose to live a little.

Tonight had driven us from friends to something more.

I was single.

He was single.

So what if the romance of sharing a storm ended with us in bed?

X wouldn't be creeping through my window tonight or any other night.

He'd made it perfectly clear we were done.

Pain pinched, followed by a hot, violent thrill.

What did that say about me that I was happy to kiss another guy after being with one a few days ago?

"It makes you a slut, that's what."

Clutching Zander's hand, I marched bravely at his side, my gaze locked on his front door. Did I have the courage to do this? What would happen when he got me inside? Should I cut to the chase and kiss him or wait for him to kiss me?

Zander cut in front of me.

I ploughed right into him, all my focus on his front door.

"*Ooof.*" He tripped and almost took me down with him, stumbling over the grass verge bordering his property from mine.

Grabbing me around the waist to keep me upright, he held me

close, our soaking skin sticking together. "Shit, Sailor, are you okay?"

I blinked.

I frowned.

I couldn't catch my bearings.

His eyes searched mine, slowly darkening as he looked back at his house and the trajectory I'd been on. He swallowed hard, his throat slicked with rain. "Eh...I was walking you back to your place, but...did you want to come in? I just assumed it was late, and you'd want to see Peng. But—"

"No! No, you're right!" My cheeks blazed as hot as the sun. "Of course, I want to see my kitten. I was cruel to go out for so long! I better go. Thanks again for the help and the ride and—goodnight!"

Wrenching my hand from his, I bolted up my front path.

He hadn't been dragging me to his house.

He'd most likely taken my hand to stop me from slipping in the puddles. He was a gentleman. Not a sexual deviant. *Of course* he was walking me to my door. *Of course* he wasn't going to rip off my wet clothes and warm me up with his tongue.

God, Lor, what were you thinking?!

"Thanks so much for the ride!" I fumbled for my keys. "And for your help. I-I already said that but thank you!"

Come on. Come on, where are you?

"You better get some rest!" I couldn't stop speaking. "I know how tired you were earlier tonight. I'm so sorry you had to come get me!"

A-ha, finally!

Snatching my keys from the bottom of my little purse, I flicked through to find the right one only—

My nape prickled.

My heart pounded.

And Zander gently claimed my hips, then spun me around to face him.

Our eyes locked.

We both struggled to catch a breath.

He made me want to melt into the ground as he asked ever so softly, "Why are you running away from me?" His voice turned thick with gravel, sounding painfully familiar. "Is it because you've had a flashback from what Milton did or..."

I swallowed hard.

Don't ask. Don't you dare ask.

"Or?"

Dammit, Lor!

"Or because you thought I didn't want you when every bone in my body is begging me to kiss you?"

My insides wrung inside out.

My heart turned into a chaotic butterfly.

I had no words.

Poof. All gone.

He stepped even closer. "Tell me why you were heading toward my house, not yours."

I gulped.

I couldn't.

I wasn't that brave.

"Tell me why I feel like I did something wrong. That I just missed an opportunity that I've been waiting for forever." He crowded me against my front door, sheltering me from the rain but not the storm he caused in my blood. His gaze dropped to my mouth. "Tell me to go, and I'll go."

Tell me to stop, and I'll stop.

Zander's voice blended with X's in my head. So similar. So deep.

I couldn't breathe as his fingers captured my chin and tipped my head back. With my spine against the door and his hips millimetres from pressing into mine, I couldn't move as he hovered over my lips.

Our eyes locked; his glasses caught the light I'd left on for Peng. His mouth hovered over mine with delicious drawn-out torture.

I quaked in my soaking shoes and waited and waited and...couldn't wait anymore.

Soaring up on my tiptoes, I smashed my lips to his.

He shuddered and collapsed against me.

The door creaked as our weight slammed against it.

I cried out as the knocker caught me right in the shoulder blade. "*Oww—*"

"*Shit.*" Wrenching away, his eyes flared with panic. "Damn, I'm so sorry. I...I didn't mean—"

"It's fine. It was just the kno—"

"It's not fine. I got carried away. I just...fuck, I don't know what I was thinking. He hurt you because of me. It's too soon. I should never have—"

"Zander, it's okay—"

"I would never hurt you, Sailor. You know that, right?" His eyes gleamed with fear and stress and guilt. His glasses slid down his nose only for him to shove them back into place. The tic was so him, so full of nerves, that any hope of him being X dissolved with the last of the rain.

I slouched against my door.

A chill crept into my heart.

I accepted that Zander might want me, but he was far too shy to claim me.

And I wasn't ready to be the brave one. Not yet.

Turning around, I unlocked the door and stepped inside.

Dripping over the rug where I'd had my first panic attack, I looked back and forced a smile.

He hadn't moved, keeping his hands balled at his sides as if he'd forgotten how to walk. "Sailor, I—" He wiped his mouth, removing any trace of our fleeting kiss. "There's something I need to tell—"

"Not tonight." I cursed the sting of tears. "We'll both catch the flu if we don't get dry. Look after yourself, okay, Zander? Sleep well."

I closed the door and staggered back as the best kitten in the world leapt into my arms and attacked me with love.

Doing exactly what I'd hoped Zander would do but didn't.

"So you kissed my twin tonight, huh?"

I smiled as X stepped through my kitchen and into my newly renovated living room. His brown eyes glowered above his skull-painted mask. His blue-black hair and eyebrow piercing made him the quintessential bad boy. A protective monster who stomped around in heavy boots and made me break apart on his fingers.

I stretched on the new couch, bold and far too brazen. "Who? You mean Zander?" I shrugged with a wink. "I can't help that I like you both."

Stalking toward me, X reclined against the threshold. "Did you stop to think that it would make me jealous?"

The faintest coil of worry worked through me. "Can you be jealous when I was hoping you were the same person? I didn't realise he was your brother."

He sniffed coldly, cruelly. "And now that you know we're not the same…what are you going to do? Be with me or him?"

I sat up, fear prickling down my spine. "You're the one who broke up with me, remember?"

"I didn't expect you to throw yourself at another man the second I was out of the picture. In fact, I tend to agree with your ex." Stalking toward me, he pinned my shoulders to the couch, yanked his mask down, and bared his teeth. "You are a slut—"

I choked and shot upright.

Just a dream.

Just a dream.

Rubbing my rabbiting heart, I squinted in the bright sunshine streaming through my window. Peng meowed where he blinked from my pillow, his ginger coat so much shinier than when I first got him.

Scooping him into a hug, I lay back down and placed his soft, warm weight on my chest. He kneaded me, no doubt feeling my racing heart beneath him.

The longer he made biscuits on my Sailor Moon t-shirt, the slower my pulse became.

Just a dream, that's all.

I'd done something very out of character last night. It was only natural my conscience decided to punish me.

X would never hurt me.

Even if he did get jealous, it wouldn't drive him to do what Milton did.

I'm safe.

So why did I reach for my phone to check if he'd messaged me? Why did I feel both sad and angry that he hadn't replied to my panicked thread from last night?

For all he knew, I was still in the movie theatre, curled in a ball in the corner.

Even Zander hadn't messaged me.

But Lily had.

OMG, pick up the damn phone. I'm worried sick.

Why did Zander call me and demand to know where you were last night?

Are you dead? Because you're going to be for ignoring me.

Sailor, you call me back right now!

Sails...I'm super worried about you.

"Uh-oh." Shifting Peng off my chest, I went to call her—

Someone pounded like a crazed animal on my front door. "Sailor Moon, you open this door *right now!*"

"Eep, I'm in trouble." I winced and nose bopped Peng. "Can you protect me? She's super scary when she's mad."

He yawned, showing me his sharp little teeth.

"I'll take that as a yes." Scooting out of bed, I grabbed my kitten and darted down the stairs in my night shorts and oversized tee. Lily kept knocking, the banging echoing down the corridor as I flicked the dead bolt and wrenched it open.

Her eyes roved over me. She looked flawless in a power suit of rich grey with a black shirt and heels, her hair coiled and perfect. "Well, you're not dead then."

Throwing myself at her, I hugged her, squishing Peng between us. "I am *soooo* sorry, Lils. I have no excuse. But after what happened in the movies and then in the car park and then with Zander, exhaustion swamped me the moment I got home, and I crashed. I crashed *way* harder than I thought I would and—"

"Whoa, what? What happened with Zander?"

"*That's* what you decide to focus on?" I huffed, pulling away.

Kissing my cheek, revealing she wasn't *that* mad, she moved me aside and stomped toward the kitchen. "Fine. What happened in the car park? What happened in the movie? I demand to know every minute of last night, and then you're going to tell me everything that you've been hiding."

Following her, I plopped Peng onto the countertop, then scooped up his bowl and put his morning rations into it. The orange furball ploughed headfirst, ignoring both of us as I added water to the kettle and two lemongrass-ginger teabags to big chunky mugs.

While the kettle boiled, I gathered my hair into a messy ponytail and figured out how to tell her that I'd fooled around with my stalker, had the hots for my neighbour, and beat up a guy who'd tried to rob me.

But…I froze.

My mind finally caught up to what I'd seen outside when I'd answered the door.

Something that shouldn't be there.

"Hang on." Racing back through the house, I ripped open the door and tripped onto the front deck.

My car slept peacefully on the driveway as if it'd been there all night long.

How is that possible?

Glancing at Zander's house, I saw no evidence of him being awake so early. Not that eight o'clock was early. With his crazy shifts, he could already be elbow-deep in a surgery.

Huh, that's strange.

The camera on his veranda that usually pointed at his garage had been angled to point at my front yard. Had the wind done that? Why would it—?

"You better start talking, Sails. Otherwise, I'm going to hold you down and tickle you like we did as kids until I get answers." She wriggled her fingers. "I haven't forgotten how quickly you squeal when I find that spot between your ribs."

I flinched away from her. "No need for threats. I have every intention of telling you. But…hold that thought."

"Oh my God, you're driving me mad." Lily stomped her high heel as I padded barefoot down the garden path and opened the car door. No clues hinted to how it'd gotten here on its own. No note. No answers.

Lily loomed over me, investigating my old car as if it would tell her what I was hiding. "Start spilling. Right this second."

Memories of kissing Zander last night. The ignition of blistering heat, followed by the bucket of ice water. If only the damn door knocker hadn't jammed into my back. If only he'd asked if I was okay instead of assuming that I wasn't.

My heart picked up its exhausted beat again. Even if I had ended back at Zander's house, could I honestly say I would've slept with him? I mean...I wanted to be free but *that* free? That unattached to jump from one man's bed to another?

Perhaps it was a good thing the knocker had stopped us.

As much as I rode the high of adrenaline last night, if I'd woken in Zander's bed this morning...I honestly didn't know how I would've reacted.

"Sailor." Lily waved in front of my face as I closed the car door and padded back toward the house.

Who brought it back for me? And how? The keys were in my purse. They hadn't left my side. Unless X broke in last night and stole them? But if he cared enough to return my car, why hadn't he messaged me?

Ugh, I'm not cut out for this.

Lily followed me through the house to the kitchen. "Earth to Sails."

Pouring hot water over our teabags, I didn't speak until I passed one mug to her and carried mine to the dining room table.

Sipping on warm comfort, I debated blurting out everything, but something stopped me.

I couldn't understand my actions.

I no longer knew who I was or who I would become.

All I knew was...X was my dirty secret, Zander was my guilty pleasure, and right now, I needed to hide what I was going through so my best friend wouldn't judge me.

Taking her hand, I squeezed her fingers. "I need you to trust me that I'm okay, and I'll tell you everything, but not today. Today, I want you to tell me about the work mess last night. Did you get it sorted? How's that builder you're seeing? Aubrey, was it?"

She sighed heavily, her eyes sad. "I know what you're doing, and I won't let you do it for much longer."

I gave her a crooked smile. "I know. Just...give me a few more days to get my head on straight. And then, I'll tell you everything."

"Promise?"

"I promise."

Forty-Two
Zander

Midnight Watching

ANOTHER WEEK FROM HELL ENSURED I had no time to sleep, let alone freak out over my lack of a love life or how many lies I'd told.

Between shifts, I spied on Sailor with my cameras and found comfort knowing she happily pottered around at home.

She hadn't tried to message X again, and when I'd contacted her as Zander two days ago, her reply had been polite and reserved instead of open and honest, and I couldn't do it.

I was too tired. Too drained.

I missed her.

I missed the way my heart would catch when a new text pinged. I missed her forwardness, pushing me to accept pieces of myself I would never ordinarily allow.

But no matter how close we'd gotten and how great the orgasms had been, it'd been based on lies. And I'd had no choice but to end it.

Hitching my satchel up my shoulder, I left the hospital and headed toward the staff car park. Honestly, I probably shouldn't drive. I could barely see straight. I think the last time I slept was fifty-three hours ago and I literally couldn't remember what my last meal was.

The thought of returning to an empty house, an empty fridge, and an empty bed almost made me turn around again to see if Colin was still in his office.

But I didn't. Because if I didn't crash soon, I'd crash not just my car but my health.

At least I have three days off.

I'd had two rostered off but added a vacation day purely because the thought of coming back here so soon almost made me want to quit. As much as I loved helping people and seeing sick people enter and healthy people leave, I was at the end of my rope.

Maybe I need a proper vacation?

Somewhere with sun and sand and two weeks of nothing but the tropics.

Unlocking my car, I slid in and rubbed my eyes beneath my glasses. A break sounded fucking awesome but the thought of being the single idiot on a deck chair with no one to share cocktails with sounded dreadfully unappealing.

Ah well.

At least I had seventy-two hours of freedom before the grind began again.

And the first thing I was doing was crawling into bed and forgetting about everything.

I woke sometime around two a.m.

Hunger pangs cut through my belly, causing enough discomfort that I couldn't get back to sleep.

Exhaustion clung to my thoughts as I hauled myself unwillingly out of bed and stumbled down the stairs to the kitchen. Yawning, I checked the fridge and lack of supplies, settling on a bag of grapes that I'd bought last week and completely forgotten about.

Rinsing them under the tap, I stuck them in a bowl, grabbed the rest of the cheese slowly cultivating its own penicillin, then carried my midnight snack out to the living room.

A crescent moon hung in the sky, dotted with silver stars. No lights shone in any of the houses. No foot traffic or car traffic. Everyone was fast asleep.

Shoving a few grapes into my mouth, I bit off a corner of cheese and sat in the chair by the window. The view angled right into Sailor's front yard, revealing she'd mowed the strip of lawn at some point and yanked out a few offending weeds.

How was she going with the renovation?

Was she still painting the living room and deleting Milton's presence?

How's her mental health going?

Seeing her appearing occasionally on my cameras between surgeries wasn't enough to know if she was happy. Alive yes, but anything else...I had no idea.

Movement caught my attention as I worked my way through the grapes and cheese.

Sailor.

I froze as she stepped out of her front door and headed toward the swinging egg chair by the railing. Scooting onto the swing, she nursed a cup of something, wrapping both hands around it as if it was snowing outside and not hot enough for crickets to chirp.

Her face tipped toward my place. I couldn't make out her features in the gloom, but I swear she stared exactly where my front camera was. Shrinking into the shadows, I hoped she couldn't see me.

What was she doing up so late?

Had she had another nightmare?

A panic attack?

My heart pounded at the thought of her struggling on her own. I should never have cut contact with X. What if she still needed to vent? To talk to a faceless stranger and get rid of all the darkness inside her?

Fuck.

Putting my empty bowl down, I padded back to the kitchen where I'd left my phone.

Swiping on the device, I scanned a text from Colin and my younger sister before clicking on the thread with Sailor.

I couldn't let her sit out there alone.

It just wasn't possible.

I'd text her as Zander.

I was her neighbour, after all.

I'm allowed to spot her out the window without it being creepy.

My thumbs flew over the screen as I made my way, in my boxer-briefs, back to the living room. I didn't go near the window, just in case she saw me.

She'd tucked her legs up and sipped her drink. Peng had joined her and sat curled on her lap. She looked so young, so innocent.

Just as alone as I felt.

My chest ached.

Turns out, we're both night owls. If you can't sleep, you can talk to me.

I pressed send and watched for her reaction.

She didn't move.

She didn't reach for a phone, hinting she'd probably left it inside.

Minutes ticked past, then half an hour.

My eyelids drooped and my shoulders sagged. I swayed on my feet, doing my best to stay awake all while fighting a losing battle.

Finally at three a.m., she vanished back inside, and I tripped up the stairs.

I barely made it back to bed before I was out cold.

Next time I woke was to brightness and noise.

My phone screeched with its obnoxious ringtone, flooding my system with adrenaline.

God, please don't let it be work.

If I got called in, I honestly didn't think I'd make it through the day. I'd never been this...*sore*. Not just physically but emotionally. It felt as if that proverbial train had come back and not just run me over but dragged me behind it for miles.

Fumbling in the bedcovers, I found the wailing device and swiped it on.

"Dr North speaking."

"Oooo, hello Dr North speaking. Don't you look at caller ID?"

I scowled and flopped back onto my pillow. "What the hell are you doing calling me so early?"

"It's eleven o'clock." Colin snickered.

"Fuck, is it?" Stretching, I reached for my glasses. My foggy eyesight suddenly became crisp, revealing the sun was high in the sky. "Shit, so it is."

"I take it you crashed hard?"

"If you told me the world ended last night and you're the last person alive, I wouldn't be able to argue."

"Love those nights when you're dead."

Sitting upright, I scratched my scruff and shoved a pillow behind my back. "Still feel like I've been run over, though."

"I have the perfect cure for that. A friend of mine is going out on the lake with his boat this arvo. I asked if I could bring a plus-one."

"Aw...and you thought of me." I yawned. "So sweet."

Placing the call on speaker, I brought up my inbox, making sure I hadn't missed anything urgent.

Christina and Jolie had messaged me in the family chat, along with a couple of colleagues at work. Colin's text loomed unanswered from an hour ago when he presumably tried to contact me.

"If you're keen, you're welcome. All you have to bring is yourself and some beer. I could swing by and pick you up on my way?"

I kept scrolling.

"Sure, sounds—" I choked as my eyes locked on a name.

A name that shouldn't be so recent in my inbox.

Lori.

What the fuck?

Colin's voice echoed as he spoke, but I couldn't understand him. I couldn't focus on a single thing apart from tapping on the message.

Turns out you're not just a stalker but a liar too. How do you know I'm up right now if you aren't watching me? Tell me, X, do you still spy on me all while forbidding me to see you again? Because that's not fair. I might've been okay with you watching me on a mutual basis, but if you think I'm going to put up with this being one-sided, think again.

"Oh, fuck, what did I do?"

"What?" Colin asked. "What did you do?"

"I fucked up, that's what."

"How?"

"I messaged her as X last night in my half-comatose state. I thought I'd messaged her as Zander. I completely blanked I have two goddamn phones."

"You are definitely not cut out for this spy shit, Superman."

My heart plummeted as I read Sailor's second message, sent at three thirty a.m.

I'll give you twelve hours to tell me where you put your cameras so I can rip them out. If you don't...I'm going to the police. And this time, I'll give them my phone, and they can deal with you.

"Fuck, I have to go."

"What do you mean *go*? I'm coming to get you, remember?"

"No, I mean. I can't come to the lake. I have to…. Shit, something super fucking important just came up."

"Super fucking important, huh? Does this important task begin with an S and end with an R?"

Launching out of bed, I dashed to my window and looked into Sailor's back garden.

I froze.

There she was, lugging a ladder twice the size of her from the back gate to the corner of her house where weeds grew out of the veranda gutters.

She didn't mean to clean them herself, did she?

Didn't she know how many accidents I saw in the ER, thanks to idiots and ladders?

Fuck.

Hanging up on Colin, I tapped Sailor's number and called her.

I paced while the ring tone echoed in my ear and watched her marching toward her house with a life-destroying ladder.

She never answered.

Forty-Three

Sailor

All Boys Suck, Especially the Masked Ones

SHOVING THE LADDER AGAINST THE side of the house, I tried to remember what Jim had instructed. I'd gone round this morning with another peach cobbler, exchanging sugar for tools.

What had he said?

Lock the legs, hoist the middle, brace the joints?

The clunky wooden thing weighed a freaking tonne. My arms already shook before I'd climbed one rung.

That could partly be thanks to the struggle of carrying it over here but also mostly thanks to X.

How *dare* he message me last night?

How dare he spy on me, contact me, and then ghost me when I'd replied?

He'd cut contact for almost two weeks and then out of the blue, I get a message that he's watching me and we can *chat*. What sort of game was he playing? In what world did he think that was acceptable?

My phone pinged in my back pocket of my jean shorts.

I'd heard it ringing while carrying the ladder over the lawn, but had no intention of answering it. I didn't want to run the risk. I'd already answered one call that rattled me this morning; I wasn't ready for another one. I flinched despite myself, recalling the case officer handling Milton's incarceration telling me a court date had been set a few months from now.

I would have to testify.

That chat had almost, *almost* sent me spiralling backward.

I'd hovered my fingers over my phone, desperate to message X even though I was furious with him. He'd opened communication between us again, and the temptation to share the scratchy, scared feeling inside at seeing Milton again almost overwhelmed me.

But he hadn't messaged me back even after I'd threatened him.

He'd sent me nothing, and I refused to put my hurt out there only for it to hang in neverland.

Curling up the sleeves of my paint-splattered shirt, I sagged in the blistering hot morning. Ever since the call about Milton, I'd stayed busy. I'd baked cakes for Jim and Zander. I'd played with Peng, added a final coat of paint to my skirting boards in the living room, and now decided to attack the gutters where arrogant dandelions grew.

Autumn was coming, which meant bad weather and rain, and no way did I want my newly decorated house to leak.

I marched back inside and grabbed a pair of rubber gloves and a few trash bags. Peng came trotting from where he'd been cooling himself on an ice mat I'd bought him. I'd learned he didn't like the heat, and after freezing the mat overnight, it stayed nice and cool for most of the day, giving him a reprieve.

He meowed and wound himself around my ankles.

Ducking, I scratched his chin. "You don't want to be out there today. It's roasting." Standing upright, my cell phone fell out of my shallow back pocket, clattering to the floor.

The SIM inbox from the phone X had given me—the one I shouldn't still care about—flashed with a new message.

I moved embarrassingly fast.

> *Please don't go to the police. I'm within your twelve-hour deadline. And I'm sorry for messaging you last night. It was a mistake. It won't happen again.*

Frustrated anger roared through me. I almost punched my screen.

A mistake? What was the mistake? The fact that you got caught spying on me or that you can't seem to stop?

Glowering at my phone, I wished I had the willpower to block him and throw away the device. I wouldn't go to the police. I wasn't the type to hurt someone who'd helped me. But I also couldn't stay in touch with someone who'd broken up with me.

He didn't break up with you! You weren't going out, for goodness' sake!

Every emotion I'd done my best to pretend wasn't real raged into being. I'd shoved X out of my head and heart and replaced him with Zander. I'd baked my neighbor a vanilla sponge this morning to thank him for Peng but also because I was going to be brave and ask him out.

It might be too soon, and my triggers might still flare, and I might have unresolved feelings for another man, but...BUT...I was ready to move on and get out of this house and start living again.

You're right. I shouldn't still watch you. But I had to know you were okay.

And you don't think I deserve to know that **you're** okay? You don't think it's cruel to barge into someone's life, make them care, then vanish like you never existed?

I'm sorry.

That's it?

I don't know what you want me to say.

How about you tell me your name and where you live? Tell me why you went so cold? Tell me how you could be with me the way you were and then just disappear?

Angry tears pricked my eyes, but I didn't let them fall.

Peng meowed again, headbutting my ankle. I wasn't done. I sent another message.

You said you had a crush on me, yet you walked away so easily. That makes me think you never felt anything toward me or you're utterly heartless because no one who said those things and did what you did could walk away without a goodbye.

I agree on all those points. I'm not a good guy. I did warn you. I started watching you to keep you safe and by staying with you I put you in danger. I did the only thing I could.

Do you honestly think I'm buying this nonsense? How did you put me in danger?

It took him a few minutes, but my phone finally vibrated.

I put you in danger because when I'm with you, I lose control. You make me become someone else. And after everything you've survived, no way could I ever do that to you.

So you're saying you'll snap like that bastard did and strangle me to death?

319

No, of course not.

You're saying you'll beat me black and blue just for talking to my neighbor?

Never. I'm not a lunatic.

I kinda think you are actually, because if you wouldn't strangle me or beat me, then how would you put me in danger?

Christ, don't you get it?
Do I have to be black and white with you?

Yes. Be VERY black and white.

Fine. I can't be around you because when I'm with you, I want you. I want you so fucking badly, and I honestly don't know if I'd be able to stop myself.

A full-body shudder woke up every nerve ending and desire.
My heart burned like a comet.
My core clenched.
I grew wet and needy and angry. Very, *very* angry that, for the first time in my life, I'd responded to a man the way I'd always hoped. He'd delivered pleasure in ways I'd only read about, and then he'd left because he thought I was a fragile little victim who would break if he let loose.
Stupid, idiotic man.
He sent another text while I stewed in lust so violent, so vicious, I snarled at nothing and paced the kitchen.

That night in your bedroom, when I helped you come for the first time, drove me into some pretty nasty places. I meant what I said when you'd be fucked five ways to Sunday and that isn't how you should be treated.

I almost convulsed at the imagery.
Of X taking me without apology. Driving into me. Freeing me from the chains Milton had wrapped me in.
I needed sex to shatter my rickety prison.

I needed to replace my past with the present, and I didn't want quaint missionary in the dark. I didn't want someone to whisper sweet nothings and touch me with velvet gloves.

I wanted bruises to replace old bruises.

I wanted real and messy and hard and fast and *connection*.

And that hurt because as much as I crushed on Zander, I couldn't see him delivering the type of explosive, obsessive, animalistic chaos that I needed. And I didn't think I could move on until I'd been thrown around in pleasure instead of pain. I didn't know how to fully heal until another man made me feel as weak and as vulnerable as Milton had that night, only to deliver mind-splintering orgasms instead of life-stealing horror.

Did that make me messed up?

Would it make sense to anyone but me?

I didn't know, and I was sick of not knowing, but I *needed* to know. I wanted to be taken, and ruled, and protected, and pleasured, and the fact that X had woken all these dark colliding, chaotic needs inside me pissed me the *hell* off. He might be man enough to make me come, but he wasn't man enough to make me heal, and that was fine.

It's fine.

It's not his job.

I don't need him.

I'm done.

You know you could've just asked what I wanted instead of assuming for me. If you had, you would've known I wanted everything you just said. But it's too late now. You left, and I'm busy. You have twenty-four hours to remove those cameras or else.

He responded within a few seconds.

Or else what?

Fury made me grin like a madwoman. I didn't know how he did it, but good God, he turned me on. Just a few messages, and I was as wet as I had been on my couch when he'd kissed me.

Or else I'll take the gift you gave me and masturbate in my back garden. I'll show you just what you're missing all while I prove that I don't need you.

"There." I grinned at Peng. "That'll teach him." Swiping away my ponytail, I marched toward the back door. "If he didn't see how I responded to him or how much I wanted him, then he's as blind as a freaking bat and good riddance."

Stomping to the ladder, I shoved the bin liners into my waistband, then wrapped one hand around a rung.

My phone buzzed.

If you climb up that ladder, I'm going to snap.

My heart added feathers to its burning comet, turning into a flying fireball.

I can do whatever the hell I want.

Like hell you can. I didn't put this much time and effort into keeping you alive only for you to kill yourself.

Stop watching me. Stop messaging me. Leave me the hell alone.

Last chance, Lori. Hire someone else to clean your gutters. It's not safe to do it on your own.

The fact that he cared so much about my well-being. The fact that a text about something as mundane as house maintenance could somehow become foreplay ought to have warned me not to push any further.

But…screw it.

It was my turn to snap.

My turn to be ridiculous and wild and stupid.

The only way I'm not going up this ladder is if you make me.

And then I tossed my phone onto the chair and scurried up to the roof.

Forty-Four

Zander

Threats Have Consequences

MY EYES STUNG FROM SHOVING BROWN contacts in. My hair still reeked of black hair dye. And I'd dressed so damn fast, I honestly didn't know how I wasn't wearing two different shoes.

Bolting out of the conservatory, I breathed hard behind my mask and slipped through the fence palings. Racing over her lawn, I caught sight of her as I cut around the side. She balanced precariously with one arm wrapped around the ladder and an open bin liner in the other. Her rubber gloves were already covered in decaying muck from reaching into the gutters.

"*Lori*! Get your ass down here, right the fuck now!"

Peng meowed and charged from inside, almost making me trip. Leaping over him, I skidded to a stop at the bottom of the ladder just as one of the old wooden rungs cracked and splintered.

My heart seized.

Sailor let out the quietest, "*Oh.*"

And then she tumbled, mud and weeds flying, bin liner fluttering, and her highly breakable body tipping backward.

I didn't think. I just acted.

Spreading my arms, I judged her trajectory and braced myself.

She landed as a dead weight, sprawling like a bride in my embrace.

"*Oof.*" Staggering backward, I struggled to keep my balance so we both didn't plummet into the flowers. My shoulders screeched. My arms trembled. I fought to find her center of gravity.

Her panicked eyes met mine as I finally stabilised and clutched her close.

For a moment, she didn't move. She panted hard, shock switching to realisation of how close she came to breaking her back or worse.

I drowned in her vibrant blue eyes. I crippled beneath the thundering of my heart.

Emotions *surged* through me. Protective ones. Possessive ones. Grateful and angry and needy ones.

Christ, I'd missed her.

I hadn't been aware how wrong life felt without her in it. How empty my arms were. How painful my loneliness had become.

I needed to kiss her. Touch her. Make sure she was okay.

But all I could think about was her deliberately putting herself in harm's way. She'd been pig-headed and reckless, and it made me far too fucking angry. All those sleepless nights of watching out for her. All those moments I put my own well-being on the line to heal hers.

She owed me, goddammit.

She owed me for caring, and this was how she repaid me?

No.

Just no.

Not gonna happen.

"*You!*" She shoved both hands against my chest, smearing my black t-shirt with gunk.

I tripped backward and dropped her. Her feet swung down just in time to keep her standing. Tripping away from me, she ripped off her dirty rubber gloves and tossed them onto the grass.

Balling her fists, she hissed, "What the *hell* are you doing here? How dare you—"

"What the hell am *I* doing here? What the hell are *you* doing?" I flung an arm at the decrepit ladder. "That relic is rotten to its core. It could've killed you!"

"Don't be so dramatic. It wouldn't have killed—"

"How about I finish the job? Seeing as you're so determined to put yourself at risk!"

"Don't you dare threaten me—"

"Why?" I stalked into her, seething behind my mask. "If your life means so little to you, then why should I care? Why should I do my best to keep you safe?"

What the fuck are you doing?

This wasn't me.

I didn't mean any of this, but…I couldn't stop.

"I didn't ask you to keep me safe, you asshole!" She bared her teeth. Peng bounced around with unhappy meows. Neither of us paid him any attention. "You're the one who appointed yourself my protector!"

"And good thing I did. Otherwise, you'd be in fucking pieces right now!"

"I was already in pieces, you prick!"

"Then you're welcome! I seem to have done such a bang-up job looking after you that you're now healed enough to do idiotic things like cripple yourself!"

"I would *not* have crippled myself!" Her cheeks shot red with rage. "And you lost any right to worry about me the moment you ghosted me! You never showed at the movies. You never even replied!"

"I wouldn't have had to ghost you if you hadn't made me want you!"

"Oh, so this is *my* fault, is it?" She threw her hands up in the air. "Of course. Go ahead. Be the typical cliché moron blaming a woman for his behavior. His stalking, spying, shady *stupid* behaviour!"

Snatching her around the shoulders, I held her tight. "Careful, Lori. Be really fucking careful."

"Or what? You'll leave again?"

I panted hard behind my mask, my fingers digging deep. Beneath my fury, bone-breaking gratefulness flooded me. She was still alive, still whole, still mine.

Mine.

She's **always** *been mine.*

My voice lowered to a growl. "Or I'll take you into the house and show you *exactly* how furious I am."

She quaked with a full-body shudder then shoved my hands off her. Her eyes flooded with heat. "No, you won't. You would never lay a finger on me and that's the damn problem!"

"I remember laying three fingers on you if I'm not mistaken," I hissed, uncontrollable lust arcing through me. "And a tongue."

A wicked glint appeared in her molten stare. "Funny, I remember begging for more and you refusing."

"You weren't ready."

"Don't tell me what I was or wasn't, you pompous jerk."

"You were still covered in bruises—"

"And I wanted you to paint me with new ones. Ones I chose!" Her rage billowed to match mine. Curling her fist, she struck me in the chest. "You were so intent on fixing me, you didn't see what was right in front of your face. Why did you have to make me feel that level of pleasure, huh? Why did you awaken me to all these feelings and then have the *audacity* to just *vanish*." Hitting me again, she snarled, "I'm so pissed off at you. I hate that you're here. I hate that you're still trying to protect me all while being so stupidly blind." Laughing, she shrugged. "But you know what? It's fine. I'm *fine.* I don't want you anymore. I'm not some victim anymore. I'm not some breakable doll to wrap in bubble wrap. I'm alive and horny, and I'm done playing whatever game this is. So go away, X. Vanish like you always do. Leave me alone so I can find someone else who will give me—"

"You're not finding anyone."

"You can't stop me. I'm going to pick a guy who—"

"No way in *hell* is that happening. No fucking *way* am I letting another man touch you. *Ever.*"

"You don't own me! I can do whatever I damn well want!"

My heart pounded as I gave in to the possession, the obsession. "Try me and see what happens."

"Okay, fine. Let's see what happens. Tell you what, I'll go out right now and find a guy to do what you refuse to do, and you can damn well *watch.*"

"Last warning." My voice resembled tar and gravel. "I'm not in the mood to fight with you."

"Well, I am. I've been in the mood ever since you first touched me!"

"I need you to go inside. Right now."

"More demands, huh? Alright, two can play at that game." Stepping toward me, she hissed, "What *I* need is for you to come here and kiss me."

My cock almost crawled out of my black slacks.

I shook and shattered and clung to the last shreds of my self-control. "I don't come on command."

"You sure about that? Pretty sure you came last time."

"Careful—"

"No, *you* be careful." Her smile was nasty. "Just go away, alright? Your threats won't work because I know they're empty."

I went fatally still. "You don't think I'll punish you for putting your life in danger?"

Stop right now.

This wasn't safe.

The doctor in me screamed to end this. This fight careened toward one conclusion. A conclusion that would scramble all her healing and leave me as the guy who hurt her.

She rolled her eyes and crossed her arms. "Actually, I think you're repressed and afraid and would rather walk away than let yourself go."

"I let go, and this won't end well."

She sniffed with arrogance. "For you, probably. But for me, I'll get what I've been begging for all along."

It was my turn to quake and burn and *yearn.*

My thoughts turned black. If I gave in, this wouldn't be nurturing and nice. I wouldn't be able to give her sweet and soft. Fucking her when I was this angry would be like a physiotherapist allowing his patient rehabbing from a broken leg to enter a marathon.

It'll break her all over again.

"Go inside, Lori. Lock the door."

She smiled with a terrible little grin. "Nope. You know what? I'm going to do exactly what I said and find a man who's willing to follow through on his threats." Spinning away, she flounced toward the back door. "See ya."

My teeth cracked I clenched so hard.

What the fuck are we doing?

This didn't even make sense.

"You dare approach another guy, and I call in all my debts."

She turned back to face me slowly. "What's that supposed to mean? Debts? What debts?"

I tried to stop words from forming.

I did my best to be better.

I failed.

My boot-encased feet thudded toward her as the politeness and professionalism I'd clung to all my life cracked piece by piece. "Did you honestly think I've been keeping you safe all this time for *free*?" I cocked my head. "That I've invested so many hours into making sure you were whole again just so another man could have you?"

Fuck, what are you doing?

Her eyes bugged, desire pooling like blue addiction. "W-What are you saying?"

"I'm saying that you are *mine*. If you want a man—an undeserving man who might hurt you, use you, and disrespect you—then I suppose that man will have to be me."

She gulped and backpedalled toward the door.

I waited to see fear. To see panic. All I saw was her chest heaving and lips glistening and her surrendering to everything that I'd promised.

I hunted her. Slowly. "Where are you going? Suddenly afraid?"

She scrambled for words. "O-Of course not. I'm not afraid of you."

"Good. Then come here and prove I'm the only man permitted to touch you."

Her nose stuck up. "I'm not yours, you jerk. I'm my own person. I'm—"

"You might think that, but you're not. You're *mine*, Sailor Rose. And you owe me for every night you made me hard watching you through the window. You owe me for every morning you made me fall in love with you watching you in the garden. You owe me for every smile and touch and moment. You've driven me insane. You've turned me into someone I don't even recognise. And I'm done. You want to see me snap? Congratu-fucking-lations. You're about to get your wish."

"H-How do you know my full name?"

Black spots in my eyes.

Faintness over my thoughts.

Fuck, I just slipped. I should apologise. I needed to get a grip on myself and stop being this asshole.

But...I'd given in.

There was no going back.

"You know what?" I bared my teeth. "I'm done with this." Stepping into her, I grabbed her around the waist and hoisted her over my shoulder. Spanking her ass, I stalked toward the back door and sidestepped the orange kitten chasing us.

"Put me down!" She pummeled my back. "X, what the hell?"

I couldn't talk.

I literally couldn't string two words together.

I was too afraid, too annoyed, too worked up. I shook my head and spanked her again. Not hard but not gentle either.

Carrying her inside, I waited until Peng dashed over the threshold before slamming the door and tossing her onto her feet.

The second she was free, she backed up and shoved a finger in my face. "Get out. Right now."

"No." Balling my hands, I stalked her. Any remnants of who I was, the oath I took, the decisions I'd made to be the best guy I could be were shredded by my feet by the very real knowledge, the very painful *agonising* knowledge that if I'd been just a second later, she would've been hurt so, so badly.

And it would've been her fault.

Her stupid, stubborn fault because she didn't want to rely on anyone.

I was so *sick* of people relying on me, but in one idiotic move, she'd proven she didn't need my help anymore.

And I was done.

Done protecting her.

Done mollycoddling her.

If she was brave enough to climb up a ladder and flirt with certain death, then she was healed enough to deal with me.

Her back crashed against the wall by the fridge in the same spot where I'd kissed her the last time.

I'd found a limit to my self-control that night.

I'd strayed over a line and kissed her harder than I'd ever kissed anyone.

And now, I found another limit.

I found a temper I never knew I had.

A temper that chewed through all my politeness and made me fucking *rage*.

Slapping my hands on either side of her head, I trapped her against the wall. "Does this feel like an empty threat to you?"

Her palms landed on my chest, trying to shove me away.

I absorbed her push, barely rocking on my feet.

Her eyes narrowed. "Stop crowding me."

"I'm done taking orders from you. I'm done treating you gently. If you can put yourself in danger, then why the fuck can't I?"

"W-What do you mean?"

"You want me to give you what you want? Alright then." My gaze dropped to her parted lips. "I'm going to give you everything you asked for, and I'm not going to stop until both of us are broken."

Clamping my hand over her eyes, I wrenched down my mask with the other. "Oh, and by the way, you should probably pick a safe word."

Forty-Five

Sailor

Emotional Explosion

I SQUIRMED AND THRASHED AS X blindfolded me with his hand, then smashed his mouth to mine.

He claimed me in one vicious, *violent* kiss.

Collapsing against me, he made my heart stop, my mind snap, and my soul flutter into tatters at his feet.

He kissed me painfully hard, *exquisitely* hard.

With a single kiss, he bulldozed through the fortress I'd painstakingly built. A fortress I didn't even know existed until its bricks shattered into dust and I snapped into a creature I didn't recognise.

I switched from fighting him to kissing him back.

Our fight sharpened the air. The tension and frustration. The freedom I'd felt at speaking up for myself and embracing wildness. The chaos and need, the crazy and desperate. I didn't have to hide with him. I could yell at him without fearing he'd strike. I could strip away all my lies and be mean and needy and wrong.

God, I'd never gotten this angry before over something this trivial. Never let myself feel these levels of emotions.

But now?

Now I felt *all* of them.

I felt need and annoyance, betrayal and relief.

But beneath all of them, I felt love and lust and bone-aching longing.

I fought him as his tongue speared past my lips, slicing through my thoughts and setting me blissfully free. My carefully cultivated personality of likes and dislikes, limits and desires all tumbled like hollow dominos.

With a guttural groan, he attacked me in a maelstrom of nasty, nice, bruising, and blissful. We kissed hungrily, savagely. I lost the ability to think as he touched me, kissed me, then kicked my legs apart and pressed his hips into mine.

He thrust up as he shoved his tongue in my mouth.

I no longer knew if I fought him off or dragged him closer.

I lost track of his hands, his lips, his tongue. He touched me with rabid fingers all while holding me reverently.

I wasn't afraid.

I was *liberated.*

I kissed him back.

Harder, deeper, meaner.

I bit his bottom lip until I tasted blood. I clawed at his neck until I left my mark.

He snarled and almost shoved me through the wall with his need.

My fists pummelled his shoulders, siphoning all my feelings into physical form. But he didn't stop. He just accepted my violence. He let me punch him all while he kissed me like a man intent on consuming my every thought and wish and dream.

And I loved him for that.

I loved that I could give in to this lunacy and embrace my need to stand up for myself all while giving in. I loved that he dominated me, but I never, *not once,* felt unsafe.

He was everything I'd been looking for and the thought of him vanishing after this? It made me grab fistfuls of his hair and yank him painfully close. To hold on tight. To jerk and punish and *hurt.*

He snarled into my mouth, relinquishing all his power to me, all while forcing me to submit to him. I surrendered to his control and shivered at his sacrifice to be my punching bag while he dragged me, kicking and screaming, into freedom.

I would never be the same after this. Never want another man after this—

"Slut!"

I gasped as Goblin-Milton sliced through my thoughts.

"Always knew you were a whore."

I fell backward through time.

Past and present combined, delivering every one of Milton's punches, kicks, and suffocation. I went rigid in X's arms. Phantom pain ripped through my limbs. Tears leaked against my control.

He froze.

His fingers tightened over my eyes, keeping me blind all while he wrenched his mouth away.

"No, don't—" I mewled. "Don't stop."

"How can I not?" he choked.

Our mania turned to agony. We stood in the eye of the storm, breaking each other apart.

"I didn't mean to...it's not you." I squirmed beneath his fingers.

"Let me see. Drop your hand."

He didn't reply. Didn't move.

Trapped, my heart seized, breasts ached, and legs struggled to stand. More tears slipped beneath his palm, brimming with frustration.

I wanted to *scream.*

Why did I have to cry?

Why did Milton still have this hold on me?

Why did you have to stop?

"Hey…it's okay." He shuddered, nudging his nose to mine, softly, gently. "It's just me. I know I'm angry with you right now, and you're furious with me, but…I would never hurt you. You know that, right? This stops the second you change your mind. Just say the word, and I'm gone."

"It's not that." I sagged against him, giving in to him keeping me blindfolded. "It's not even him. I…" I struggled to put into words to describe the sweetest ecstasy he'd given. "I was free for the first time. I stepped into someone I've always wanted to be."

He stayed quiet, letting me sift through my truth.

But then he shifted as if to let me go.

I dug my nails into his waist. "If you leave, you will never be welcome back here again. Do you hear me?"

His fingers flexed over my eyes. "But if I'm making it worse—"

"You're not. You're making everything better." Swallowing hard, I tipped up my chin. "Kiss me."

"We should talk about—"

"I'm done talking. What I want is for you to finish what you started."

He let out a harsh growl. "Lori, I—"

"Wait."

Lori.

He called me Sailor Rose before.

How?

Sucking in a shaky breath, I whispered, "You called me Sailor. In the garden."

He went deathly still.

Cold water trickled down my spine. "X…h-how do you know my real name?"

A tortured noise sounded in the back of his throat. His hips rocked into mine almost as if he had no control over the obsession we'd started.

Blinded by him, my other senses kicked in until I swore every part of him throbbed with guilt and regret and grief.

I hated it.

I hated that our passion switched to self-consciousness, ruining everything.

And in that moment, on the precipice of getting everything I wanted, I didn't want to know. I didn't want to see his face or know his name or have reality ruin this.

I suffered my own guilt that I'd chosen to sleep with a stranger instead of dating my kind-hearted neighbour, but...I couldn't deny that pieces of me had fallen for X.

I'd tripped the night he'd watched me cry in the garden, then wrapped me in a blanket to keep me warm. I'd fallen with every message and whisper, every touch and text.

I'd fallen for a stranger all while falling for my neighbour, and now my heart tore in two because I didn't want to stop.

Anger returned, filling me with spark and fire. I dug my fingers over his thundering heart, fighting the urge to gouge my way through his chest to see if he felt as confused as me. "Actually, don't answer that. I don't—"

"I've watched you for a while," he groaned as if the words were torn out of him. "I've heard your friend Lily call you by your full name. I..." He swallowed hard as if scrambling for half-truths. "I've seen your mail too."

The darkness from his hand was absolute; I couldn't see if he was lying.

His fingers threaded with mine against his chest. Without a word, he pressed my palm down until it felt as if I held his pounding heart. His body trembled with heat. The closeness of his lips made me tingle, all while my stomach flipped upside down as a bolt of lust arrowed like lightning.

Why did he feel so familiar?

Why was I so drawn to him?

It was too much. Too intense. Too *painful.*

He shifted and pressed his lips to my ears, making me break out in goosebumps. "I've also watched your neighbour."

I melted.

I *wanted.*

"You have?"

The tip of his tongue traced the shell of my ear, making me shudder. "He's an idiot. If he had any guts, he'd tell you that he loves you. He'd admit he's wanted to touch you like this for years."

"How could you possibly—"

"Know that he loves you?" A broken chuckle fell from him. "You just have to look at him to see it."

My heart twisted in my chest. "Why are you telling me this?"

"Because you should order me to leave and be with him instead."

I trembled at the thought of stumbling next door and kissing

Zander this way.

I couldn't picture it. Couldn't see him ever being this rough with me, this hungry with me.

And that made me sad because Zander must never know about this.

Lily must never know.

X had promised to be my dirty secret, and he would stay that way.

"Stop talking about my neighbour."

"You should give him a chance," he murmured. "He would treat you far better than——"

"And there it is. I *knew* it." Defiant annoyance surged, followed by aching frustration. I struggled to get rid of his blinding palm. "I knew your threats were empty. You have no intention of——"

"Fucking you?" He drove his hips into mine, branding me with his hardness. "Are you so sure about that?"

I shivered, lust dragging me back into its dark whirlpool. "Words are cheap."

"Words are safety." His lips skated from my ear and along my jaw. "Did you think of one, by the way? Seeing as you're so determined to make me do this, and you've just proven you'll have flashbacks, I need a word. Give me a word that will make me stop the second you say it. Because without it, I won't. I won't check in with you next time you flinch. I won't ask if you're okay when I'm balls deep inside you. That's my promise to you. I messed this up by stopping now. And I won't have the strength to do it again. When I kiss you next, nothing will make me stop." His voice dropped to a rough snarl. "Nothing but a word, so give me one…before it's too late."

"Are you trying to scare me off?" My heart raced. "Because it's not working."

"Don't you get it?" he hissed. "I'm scaring *myself.* This isn't for you, it's for me. Give me a goddamn word, so I have a line not to cross because I'm losing myself to everything I've ever wanted, and I honestly don't know how I'll cope." Pulling back a little, cotton rustled as if he went to pull his mask back up. "A word, Sailor, or I'm leaving."

Sailor.

It felt so strange to have him call me that. To hear his voice ache with despair.

It clutched me around the heart and made me leap off the last of my trepidation.

I chose the first word that popped into my head.

"North," I panted, my fingernails stabbing into his chest. "My safe word is north."

An animalistic grunt wrenched from him. *"That's* the word you chose?"

My eyes tried to flare beneath his hand.

Oh God.

Why?

Why did it have to be that one?

Why did I link Zander to this?

Why did I say his last name?

I opened my mouth to change my answer. To pick any other stupid letter but X made a noise that arrowed straight through my heart and left me in pieces.

"North it is." He slammed his mouth back on mine, wrenching a moan from the depths of my soul. I cried out as he drove his tongue inside.

He lost control, broke every resistance, and *devoured* me.

And I let him.

I clung to his hair as he delivered the same mind-twisting pleasure he'd given the first night he'd made me come. His every lick, his every breath, his every rock drove me past flashbacks and fears and straight into freedom and fantasy.

I wasn't afraid or scared.

Because I trusted him.

I trusted him to hurt me as well as heal me.

I *trusted* him, and good *God*, that was the best feeling in the world.

I no longer worried or took responsibility for my own protection because *he* was here. This man who'd walked into my life as if he'd always belonged. This man who caged me in his arms and imprinted his very soul onto my lips.

His heart pounded against my ribs as if it fought to crawl inside me. He pawed at me as if I'd vanish at any moment.

I cried out as he suddenly lifted me with one arm and waited for me to wrap my legs around his waist. We both hissed as the throbbing heat of his erection branded between us.

Keeping his palm over my eyes, he carried me into the living room, never stopping our kiss.

Dumping me onto my feet again, his lips turned demonic.

I answered him back with feral starvation.

The deeper we kissed, the more nothing else mattered.

Not names.

Not pasts or mistakes or truths.

Just this.

Just heartbeats and blood, need and belonging.

Throwing my arms around his shoulders, I hung on as his head turned, his lips slid, and he yanked our kiss from insanity to cruelty.

Tears welled and fell, streaking down my cheeks as I surrendered every piece.

I needed him to break me. To break *with* me.

I needed violence because I was strong enough to survive.

I needed bloodshed and brutality because those were proof of life and living.

"I'm not going to stop just because you're crying. You haven't said the safe word, so I'm going to take everything you have to offer me." Spinning me around, he pinched my nape and kept my eyes facing the living room wall.

The fresh white paint I'd used gleamed gold from the sun. The ancient box TV hissed with snow, turning itself on at some point in our mauling. Peng huddled on the windowsill, looking at us with wide green eyes.

X hissed into my ear from behind. "Don't turn around. You do, and I'm gone."

Panting hard, dripping wet with need, I swayed in the centre of the living room while he stomped down the corridor. He moved about in the laundry. The sounds of him raiding Nana's old boxes of supplies echoed, just before he marched back and set my skin alight with sensitivity.

Just having him in the same room as me caused my entire body to break out in mind-searing flames.

Crowding behind me, he pressed something soft and heavy over my eyes. Without a word, he tied the butterfly bead mask in place, repeating what we'd done the night he'd finally snapped and permitted me to make him come.

I trembled as he spun me around and tugged at my shirt. "Off."

Raising my arms, I didn't speak as he removed my black shirt and unhooked my bra beneath. My nipples pebbled at the sound of my clothing being tossed away.

My heart leaped into my throat as his fingers brushed my bare belly, undoing the button of my jeans shorts and unzipping me. "Hold onto me if you need to."

I fumbled for his shoulders, blind and completely at his mercy. Balancing on one leg, I bit my bottom lip as he stripped my shorts off, then slid my underwear down.

My pulse skyrocketed as I stood before him, unable to see and utterly nude.

Pulling my hands off his shoulders, he commanded, "Stand there. Don't move." Clothing rustled as he undressed. His boots thudded as if he'd tossed them aside. The sounds of my curtains being drawn and the sudden disappearance of the sun on my skin hinted he'd cocooned us in our own private world.

I breathed hard as he came close.

My skin broke out in searing goosebumps as he cupped my chin and pushed me down. "Kneel."

I gulped as a ricochet of womb-clenching lust had my knees wobbling.

My mouth watered to suck him.

But the moment I was on my knees, he pushed me until I sprawled backward, kicking my legs out, and landing on the nest of cushions I'd scattered on the floor while waiting for a new couch to be delivered.

Disappointment filled me.

I wanted to suck him.

I wanted to make him break as much as he was breaking me.

"Why do you have to be so gorgeous?" he whispered, his finger tracing the seam of my core.

I flinched at the intimate touch.

I moaned as he penetrated me with a single finger.

I thrashed as he drove in deep, testing my readiness, driving me straight into hell.

"Fuck, you're wet. So incredibly wet."

I had no words.

None.

I didn't care what I looked like, sounded like. With my eyes blindfolded and every sense blazing, I didn't know how much longer I could stand it.

"Do it," I groaned. "Please."

"Do what?" He inserted a second finger. "Make you come?"

"Fuck me. I-I'm going out of my mind."

And there, in my X-induced delirium, Milton couldn't find me. The past didn't exist. The future didn't matter. I had no bills to pay, no walls to paint, no healing to solve.

I was just his, and I really, *really* needed him to fuck me because my heart was about to burst and my sanity about to shatter.

Shaking so hard my teeth clacked, I reached for the mask blinding me. I needed to see him. To watch. But his fingers withdrew, and he tapped them warningly against my thigh. "If you want me to fuck you, you'll leave the mask where it is."

I pouted but dropped my arms. "It isn't fair. I want to see you."

"Next time." His voice resembled brimstone and broken glass.

The promise of a next time made an orgasm build. Heavy heat coiled around my bones, tingling in my blood.

Something rustled again, followed by the telltale sound of a condom wrapper. The slap of his wallet on the floor hinted he'd come prepared.

I was both grateful and jealous.

If he ever tried to use those supplies on another girl, I would break far more laws than he had while stalking me.

The cushions shifted a little as he moved between my legs, but he didn't lie down. Instead, he wrapped his arms around my shoulders and sat me up. His palms cupped my cheeks as we sat facing each other.

His lips found mine again.

I melted.

I burned and burned and *burned* as he bit my bottom lip and kissed me.

With a soft cry, I crawled onto his lap and slung my arms around his neck.

He didn't stop me.

With a snarl, he clutched me painfully close and plastered our stinging, searing nakedness together. My breasts to his chest, my wetness against the hard length of his erection stabbing upright between us.

Our kiss turned as deep as before. As demonic as before.

I felt endlessly safe, tragically adrift, and incredibly, wonderfully *free.*

A grunt tore out of him as our kiss turned savage.

Lick for lick, bite for bite.

But that wasn't even the best part.

The best part was how he *hugged* me. Squeezed me. Suffocated me in his arms as if he'd never let me go.

I hugged him back. Our heads tilting, our breaths merging, our bodies fighting to become one.

His hips rocked against me, pulsing with hungry little thrusts.

I tried to reach between us, but he grabbed my wrist and planted my palm on his chest again, granting his thundering heartbeat into my control. His mouth opened wide, kissing me, binding me, keeping me his prisoner to plunder.

I couldn't fight.

Couldn't run.

But unlike the harrowing helplessness of the night I'd almost died, I wasn't afraid.

I was ecstatic, electric, and enthralled.

I needed more.

So much *more.*

Looping his fingers around my throat, he squeezed just a little.

I froze as the past did its best to splice over the now.

Another man had once touched me there.

Another man had almost killed me.

But he was gone, and X was here, and I wasn't responsible for my reaction.

Pressing my throat deeper into his grip, I dropped my hand from his chest and wrapped my fingers around his condom-slippery cock.

He grunted as I squeezed him. His fingers flexed around my neck in time with mine.

It made me wild.

We became mirror images—plugged into the same mania, mimicking each other with matching finger pulses.

My breath caught as he squeezed me.

His breath choked as I squeezed him.

We writhed together, desperation becoming not just a word but an existential crisis.

"Please," I moaned. *"Please—"*

"Fuck, what are you doing to me?" His forehead pressed against mine as his lips parted wide, sucking in air as I jerked him up and down. "I can't think. I can't move. I can barely function with how much I need you."

"Then take me." I fisted the base of his cock.

He let out an explosive breath, his erection throbbing in my hand.

"Sailor...*fuck.*" He kissed me again, meanly, desperately. "You're making me lose my goddamn mind."

With the blackness blinding me, my other senses turned ruthlessly sharp.

His voice. His smell. His energy.

They weren't unknown.

I'd heard his voice for years. I'd smelled his crisp, clean scent on the summer breeze. I recognised the electricity of his soul almost as if it were mine.

Something bound us together with familiarity while he kept me blind and dined on me.

Was this what people meant when they said they found their soulmate?

Was it normal to feel as if you knew someone to the depths of their being when you didn't even know their face?

"Put me inside you," he whisper-choked against my ear. "Now. Before I come all over you."

I shuddered as every part of me turned into molten obedience.

Arching up on my knees, I angled him and hovered.

When I didn't sink down, he groaned, "Are you trying to kill me? What are you waiting for?" His hand fell from around my throat, trailing to my breast and squeezing hard. "Do it. Before I break."

"I can't see." I licked my lips. "I don't know where—"

"Let me." His large hand wrapped around my smaller one, making me squeeze him extra hard. Pushing forward a little, he kissed the tip of my nose. "Now sit."

I obeyed.

I went slow until I felt absolute heaven.

His crown pressed against my entrance, unapologetically thick and hot and hard.

"Christ, you're killing me." His other arm wrapped around my waist, pulling me forward and pushing me down.

I smirked despite my heart flying out of my chest. I cried out as the first inch of him sank inside me. "Do you want me to stop?"

He let out the hottest, sexiest groan. "You stop and I die. It's as simple as that."

"Well then..." I clung to his shoulders and sank a little deeper. "We can't have that."

Another inch.

Another madness.

We both cried out. Trembling hard.

We couldn't speak as I sank down and down, stretching over him, claiming him deep, *deep* inside me. Yanking our combined grip off his cock, he captured my cheeks again and smashed his mouth to mine.

He kissed me between snatches of air and tortured groans.

He kissed me as I kept sinking.

His size pinched me with his ownership. His body twitched as if he was seconds away from losing control.

The moment I sat on his thighs, joined in every way possible, we both froze.

My core slowly accepted his intrusion.

Our bodies quickly became one.

His arms wrapped tight and held me down, his mouth found mine and kissed me deep as he thrust up with ferocity.

He fucked me slow and hard, burrowing his face into my shoulder and biting me with need.

"More..." Raking my fingernails over his back, I gave into his thrusts and threw myself into begging. "Please."

He snapped.

Launching forward, he shoved me down and pinned me to the floor. Grabbing both my hands, he slammed them above my head and gripped my wrists.

"You know what word to give me if this becomes too much." He kissed his way down my throat. "If you don't say it, I don't stop."

My skin misted with sweat. My pulse skyrocketed. I bordered on obsession as he held my wrists, and plunged his cock inside me.

I waited for an injection of terror. To remember Milton's abuse and have this incredible experience ruined.

But nothing.

I felt nothing, saw nothing, heard nothing but *him.*

His mouth found mine again, kissing me just as hard as before.

I flung myself into his control and surrendered, opening wide for his possessive tongue.

His hips pulsed between mine, his cock pressing against my clit.

I writhed as he nipped and licked me. My legs wrapped tight around his waist, caught up in the dance, the hunger and thirst and yearning.

His back strained as I clung to him, his hips grinding deeper into me.

He bit my bottom lip.

Hard.

Too hard.

I cried out, automatically struggling.

He held me down and fucked me harder.

My mouth fell wide as he speared again and again inside me, claiming me like spoils of war.

He was ruthless and merciless, and I'd never felt anything so *good.*

The two sides of me—the fighter and the fragile—collided in a chaos of sparks. He took me like he hated me, all while his kisses said he loved me. He gave me violence and salvation.

I transcended thoughts and feelings. I became nothing more than his as he plunged again and again. Taking everything I had to offer all while giving himself in return.

My back arched.

I ruptured with overwhelming completion.

This was sex.

This was freedom.

Togetherness.

Trust.

Total annihilation of self.

Everything ached.

My heart, my bones, my soul, my core.

He filled every corner of me and broke apart every shadow.

He withdrew and drove back where he belonged, shoving me harder and harder against the floor. The cushions scattered. His fingers lashed tighter on my wrists.

But he didn't stop.

He kept taking me, breaking me, freeing me.

"Holy *fuck*," he snarled in my ear. "Why…*how*? How are you doing this to me? Why do you feel this *good*?"

The sensation of being too full and ruthlessly ridden brought out every primitive instinct.

My hips rocked up, forcing him even deeper.

He growled and fucked me in answer.

We strained against each other. Trembling and sweating and going out of our minds with need.

His pulses came faster and faster, stabbing into me again and again, setting my blood on *fire*.

I tensed as stars popped in my veins.

I gasped as he conjured pure heaven.

My eyes snapped closed behind my blindfold as everything coiled to erupt.

I couldn't stand it, couldn't survive it.

I wanted to shatter. I could barely speak as I fought where he held me and begged, "Please...*please*."

Collapsing over me, he found my mouth again and kissed me.

He never stopped taking, his hips pumping with savage need.

We were infected with the same violent sickness. The same uncontrollable connection.

"I can't...I can't wait much longer." He licked my bottom lip. "You need to come for me. Right now."

A full-body shudder had me so close.

Angling his cock, we both groaned as the depth changed and he pressed against a tingling spot inside me. The base of him rubbed perfectly against my clit.

"Oh God. Yes...right there. Don't—" My voice cut off as he shoved me face first into something sparkly and sharp and delicious. "Don't stop. God, *please* don't stop."

"Never." He grunted, driving again and again. "I can't."

I saw literal shooting stars.

My thighs trembled around his hips. The sounds of him fucking me made me spiral that final hill.

Sucking in a breath, his lips brushed my ear as his hands let my wrists go only to land in my hair and hold me down. His weight smothered me against the floor.

Nowhere to go.

No way to stop him.

For a horrifying second, I panicked but then his whisper set me free. "I'm the one inside you, Sailor. I'm the one fucking you. From now on, I'm the only one. You belong to me and you're going to come for me. Because the moment you do, I can join you and, ah *fuck*—"

I came.

I shattered.

He felt me.

He swallowed a curse as I cried out, convulsing with body-fisting waves.

Clench after clench, I exploded with the best orgasm of my life, milking him, gripping him, making him—

"Jesus *Christ*." His pace switched to shallow rutting pumps, captured by his own release. His back locked beneath my fingers; his groan echoed in the room.

His release added another level to mine and I lost myself to it.

We clung to each other as we fell and shattered and when the explosion ceased, we flopped into a sticky, sweaty mess and didn't say a word.

We couldn't.

There weren't any to say.

It was just…perfect.

Forty-Six

Zander

Who Needs Furniture

I'D DONE A GREAT MANY THINGS that were severely bad for my health the past month or so…and that long list started and ended with Sailor Melody Rose.

I'd broken the law for her, disguised myself for her, realised I wanted more with her, and become slightly unhinged. She'd conjured needs in me that I'd never felt before and forced me to come face to face with the fact that I was sick to death of being the good guy.

After almost three decades of convincing myself I could never hurt anyone, I now had the undeniable urge to go on a rampage and let loose all this confusing, clawing, crippling fury, starting with her for putting herself in harm's way.

I'd never been that free in bed before. Never felt that black obsession to consume and dominate. But with her? It'd taken all my willpower not to fuck her into the floor with no apology.

Kinda did that anyway.

Sighing heavily, I gathered her closer where we lay sweat-sticky and breathing hard on mismatched cushions. The living room smelled of fresh paint and she'd gotten rid of the couch and furniture. I liked that the bare bones of the room no longer held memories of what that bastard did to her and had been replaced entirely by what I'd done to her.

I'm also a bastard but at least I killed her with an orgasm instead of jealousy.

Sailor moaned and threw her leg over my thighs. Her arm flung over my waist as she nuzzled deeper, plastering us together. Her heart tapped the same chaotic rhythm mine did.

I'd heard that sex could be the greatest sedative, but I'd never experienced it. Now, I felt as if I'd chugged an entire bottle of sleeping pills.

Licking my lips and trying to get my breath back, I forced myself to be a man again and not the monster who'd just done dirty things to her. Kissing the top of her head, I groaned, "What did you just do to me?" Every part of me felt as if we'd punched each other in a boxing ring until we'd passed out.

Her heavy sigh sounded utterly content. "I believe you finally gave in and took what you wanted for a change." She hugged me tighter. "Feels good, huh?"

"Good?" I could barely keep my eyes open. "That word is nowhere near adequate to describe how I feel."

"And to think I almost had to hog-tie you last time just to give you a handjob."

I choked on a laugh. "How did I not know you were such a temptress beneath all that primness?"

Kissing my chest, she whispered, "You haven't been watching me for that long. It's forgivable that you thought I was just some abuse survivor."

My heart seized.

I'd almost forgotten.

Christ, I'd almost forgotten that I'd fucked her as X. That I was lying here, naked in her house, with black hair and brown eyes and a false identity.

Nausea gushed up my throat.

Protecting her as a masked stranger could be forgiven if my secret ever got out. But fucking her the way I did without telling her who I truly was?

Jesus Christ, she'll hate me for eternity.

It wasn't just the lies at this point. It was the betrayal of the incredible trust she'd given me. I'd felt her flinch a few times. Tasted the salt of her tears as I bulldozed my way through her trauma, but she'd trusted me not to hurt her and I'd trusted her to use the safe word if she wanted me to stop.

But she hadn't said it.

She'd been brave and perfect and wonderful and…*I'm fucked.*
She used your last name as her safe word…

When she'd said it, I'd almost gone into cardiac arrest. Blistering hope bolted through me that perhaps she'd known it was me all along, and that was her way of confessing. That she knew and forgave me and wanted me anyway.

But that was just a dream.

And now I'd woken up and come face to face with the fact that it'd been a slip on her part. A Freudian slip revealing she might have feelings for me as Zander, but whatever crush she had would tear apart the moment she found out just how badly I'd betrayed her.

Fuck, what have I done?

My arm shook as I hugged her harder. Terror I'd never felt before bled through me. I'd lost her. I'd given in to my anger and taken her without telling her the truth, and now...*now*? Fuck, now I'd have to move far away just so I never had to see the disappointment and betrayal in her eyes.

Sailor pressed a kiss to my chest. "Your thoughts are loud again. Are you okay?"

I forced myself to stay calm when all I wanted to do was explode. "Sorry, I..." Truth coated my tongue, painting over my many lies. I might never be able to have her like this again, but while I had her, I couldn't pretend I wasn't deeply, madly, *stupidly* in love with her. "I can't stop thinking about you," I whispered. "How good you felt. How that was the best sex of my life, and I want to do it all over again."

She puffed up with pride. "You sure know how to squeeze my heart. Hearing you say that means the world to me." She grinned. "And I feel the same way. I've never experienced what we just did. *Ever.*"

Goddamn tears pricked my eyes.

Despicable jealousy roared through me.

I was jealous of myself.

Cursing the two versions of me who got totally different sides of the same girl.

Why had I done this? Why had I come here? Why had I ever put on a mask and thought I could survive the fall-out?

Stiffening, I did my best to gather enough strength to stand. To say goodbye. To leave forever. But she clung to me like a baby sloth and buried her face in my neck. "You're not leaving. No way."

The butterfly blindfold hid her stunning blue eyes, keeping my secret. My mask lay in a discarded puddle beside us, mocking me with its skeletal grin.

You can't let her find out.

If she ever learned who I truly was...going to jail would be paradise compared to the way she'd hate me.

My heart slowed with single-minded determination.

I only had one way out of this mess.

X would have to die, and Zander would have to grow a pair of goddamn balls and tell her how he really felt instead of talking about myself in third person.

Colin's warning echoed in my head.

He'd cautioned me not to separate X and Zander as two different people because it would be harder for her when she knew the truth. But now that I'd fucked her like a madman all while telling her to date her neighbour, I'd destroyed any hope of a happy ending. The only way out of this mess was to make my alter ego die a miserable death and be done with it.

God, why did you have to make me fall in love with you?

Why did our grandmothers have to shove us together again and again?

Why was I so weak not to pursue her as Zander when I had the chance?

"You're doing it again," she whispered drowsily. "Now what are you thinking about?"

I shuddered with shame that I couldn't be honest even while being more truthful than I'd ever been. "I'm thinking that I don't want to let you go."

She sucked in a breath. "Then don't."

I squeezed my eyes closed and cursed the agonising fisting of my heart. "I need to leave. I shouldn't be here. I shouldn't have—"

"If you say you regret sleeping with me after just confessing it was the best sexual experience of your life, you're going to make me really mad." She pulled away and went to yank off her blindfold.

Soaring upright, I grabbed her wrists and jerked her hands down. "Don't." Glancing at my mask on the floor, I ordered, "Give me ten seconds, then I'll give you back your sight." Letting her go, I snatched my scarf balaclava, yanked it over my head to bunch around my neck, then pulled up the black material until it almost touched my eyelashes.

Gritting my teeth, I reached around her head and undid the bow. The butterfly wings fell away, leaving her blinking.

The moment her gaze caught mine, she shifted to sit on her knees and balled her hands.

She sucker-punched me with how stunning she was. Naked and sated and so full of fire.

My cock reacted before I could stop myself.

Launching to my feet, I plucked the condom off and headed into the kitchen to dispose of it.

Peng appeared from wherever he'd been hiding, trotting and meowing by my ankle.

Sailor muttered from behind me, "He's still obsessed with you."

I didn't dare acknowledge the orange kitten or the woman who'd successfully made me break. Instead, I padded barefoot and bare into the kitchen and slammed to a stop.

"Eh..." I blinked. My eyes struggled to see what was right in front of me. "Did you get robbed while we were busy?"

"What?" A rustle of limbs and the pad of her feet as she left the floor and came to join me. Her jaw fell. "Oh my God. What on earth?"

Every cupboard was open. Every drawer ajar. Even the fridge was open, spilling icy air all over the floor. Peng meowed and headed toward it, searching for dinner.

In a daze, Sailor scooped him up and cradled him in her arms. The sight of this beautiful naked woman cuddling an orange kitten—a kitten I'd given her—was too much.

My temper flared, protecting me from emotions I just couldn't function feeling.

Stalking forward, I tossed the condom into the trash, then slapped every cupboard closed and shoved in every drawer. Only once the kitchen was back to normal did I shudder with horror by the sink.

Mary and Melody.

Two matchmaking highly meddling ghosts had—

"I mean, I've heard of hauntings and am well used to my TV turning on without me, and Peng regularly has conversations with things I can't see, but this...?" Drifting forward, Sailor placed the cat on the dining room table and stood bravely bare. "This is on another level. If I hadn't seen it, I wouldn't believe it. In fact, I barely believe it even though I just watched you close everything."

My fists curled. "They just can't leave us alone, even when they're dead—" I cut myself off with a grunt.

Fuck.

X wouldn't know about Mary and Melody's lifelong pact to join their bloodlines. To marry a Rose to a North and forever be family.

Spinning to face Sailor, I choked on my heart.

Had she heard? Did she know?

My shaking hand strayed to my mask, making sure it was in place.

She gave no indication of noticing, chewing on her bottom lip and staring at her kitchen in a daze. Slowly, a sly smile crossed her red-kissed lips. "I think Nana just gave us her blessing."

I stumbled backward. I couldn't speak. I didn't trust myself. Once again, jealousy poured through me that Sailor was choosing X over me. She looked at me as if we had a future. She had no qualms about breaking my heart as Zander because her connection with X was so much stronger and *fuck* that hurt. It *killed.* It butchered me because how could I stay living on Ember Drive after this? How could I spy on her through her windows and see her grieving for X after I killed him off?

I wouldn't stand a chance as Zander because I'd break her heart just like she was breaking mine and *good God what the fuck have I done?*

Self-protection made me shut down.

I couldn't stay here anymore.

Marching past her, I headed toward my clothes scattered around the living room.

"Hey!" she squeaked as I brushed past without looking, our naked skin zinging with chemistry. "Where are you going?"

"I-I just remembered. I have something urgent to do." Rage

percolated, tangling with the very real, very scary ability to be cruel all in order to save myself. "I told you we were over. Just because we slept together doesn't make that any less true."

She slammed to a stop on the threshold.

I did my best not to look at her, but I couldn't help throwing her a glance as I snatched my black slacks off the floor.

For a second, she looked as if she'd burst into tears. The next, I wouldn't put it past her to beat me with a frying pan. In the end, she straightened her shoulders and stalked toward me with blue heat in her stare. "Bullshit."

"Excuse me?"

"You're running away again."

"No, I—"

"I'm telling you, X, if you leave, I will *never* speak to you again."

"I'm aware." I fisted my trousers, trembling with the need to pull them on. "This is the last time we'll see each other. This was a mistake—"

"A *mistake*?"

"You're the one who forced me to come over here. You're the one who almost killed herself. What happened afterward was both our faults, but it's over now and—"

"No."

"*No*?" My eyebrows rose, the mask hiding my shock. "What do you mean, no?"

"I mean, I might not know your name or address or a single thing about you, but I do know that when you're afraid, this is what you do." She bared her teeth. "You run the moment you feel anything."

I sneered. "I'm not running. I'm just done with—"

"Protecting me?" She stuck her nose in the air. "Good. I'm glad you're done playing the role of my guardian. It means you can stop treating me as if I'll break."

"Did I treat you as if you'd break when I was fucking you on the floor?"

"No." She smiled a sexy, dangerous smile. "You didn't."

"Well then." Snapping out my trousers, I lifted up a leg to get dressed. "We both agree that you're in charge of your own healing from now on. Whatever we had has run its course."

Dashing to me, she wrenched the trousers out of my hand and tossed them over her shoulder. "*Argh*, you're a stubborn pain in the ass."

"What did you just call me?"

"I called you an idiot."

"And you think calling me names will stop me from walking out the door?"

"I think you need a good slap to acknowledge you were free for just a little while. You let yourself go. In the weeks I've known you, you stiffen up the *moment* I try to care for you in return. You get prickly and cold and say things you don't mean all because you don't know how to lean on others."

"What are you? My psychologist all of a sudden?" Pushing past her, I reached for my pants again.

She kicked them away and shoved her hands against my chest, making me stagger back. "I'm trying to help you the way you helped me, you frustrating idiot!"

"Again with the idiot." My hands curled, pulling on the faint bruises I still had from beating up Chad Harris. She hadn't noticed the marks on my knuckles. So blinded by the disguise that Colin had promised would hide me in plain sight.

For a second, I contemplated ripping my mask off and confessing.

I didn't know how much longer I could do this.

How I'd be able to keep this secret for the rest of my life.

But I had to try because after the things I just said, after the hole I was determined to dig, she'd never look at Zander while X was in her life. And if she ever figured it out, she'd never forgive me, and *I'm done.*

"Get out of my way, Sailor. I'm leaving—"

"You're staying." With the softest gasp, she dropped to her knees and placed her hands on her thighs. Peng scurried from the kitchen, headbutting her for affection, but her eyes never left mine. "Tell me what you want, X, because I owe you another debt. You showed me how much I like being taken with anger, but only by a man I trust implicitly. You shattered every fear I had of him strangling me and gave me a new memory of lust and desire. You've done more for me this afternoon than all the weeks combined and so...I owe you."

Her gaze dropped to my hard cock. She looked older, wiser...sexier with a hint of a dangerous rebellion.

"I'm not letting you walk out that door until I do for you what you did for me. And if that isn't black and white enough for you, I'm telling you, you stubborn pain in my ass, that I *want* you. I don't care who you are. I don't care about tomorrow. I don't care if your name starts with an X or an A or a Z. All I care about is staying this free and so..." She sat higher on her knees. "You have to make another choice."

"What choice?" I strangled, my breath coming short.

"The choice to be free. The choice to drop all your pretences. I don't know why you're terrified of admitting who you truly are, but...you don't have to be afraid with me."

Every part of me *ached.*

It was agonising.

Blinding.

I clung to doing the right thing. "You're making this impossible for me. I'm trying to *protect* you. Even if that means protecting you from myself—"

"And I'm telling you I don't want protecting. Not anymore. Not here. What I *want* is for you to break me. Break *with* me."

My entire body clenched.

My cock ached so badly, I wedged a fist in my stomach trying to ignore the relentless craving to give in. "You're going to kill me."

"If that's what it takes for you to agree, then fine."

I resisted the urge to grab myself and relieve the agony she conjured. "I'm not going to—"

"You know, until today, I didn't know my blood could sizzle like that. I didn't know my insides could turn liquid or that my mind could blank into nothing." Her voice turned to a hot whisper. "I want to show you what that feels like."

"I already know. I felt it. With you."

"Then let me make you feel it again."

I gagged on a groan as my body spasmed with excruciating lust. "Sailor, I'm begging you."

"And *I'm* begging *you*." Her face fell a little as her courage faltered. "Stop thinking about others, X. Stop putting yourself last. Stop being afraid."

My feet moved of their own accord.

Standing over her, I bent and sifted my fingers through her hair. My voice crawled through river rock. "I'm not afraid. And I won't let you antagonise me into touching you again. Are you not listening? I *can't*."

She shrugged. "You're touching me right now." She studied my mask, her beautiful face unreadable. Her smoky eyes and kiss-swollen lips looked so different to the sun-kissed, make-up-free look she usually wore when harvesting her herbs and cooking her concoctions.

I'd known her as the shy girl next door and now as the kneeling vixen offering herself to me.

The two versions of her scrambled the two versions of me.

The right and the wrong.

The saint and the sinner.

The martyr and the monster.

"You've just been given the vote of approval by the one person I loved more than anyone," she whispered. "My nana knows you're a good person and I'm not letting you leave while you're hiding and hurting and being utterly ridiculous. Tell me what you want, X. Tell me how you want me and I'm yours. An orgasm for an orgasm. Isn't that how this game goes?"

I shook my head like a crazy person, trying to get my bearings. My cock went full mast. My balls drew up. My stomach clenched. All that lust, that longing, that lifelong denial of what I truly needed throttled me. "I can't. I-I…shouldn't."

"Why shouldn't you?"

"Because…" All reasons flew out of my head. All the excuses of being the good guy, the caring doctor, the kind friend. I was all of those things, but I was also more. I was lonely and angry and so full of goddamn need I couldn't fucking see straight.

But I'm not Zander.

My breath caught in my lungs as I studied her on her knees.

It would be so easy.

All it would take was a single command.

Two little words I'd never be able to say as Zander but as X? With this mask on and hidden identity…why couldn't I?

I was going to hell anyway.

I'd decided to make X take a flying leap off a cliff.

Come tomorrow, he would cease to exist, I'd block her number, and she would never know that she'd been fucked by her neighbor.

And I would carry this dirty, despicable secret for the rest of my life, reliving this afternoon over and over again, desperate to be this seen, this free, this *wanted.*

I straightened slowly, sifting her hair through my fingers.

Her nostrils flared, looking at me from where she knelt.

Without her blindfold, the connection between us reached another level. A soul-deep, heart-wrenching level and I lost.

I lost to her submission.

I broke under my addiction.

And those two haunting words spilled free in a rush of shadows and sparks. "Suck me."

A slow smile crossed her lips. Her eyes lit up with triumph. And then she reached for me, bent her head, and did exactly as I commanded.

My eyes snapped closed as her hot, wet mouth encircled me.

I almost jack-knifed as she sucked hard.

She broke me with one incredible lick, and I struggled to stay standing as I gathered her hair and held on.

I couldn't speak as her head bobbed over me, taking me as deep as she could manage. Using her spit, she coated my length and corkscrewed her hand up and down.

She moaned and licked and drove me into fucking insanity.

Peng screeched and took off.

The curtains fluttered as if the ghost who'd rearranged the kitchen still watched.

I didn't care we might have an audience as I gathered her closer and pushed her head down. I didn't ask if she was okay. We'd established the rules. She knew how to stop me. She'd forced me to become this beast, and now...now, I would make her pay.

"Harder," I grunted, my eyes rolling back in my head as she squeezed me to the point of pain. Her tongue teased my crown. Her hot breath tickled my belly.

I shuddered with shame at how filthy I wanted her.

I groaned with how good it felt.

She kept blowing me, shoving me higher and higher up the climax cliff. I deliberated coming in her mouth, making her swallow, but this was the last time. I would never be this rough, this selfish again, and...if I was going to embrace every dark and desperate shadow inside me...fuck it.

Holding her hair, I thrust.

She gagged.

I winced as her teeth caught me.

"Don't bite, or I'll bite right back," I choked.

She shivered on her knees and sucked me deeper.

The percolating bubbles of warning gathered between my legs. It was too soon.

I wasn't ready to say goodbye just yet.

Wrenching her mouth off me, I grabbed her elbows and yanked her from the floor. Tossing her over my shoulder, our bare skin stuck together as I returned to the nest of cushions and placed her down.

She immediately kneeled again, her lips glistening. Fumbling for my wallet in the mess of clothes, I flipped it open and searched for another condom.

My heart plummeted as I found none.

Christ, I thought for sure I had two. My background in medicine always ensured utter strictness whenever it came to sleeping with someone. I'd never gone without protection. Never had the urge—

"Are you out?" Her quiet question made me want to snarl.

My shoulders sagged, all while I fought the debilitating need to release. "I thought I had more." My eyes met hers, my mask feeling so restrictive. "Do you have any?"

"No." She winced. "I threw them all out when I removed Milton's things."

"Well, shit." Pinching the bridge of my nose, flinching at not finding my glasses, I did my best to pull myself together. "That's that then." Tossing her the nearest piece of clothing, I ordered, "Put that on. I can't look at you."

She caught it but didn't obey. Her tongue ran over her bottom lip, her forehead furrowed. "You know…I've never…I mean…even with Milton, I always used…um…what I'm trying to say is…"

"No." I shook my head. "Absolutely not."

Her eyes met mine, slightly bashful, her cheeks slightly pink. "Have you ever…?"

"No, but that's beside the point."

"So we're both virgins in that respect? We'd be safe to…"

Ah Christ, no one else had made me feel so out of control. This angry, this lost, this *hungry*.

"Sailor, I'm not—"

"I follow my cycle. I don't take the pill, but I take my temperature every day, and…I know I'm in the safe range. I-I'm okay with it if you are." Crawling toward me, she stood upright on her knees. "I wouldn't offer if I wasn't sure. My nana taught me all the olden ways of birth control. I've been doing it for years. And I…I really don't want you to stop."

God, her body heat. Her bare breasts. Her seduction and innocence and need.

How could I compete with that? How could I ever find the willpower to walk away?

"What do you want, X?"

I want to keep you.

I want to tell you everything.

I want you not to hate me.

I lowered my head, watching her with half-hooded eyes. "I want to fuck you."

"Then do it."

"If I do…you'll be the only girl I'll ever be bare with."

She shivered. "Then definitely do it."

I groaned, watching her skin pucker with goosebumps. "God, I love seeing you like this."

"Like what?"

"Hungry…like me."

She swallowed hard. "I'm starving."

Damn, I'd messed this up so badly.

I'd been searching for something all my life, and it had been under my nose the entire time.

Her.

My neighbour, friend, and soulmate.

I moved before I could think.

Lurching forward, I collided with her.

Dragging her close, I planted my hand over her eyes and ripped my mask down.

And then, I kissed her.

I kissed her hard and deep, driven by instinct and insanity.

Plunging my tongue into her mouth, I didn't just give in; I broke.

My self-control snapped.

My morality splintered.

I kissed her like a madman.

She cried out as I forced her lips wide.

But I didn't stop.

I didn't stop as I grabbed her jaw and held her firm.

I didn't stop as I bit and licked and *devoured* her.

All those urges I'd pushed away. All that hunger I'd done my best to ignore.

I forgot about my rules and reasons.

I didn't care what this made me or what we would become once we were through.

The only thing that mattered was getting inside the girl I'd watched for most of my life. The girl I'd spied on, longed for, and needed more than anything. The girl who'd leashed and collared me the moment she was born.

Licking her deep, she moaned and licked me back. Her hands found my hair, tugging hard. I didn't know if she was trying to pull me off her or pull me closer, but I was past the point of reason.

Stopping the kiss, I jerked my mask back up and grabbed her by the waist.

She cried out as I flipped her to face away, pushing between her shoulder blades so she landed on her hands and knees.

Her back arched, teasing me, taunting me, making me groan.

My skin exploded with hypersensitivity. She threw me headfirst into a place I'd never been before. Somewhere dangerous and selfish and I couldn't stop.

I can't stop.

I didn't ask if she was okay being taken this way. I trusted her. She trusted me. And I hated that all of our wonderful connection was based on lies.

Grabbing her hips, I held her firm as I rose behind her.

We turned breathless and shaky. I snarled as I angled myself to that perfect glistening spot. The sharpest electricity crackled through my bones, blasting through my legs.

I was naked.

With Sailor.

I was about to fuck her.

Bare.

I'm about to have a heart attack.

My hips pulsed forward.

She cried out as I fed her a single inch. Her head fell forward, revealing her nape as her hair tumbled around her face.

I had no control as I cupped the back of her neck and held on.

I lost all sense of self as I tensed every muscle and stopped thinking, trying, hoping.

I pulled her back at the same time as I mounted her.

Fiercely. Fully. Meanly.

One moment, we were two separate people.

The next, we were joined in an excruciatingly mind-shattering way.

Silky-hot wetness and nothing else.

Her bareness to my bareness.

My body inside hers with no barrier.

It was the most *incredible* thing.

The most dangerous thing.

I hissed between my teeth as her core flexed around me, rippling with welcome.

We both lost who we were as we moved together. Deep and ruthless. I thrust into her while holding her nape. My other hand locked on her hip, keeping her in place. My pace increased, faster and faster, harder and harder all while she moaned and whimpered and met me rock for rock.

I lost track of time as I fucked her.

I never wanted it to end, all while knowing I was too close.

My climax didn't just originate in my balls but in every droplet of blood. It felt as if our skin evaporated, and we fed energy to each other, our bodies siphoning with the same delicious need, the same heart-rendering passion.

"Deeper," she begged, arching her back and dropping to her elbows.

I obeyed.

Running my nails down her spine, I grabbed her other hip and rode her.

Again and again.

Over and over.

And when she broke apart and came around me, I roared and let go.

For the first time in my life, I was utterly free. Completely mindless.

I took her, ruled her, and the explosion of my orgasm stole my breath, my soul, my heart, granting everything I was to her.

Forever.

Forty-Seven

Sailor

The Floor is the Best Nest

I WOKE TO PENG LICKING MY nose.

His soft meow was barely audible in the dusk-filled living room. I shifted to move, then froze. *Everything* ached. Inside and out. But it wasn't the discomfort of moving that made me still but the fact that X was still here.

His arm slung over my side while he spooned me from behind, his fingers cupping my breast with a protective hold. His breathing came slow and steady, heavy with exhaustion and dreams.

Peng went to meow again.

"Shush," I whispered, grabbing him and cuddling him close.

His annoyance turned into a purr. He snuggled against my neck and made biscuits in my hair.

He was probably hungry, but also looked a little concerned. The way he clung to me said he was highly suspicious of why his human companion was out cold on the floor, all while a masked naked man shared his body heat like some kind of primitive blanket.

I grinned and kissed his silky ginger fur.

Sleeping with X had been mind-blowing.

Doing something as reckless as being with him without protection made me feel naughty and sinful. Everything I'd done with him today had been completely out of character.

I would *never* do this with someone else.

I would never ask to be treated so roughly or be thrilled when he commanded me to serve him.

But it'd been the best experience of my life.

He'd changed me.

He'd changed me and awoken me and proved that I'd *always* been a sexual creature just waiting to find the perfect playmate. I'd never been so honest with what I wanted or shared what turned me on. I'd never been set on fire so badly or shivered with power as I made him come.

He'd covered me in flames with his every thrust, leaving me rising from the ashes as we lay in pieces on the floor.

My mind skated to Zander against my will.

Guilt ate away at my satisfaction.

The woman I'd become today would never fit into his world now. As sweet and as wonderful as he was, he probably made out with the lights off and asked permission for every touch.

And...I needed the opposite.

X hadn't just gotten under my skin; he'd burrowed into my heart.

He'd made me feel both vulnerably small and femininely powerful. And I hated that he still thought there wasn't a future for us when I had no intention of letting him go.

Look at what happened in the kitchen.

Look at the message Nana had left behind.

She approved of the hussy I'd become. She didn't admonish my evolution and gave me her blessing.

Therefore, X wasn't going anywhere.

I would lock him in this house, rip off his mask, and force him to confess everything.

I'd gotten to the point where I didn't care what secrets he had.

If he had a criminal background, oh well.

If he secretly killed people, hopefully they deserved it.

If he turned out to be on the run or embezzled funds or hoarded any number of sins...I didn't care.

Because I loved him.

And love could overcome everything.

Forty-Eight

Zander

Sneak of Shame

I WOKE TO THE WORST CHEST pains of my life. A daggering sort of loss that made me gasp for air. The nonsense dream I'd had dissipated the quicker I came back to reality, but the pain didn't fade.

It only grew worse.

I still had her in my arms, yet...I'd dreamed of her finding out everything. Of all the affection she felt for me bleeding into absolute hate.

Shuddering, I did my best to snap out of it.

I have to go.

Evening had fallen, and the fairy lights strung up over the hexagon shelving on the newly painted wall clicked on as if on a timer.

I froze, waiting for her to wake.

However, she merely snuggled deeper into the cushions, her hips scooting back to steal more of my heat.

Just that one movement made me hard again.

It would be so easy to roll her onto her stomach and take her one last time. To slip inside and—

What's stopping you?

She wouldn't be opposed.

But...if I woke her, I lost my opportunity to sneak out of there. I'd have to make up yet more lies about where I was going and why I was never coming back.

Christ, why does this hurt so much?

Peng yawned and popped his little head up from where he lay in an orange ball on a cushion above Sailor's head. He eyed me as he sniffed with bristling whiskers.

I tore my gaze from his. I had no power to win a cat stare down thanks to the level of guilt I suffered.

Sailor sighed in her sleep, sucker-punching me in the heart.

The thought of never talking to her again, sleeping with her again, being this free with her again almost had me lowering my mouth to her shoulder to kiss her. I didn't care that I still wore my mask—that the cotton would absorb my kiss not her skin.

I just had to touch her.

Hold her.

I'm so sorry.

Hovering behind her, my eyes went to half-mast as I inhaled the floral scent of her skin and gave in to the insidious creep of lust.

My eyes caught on a shadow.

A finger-shaped shadow on her skin.

Another dagger stabbed directly in my heart.

Bruises.

Colourful bruises marred her nape from where I'd held on while riding her. A few scratches down her spine. A hand sized bruise on her hip from where I'd held her in place.

I almost threw up.

It took all my strength to inch slowly away instead of tearing myself off her with aversion. I trembled with self-hatred as more bruises appeared along her stunning body.

From me.

I did that.

Like him.

She frowned in her dreams as I kneeled above her. She shivered and curled up tighter as if feeling the cold.

Grabbing the blanket folded against the wall, I carefully draped it over her all while crawling farther away.

Too many bruises decorated her.

Bruises so similar to the ones she'd presented with in the ER. Sure, she didn't have ligature marks or hematomas like that bastard had left her with, but I'd marked her, injured her, and caused physical harm all because I'd lost control and been the worst version of myself.

Fuck.

Launching to my feet, I grabbed my trousers and yanked them on. I didn't bother finding my t-shirt amongst the rubble of clothing.

This stunning, amazing girl had introduced me to a number of my limits and now she'd just shoved me into the final one.

This was my ultimate line.

I'd made a vow.

Thou shalt do no harm.

And I'd crossed it.

I would never forgive myself. I'd been raised better than this. Gran would be so disappointed in me.

With rage directed entirely at myself and agony breaking me apart, I made sure I had my wallet, snatched up my boots, and took one last look at the damaged angel on the floor.

Then fled out the back door.

"'Sup?"

I swayed from the kitchen, focusing way harder than normal just to do a simple task like walking. I still managed to trip over the tiled lip on the threshold leading into the conservatory.

Stupid whiskey.

"'Sup?" Colin yawned in my ear. "Who are you and what did you do with my friend?"

"Killed him off. That's what." I swallowed hard. *Why is the room spinning?* "He's gone."

"If you're calling to make me become an accessory to murder, I have to tell you, my limit is aiding and abetting stalking. That's as far as I'm willing to go in this friendship." He snickered, thinking he was funny. "Why are you calling me at ten p.m.? I thought you'd be gallivanting around town, enjoying your few days off. Or better yet, in bed with a certain neighbour."

I groaned and collapsed into one of the rattan chairs that Gran used to love to knit in. The wind chimes hung above, silent in the still air. If they suddenly started singing, I was going to freak the fuck out.

The incident in Sailor's kitchen still sent goosebumps down my spine.

I'd never believed in the supernatural. I was a man of science not superstition, but I had no explanation for what happened over there.

"Did you know I'm haunted?" I hiccupped, wiping my mouth with the back of my hand and reaching for the Johnny Walker again.

I'd long since stopped pouring it from the bottle into a glass. What a waste of time. It was way easier to drink straight from the source.

Colin's tone sharpened, losing his humour. "You're haunted? What the hell are you talking about?"

"I mean..." I licked my lips and closed my eyes against the spinning conservatory. "My grandmother and her grandmother are still playing tricks on us, even now."

"I have no idea what you're talking about."

"I've fucked up shoow bad," I groaned, leaning forward and digging my elbows into my knees. Taking another mouthful of sharp liquor, I wrenched off my glasses and tossed them onto the side table where a stack of crossword puzzle books used to tower from my granddad doing four a day.

"Uh-oh, now it makes sense." Colin clucked his tongue. "You're drunk."

"Am not."

"You're slurring."

"It's shbetter than hurting."

"What's hurting? You okay?" Something shuffled in the background. "You know not to operate heavy machinery when drinking."

"I hurt her," I whispered, my voice catching.

"Hurt who?" His tone instantly switched to the supportive doctor vibe I'd heard him use with his patients. Cajoling and kind, but no-nonsense at the same time. "Sailor? You're saying you hurt your neighbour?"

"I-I'm just like him."

"Like who?"

"I really messed up, Col."

"Fuck, you're legit starting to scare me. Look, come here and sober up, yeah? Grab an Uber and we'll have a late dinner. Probably best you don't sleep there tonight."

"Nah…" I swallowed another bitter mouthful of whiskey fire. "I need to tell her I died and then I'm just gonna crash."

"Wait. Who's dying? Don't do a damn thing until you've slept the booze out of your system."

"Can't. Need to do this before it's too late."

He cursed under his breath. "How much have you had to drink, Zan?"

I eyed the bottle with blurry eyesight and shrugged. "No idesha."

I took another sip.

I hadn't meant to call him.

However, the drunker I got, the sadder I became, and I desperately needed someone to figure out how to remove the agonising dagger that'd permanently wedged itself in my heart before I went insane.

Leaning back in the chair, I ran my hand through my hair.

At least it was back to being red.

I'd had a shower and dressed in black track pants and a white tee before aimlessly trying to figure out what to eat.

That was where the whiskey came in.

I'd found no food, only this bottle.

And drinking on an empty stomach and a broken heart did not mix well.

"Do you think she'll hate me forever?" I mumbled. "Like…if I turned myshhelf in, do you think I could make this all go away?"

"Right, that's it. I'm coming over."

"No." I sloshed the bottle around, making the amber liquid bubble. "I like being alone. I'm *meant* to be alone. I don't deserve anyone after what I've done."

"Wow, you're a depressive drunk. Anyone ever tell you that?" The sound of a key fob beeping echoed down the phone line, followed by the slam of a car door. "Tell me what's happened. Why are you drinking? And use full sentences instead of this cryptic crap."

I laughed as if that was the funniest request in the world. And then almost broke into tears because I'd lost the best thing I'd ever found. "I fucked everything up. I just shtold you."

An engine roared. "Come on, Zan, this isn't you. You need to sober up and talk to me."

I sighed heavily and sagged in the chair. "Stop nagging."

"You never get drunk. Remember why? You don't get drunk because of your patients. You told me you'd never kill off brain cells doing something as stupid as drinking when it's clinically proven to murder quite a few of them with every level of intoxication."

"You're annoying."

"I'm right, that's what's annoying." He huffed. "I'm ten minutes away. Put the bottle down and go eat something."

"I have no food." I sighed heavily. "No wonder she doesn't want to be with me. I can't even stock my fridge."

"Okay, new plan. I'll be there in twenty, and I'll pick up a pizza. But I'm warning you, Zander, stop drinking right now. Whatever's bugging you, you can talk to me about it when I get there."

He hung up.

I sucked back more whiskey.

If only the burn in my throat would erase the burn in my heart.

Forty-Nine

Sailor

Accidental Spying

I WOKE WITH A START, FEELING as though something was terribly wrong.

Sitting upright where I lay on the floor, the blanket that I'd kept after X covered me in the garden slid off my shoulders and pooled around my waist.

He did it again…

Cool air licked around my nakedness.

For a second, I couldn't remember why I was bare in the middle of my equally bare living room.

But then, I remembered.

X.

Sex.

Best day of my life.

Spinning around, I looked behind me to where my stalker turned lover had been sleeping.

And froze.

Empty.

I brushed my fingers over the cushions and recoiled.

Cold.

He's been gone a while.

Scrambling to my feet, I glanced at the clothes scattered on the floor. His t-shirt tangled with mine, but his trousers and boots were gone.

My heart turned into a lump of ice.

No…

Wrapping the blanket around my shoulders, I stumbled into the kitchen. The cupboards were still closed, the fridge tucked tight instead of flung open by a ghost. Scanning the countertops, I searched for a note or a sign that X hadn't vanished. That he hadn't upped and left without a goodbye.

My phone.

Darting back into the living room, I grabbed my jean-shorts and fished my phone from the pocket. Swiping it on, I scanned the social notifications and noticed a few messages from Lily but nothing from X.

Not a single word or apology or explanation.

A slithering, stinging agony crept through me, coiling around my organs and climbing up the step ladder of my ribs.

He couldn't just leave…not after what we'd done.

Not after what we'd *felt*.

Hot, blistering tears threatened to fall, but I sniffed them back.

No.

I wouldn't cry.

Not over this.

Not because of him.

He might be coming back.

I clung to my mind's excuse.

That's right.

He might have left to grab some dinner. He was coming back and—

He didn't take his t-shirt.

Where could he go at this time of night shirtless?

He might be upstairs…

I gasped and tore toward the corridor. Taking the steps two at a time, my blanket flaring like a cape, I careened into my old bedroom, the office, and finally my new room at the front.

Each empty.

Each dark and dangerous with shadows.

Goblin-Milton stalked my thoughts, ready to throw nasty slurs into my ears. The house cracked and settled, making me prickle with the urge to check behind the doors and hide in the bathroom.

But…I was better now.

I wouldn't let him win.

Balling my hands, I stood in the dark and dared the phantom of my past to mock me.

And nothing.

The only thing I heard was the pounding of my heart and silence. Painful, heavy silence that I hadn't heard since I'd gotten Peng. Just having his little soul in the house had eradicated that emptiness. That cavernous loneliness that seemed to have its own frequency.

Fresh horror filled me. "Peng?" Racing back down the stairs, I turned on all the lights. My eyes scanned every nook and cranny, searching for the ginger fluffball.

"Penguin?"

Not in the kitchen.

Not in the living room or snug or laundry.

"Peng?!"

Bolting outside, I stood on the deck and blinked into the overgrown garden. "Peng!"

No meow.

No hiss.

My knees threatened to buckle. Tears broke my control and rolled.

"Here, kitty, kitty. Where are you?"

I stood trembling, waiting, begging him to answer me.

I-I have to find him.

Flying off the deck, I ran barefoot over the grass. The blanket flared out; my fingers lost their grip. The heavy protection plummeted to the ground, leaving me completely nude beneath the stars.

Shit!

I couldn't go running through the neighbourhood naked, no matter how closeknit we all were.

"Peng!"

Still no reply.

Had he run away? Got hit by a car? Stolen?

"Penguin, please!"

Fear choked me as I galloped back inside. Gritting my teeth so I didn't give into my sobs, I wrenched on the same clothes I'd been wearing before X stripped me, then shot back into the night.

Slamming through the back gate, I skidded down the garden path and tripped onto the road. "Peng? Come here, little man. Where are you?"

Turning on the spot, I looked up and down Ember Drive.

No flash of a tail.

No gleam of green eyes.

Doing another circle, I spied a car parked next to Zander's on his drive. I'd seen it before. It belonged to Colin, his colleague.

Perhaps they've seen him?

Jogging up Zander's front veranda, I rang the doorbell.

I tapped my foot and kept scanning the street.

Come on. Hurry up.

No one came.

"*Argh!*" Charging down the steps, I paused on his driveway. I could door knock all my neighbours, but Peng knew Zander. If he was going to visit anyone, it would be him, right?

Feeling a little guilty for trespassing, I ran down the side of his house, heading toward his back garden. I wouldn't be interrupting too badly. He couldn't be asleep if he had company. So why hadn't he answered the door?

Weaving my way around the intricate box hedging some landscape designer had done for him, I looked up just in time for Colin to force a large glass of water into Zander's hands.

Zander sat slouched in a rattan chair in the conservatory. The all-glass walls gave me a perfect view of the potted ferns and redheaded doctor who looked as if he'd been run over.

Sympathy clenched my aching heart.

He worked too much.

He cared about others too much.

Did something happen in surgery?

Had he lost a patient?

He must have because he looked as if he'd lost something desperately important. His eyes pinched, and jaw clenched, and when he tossed his head back, he spilled most of the water on his leg then almost dropped the glass. "That was her. I know it was."

Colin slid into the matching chair and reached over the small table to keep him upright. Extracting the glass from his friend's fingers, he placed it safely on the table and shook his head. "I wish there was a miracle pill to cure drunken idiots like you."

I froze in the garden, hidden behind a trimmed bush.

I didn't want to intrude if Zander was having a bad night. I'd heard doctors hid their mental health to be the best they could be for their patients. But if Zander was this bad, it meant work had gone *very* bad and I had no right to—

"I should've opened the door," Zander groaned. "I need to start making her want me like this so I don't lose her."

The open door of the conservatory delivered their voices directly to me.

I shouldn't eavesdrop, yet…I couldn't seem to stop.

"Yeah, no one is gonna like you like this, believe me. You definitely shouldn't let her see you in this condition," Colin muttered. "You're a mess. The moment she saw you, she'd figure everything out."

"Nope." Zander tried to shake his head but slouched deeper in the chair. "She wouldn't. Like you said, Superman worked. She has no idea. None." He zipped his lips with a drunken grimace. "That's why when he dies, she will never know."

"And you're back to talking gibberish." Colin stretched, kicking out his legs with a groan. "How about you tell me what's eating you, and then I'm going to stuff half that pizza in your face, and you're going to bed."

Zander threw him a scowl. "I brought her car back."

Colin groaned. "Dude, we just talked about this. Stop talking in cryptic code. It's frustrating as hell."

"I'm not." Zander struggled to sit taller. "I'm trying to tell you what happened if you stop interrupting."

Colin smirked. "Sure, by all means. Go right ahead."

Zander nodded sagely. "I have a spare set of keys for her car. Her granddad gave them to Gran decades ago, saying she could use his car whenever she needed to. Which was a mistake 'cause I'd banned her from driving the day I caught her pressing the accelerator instead of the brake pedal. She almost flattened the garage and herself."

"Interesting. Does this little story have a point?"

"The point—" Zander swayed and closed his eyes. "—the point is, I had the keys, so I went back to the movies and drove her car back. It was my fault it was stranded there after bringing her home on my bike. Do you know I kissed her that night? Did I tell you?"

"You didn't. How did that go?" Colin crossed his arms.

"About as well as you'd expect." Zander sighed. "It couldn't even be called a kiss. I should've asked permission, right? I tried kissing her, and she freaked out, and fuck, I should've asked before I did it."

My worry over Peng overrode my desire to listen to my neighbour have a drunken moment. He hadn't told me he'd been the one to return my car. It was yet another favour he'd done, all while expecting nothing in return.

Tomorrow, I would pop round and deliver the vanilla sponge I'd made him. I'd look him in the eye and thank him profusely for all he'd done for me, but then I'd tell him we could only be friends because I'd fallen in love with a masked flight-risk of a man, and it wouldn't be fair to lead him on. As incredible as he was—as sweet and kind and thoughtful as he'd proven to be, now that I'd tasted the level of freedom with X...I didn't think I could be with a man who asked permission for every kiss.

Backing into the shadows, I held my breath in case they spotted me.

God, that would be next-level embarrassment after what I'd heard.

Taking another step backward, I swallowed my yelp as something squeaked.

Twisting around, I narrowed my eyes in the dark...then dropped to my knees in absolute relief. "*Penguin!*" Snatching my wayward kitten into my arms, I made sure to keep my exclamation to a whisper. "Where have you been, you naughty cat?" Burrowing my face into his scruff, I rocked and squished him. "Good God, I was so worried."

He purred and wriggled, his little body as fizzy as I felt inside.

Pulling him away from me, I held him upright—his little legs dangling and green eyes blinking innocently. "Don't you ever do that again; do you hear me?"

He meowed quietly.

Gathering him against my chest, I struggled to my feet and went to head toward the fence palings to go home. Damn kitten probably ran away because he was hungry. I'd neglected him all thanks to X's distraction. Therefore, I would feed him until he was too fat to waddle anywhere. "You're grounded, Mr Fluff—"

"—and it was the best sex of my life."

I froze, my gaze whipping back to the conservatory where Zander sat slouched with his elbows on his knees. His voice echoed in the garden, licking around my feet. "I've never felt that way...with anyone."

Stinging jealousy hit me.

Which made no sense as I'd just made up my mind to establish boundaries between us, yet...hearing that he actually had a life outside of this suburb?

It hurt.

Like...really hurt.

W-Who did he sleep with?

Not that I had any right to be possessive after what I'd just done.

"Okay, so you're in love with her. I could've told you that years ago. In fact, pretty sure I did. Multiple times." Colin sniffed, looking at Zander with very little sympathy. "I told you to ask her out, and what did you do? You decided that falsifying your identity was a better idea."

Wait, what?

My arms stiffened around Peng as Zander raked his hands through his hair. "I've messed everything up so bad."

"Meh, don't beat yourself up. These things happen. Just come clean and—"

"I *can't* come clean." Zander's red-rimmed eyes shot up. He wasn't wearing his glasses, and a pang of familiarity kicked me in the gut.

An image of X spliced over Zander. Replace the red hair with black and—

"I hurt her tonight, Col. I-I bruised her like he did, and—"

"Hold up." Colin adopted a patient-doctor pose, eyeballing his friend. "You said that on the phone. I know I've been supporting you with this crazy idea, but only because you did it for the right reasons. You were supposed to help her, Zan, so...how did it go from helping her to hurting her?"

My heart rate picked up.

Something itched inside, growing more and more intense the longer I stood there. Even Peng didn't struggle, lolling in my arms and watching the two men.

"I-I let go." Zander groaned. "She told me to stop thinking of others and put myself first for a change."

"Sounds like wise advice. Go on."

"I went over there angry as hell. And…I did something."

"You fucked her, you mean."

Zander didn't respond.

The itch grew worse and worse, intuition flaring brighter and brighter. The rasp of Zander's drunken voice sounded so similar to the gravel whispered into my ear when X took me from behind. The way Zander suddenly launched out of his chair and paced the conservatory as if needing to run, unable to stay…

No… My arms wrapped tighter around Peng. *It can't be.*

"I snapped, alright?" Zander spun around, agony etching his face. "Fuck, what have I done, Col? Why did I think I could do this? Why did I go this far? Why did I go over there when I knew I was at my limit? She absolutely petrified me by climbing up that ladder. I should've walked away the moment she was safely on the ground. I should've torn off my mask and told her. I mean…I'd already gone too far, but at least I hadn't slept with her. *Fuck!*"

Wiping his mouth, he continued to pace with jerky, horrified steps. "I told her to pick a safe word for Christ's sake. I fucked her without telling her who I was. I don't care that it was the best experience of my life. I had no right to do that. *None.* And now I've fucked everything up because there's no way in hell I can tell her, and I have to move. I'm going to leave because I can't look her in the eye, and when X doesn't come back, she'll swear off men anyway. I took my chance, and I blew it. And I deserve to have blown it. What sort of bastard does what I did? What sort of asshole bruises her that badly when she's only just healed from another asshole's marks?"

Storming into Colin, he snarled, "I'll tell you what sort of asshole. Me. *I'm* the asshole. And if she finds out, she'll call the police and, fuck…I'm still being selfish. *I* should call the police. I should turn myself in on her behalf because what I did was wrong, and that isn't me, and fuck me, I can't *do* this."

Throwing himself into the chair, he buried his face into his hands.

Colin sat there unfazed, watching his friend have a breakdown.

I couldn't move.

Couldn't breathe.

I'd heard every word, yet I couldn't compute.

He knew things he shouldn't if he wasn't X. His voice was the same. His mannerisms the same. Yet my mind and heart still saw him as two completely different people.

I literally couldn't combine them.

I couldn't see my slightly standoffish doctor who barely slept and did house calls asking me to kneel and suck him.

It…just…*they're not the same.*

Peng squirmed closer, no doubt feeling my thundering heart. I kissed the top of his head, my mind spinning. Every moment of X interacting with Peng collided. Of Peng clinging to X. Of Peng acting as if he knew him.

"Oh my *God*! You knew all along," I gasped, glaring at the kitten. "You little traitor!"

He yawned as if this was old news, and I was just an ignorant human.

He'd probably followed him when Zander left earlier tonight, sneaking to his house as if he belonged.

The movies.

The messages.

I gasped as every clue slipped into place.

I'd messaged X at the cinema, but Zander was the one who turned up.

I'd been afraid of being alone, and Zander gifted me a cat.

I'd been at the market with X messaging me, but Zander had been there too…

I'd screamed in my sleep, and X turned up…in bare feet.

He knew all the right things to say to me.

Knew my routines. My habits. My likes and dislikes and…

H-He bought me a dildo.

I froze as more memories crashed into one another.

He knew where my spare key was.

He knew where my bedroom was to sneak beneath my covers and hold me.

He knew how much Milton broke me because he was there. In the ER. As a *doctor.* He'd seen with his own eyes the mess I'd been and…

Oh my God.

He gave me an orgasm after I begged him.

He tried to refuse me because of his lies.

He led me on and fibbed to my face, and…every night he said he watched me, he hadn't done it by camera but through a damn window.

How was I so blind?

My eyes shot to the side of his house beneath the gutters. His home security blinked a red dot in the dark. Just like the camera at the front of his house pointed at my place, the back one did too—the angle perfectly in line with my garden.

Okay, not just via a window.

He used his home network to record me. He didn't stand on the street or peer through my bushes; he literally had me on a video feed no matter where he was.

Anger bubbled, hotter and hotter.

How dare he.

How damn well *dare* he stalk into my life and spin a web of lies.

The house of flimsy cards he'd built around me came tumbling down in a puff of wind.

The plate in my letterbox.

The forced scratchy voice to hide his true baritone.

The way he knew the layout of my house.

The uncanny timing whenever I wasn't coping.

I…I felt violated, all while protected. Betrayed and confused and—

"Now that you've got that off your chest, let's get rational instead of emotional, alright?" Colin sniffed with faint annoyance.

Zander didn't respond, keeping his face buried.

Standing, Colin held up his hand. "Let's look at the facts, shall we? I'm sure you'll see it's not nearly as bad as you think it is. First…" Holding up a single finger, he smiled. "You've loved her since you were a geeky little teenager, and seeing her hurt after what that cunt—and yes, he's a cunt, not an asshole—did to her, you knew she wouldn't know how or be willing to accept your help, so…you did what you thought was best."

Holding up a second finger, he added, "Secondly, you put your reputation, mental health, and heart on the line the moment you gave her a phone and offered to be the therapist she didn't know she needed. You were being the best kind of doctor and human by giving her an outlet to talk because you were right…she was sinking into agoraphobia and claustrophobia and it would've only gotten worse unless she addressed it."

Up went finger number three. "Thirdly, it was me who suggested you be prepared for seeing her in person, and I'll take the blame that I gave you the disguise you needed. I hate to say I told you so, but even if all her instincts said it was you behind the black hair and contacts, those two things, plus the mask, were enough to keep you hidden in plain sight. Don't feel bad about that, Zan, it's just biology. We humans are stupid creatures."

Taking a deep breath, Colin held up a fourth finger. "Fourthly—is that even a word? Doesn't sound right. Doesn't matter. Apart from work, I've never seen you have a hobby or interest outside of the hospital. Sure, choosing stalking as your favourite pastime might not be the best thing, but it's forgivable because your intentions were pure. You were there for her. You were there when she had those panic attacks. You had more sleepless nights than usual because you put her needs before yours. And you did absolutely everything—including giving up your own peace of mind—to heal hers which leads me to my fifth and final thing."

Zander slowly lifted his head. "And what's that?"

Colin smiled gently and lowered his hand. "You say you hurt her? That you let go? I say bullshit and good for you. In the same sentence."

"What the fuck, Col? I-I bruised her and—"

"Was she begging you to stop?"

"No, but—"

"Was she fighting you off?"

"No, but that's—"

"Was she screaming for someone to save her?"

"No, she—"

"I rest my case." Sitting down with a smug smile, Colin patted Zander on the shoulder. "You, my friend have finally learned to let go and put yourself first for once, and it sounds like you both had a *fabulous* time."

"But I hurt—"

"Dude, give it a *rest*." Colin threw his hands up. "So you roughed her up a bit? You said you gave her a safe word. She knew what she was getting into. Did she use it? Did you ignore her? Are you saying you raped her because if you did, I'll take you to the police myself, but if you didn't, then I'm seconds away from beating some sense into you because you have got to realise you can't keep living your life like this. You can't keep putting everyone else first. You did it with your grandparents, with your sisters, and with her. You need to be cared for just as much as the next person. You had rough sex. Big deal. Everyone does it. No matter how much we love someone—in fact, I'd probably say the more we love someone, the more primal those instincts get. Sex is where all that violence and desperation comes out, and it feels good. For *both* parties."

Zander slowly exhaled. "Why did you have to come here with your stupid voice of reason?"

"Because you're drunk and ridiculous, and that's what friends do." Colin cracked his knuckles and punched his other hand. "However, it doesn't mean I won't hit you a few times if you don't sober the hell up and stop being an idiot."

"It doesn't fix the fact that I lied to her."

"No, it doesn't. She'll have every right to be pissed, and you're going to have to grovel. *Big* time."

Zander sniffed and rubbed his nose. "You're saying I should tell her? Even after I slept with her under false pretences?"

Colin shrugged. "Remember a few weeks ago when you told me she asked you to sleep with her and you didn't know if you could cross that line?"

"I flatly said I wasn't going to."

"Yeah well, life finds a way, my friend." He sighed and shook his head. "You're meant to be together, Zan. And if you haven't learned that by now, then you deserve to lose her."

Silence fell.

Peng snuggled closer. I struggled to breathe.

I didn't know what I was feeling.

Anger, definitely.

Betrayed, of course.

But…what Colin had said was true. Without X, I didn't know how far I'd be in my healing. I'd probably still be rocking in the corner of my old bedroom, too afraid to stay and definitely too scared to go out.

I would've been trapped in a completely different hell, and the fact that Zander had known he'd become a trigger for me and done what he could to help me behind a mask was so…*him.*

Quintessentially him because he was the best kind of doctor, neighbour, and friend and…

I have to go.

I needed to leave before I was caught.

I needed to think about this, deliberate over this, and decide if this was forgivable.

Scooting Peng higher in my arms, I turned to go, but Zander's soft confession had my feet rooting into the ground.

"I love her. I think I always have. I know I always will. The very thought of never being able to talk so honestly with her? The idea of living beside her and never touching her again? God, it rips out my heart." His voice thickened. "I didn't know how lonely I was until I started going around to her place. The night after our first bike ride, all I wanted to do was invite her in. Not to hook up, but just because I couldn't bear to be away from her. But she declined my offer and messaged X instead. She gave him cake and kissed him and—"

"And you're back to talking about yourself in third person." Colin reached over and patted Zander's hand. "What did I tell you about that nonsense?"

Zander actually smirked. "Fine, you smart-ass. *I* got to hang out with her that night as X but when I came home, it wasn't just loneliness that cut me but gut-ripping jealousy. I was so fucking jealous because this alter ego earned everything I ever wanted."

"Isn't that saying something, though? She likes this version of you. This version that you've pretended doesn't exist all because it doesn't fit in with your idea of what a 'good guy' should be?"

Zander ignored him, muttering, "X got to be everything I was too afraid to be. I was free when wearing that mask, Col, and…she's never looked at me the way she looked at X, and honestly…I don't think I have the strength anymore."

Colin's eyebrows shot up. "What are you saying?"

Zander took his time replying. "I'm saying I love her. I'm *in* love with her. But…she's not in love with me. And because I don't have the courage to have her hate me, I can't tell her. This secret will eat me alive for the rest of my life, but I'm done. I function better on my own anyway. I should never have thought I could deserve her." Sitting stiffly, he nodded as if he'd made up his mind. "I'm going to kill X off and be done with it."

"So…wait." Colin scowled. "That's it? You're not even going to try to date her as yourself? Red hair, glasses, and all?"

Zander bowed his head and dug his fingers into his eyes. When he looked up, they were suspiciously wet. "I can't. I'll never be able to forgive myself."

"Then how about you tell her everything and let *her* forgive *you*."

"She won't forgive me, that's the problem. And I don't blame her. What I've done is unforgivable." Standing, Zander headed up the two steps toward the kitchen. "Thanks for coming round, Col, but I've sobered up and really want to go to bed, so…I'll walk you out."

Colin swooped to his feet and balled his hands. "You're a frustrating son of a bitch, you know that?"

Zander didn't reply.

Stalking into him, Colin threw a single fist right into Zander's stomach.

Zander doubled over with a groan. "What the—?"

"That was for Sailor." Rolling out his wrist, Colin stomped through the house and disappeared.

Zander slowly kneeled where he stood, cradling his middle.

And I faded into the night as a single tear rolled down his cheek.

Fifty

Zander

Time to Immigrate

"DAMN, ARE YOU SURE?"

Doing my best to stop my knees bouncing where I sat before the desk of the hospital hiring department, I nodded. Every muscle ached like I had the flu. Every day was worse than the last. Somehow, a week had passed since I'd been with Sailor, and she hadn't sent me a single message.

Not to X or to Zander.

I'd drafted so many texts to her, coming up with the quickest, surest way to make her hate X and cut him out of her life completely, but each time I wrote something—each time I typed lines like: 'I'm sorry', 'forgive me', 'this is the only way', 'I didn't mean to hurt you'—I hated myself a little more.

"How about you think a little more on this and—"

"No, I'm sure." I wedged my palms on my thighs. "I'd like to be transferred. I'm happy to consider any hospital you recommend. I'm even open to overseas."

"Well, okay then." The director of recruitment nodded. His greying hair was slightly balding on top. "It will take me a few months to put out the necessary feelers and find someone to replace you."

"That's fine." Standing, I headed toward the door.

"Hey, Dr North?"

I turned and forced a smile. "Yes?"

"Why the sudden decision to move? Forgive me but I thought you were born and bred here? I don't mind admitting that due to your young age but already impressive record, I've already earmarked you for taking over as medical director one day."

I nodded politely. "Thank you for your trust in me, Dr Parker, but things change."

"They do indeed." Shuffling some paperwork, he nodded with a sad smile. "In that case, I guess I'll be in touch."

"Thanks."

Slipping out of his office, I headed back downstairs to the staffroom where I had ten minutes before checking on a patient.

I checked my phone for the millionth time, hoping, wishing, fearing a message from Sailor.

But nothing.

I didn't have the courage to send that final text from X ending things.

And I couldn't survive the pain of messaging her as Zander, knowing what she'd done with X.

I couldn't be mad at her for sleeping with another man who wasn't me.

She *had* slept with me.

But she'd also shown that I didn't mean as much to her as X did, and now, I had nothing left.

Fifty-One

Sailor

Cupcake Confessions

"SO…ARE YOU READY FOR ME to tell you all my secrets because I'm only saying this once and only once and then I have a plan to put into action but I didn't want to put it into action until I'd spoken to you because I need your advice and I've been thinking about this non-stop for eight awful days and it's doing my head in until I can't see straight anymore and so yeah…only saying this once."

"Whoa, jeez Louise, did you breathe at all in that terrible run-on sentence?" Lily grinned. "No more coffee for you." Taking away my empty cappuccino cup, she shoved another tiny vanilla cupcake onto my plate instead.

My first outing to a local café, and it was to the one closest to Lily's real estate office. I'd driven here by myself, parked in an alley, walked down a crowded street, and waited for her in a bustling restaurant with no problem whatsoever.

Goblin-Milton never said a peep.

I didn't jump or flinch or freak out if someone looked at me or got too close.

I was back to myself.

And I only had Zander to blame.

"If I'd known you wanted to spill the beans when you called me this morning, I would've chosen a quieter place."

I shook my head, fiddling with my napkin. "This is perfect. I can blurt it out, suffer your scorn, and then go. At least you can't berate me for hours."

"Uh-oh, what's going on?"

"Oh, you know…nothing much. I just had the best sex of my life with a man who I didn't know his name and just found out he's been lying to me this entire time, but for some reason, I can't stay mad, and now…now, I'm seriously considering running after him."

Lily dropped her cupcake. Icing down. White frosting splashed her pale pink suit. "Okay…you can*not* just dump that on a girl."

I passed her my dogeared napkin. She took it and scrubbed her blazer. "Start from the top, Sails. Don't leave anything out."

I kept my eyes locked on the table and tried to figure out how best to say this.

I'd gone over every detail of X and Zander and Zander and X and *ugh.* I couldn't keep torturing myself this way. I'd made a thousand lists. Made a million excuses. Tried my best to cling to my righteous anger all while I saw it from his point of view.

I played devil's advocate late at night when I couldn't sleep. I became the bad guy needing someone to save me, only to be rescued by the boy next door who'd put his own morals and sanity on the line.

He'd put me first.

He'd given me an outlet, a safety net.

He became my protector and guardian and…*God.*

Who was I kidding?

I wasn't mad.

How could I be mad when my wish had come true?

Hadn't I wished that Zander and X were the same person, all so my heart wasn't torn in two? Hadn't I been drawn to both? Confused and hurting to be attracted to two men when I was always hardwired to be loyal to just one?

I hadn't understood then, but my body had. My heart had. Both of those had known all along, just like Peng. It was just my stupid eyes that hadn't seen.

"Are you going to speak, Sailor Moon, or do I need to slap you back into the world of the living?"

I blinked and forced a smile. "You can't judge me."

"Oh, I'm judging." She smirked and crossed her arms. "And I want to hear every detail. Who the hell did you hook up with? How was it the best sex of your life? How did you not tell me this?"

Using her questions as stepping stones to everything else, I said, "His name is X. It was the best because I asked for what I wanted, and he gave it to me with no shame or fear. He bruised me but in the best kinds of way, and…I couldn't tell you because…he was my stalker."

"Your *what*?" Her jaw fell on the table. "He was stalking you?!" Her eyes narrowed into slits. Pointing a finger in my face, she hissed, "I *knew* it! The phone in your letterbox, the 'care' package you didn't explain. That was him?"

"Yes."

"And you *slept* with him? Are you insane? Do you not watch crime TV?"

"Believe me…I had those same thoughts when he first started

messaging me but…"

"But?"

"I grew to trust him."

She crossed her arms. "Explain. Immediately."

So I explained.

About everything.

Every moment, every message, every mistake and triumph and fall.

And when I was done, Lily ordered two glasses of wine instead of coffee, claiming she needed alcohol.

We both waited until the crisp white wine had been delivered.

After taking a huge gulp, she coughed around the sharpness. "You know he called me looking for you. Zander, I mean. The night I stood you up at the movies." Her face fell. "By the way, I'm so, so sorry that creep attacked you in the car park. If I'd gone you would never—"

"Zander was there to save me." I shrugged. "And I think…I think I needed to see him in that way. You know…being violent toward someone? Protecting me like X did. If I hadn't, I would still have a super hard time admitting he's the one who's been stalking me all along."

"Not surprised. He went as far as to dye his hair and change his eye colour. That's commitment. *Freaky* commitment."

I nodded along, sipping my wine.

Her voice softened as her eyes met mine. "I should've guessed something was going on with you two. The night he called me looking for you, his voice said it all."

"What did it say?"

"He was panicking. Desperate." She smiled gently. "He's in love with you."

I ducked my head, fighting a blush. "So…you don't think I'm crazy?"

"Oh, I think you're batshit crazy." She laughed. "But then again…so is he. It sounds as if he's turned himself into knots for you. Coming over in the dead of night, giving you an orgasm under duress, gifting you a damn kitten for goodness' sake. I mean come *on*." She pressed her wrist to her forehead and fake swooned. "He's a walking romance trope."

I laughed, surprising myself. "And you're not mad at me?"

Her smile fell. "Honestly? Yeah, I am a little."

I flinched.

She took my hand and squeezed it, all while she scolded me. "I'm happy for you, Sails. I truly am. He wouldn't have gone to such crazy extremes if he wasn't head over freaking heels for you. I'm grateful he gave you an outlet to talk. That he was smart enough to know you needed a stranger to confess to. He helped you find your feet again, but I can't help feeling like…you didn't trust me enough to confide in me. I'm hurt that you thought I wouldn't accept you. I would've loved you no matter what state you were in—"

"I know. And I love you for it. I know every word of that is true, but…I was a little lost, Lils. I was afraid of my own shadow, and you looked at me as if I was so strong, and I needed to believe that. I don't think I could've coped if you'd seen how much I struggled."

Tears glimmered in her eyes. "I get it. I do. But I just need you to know I would *never* think you were weak for having panic attacks. Milton tried to *kill* you, Sails. Even if you hadn't almost been strangled to death, something like that stays with a person."

I sipped my drink and let her continue.

"No matter that Zander lied to you and stalked my best friend, I'll always be grateful to him for helping you, and I can even understand why he used a fake name and wore a mask, especially now that I know that Milton hurt you all because he caught you spying on Zander in a towel—"

"I wasn't spying." I swallowed a mouthful of zesty alcohol. "I was thinking about work and—"

"I'm sorry, moonbeam, but that's a lie."

I reared back, breaking our handhold. "What? How could you—?"

"I'm your best friend." She smirked kindly. "I'm around at your place all the time. I've been popping over well before Milton ever moved in. Do you honestly think I haven't caught you checking out your neighbour?"

"What? No, I—"

"You might not be aware of it, but whenever Zander appeared in his living room or kitchen, every part of you knew. You're like a damn antenna picking up his whereabouts." Her smirk turned into a laugh. "Do you remember the night we were playing Monopoly and you—for the first time ever, I might add—had all the hotels, and I landed on your squares and had to pay an exorbitant amount of money?"

I scowled, going back over our fun game nights that'd become a bit of a tradition. We'd taken up playing Monopoly as an ode to my grandparents but also because Lily said it would help her get in touch with her developer side. We'd kept playing it because it was fun to bicker and taunt, all while eating snacks and sugar.

But try as I might, I couldn't remember that night. Usually, I lost. I would remember wiping out her bank balance. "I'm guessing you cheated because I don't remember you losing any game."

"And there you have it. I rest my case."

I frowned. "I don't follow."

"You didn't remember to charge me because you were too damn busy perving at Zander as he paced through his house on his phone. He was wearing a pair of track pants that hung *real* low and no shirt. Even I did a second-glance. But you?" She fanned herself. "You practically crawled to the window to watch."

"What?" My cheeks caught fire. "I wouldn't. I didn't—"

"You did, and it's okay. You've wanted him for years. Even if you couldn't admit it."

My stomach clenched.

I have a crush on you.

This stupid crush is getting out of control.

I like you...

X and Zander's voice braided into one in my head. A gush of goosebumps shot down my back.

In a split second, everything ceased to matter.

The lying. The sneaking. The stalking.

Nothing mattered.

Because he was *him.*

I stood so fast, my chair fell backward.

Lily just smirked and waved a hand like a princess shooing me away. "Let me guess, you have something you need to do?"

Rushing around the table, I kissed her on the cheek. "I love you, Lily McBride."

"Yeah, yeah. Go get that Dr Stalker of yours."

I flew out of the café.

Oh, Zander, Zander, Zander...whatever am I going to do with you?

I had a new plan.

One where I'd enjoy the tiniest bit of revenge. Zander would get a serious wake-up call. And every obstacle keeping us apart would shatter.

Dashing to my car, I threw myself inside, locked my doors because...safety...and then called the hospital.

I jittered and shivered, willing the line to connect.

My voice cracked as I asked to be put through to Dr Colin Marx.

And when it connected, I blurted a question, "Did you or did you not give Zander North black hair dye and brown eye contacts so he could become incognito to stalk me?"

Colin coughed. "Uh...well, shit. I'm guessing this is Sailor Rose?"

"It is. Are you going to answer me?"

"Guilty as charged." He sighed. "Are you gathering information to file a report on him? Because I have to warn you, he did it out of love. He loves you, Sailor. He always has and—"

"Does the dye wash out easily?"

He sighed again. "It's completely water based. Doesn't even need soap."

"Perfect."

"Look, Sailor. I know you have every right to be pissed, but please—"

"Don't tell him I called you. You have my word I'm not going to hurt him. I heard you both. A week ago, when he was drunk and you came round."

"Ah, crap...you did?" His voice turned into a whisper. "So you'll know how much he's suffering over this? He hates that he lied to you. That he lost you. He's even asked for a transfer. He thinks it's for the best and—"

"He's not going anywhere." I clutched my steering wheel. "I'm going to enjoy a tiny bit of payback, then I'm going to ensure he has someone to take care of him for the rest of his life."

He exhaled in a rush. "You mean it? Ugh, that's the best news I've—wait." His tone turned suspicious. "What do you mean? Payback?"

"You'll see."

I hung up and drove with a mad smile all the way home.

Fifty-Two

Zander

Be Careful What You Wish For

COME ROUND TONIGHT. That isn't a request.

I stared at that message all day.

It'd come through while I was at work, and it'd taken every shred of professionalism I had to ignore it while dealing with patients and surgery. To pretend my gut didn't knot into barbwire or my heart didn't palpitate every time I thought of going to see her.

I managed to ignore her message until I got home.

I refused to obsess about it as I dumped the small amount of groceries I'd picked up and devoured a simple Greek salad from the deli.

I headed upstairs, convincing myself I was just going to have a shower, watch some shit TV, then fall into bed and sleep.

The same thing I'd done the past eight days.

Eight long days of no contact, no hellos or goodbyes or spying Sailor in her garden. I'd had lots of early shifts and forced myself to angle my cameras back to watch over my place so she no longer triggered them.

I had no way to indulge in my addiction to her and going cold turkey was *way* harder than I thought it would be. It gave me better appreciation to those patients who came in high. Those who needed help getting off the substances that'd ruined their lives.

I didn't think I'd ever be able to wean myself off Sailor, and that was why I needed to move.

I wouldn't sell this place, but I needed time.

Time to get my head on straight and figure out how not to be the jackass secretly in love with his neighbour.

All of those thoughts and all of those convictions splintered the second I went to my bedroom window and saw Sailor standing in hers. Hiding in the shadows, I couldn't help myself as I watched her smooth down a little black dress. Slinky and elegant, it skimmed her knees. Thin spaghetti straps clung to her shoulders. Her sandy hair hung in soft curls and her eyes darkened with eyeshadow.

I'd never seen her look more delicious or more dangerous.

She dressed up for me.

She'd texted X, commanded his presence, and dressed up for his arrival, for *my* arrival—

Goddammit, why was this so hard?

I went to yank my glasses off and rub my stinging eyes but froze as she lifted something off her dressing table. Something long and silver and...

The dildo I bought her.

Her gaze shot to my bedroom window; I tripped backward.

I tripped so badly, I ended up on my ass on the floor.

I gave up.

Falling onto my back, I snarled at the ceiling.

Fuck, can this get any worse?

She'd summoned me to go around, dressed in a sexy black dress, and fondled the toy I'd bought her. If I didn't go, she'd use it. She'd get off on something that wasn't me, and the sudden jealousy fucking crippled me.

Lying on the floor, I reached a new low.

I was officially jealous of an inanimate object.

I moved before I could stop myself.

Tripping into the bathroom, I ripped off my tie, jerked off my shirt, and reached for the box of hair dye.

Fifty-Three

Sailor

Revenge is Best Served with Dessert

PENG ALERTED ME TO HIS ARRIVAL.

With a happy meow and flicking tail, he bolted to the back door just as X opened it and stepped into the kitchen without an invitation.

"You made it." I beamed the biggest, over-the-top smile of my life.

He froze, his eyes locking on mine where I stood by the counter, icing the final corners of the hazelnut chocolate cake. On the top, I'd piped an intricate X covered in flower petals.

Peng clawed his way up X's jeans, distracting him.

With a softly muttered curse, he plucked the kitten from where he hung on his belt and bundled him into his hands. "You're a pest." He held Peng away from him, all while the cat did its best to headbutt every finger and purr like a chainsaw.

I should've figured out who X was the first time he'd come round for cake. Peng couldn't hide his obsession with Zander all because he'd been the one to turn his life into a happily ever after. If I didn't love Zander just as much as Peng did, I would be obscenely jealous.

But now…we can share.

I snickered to myself, all while watching Zander/X wrangle Peng off him.

Now I knew who he was…it was obvious—even with the black hair and brown eyes. The shape of his forehead, the fall of his thick hair, the faint lines around his eyes, the breadth of his shoulders, his lean powerful height and strong elegant hands…even his energy was the same. The same protective, sweet, caring aura that made me feel instantly at home.

"So." I grinned another megawatt smile. "How was your day, dear?"

"Dear?" He rocked backward on his heels, his eyes narrowing above his skull mask. "Who are you and what new trap have you come up with?"

"Can't I call you something other than X?" I wrinkled my nose. "I mean...it's not even a nice letter. Kinda harsh if you ask me." Spinning on the spot and brandishing the spatula covered in icing, I grinned. "You know what? You could just tell me your real name, and I'll call you that."

He huffed and managed to escape Peng's love attack. "I see what you're doing, and it won't work."

"What won't work?" I blinked innocently.

"You know what."

"How about I guess?" I tapped a finger against my bottom lip. "Let's see. You could've chosen any letter to go by but you chose X. So that leads me to think there's an X in your real name somewhere."

He coughed and balled his hands. "That's ridiculous—"

"You don't look like a Max." I cocked my head, studying him. "Or a Jaxon or a Braxton or an Axel." I tossed the spatula back into the bowl, making him flinch with the noise. "I've got it. Alexander."

He went deathly still. His eyes pinched into a sniper stare. "Why Alexander? I could be a Felix or a Dexter."

"True. You could be. Alright, I'll just randomly choose one until I figure it out." Smiling as brightly as I could, I asked my question again, pretending to be the dutiful housewife welcoming her hard-working husband home after a long day. "So, Hendrix...how was your day?" I waved the question away. "No, that doesn't suit you. Oh, I know." I paused for dramatic effect. "How about Lex...you know? From Superman? He was the villain all while Clark Kent wore sexy glasses only to transform into a sexy alien who could fly?"

He choked and swayed on the spot.

I snickered, enjoying my revenge a little too much. "Oh, did I guess right?"

"Think I'd prefer Bronx."

"Nah, that one isn't very sexy. Oh, I know." I giggled. "Pax. How about that?"

"I think this is getting old, and I'd like to know why I'm here."

"Okay, fine." Bowing my head, pretending to accept defeat, I asked my question the third time. "But first...how was your day?"

He sighed heavily. "You're suddenly very interested in my daily activities. Why?"

"Because I'm curious. I want you to share with me."

"If this is why you texted me—"

"Wow, you really don't know how to let someone care about you, huh?" I pouted. "You're going to have to get over that."

"Get over what?"

"Being on your own."

He scowled. "What the hell has gotten into you?"

"Nothing much." My gaze struggled to unlock from the mocking skeleton covering his mouth. The same mouth I'd kissed and tasted. Even once I'd demolished his disguise, I would let him keep the mask. I would even ask him to wear it sometimes because…even though I was accepting that Zander had layers he'd always hidden from me, even though I was ready to forgive every lie he'd ever told because everything he'd done spoke far louder than words, I didn't want to say goodbye to X.

I didn't want to choose.

If Zander tried to kill X off…*well, we're going to have a problem.*

Picking up the cake, I carried it to the dining table where a candelabra flickered with three candles. Pressed cloth napkins waited beneath polished silver cutlery, and two china plates like the one he'd left in my letterbox waited to be used.

Placing the cake on the intricate stand in the centre of the table, I motioned for him to sit down. "Are you going to answer me?"

He blinked and shook his head as if utterly confused. Ignoring my question for the millionth time, he eyed up the X on the cake, then grabbed the back of the nearest chair. Strangling it, he asked, "Are you…are you not mad at me for leaving that night?"

"Should I be?" I shrugged.

His brown eyes searched mine.

That was the only part of my little sting operation that I couldn't figure out how to tamper with. I missed Zander's emerald stare. The muddy brown had to go. However, the blue black in his hair would be my first victim.

Luckily, he'd worn a black t-shirt tonight, and I'd yet to renovate my kitchen because I was about to cause a hell of a mess.

His knuckles turned white as he continued trying to murder my chair. "I don't understand. You haven't messaged me for a week. You're acting strange."

Getting into character and going over the lines I'd prepared, I headed to the freezer and pulled out the vanilla ice-cream. Carrying the tub to the table, I placed it beside the cake and sat primly in my little black dress. "Me strange? Never."

The sheer satin meant I wore no underwear to avoid bra and knicker lines, but it also meant my nipples were rather visible.

And of course, he noticed.

His gaze dropped to my breasts, making them pucker with need.

Swallowing hard, he nodded once and sat down. "What's going on, Lori?"

"Nothing." I giggled, laying it on a little thick. "I just missed you and figured…why use the dildo you gave me when I could have you instead?"

He coughed. "Excuse me?"

"Oh, I'm sorry, did I talk too quietly?" Leaning forward, I cupped my chin in my hands and smiled. "You appointed yourself as my faceless therapist to help me heal and…seeing as you've done such a bang-up job, I'm firing you from that position and hiring you in a new role."

"What new role?"

"My orgasm delivery boy of course."

He frowned. "That's why you commanded me to come?"

"Careful, X." I ran my finger over my bottom lip. "When I command you to *come*, you'll know about it."

He shivered. His eyes dropped from mine to the cake and back again. "Lori, whatever you're doing, it won't—"

"I'm giving you another two choices, dear." Wedging my elbows on the table, still cradling my chin with my hands, I smiled. "It's up to you, so I suggest you choose wisely."

He stiffened. "I don't need you to give me another choice. We're over, Lori. I told you that the last time I was here." His eyes flashed with guilt. "I apologise for how I treated you. I-I hate that I left bruises when I always promised I would never hurt you, but…I only came here tonight to tell you that I'm leaving."

"Oh?" I blinked like a brain-dead owl. "Where are you going?"

"Doesn't matter. All that matters is—"

"I thought you were going to kill yourself off? That option would've been far more final, don't you think?"

"What?" His eyebrows shot up. "How did you…?"

Leaning back, I shrugged. "If you wanted to end things dramatically—if you wanted me to give up trying to find you—then you should've told me you were terminally ill and only had a week left to live. I would've mourned you of course, but I would've given up looking in a month or two because why would I search for a dead guy?"

Peng leaped onto the table. Prowling toward the cake, he batted it. Icing covered his claws, making the little demon kitten sit and lick his paw.

X never took his eyes off mine. "I can't read you tonight. What are you saying? What's wrong? Did something happen?" His voice turned thick with protection and rage. "Is it Milton? Did he get in touch?"

I grinned, never letting my act slip. "I received the summons to testify against him, but that's not what tonight is about."

He moved before he could stop himself. His hand reached for mine across the table. He squeezed my fingers tight. "How can it not be? Knowing you have to see him? Are you doing okay? I know you're strong enough to face him...but do you know that?"

I squeezed him back, my heart fisting all over again.

I'd invited him here to pick a fight and strip his disguise halfway through. My revenge plan was to show him I knew all along and forgave him, but...I'd never been good at confrontation and had no intention of making him hurt more than he already was.

He was too nice.

Too caring.

Even now...even highly suspicious and on guard, he still put my well-being above his own.

Oh, Zander, Zander, Zander. You just keep messing up my heart, and I just keep on letting you.

"I'll be fine." Squeezing his fingers, I stood and headed to the butcher's block. Sliding out a large blade to cut the cake with, X stiffened as I carried the knife back and placed it slowly on the table.

"When will you have to go to court?" he asked quietly, never taking his eyes off the knife.

"Why?" I sat back down. "Will you come with me? I hate to tell you, X, but I don't think you'll be allowed a mask in there."

"I won't be there, Lori. I've told you this. After tonight, you'll never see me again."

"Is that right?" I nodded along. "In that case, I better get to the point quickly then, huh?"

He sighed heavily as if I'd drained him of every strength. "That would be great. Thanks."

Grabbing the knife, I plunged it right in the middle of the X, slicing through the cake with murderous precision. "Alright then..."

He jerked. "Was that meant to be a threat?"

"Did it work?"

"Kinda, yeah." He chuckled. "Anyone ever tell you you're scary when you're secretive?"

"Guess there are things about me that you don't know, after all." I smirked. "Even after all your stalking."

He scowled. "I deserved that." Shifting as if to stand, he muttered, "Look, I know I've pissed you off with what I did last time I was here. I left when you asked me not to. I was too rough and took too much. I haven't messaged or—"

"Meh, let's not talk about the past, shall we?" I winked. "I'm far more interested in the future."

"There *is* no future, Lori—"

"Call me Sailor. Every time you call me Lori, it reminds me of my neighbour when he pulled my pigtails when we were kids."

He stopped breathing.

I smiled full of sugar. "That's why I told you to use that nickname. I've had a crush on Zander North basically my entire life. Did I tell you that? Probably not because I've only just figured it out myself. Until recently, I wasn't even aware how much I watched him. I always thought I kept a respectable boundary between us. That I always looked away. Turns out...I didn't."

"What's that supposed to mean?"

"It means, I've been a bad neighbour. After all, he can't help moving about in his own house, right? He shouldn't have to put up with his neighbour ogling him when he's just come back from the gym. He should have privacy instead of realising that the girl next door once stood for a full hour watching him nap on the couch because he looked so exhausted and all she wanted to do was go over there and give him a hug."

"W-Why are you telling me this?" His hand strayed to the bridge of his nose—the tic so Zander, my heart fluttered with love. But then he realised what he was doing and yanked his mask a little higher instead. "Are you trying to make me jealous?"

"Is it working?"

"Doesn't matter what I think." His voice came out all scratchy. "I'm leaving."

"Not yet, you're not."

His forehead furrowed. "You think you can keep me here against my will?"

"I'm willing to try." I ran my finger over the knife with a crazy smile.

He gulped. "Look, Sailor...I don't know what you want—"

"I want you to sit there and listen. Do you think you can do that?" I scowled. "And then you can go. You can leave and never come back if that's truly what you want."

"I won't change my mind—"

"We'll see."

He shuddered as his gaze shot to the back door.

If he left, I had every intention of spraying him with the hose until his hair turned red, but...he resisted the urge to run and turned back to face me. "Fine. What do you want to talk about?"

"Oh, I don't know. How about we get straight to the juicy stuff and confess our deepest, darkest secrets?" Cutting a piece of cake, I placed it on the plate in front of him.

He scowled. "You know I can't eat that with my mask on."

"Oh, I know."

"Then why did you—"

"Hospitality? Hope that you'll trust me enough to take off your mask once we've finished talking?" I laughed, enjoying taunting him far too much. "However, if you want to keep it on while doing bad things to me again, that would be perfectly acceptable." I licked my bottom lip. "One of my secrets is…you've successfully given me a mask fetish."

He twitched and cleared his throat. "Sailor, I—" His gaze dropped to my breasts again.

His chest strained with a heavy breath.

I blushed.

Zander might've been hiding the darker parts of his personality that only ever came out when he was X, but…so had I.

I might have gone my entire life pretending that I didn't have urges—normal, *simple* urges. Now I was happy to admit, I wanted a man to adore me but also rule me. I was both a feminist and a traditionalist. I craved to be taken care of by a man who I trusted to fight off monsters, but also become that monster in bed when it was just us. In return, I wanted to be the hearth he came home to. I wanted to care for him, protect him, and be the one he could be both man and monster with.

And if I couldn't convince Zander that he needn't be afraid of wanting those same normal, *wonderful* urges, then…drastic moves would have to be taken.

Gathering every shred of courage I had, I sniffed. "Okay, I'll go first." Placing my hands on my lap, I forced myself to meet his stare. "Secret number one is…the night Milton tried to kill me…I told you he accused me of watching my neighbour when I'd been distracted and thinking of work. That's…a lie. A lie I couldn't even admit to until today. My best friend forced me to realise just how aware I've been of Zander North my entire life. Yes, I moved into this house to care for my nana, and yes, I love this home more than any other but…the real reason was *him*." I shrugged, my back prickling with the hard-to-swallow truth. "I missed him when I lived in the city. I missed him every time I returned from a visit here. I loved every time our grandparents whispered about us getting married and felt physical pain at the thought that he'd end up with someone else. Living close by— being able to see him, even from a distance—was a temptation I wasn't strong enough to ignore."

X didn't say a word, frozen in his chair.

It still felt odd to talk about Zander as if he wasn't here, but I threw myself headfirst into making him break, allowing myself to break in the process. "I'm not taking responsibility or excusing Milton's behaviour that night. I will never forgive him, and there will never be a good enough reason for a man to try to kill his significant other, but…I will admit that it wasn't just him at fault in our relationship. I went along with it because I thought I couldn't have the man I wanted. The man I didn't even admit I wanted. I made do and settled for what I thought I deserved, all while craving someone else. I thought I was so stealthy whenever I'd spy on my neighbour, but it turns out, I wasn't. Lily noticed. Milton noticed. And that's when cracks started appearing. The night Milton found me watching Zander in his bedroom, he didn't say a word. He watched me watching my neighbour and saw how I reacted when he dropped his towel."

I blushed, confessing this to the very man I'd spied on, doing my best to keep talking about him in the third person. "That was the first time he ever exposed himself in full view of the window. He showed me exactly what I've been wanting all these years. I think I must've gasped or done something to give myself away, and…Milton retaliated."

I trembled as the phantom pain around my throat returned. The kicks and the punches, the slurs and the curses. "He tossed me around like a lump of meat that night. He would've taken my life if it hadn't been for Jim, but…the biggest secret beneath all of that horror is…Zander wasn't my trigger. My feelings for him were."

"Sailor, stop. You don't need to—"

"I do. And you need to listen."

He slouched in the chair, his eyes infinitely sad.

Sucking in a breath, I continued, "All this time, I placed the blame on Zander. I willingly let blindness keep me from understanding that I was partly at fault even though what Milton did was inexcusable. But then *you* came into my life. A faceless, nameless guardian who held my hand through the panic attacks and hugged me through the terror, and somehow, you made me come alive again. However, what you don't know is…you also made me become someone else. The night you bruised me and commanded me to kneel was—"

"Wrong—"

"The best damn night of my life." I balled my hands on the table. "You showed me that I've been lying to myself all this time. I might want my sweet neighbour, but the one thing holding me back from attempting a relationship with him was…I don't want sweet in the bedroom. I want what *you* gave me. Primal and passionate and so full of emotion that the bruises you left behind were talismans of connection, not abuse. Milton left me with scars but you…you left me with memories I will never forget, which brings me to my second secret."

X rubbed his eyes with a groan. "I can't handle hearing another one. I know I said I'd always be there to hear whatever you wanted to tell me, but, Sailor, I can't hear this. I can't because I'm not the man you think I am, and—"

"It will be your turn to confess soon enough. Let me finish."

His eyes flashed the wrong colour, but finally, he nodded. "Go ahead."

Arching my chin, I said, "I'm in love with both of you. I love Zander, and I love you. My heart has been torn in two over this, and it's made me feel like a terrible person, but now I know how I can fix it."

"How?" he asked helplessly.

Tapping my throat, I smiled. "Sorry, confessing is thirsty work. I'll just grab a glass of water. Be right back." I stood and Peng trotted over the table from where he'd been lounging beside the ice-cream tub, chilling his tiny tummy and getting his fur all frosty.

Grabbing him, I moved him to the floor. He wouldn't appreciate this next bit.

While I went to the cupboard and grabbed my mixing bowl, X burrowed his masked face into his hands and slouched.

He didn't see me fill the bowl to the brim.

Didn't even look at me while I pretended to slake my thirst.

He still had his head bowed by the time I carried the bowl of water toward him, staying behind him the entire time.

My arms trembled beneath the weight as I whispered, "You know, after a lifetime of being scolded by my nana and raised with the same marriage promise that I have, you should know not to mess with a Rose, Z."

And then, I dumped the entire bowl of water over his head.

Fifty-Four

Zander

Unravelling by Water

ICE, WET, COLD, *FREEZING*.
I shot to my feet, spluttering and coughing.
Water went everywhere, quickly switching from clear to black.
No.
Fuck.
It soaked into my mask, making it hard to breathe. It ran under the collar of my t-shirt and dripped off the ends of my hair. In the reflection of the windows, I watched in horror as the blue-black box dye quickly rinsed back to North-condemning red.

Spinning around, I faced Sailor as she placed the bowl back on the counter with a smirk.

Black droplets continued to drip off my eyelashes and down my face, but I couldn't think, couldn't focus. I fixated on a single letter. One tiny uncommonly used letter and my heart threatened to burst in all directions.

"What did you just call me?"
Her smirk dropped.
She stalked into me.
I backpedalled until I crashed against the table. Without a word, she reached up and ran her fingers through my dripping hair.
Her hand came away black.
"Why?" I breathed. "Why are you doing this?"
Biting her bottom lip, she reached up with her black-streaked hand and gathered the material by my chin.
Her eyebrows rose.
I almost passed out.
She tugged gently.
And…I nodded.
I gave in.
I gave up.
How could I not?
She'd spilled her secrets.

She'd told me so many things that set my soul on fire and hope ablaze like stardust.

Ever so slowly, *agonisingly* slowly, she pulled my mask down. It slithered along my nose, clung to my cheekbones, then cascaded over my lips in a rush.

She let go the moment it gathered into a soggy mess around my neck.

I couldn't catch a proper breath as I stood before her, all my lies exposed.

My knees threatened to buckle…the despair that'd haunted me for weeks at the thought of losing her slowly morphed into something else. Something sharp and stinging and so full of yearning I could barely talk. "Why?" I asked again.

A simple word that hid so many within it.

Why did she expose me?

Why did she tell me those things?

Why did she forgive me?

Why did she love me?

Christ, she loves me.

I staggered against the table, slapping my palm over the cutlery and stabbing myself with the fork. Hissing between my teeth, I—

"I called you Z," she whispered. "And I did it because…I heard you last week. I was looking for Peng. I rang your doorbell and ran into your back garden searching for him. It was an honest mistake—this one I'm not lying about—I honestly didn't mean to watch you that night. But…true to my history of being unable to tear myself away whenever you're in a window, I stayed. And I saw. And I heard. Everything."

"*Everything*?" I groaned.

Stepping into me, she planted her palm over my painfully chugging heart. "I heard why you did what you did. Why you disguised yourself. Why you put your own sleep and health on the line. Why you put me first, like you always do, and why…why you've made it impossible for me to let you walk out that door because…you're everything I've ever wanted, Zander. I've loved you since I was a silly little girl with pigtails, crushing on the boy who called her Lori, but only recently did I fall into lust with the very masked protector who touched me because I begged him to. The kind-hearted villain who went against his morals and his unflappable rules of right and wrong. I did it because…by freeing me, I think you freed yourself, and you're afraid that you can't be the guy you used to be if you embrace this new version of yourself. But…" Her fingernails dug into my chest. "I'm telling you, Z…you can. You can still care while being erotically cruel to me. You can still protect me while punishing me. And you can have exactly what you need because I want to give you everything, just like *you* give *me* everything."

Tears welled and spilled down her cheeks. "You've looked after me my entire life and...I want to look after you now. I want you to come home to a home-cooked meal, so I know you're getting enough food after you work so hard. I want you to help me renovate because your house looks way better than mine, and it's time to step into the future. I want a relationship with you...the good, the bad, the safe, the sinful...I just...I just want you. All of you."

For a second, only white noise filled my ears. A hissing, annoying snow that drowned out my thoughts.

Sailor rolled her eyes in the direction of the living room. "Bloody Nana turned the TV on again." Swaying backward, she laughed softly. "I'll just go turn it off and—"

I snatched her wrist.

I jerked her into me.

I reached another limit.

The last one.

The one that would always be the finish line and the starting line, the before and after.

Snatching a fistful of her hair, I yanked her head back and kissed her.

Hard.

Painfully, *deliciously* hard.

She exploded.

She opened wide and let me plunge into her mouth.

She fought me back, fire with fire.

Kissing, nipping, slipping, sliding.

She squirmed as I grabbed her jaw and deepened the kiss with brutal lust.

Spinning around, I picked her up and tossed her onto the table, never stopping our connection. Our tongues fought. Our breaths caught. My hands roamed all over her body, the slipperiness of her black dress sending me straight to fucking hell.

Cupping her breasts with punishing fingers, I let loose all those needs inside me. The need to maul her and corrupt her. The desire to break her for having the power to break me.

Her back arched, pushing more of her flesh into my hold.

Her legs spread, cradling me as I stepped into her and ground myself against her.

Water continued to drip off my hair, splashing her with midnight droplets.

Her hips rocked, seeking me as I grunted with the need to be inside her.

A flicker of persecution told me to stop.

Not to be this manic.

But then she clawed at my back, and I snapped.

Burrowing my face in her neck, I bit her. I sank my teeth into the spot where Milton's fingers once bruised her gorgeous skin and marked her unapologetically with my own autograph.

She clung to me as I kissed my way back to her mouth, unbuckling and unzipping as I went.

Our lips found each other again.

She bit my bottom lip, drawing the tang of blood.

I snarled and bit her back, rocking my hips between her legs, letting her feel just how badly I needed her.

Squeezing her breast, I ran my thumb over her pert nipple. "Tell me now if fucking you on this table is going to be a problem."

Her head tipped back with a throaty groan. "God, no problem. No problem at all."

Grabbing her dress, I bunched it around her hips.

My gaze locked on the bareness between her legs. "Goddammit, you're not wearing any underwear."

She smirked. "I had planned on torturing you a little more than this. I wanted payback, but…screw it." Grabbing my undone jeans, she jerked me forward and stuck her hand into my boxer-briefs.

I snarled as she found me. I shuddered as she jerked me.

In a few savage pumps, she almost made me come.

Fisting her wrist, I wrenched her hold off me and shoved my pants down.

My erection bounced free. She licked her lips. Her gaze met mine as she whispered, "Can you…can you do me a favour?"

"Anything," I breathed. "Always."

"Can you take the contacts out?"

A lopsided, stupid smile spread my lips. "Miss the green?"

"I want to sleep with Zander tonight. Not X."

Fuck, how had this happened?

I thought I'd been the one sneaking into her life, but she'd been the true thief. She'd successfully stolen every shred of my soul.

With shaking hands, I reached up and pinched the film over my pupil. I sucked at this in front of a mirror, let alone broken with lust. I struggled and winced and poked myself, making my eye water.

She wrinkled her nose. "Jeez, I didn't realise they were so hard to take out."

"They're not. I just suck at it."

She swooned into me. "And you still put them in for me? Be still my beating heart."

I finally managed to grab the slippery sucker. Removing the left contact with triumph, I squished it between my fingers and flicked it onto the floor.

Peng immediately went to investigate.

With a grimace, I reached for my other eye, but Sailor grabbed my arm and stopped me. "Don't. I don't want you to injure yourself."

I looked up.

We made eye contact.

She gasped. "Oh wow...that...yeah, that does things to me."

I frowned. "What do you mean?"

Peering closer, she broke out in goosebumps. "One green, one brown. It's like...it's like I'm sleeping with both versions of you at once."

There were many things I could say to that.

I could laugh it off or tease her, but the only thing I could do was finish what I started.

Grabbing her cheeks, I bent over her and kissed her. "Tell me to stop," I begged into her mouth. "Tell me this is a dream, and I'm about to wake up."

"Why? Because you don't think you can have me?"

"Because I'm petrified this isn't real." She'd already spilled her secrets. Now mine torrented off my tongue. "Actually, the truth is...I'm afraid I haven't worked hard enough for long enough to deserve you. I'm afraid that if I show you who I truly am, you'll think I'm a fraud. I'm afraid that if I choose happiness over my career, my patients will suffer because I'm selfish for wanting my own life. I'm afraid that if I learn to rely on you, I won't survive when you decide to leave me. I'm afraid of death taking the people I love the most. I'm afraid of not being good enough to heal them. I'm afraid that if I stop trying to be the best I can be and invite the worst parts of myself, I'll lose everything."

She went to speak, but I planted my hand over her mouth.

"I think..." I said softly. "I think that's what I'm most afraid of. I have this hunger inside me that only gets worse the more I'm around you. The more I fall in love with you, Sailor, the more I want to keep you, and I know in myself that it could lead to a spiralling obsession. I-I don't know how to take from you and give to you. It's one or the other for me. And I need...I need—" I swallowed hard. "I need you so fucking much that I'm flat-out terrified of hurting you. Of you hating me. Of you leaving me. Of you knowing exactly who I am when I've been hiding, even from myself."

Silence blanketed us, sticking to all my confessions.

My pulse skyrocketed when she didn't say anything.

Finally, she pulled away my hand and whispered, "Zander?"

"Yeah?"

"Shut up." Her lips found mine.

She kissed me.

I surrendered.

Slinking my fingers into her hair, I held her steady, accepting her kiss before deepening it. The chaos in my chest slowly tamed, and by the time we pulled away, I felt a little more sane. "Sorry...I—"

She pinched my arm. Hard.

"Ow, what the hell?"

"Did you wake?"

I scowled. "No."

"Well then, this is real. This isn't a dream. And everything you just said is ridiculous. I'm not going anywhere, you aren't selfish, and I can't tell you to stop." Her breathy tone made my gut clench. "I literally can't because I want you as much as you want me, and if you don't give in soon, I'm—"

"I won't be gentle, Sailor. Not tonight."

"I told you...I don't want gentle. I want you to be *you*."

An overwhelming surge of possession pounded through me. With quaking hands, I pushed her back just enough and guided myself to her wet entrance.

We both looked down. She and I. Millimetres from joining.

And I couldn't do it unless she was mine.

For eternity.

I didn't just love this woman.

I loved everything about her. Her house, her bravery, her cat, her grandparents...our shared past. I always had. Always would. And if I didn't get a ring on her finger, I would always feel as if I was moments away from losing her. I'd always fear that this *was* a crazy wonderful dream, and one day, I would wake up and be all alone.

Notching myself inside her, I looked up and held her stare.

She moaned again. "You can't look at me with those multicoloured eyes and not fuck me, Z."

I suffered a full-body shiver at her new nickname for me.

I choked on two words.

This wasn't the time or place.

This was new. This was fresh. This was fate.

"Marry me," I whispered.

"*What?*" Her eyes flared wide, time screeched to a halt, the TV kept hissing, and Peng meowed somewhere on the floor.

I tensed to take the question back. To pretend I hadn't ruined the mood, but then the TV hissed louder, and I stopped being afraid anymore. I stopped putting myself last. I fought for what I wanted, regardless of the consequences.

Cupping her cheeks, I breathed, "Marry me, Sailor Melody Rose.

Exact your revenge on me every day of my life. Let me keep you, okay? Say you're mine and—"

"But this is crazy," she moaned, her eyes glazed with desire. "We're not even dating."

"We've been engaged since I was six and you were born. How long do you think we need to date when we've been betrothed for almost two decades?"

She laughed and slung her arms over my shoulders. "So you're doing this to honour our meddling matchmaking ghosts?"

"No." Tucking her hair behind her ears, I couldn't tear my eyes from her kiss-glistening mouth. "I'm doing this because you told me to. You want me to fight for myself for once? Well then…" I smirked. "What I *want* is you, and if you don't let me have you—if you don't agree to be mine, then—"

"Z…" Grazing her mouth over mine, she made me wait in purgatory. Then she kissed me, feeding me one word in response. "Okay."

I yanked away, my heart on fire. "Okay?"

She blushed. "Okay, I'll…marry you."

Her lips parted wide as I pushed forward.

We both groaned as I slid inside her, slowly, possessively, claiming her in every way possible. "You can't take it back." I shuddered as her hot, wet body welcomed mine, imprisoning me as hers. "To think I've wasted years when I could've been inside you." I groaned as I thrust the final inch. "I should've been braver. I should've marched next door and claimed you the moment you were legal."

She clung to my shoulders. "God, why didn't you? I've been missing out."

"Good question." I kissed her softly. "Maybe I wasn't ready. Maybe we both weren't."

"Are you ready now?"

My rumbling snarl had her shivering again. "Spread your legs and I'll show you just how ready I am."

She obeyed, relinquishing every part of herself to me.

Burrowing my face into the crook of her neck, I withdrew and drove inside her again, making the table rock. "You're destroying me, Lori. You always have." I rode her again, harder and harder until the kitchen filled with sounds of skin slapping and furniture creaking.

She cried out as I thrust faster, cradling her in my arms to keep her safe, all while ravaging her.

"*More*," she moaned. "Let go. Be free…with me."

I snarled and did exactly as she commanded.

I stopped worrying and started living. I grabbed her nape and dragged her into me, kissing her hard and deep.

We rode each other violently, chaotically. We were wet and messy and slightly unhinged.

And I'd never been so turned on.

Never been this free or this happy.

I couldn't catch my breath as I found her clit and rubbed.

Her back arched the second I found the right spot. Her legs snapped around mine, forcing me to switch from deep long pumps into savage little pulses. "Oh God! *Yes*, right there."

I captured her lips in another kiss. I plunged my tongue into her mouth in sync with plunging between her legs.

It'd taken a mask to accept that I wasn't okay with being the boy next door anymore. I wanted to slay her nightmares, carry her through her hardships, and fight off every motherfucker who ever laid an unconsented hand on her.

And I wanted to do it as her husband.

Her nails punctured my ass, riding with me as I rode her.

Every rut and grind of my hips, she matched me.

"Z!" Her pussy locked around my cock, her legs spasmed around my hips, and the delicious heat of her orgasm milked me in clenching waves.

I lost everything that made me human.

I only lived to make her happy.

To be hers.

My answering orgasm tangled full of agony and exquisite intensity.

My heartbeat thundered as aching need pushed me over the edge.

We clawed and snarled and rocked and fucked, and every shackle of loneliness fell away as my soul ceased to be mine and became hers instead.

A lifetime of being promised each other.

A childhood of fighting such a stupid decree.

Followed by the unarguable knowledge that our ghosts were right, we were destined, and now we were finally exactly where we belonged.

Together.

Epilogue

Sailor

Can't Fight Destiny

I STOOD AT THE TOP OF the quaint little church with the sun beaming through stained-glass windows. Pews full of young and old neighbours from Ember Drive watched us with bated breath, and the ghosts of the North and Rose family watched me pledge my life and love to the boy next door.

Two months since he proposed and now he had me at the altar.

It'd been a whirlwind, but…every step had felt absolutely right.

Fate had stepped in the moment we stopped fighting the inevitable. The day after we announced our engagement to our friends, everyone came together and made it happen.

It'd seemed too easy—terrifyingly easy—almost as if this entire affair had been choreographed by the universe itself.

Lily stood behind me in a coral pink bridesmaid's dress.

Colin stood behind Zander in a crisp black tux.

Even Peng had been invited, sitting obediently in his little basket on Christina's knee, where she sat next to Zander's other sister, Jolie. He had a leash on to prevent him from destroying the decorations, and he blinked with such loving green eyes, he reminded me so much of the man I was about to marry.

"Do you, Sailor Melody Rose, take Zander North as your lawfully wedded husband, in sickness and in health, until death do you part?"

I blinked and focused on the celebrant. A lovely old priest who'd regularly had a few sherries with my nana.

Zander and I would've preferred a small garden wedding or even an elopement, but the moment the suburb learned we were finally getting married—after Melody and Mary had spoken of this auspicious day for almost three decades—the entire town wanted to attend.

The church had offered to host, the local flower shop owner (who Zander had sewn up after a nasty accident with a pair of pruning scissors) offered free blooms, and the cake had been donated by a lovely woman I'd grown close to at the market who sold cakes way better than any I could ever make.

I sighed with utmost contentment.

I felt so loved, so content, so safe.

Zander squeezed my fingers, bringing me once again to the present. I kept drifting off, floating in a wonderful dream that'd come true. "Eh, you're making me nervous, Little Lor."

Pop's nickname for me made my heart threaten to explode.

Zander regularly called me all kinds of things when he had me in his bed. And I often called him X when he wore the mask and took me roughly. I had the best of both worlds. I had a wonderful, intelligent man who'd dedicated his life to healing the sick, but only I got to see him as a ruthless, dominant lover who got hard at leaving a mark on my skin.

I adored the two sides of him.

I was eternally grateful I was healed enough to be healthy inside *and* outside of the bedroom.

And I only had him to thank.

My guardian. My stalker. My doctor. My husband.

Grinning, I tugged him a little closer. He looked absolutely ravishing in a black tux. His emerald stare sparkled behind polished black glasses, and his dark red hair glittered like fire tinsel thanks to the beaming sun.

My heart flipped, tripped, and fell into his pocket. Forever.

"I do." I smiled.

The priest let out a sigh of relief. "And do you, Zander North, take Sailor Melody Rose as your lawfully wedded wife, in sickness and in health, until death do you part?"

"Absolutely." Zander grinned. "Always."

A few laughs twittered around the crowd.

"Excellent." The priest beamed and stepped backward. "I was told you've prepared your own vows as well. If you'd like to exchange rings and share those, then I'll announce you."

"That's my cue." Leaning forward, Colin handed Zander a ring. "By the way, I seem to remember saying this exact thing would happen." He laughed. "And it didn't even take three to five years."

"Yeah, yeah." Zander scoffed. "Nobody likes a know-it-all."

"Happy for you, Zan." Colin patted Zander's shoulder and stepped back.

"Here you go, moonbeam." Lily kissed my cheek and pressed the simple gold band into my palm.

I returned her kiss, then sniffed back tears as Zander and I faced each other one last time as separate people.

"I—"

"I—"

We both laughed. "Sorry, you go."

"No, you first."

Zander blushed. "Okay." Taking my hand, he slipped the most stunning flower-shaped diamond onto my finger and kissed my knuckles. "Not a single day goes by that I'm not in awe of you, grateful for you, and head over heels in love with you. It took a false identity to realise who I truly am, and now that you're mine, I'm never letting you go. I love you, Lori. Forever."

Tears rolled down my cheeks as I slid the gold band onto his finger and whispered, "There isn't a TV here, but I know it would've turned itself on with approval that we finally did this. I've always secretly loved the boy next door, but it wasn't until he guarded me in the shadows that I realised I was in love with him too. I love every piece of you, Z. Yesterday, today, and tomorrow."

A few aw's feathered out from the older women watching us. They dabbed their eyes, giving Zander besotted looks.

Lily grinned, Colin laughed, and at the exact moment the priest said, 'I now pronounce you husband and wife', a sparrow fluttered down the aisle and landed in Zander's hair. It chirped, flittered to my shoulder, then flew into the church rafters.

It wasn't a snowing TV.

But it was a sign.

A sign of approval from two matchmaking women who finally got their wish.

Zander held my hand as the judge read Milton's verdict.

Testifying against him hadn't been easy. I'd had a few sleepless nights and one mild panic attack on the way to the courthouse, but...thanks to Zander, he'd held me through it, comforted me, and given me strength. I'd held my head high while I testified against the man who tried to strip me of my incredibly happy life.

Milton had lost weight, and his eyes no longer held any resemblance of being human, almost as if evilness eroded him from the inside out. He watched me with pure hatred the entire time I answered the lawyers' questions and studied photos that'd been taken of my wounds and strangulation marks when I'd been admitted into the hospital.

I'd feared facing him would send me back in my healing...but hearing the gavel come down and his sentence delivered, a tiny part of me that was still terrified of him breathed a huge sigh of relief.

Fifteen years with no parole for nine years.

It wasn't forever, and in a decade, I might have to face him again if he was stupid enough to come after me a second time, but…I wasn't alone anymore. I had Zander. I was safe. And as we headed out of the courthouse and back into the autumn sunshine, I tipped my head back to the sky and sent a quick prayer of thanks to all those watching over us.

"Oh no, you don't." I scooped Peng around the middle and plopped him back onto the

floor. Within a second, he was back on the counter, sniffing the garlic butter fish I'd just pulled out of the oven.

Rolling my eyes, I grabbed my favourite fluffy nuisance and smooshed him.

Instead of squirming to get down, he lolled like a boneless orange noodle in my arms and purred as I buried my face in his belly fur. "You're a terror. A wonderful, rascally, far too adorable terror."

The sounds of keys clinking on the sideboard had my eyes shooting up and a bigger smile spreading my lips. "Yay, you're home."

"Thank God." Dumping his satchel that no doubt held a few notes he wanted to review on current patients, he yanked off his tie as if he was sick of it strangling him. With a heavy sigh, Zander kicked off his shoes and prowled toward me.

Peng immediately turned traitor, meowing to be rescued as if I was the world's worst cat cuddler.

Zander grinned as he scooped Penguin out of my arms and flopped him over his shoulder. "Hello, wife." With a tired smile, he pulled me close and hugged me.

Peng grumbled in annoyance and leapt down.

I hugged Zander back, then squeaked as his strong arms circled my waist, picked me up, and placed me on the countertop beside the bowl of home-made fries and fresh garden salad.

His hands landed on my thighs, unapologetically spreading my legs.

With a hot look in his eyes, he leaned in and kissed me.

He kissed me to distract me.

He kissed me while pulling my underwear down beneath my cable dress and kissed me as he unbuckled, unzipped, then sank inside me right beside the dinner I'd cooked for him.

And I kissed him back.

I flung myself into lust and love and longing.

And when his hand came up to circle my throat, stroking me and threatening me in equal measure, I scratched his back and baited him to take me harder.

We switched from sweet hello to violent claiming.

I'd gotten everything I ever wanted.

We'd drawn up plans to renovate my place, and I'd moved into his home in preparation for some rather large structural works. We'd talked about renting out Nana's house, but…the garden was too precious. It had all my plants needed for the business, and neither of us liked the thought of strangers living next door.

So…we'd hired an architect to combine this place with that one.

Not only had we combined our lives, but the two houses would eventually merge into one too.

Zander dragged me out of my thoughts by teasing me toward an orgasm. I mewled in frustration as he withdrew, pulled me off the counter, then spun me around and pressed me belly first against it.

With a groan, he sank back inside me. Taking me from behind, he kept one fist on my lower back so I couldn't escape while his other hand sneaked around to my clit.

I went bowstring tight.

He knew exactly how to make me shatter in two seconds flat.

My release set off his release, and we almost crumbled to the floor as we slowly broke apart, straightened our clothing, and smiled at each other like naughty teenagers.

"We've been married three months, but I still can't get enough of you." Running his thumb over my bottom lip, he sighed. "Every time I come home to you and Peng. Every damn time I smell a delicious meal and know that I get to snuggle with you on the couch later and then take you to bed just…" He shook his head and clutched his heart. "It hurts, Little Lor. Right here."

Going to him, I planted my palm over his beating heart and raised on my tiptoes to kiss him. "I have the same problem. Whenever you text me that you're on the way home, I shake in anticipation."

He grinned. "So we're both obsessed?"

"I'd say so." I smirked. "Do you happen to know a cure? You're a brilliant doctor, after all."

"Afraid not." He kissed my nose and headed to the table. "We'll just have to remain incurable for the rest of our lives."

"I can live with that."

"Yeah, me too." He smirked a sinful smirk as he readjusted himself and sat down at the dining table. With a sigh, he pulled his phone from his back pocket and checked any notifications he'd missed while commuting home.

That was the one blip in our otherwise blissful marriage.

Zander still worked a lot. Some nights, I went to bed alone with my kitty, only to wake with him snaking his arms around me with an exhausted groan. Sometimes our planned days off ended with him called in to an emergency, and I did my best to be supportive all while the protective wife in me came out.

I didn't like that he worked so much, but…I understood it.

He needed to help, so I would take care of him while he took care of others, all while secretly planning for the day when he retired, and I could keep him to myself.

At least he got regular meals these days.

My own business had grown so big, I'd had to hire someone to manage the market stalls and help me ship out the online orders every week. I spent most of my time cooking Nana's recipes and making tinctures and remedies. Some of Zander's patients who preferred more natural healing than pharmaceuticals had even bought a few things.

If we met someone new who didn't know our destiny granted by our grandparents, they'd smile uncertainly at the doctor who'd married the flower child. In reality, we shouldn't really go together, but thanks to a pact made decades ago, our future had already been written.

Besides, they only saw the upstanding, risk-averse doctor while I got the slightly dangerous, mask-wearing motorcycle rider who sometimes dragged me out of bed at two in the morning to go soaring into the stars. The stalker who'd tattooed the smallest skull above his hip—hidden beneath his scrubs and only visible when he made dirty, wonderful love to me.

"Anything important?" I asked as I made up two plates and carried them to the table.

Zander didn't look up from his phone, a frown cutting his forehead.

"Uh-oh." I sat down and picked up my fork. "I know that look. Do you have to go back in?"

His eyes met mine. "Sorry, no, I…I just got an email from the staffing office."

"Oh? What did it say?" I took a bite of juicy, buttery fish.

"They wished me a wonderful time on my honeymoon. And not to answer my phone under any circumstances."

"What? I thought we agreed we couldn't have a honeymoon? You're too busy and—"

"We did." He passed his phone to me. "But somehow, I have leave booked for three weeks. Starting tomorrow."

"How?" I scanned the email, then jolted as a message from Colin popped up. "Colin's just texted you. He says to call him."

He frowned and took back his phone. "What the hell is he up to?"

I shrugged. "Better call him and find out, I guess?"

With a worried look, Zander pressed Colin's number and put the phone on speaker between us. It only rang once before Colin picked up.

"Now…before you get mad at me, there's a reason I didn't tell you."

"Why would I get mad, Col?" Zander cracked his knuckles as if his friend was here to punch him. "What did you do? Are you behind the fact that I have three weeks off when I didn't ask for any?"

"I am."

"Why?"

"Because you wouldn't have taken the time off if it wasn't for me. You would've let your poor little wife go without a honeymoon all because you're a workaholic."

"I have a few important surgeries coming up. I can't just—"

"You'll *always* have important surgeries coming up, Zan. That's the point. There will never be a break from the work. There will never be a good time to get away. Not one, do you hear me? When you're on your deathbed and someone asks what you most regret, you know what you'll say? You'll say you regret not spending more time with your delectable wife and so…you're welcome."

Zander flinched as Colin struck a nerve. Before he could reply, Colin added, "There are other doctors. Other surgeons. Your patients won't suffer, and you aren't letting anyone down by putting yourself first for a few weeks. Didn't you tell me you wanted to find a better work-life balance now that you're hitched? Well…this is me fulfilling that wish."

"I don't understand how they let you ask for it off. Isn't there some sort of—"

"Yeah, about that. I kinda had help. Of the legal kind."

"What the hell are you talking about?"

"It wasn't entirely Colin's fault, Zander," a woman cut in, a smile in her voice. "I'm half to blame."

"Christina?" Zander scowled at me before looking at his phone again. "Why are you with Colin? What the hell is going on?"

No one spoke for a second but then Christina blurted, "I'm at Colin's place because we're kind of…you know. Seeing how it goes. And before you start, Colin arranged your leave because, the day after you two got married, the family lawyer called me. He delivered a document that demanded your presence at some secretive location, and when we showed it to the hospital, they were only too happy to give you time off."

"Wait. Why did the family lawyer contact you? I'm the one in charge of the Norths' affairs."

"Because he had strict instructions from Gran to tell me over you."

Zander sat back, a dazed, almost hurt look on his face. "Why?"

"Because she knew you better than you knew yourself and

probably figured you wouldn't do what she asked."

"What did she ask?"

"Doesn't matter." Christina laughed slyly. "You'll know when you get there. But...you have to take a trip. You and Sailor."

"A trip?" I asked when Zander didn't say anything. "A trip where?"

"All I can tell you is it's in Costa Rica."

Zander and I made eye contact.

Growing up—when both sets of our grandparents were alive—they'd often go as a happy foursome on holiday to Costa Rica. It'd become a bit of a tradition. Every year, they packed their bags for a few weeks of double-dating vacation before returning browned, happy, and ready to work again. They'd promised to take us with them, but then Zander's grandfather passed away, and they'd stopped going.

"Your flight leaves tonight. You have four hours before take-off, so I suggest you start packing and get to the airport."

"What the hell?" Zander raked a hand through his hair. "You can't just spring this on us. What about Peng? We haven't got—"

"Lily has already agreed to move into Sailor's for three weeks and cat sit him. You know her boyfriend Aubrey is helping with the renovation for you. It's a perfect opportunity for him to assess the pros and cons of each house so he can figure out how to link them for you. Because we both know stuffy architects can get it wrong, and you want to get it right."

"Why do I feel like we don't have a choice in this matter?" Zander huffed.

"That's because you don't. You're getting on that plane and you're going to the address that the transportation service has when they pick you up. Just...go with it, Zan. For once in your life, lean on someone other than yourself. Trust us, alright?"

Zander slouched, all while my phone started ringing with Lily's name.

"I'll just take this." Scooting away from the table, I accepted the call and left Z to talk to his sister. "Lils, what the hell is going on?"

"I'm already in your kitchen. I can't find your pesky cat, though. Has he escaped again?"

I glanced at Peng happily sprawled on the back door mat licking his paws. "He's here. With us. At Zander's."

"Oh phew. I thought I'd already failed at this cat-sitting business."

"Why are you all ganging up on us and shooing us away overseas?"

She giggled. "Just you wait."

"So you know?"

"Oh yes, I know. I had a rather wonderful time over at Colin's a few days after your wedding. If I wasn't falling for Aubrey and Christina wasn't giving off possessive vibes, I might've been tempted. He's freaking hilarious, but…he's also kind and cares a lot about Zander so…just go with the flow, Sailor Moon, and get on that damn plane."

"This is crazy, right?" I asked for the millionth time.

I'd asked it as we'd packed and shed a few tears as I passed my wonderful cat into my best friend's arms.

I'd asked it as we climbed out of the Uber at the airport.

I'd asked it as we took off and flew across the ocean and landed in hot and steamy Costa Rica.

And I asked it again as Zander took my hand and led me into the arrivals hall, scanning the mismatch of drivers, family members, and hotel clerks holding up plaques with people's names on.

Spying a guy with *North* scribbled on a board, he dragged me over to him. "It's nuts, and I'm legitimately worried about what they're all up to, but…we're here now, so I guess we're doing this."

I didn't ask again as the driver shook our hands, helped with our hastily packed luggage, and guided us outside to an awaiting white sedan.

The journey from the airport wasn't too long. He gave us facts about how the weather had been, what events were taking place on the island, and how he was madly in love with the place where we were staying and how wonderful it was that it would be used again.

Zander and I shared a worried look.

The longer we drove down streets that became progressively worse with potholes and overgrown vegetation, the more I clung to his fingers.

"Here we are." The driver grinned, turning left at the top of a hill and bumping our way down a rutted driveway. Palm trees and tropical bushes blocked everything; banana fronds and mango trees gave me new ideas for face creams and lip balms, and when we finally broke through the wilderness, the most incredible house appeared.

A sprawling bungalow perched on the top of a small cliff; the ocean spilled out like sparkling aquamarine gemstones below. The mid-morning sun shimmered and played on the crystal sand, making everything ridiculously pretty.

Pulling our luggage out of the trunk, the driver passed us a rustic-looking key and grinned. "We've stocked the fridge and cleaned. The gardener hasn't been well, hence the state of the jungle, but rest assured, he'll pop by in a few days to tame it. There's a motorcycle in the garage, and the nearest eateries are only five minutes away. If you need anything, my number is on the counter. Fresh linens are in the cupboards. Oh…and the pool has been filled, so if you fancy a swim to wash away your travels, go right ahead."

"Pool?" Zander blinked. "W-What are you talking about?"

"It's just down the hill a little. Can't miss it." Waving at our dumbfounded faces, the guy got back into his car. "Have a wonderful vacation, Mr and Mrs North. All of us in this tight-knit community are so happy your family is back to continue the tradition. I'm hosting our weekly barbecue at my place. Please join us. It will be like old times."

"Old times?" I coughed.

But the driver closed his door, waved once more, and bounced his way back up the drive.

Zander and I shared yet another look.

Equally as lost as each other.

We opened our mouths to speak, but in the end, we just shrugged and dragged our luggage to the front door.

Inserting the key into the carved entry, Zander pushed it open and let me go ahead.

My mouth fell open.

The airy foyer spilled directly into a vast open-plan living room with huge sliding doors facing the ocean view. A pool glittered to the right, a green jungle surrounded us, and colourful birds flittered from tree to tree.

A large sandstone-coloured corridor wound like a snake to my left, while a massive granite-benched kitchen waited to the right. A large wicker basket sat beside the stove, full of fruits and vegetables, cheese and crackers.

"What on earth is this place?" Zander whispered. Propping our luggage against the wall, he drifted forward in a daze.

I followed him.

We both came to a natural stop by the long slab of wood acting as a table and room divider. Behind it rested a slouchy linen couch facing the view.

A letter sat propped up by a glass jar full of seashells.

A letter addressed to Mr and Mrs North.

Zander swallowed hard as he reached for it. The rip of the envelope made both of us tense, and the crackle of unfolding pretty flower paper made me hold my breath.

Zander licked his lips and read:

"Dear Sailor and Zander,
If you're here, then we were right.
We hoped of course, but never truly knew if you'd fall in love.
You're both so different but also perfect for one another, and we only wish we could've been there to see you get married.
You were born from best friends, and now you are best friends. We can rest easy, knowing you're both taken care of. We know you'll look after one another for the rest of your lives. We know you'll work hard and laugh often, but please remember to relax too.
We bought this house back in the sixties and have loved it ever since.
Now it's yours.
Please share it with your sisters, friends, and future family. It's been empty for far too long and it's up to you and your loved ones to fill it with laughter and love.
Please use it.
Please enjoy it like we did.
Please create so many happy memories.
Our only regret is that we didn't bring you here when we had the chance, but...surprise.
This is our wedding gift to you both.
Our dream finally came true, and now our families will always be connected.
You've made us so proud.
We'll be watching out for you in heaven.
We love you both so much.
Love your Gran, Grandpa, Nana, and Pops.
PS. Look up. You're home."

Our eyes soared to the open rafters. We noticed at the same time.
A stunning rose had been carved into the ceiling with a compass facing true north in the centre. Beneath the emblem existed three words.
The North Rose.
The final sign from the grave that our family approved of our union.

A secret house they'd kept all these years in hopes that we'd get married.

Grabbing me in a kiss, Zander scooped me off my feet, then carried me toward the corridor and hopefully a bedroom.

Behind us, the letter fluttered to the floor.

The curtains rippled.

And somewhere in the living room, an ancient box television

THE END

Thank you so much for reading Zander and Sailor's story.
I hope you liked it!
I have many more coming out soon.

Please sign up to my newsletter to receive 'New Book' alerts.
As a thank you for signing up, you'll instantly receive a free audio book for Lunamare and an ebook of The Boy and His Ribbon.

I hope you have a wonderful day and all your wishes come true.
xx

Acknowledgements

I'm ever so grateful to those who helped me edit, cover, and publish
this book!
Thank you to my beta readers: Laura, Linda, Charli, Betül, Michelle,
Danielle, Selena, Rochelle, Rowan, Melissa, and Heather.
Thank you to the artists who made the different renditions of these
covers Cleo and Farras.
Thank you to my editor, Jenny.
Thank you to Christina for your final proofreading eagle-eyes.
Thank you to Danielle my amazing friend and helper.
Thank you to everyone who read an ARC and shared this release.
I couldn't do this without you.
Nor could I do this without you, dear reader.
THANK YOU
xxx

OTHER WORK BY PEPPER WINTERS

Pepper currently has close to forty books released in nine languages. She's hit best-seller lists (USA Today, New York Times, and Wall Street Journal) almost forty times. She dabbles in multiple genres, ranging from Dark Romance, Coming of Age, Fantasy, and Romantic Suspense.

She also has IMMORTAL ROMANTASY books releasing in 2025 under FERN RIVERS.
WATER DUST will be the first to release under this new pen name and more details can be found on pepperwinters.com under Fern Rivers.

For all other books, FAQs, and buylinks please visit:

https://pepperwinters.com

Subscribe to New Release Newsletter by following QR code

IMMORTAL ROMANTASY – Fern Rivers

Water Dust
An immortal romantasy story perfect for readers who love spirit beast companions, dark gods, crafty demons, weak to strong power progression, unique magic, stacks of alchemy, slow burn steamy romance, overpowered morally grey lead, and different realms.

STEAMY STANDALONES

Spectacle of Secrets Standalones
One Dirty Night
One Stalker Night
(Steamy, spicy standalones with plenty of heat and swoon)
Plenty more to come…

Destroyed
(Grey Romance)

Can't Touch This
(Romantic Comedy)

Unseen Messages
(Survival Romance)

DARK ROMANCE

The Jewelry Box Series
Ruby Tears, Emerald Bruises, Sapphire Scars, Diamond Kisses

Monsters in the Dark Trilogy
Tears of Tess, Quintessentially Q, Twisted Together, Je Suis a Toi

Goddess Isles Series
Once a Myth, Twice a Wish, Third a Kiss, Fourth a Lie, Fifth a Fury,
Jinx's Fantasy, Sully's Fantasy

Indebted Series
Debt Inheritance, First Debt, Second Debt, Third Debt, Fourth Debt,
Final Debt, Indebted Epilogue

Dollar Series
Pennies, Dollars, Hundreds, Thousands, Millions

Fable of Happiness Trilogy
Fable of Happiness Book One, Book Two, Book Three

FORBIDDEN, EROTIC, COMING OF AGE ROMANCE
The Luna Duet
Lunamare and Cor Amare
The Ribbon Duet

The Boy & His Ribbon, The Girl & Her Ren
Spinoff Standalone to The Ribbon Duet
The Son & His Hope

Truth & Lies Duet
Crown of Lies, Throne of Truth
Master of Trickery Duet
The Body Painter, The Living Canvas
Pure Corruption Duet
Ruin & Rule, Sin & Suffer

INSPIRIATIONAL / CHILDREN
Pippin & Mo
(Picture book based on Pepper's own rabbit)

UPCOMING RELEASES

Water Dust
For 2025 titles and beyond please visit www.pepperwinters.com

RELEASE DAY ALERTS, SNEAK PEEKS, & NEWSLETTER
*To be the first to know about upcoming releases, please join Pepper's
Newsletter (she promises never to spam or annoy you.)*

Pepper's Newsletter

SOCIAL MEDIA & WEBSITE
Facebook: **Peppers Books**
Instagram: **@pepperwinters**
Facebook Group: **Peppers Playgound**
Website: **www.pepperwinters.com**
Tiktok: **@pepperwintersbooks**

Made in United States
North Haven, CT
26 January 2025

64993838R00232